Pugg's
portmanteau

UNIVERSITY OF CALGARY
Press

Pugg's
Portmanteau

D. M. Bryan

Brave & Brilliant Series
ISSN 2371-7238 (Print) ISSN 2371-7246 (Online)

University of Calgary Press
2500 University Drive NW
Calgary, Alberta
Canada T2N 1N4

press.ucalgary.ca

LIBRARY AND ARCHIVES CANADA CATALOGUING IN PUBLICATION

Bryan, D. M., 1964-, author
    Pugg's portmanteau / D.M. Bryan.

(Brave & brilliant series, 2371-7238 ; 9)
Issued in print and electronic formats.
ISBN 978-1-77385-050-4 (softcover).—ISBN 978-1-77385-051-1
(PDF).—ISBN 978-1-77385-052-8 (EPUB).—ISBN 978-1-77385-053-5
(Kindle)

    I. Title.

PS8603.R887P84 2019   C813'.6   C2018-906351-3
                                              C2018-906352-1

The University of Calgary Press acknowledges the support of the Government of Alberta
through the Alberta Media Fund for our publications. We acknowledge the financial support
of the Government of Canada. We acknowledge the financial support of the Canada Council
for the Arts for our publishing program.

Printed and bound in Canada by Marquis
♻ This book is printed on 55lb Enviro Book Antique paper

Editing by Aritha van Herk
Copyediting by Kathryn Simpson
Cover image: Colourbox 20147823, 31383713, and 16008870
Cover design, page design, and typesetting by Melina Cusano

To Richard, Joel, and Aphra

CHAPTER 1

PUGG'S NOTE, THE FIRST.

Today's weather drizzles and drops grey threads. Outside hangs like an engraved page, steely with strokes. Rain falls upon flagstones where puddles ink and flow. Inside, the tile floor of our building is dry but wintry enough to feel damp. I paw at your feet, having brought you a grimy leather portmanteau: a case round at each end and cylindrical in between. Three well-creased straps with tarnished brass buckles secure its curving lid, fastened tightly in the manner of a fist furled. The case has a well-chewed handle on the top, and this gives me the purchase I need to drag it to your feet. Now I waggle my tail from side to side and set my head at an obliging angle. I bark, once.

Your expression mirrors mine, both foreheads folding into puzzle pieces. You bend down to the portmanteau and undo the buckles. The case does not belong to you, and I worry you might scruple to open a stranger's possession, but no, without hesitation, you fold back the weather-beaten lid and expose the contents—a bundle of ragged pages, now mine, although I've made the least part of what's contained therein. You take up the top sheet and read: *Today's weather drizzles and drops grey threads.* You wonder what you hold in your hands, and well you might.

Dear reader, stay with me and I will compound marvel with marvel. You see before you an elderly pug, but in truth I am older even than I seem. When you and I first met, I was already ancient by the reckoning of animals and men alike. For more than two hundred and fifty years, I've led a dog's life here in London's courts and thoroughfares, and this city and I have aged together. I've pissed on every model of lamppost ever designed for its wandering streets. I've watched as link-lit lanes gave way to hissing lamplight and sewers were dug to flush away ordure and odour. I've dodged coaches, chairs, hansoms, horse-drawn trams, steam trains, bicycles, and motorcars. One moment, I was biting at the heels of the fife-piping grenadiers, and the next, I cowered as Doodlebugs buzzed a blitz-dark sky. Cobblestones vanished and cement spewed, curing in tough squares. Commons grew uncommon. Chickens, pigs, cattle, alpacas, and horses disappeared, until only cats and dogs remain. Until, of all the animals I knew, only *I* remain. I passed a score of years, two score, three score. My age grew improbable and then impossible. Every decade I changed families, finding myself a new home: a garret in Spitalfields, a terrace in Fulham, a council estate in Willesden, a squat in Shepherd's Bush, a houseboat on the Thames, a flat in Canary Wharf. Now, I live here with you, tucked into a white box, stored in a black tower. We live more in the cloud than on any street I recognize. And now I, Pugg—the dog who seemed ready to outlive London—catch myself at last in the act of dying.

Beginning to die changes a dog. You too, reader and master, have seen the signs: grey hairs at my muzzle, stiff hind legs, damp evidence of occasional incontinence. All kindness, you clean up after me and call me "puppy" when you ruffle the fur around my neck, but we both recognize the meaning of that extra gentleness in your fingers. You know. I know. My impending death surprises you not at all, but it astonishes me—old as I am, I have never yet died. And yet, death comes.

Yesterday a deliveryman came to the flat, his face on the picture-panel beside your door. You pressed the button that allowed him entrance and he rode up in the elevator, finding us by our number, not by a signpost, no Golden Head to mark our door. Without a footman to provide the service, you yourself opened that featureless wooden slab. The liveried—nay, uniformed—deliveryman stood in the passage with your parcel in his hand. "You're a great one for the reading," he said, passing over the package, a book-shaped cardboard oblong. The whole time, I could see him looking between you and the shelves that fill our flat, and before he turned away, he spoke

D. M. Bryan

again. "Dying art—books," he said, and then he left us standing there, neither of us with a word to say in reply.

Dying art. Dying dog. More than an accident of timing gives my anecdote its bite, for in that moment of shared silence I understood the finality awaiting me, and I knew the time had come to dig this worn portmanteau from its hiding place. I keep it near me always, and so I have become adept at finding those situations where a manky leather case need not explain itself. And today, my reader and master, while you imagined me footling overlong behind the planters on the terrace, I ran faster and lugged harder than I have in years. I fetched my treasure and dragged it to your feet. Now you have touched its mottled skin, opened its buckling cover, and rustled its papery core. You look up from this page, straight into my brown eyes, and I return your gaze. There is a question in your look: what do you hold in your hands?

What indeed. A thick sheaf of papers, of which these are only the uppermost, wrapped in a protective shell of leather—my portmanteau. Bulging, blotched, and reeking of years, the case is unprepossessing, even ugly. But if you would see it as I do, imagine fine boards covered in goatskin, with marbled endpapers and uncut pages. Imagine a volume so handsome you yearn to take it between your palms. Use your knife to part the first fold of creamy paper, laying bare the houndstooth pattern of type. Bury your nose to smell ink and paper, traces of linen and soot. This is what you hold in your hands. A book in the shape of a portmanteau. A testament to a dying dog's wish that you keep reading.

Stay with me, and I will tell you how I became the portmanteau's keeper, long ago when its leather still showed amber smooth. Reader, follow me back to 26 October 1764, to a certain house in Leicester Fields. Press past the footman, up the stairs, and into the best bedchamber. Do you see me there, a much younger pug, shivering beneath the squat protection of an armed chair? Once you have fixed that picture in your mind, reader, print around the edges a heavy black border, a funereal frame, for lying dead upon the disordered linens was my first and best, my dearly beloved Master—William Hogarth, painter, printmaker, paper-seller extraordinaire.

I was half mad with grief, growling and yipping beneath my chair. Faithful cousin Mary Lewis, just risen from her vigil in that same seat, now stood hard by, her face buried in green bed-curtains. From the depths of those stiff folds came the cries common to all creatures, guttural pleas to the eldest power. She'd done her utmost, writing to Jane, still in Chiswick, but the letter sat on a table nearby, awaiting morning and the post. Underneath that impotent missive lay a sheet of paper, part of my Master's correspondence with a printer in Philadelphia. Full of a good dinner and with a steady hand, Master Hogarth had drafted its contents, innocent of the future. Then he went to bed. Almost at once, he rose up again to ring the bell so hard he shook loose the clapper. Then followed the vomiting, the crying out at the light, the pain.

Two hours he keened and kicked. Once Mary put me on his lap, hoping to distract him from his distress, but when he looked at me I saw how one eye drooped, his features done in wet paint. He called me by all my names—Pugg, Trump—and other titles that never were mine. A moment later he could call me nothing, sinking back into the bedclothes, a pale, sweating white, all line and tone wiped from his surface. Then Mary made noises, and I smelt only death.

A brown fug, perceptible to my keen dog's nose, rose from the body on the bed. I barked, flattening my ears and showing my teeth in a grin of distress, but to no avail. The fug grew thicker and moister, pervading the close atmosphere of the bedchamber. I began to pant, swallowing the air in quick puggish gulps, and I made my decision. I intended to lie down, there beneath the chair's stout legs, and move no more. Faced with my Master's death, I myself meant to die.

Beneath the bed I crawled, all fat legs and claws scrabbling sideways. A resurgent smell, at once salty and inky, pulled me there—my Master's scent, stubbornly returning. I sniffed and sniffed again, tracing the scent to a strip of red-brown hide, tanned and gleaming. Grief has its own logic, and a wise dog knows not to question it. My teeth closed on the handle, and so deeply did I bite the leather, my tooth marks still show to this day. I tugged and tugged, emerging from beneath the bed with a large, leather portmanteau. Dimly, I heard Mary Lewis call my name, but she would not leave that empty husk that had been my Master, and neither did she part me from this new object of my attention. Growling in the back of my throat, I backed from the room, holding tight between my teeth the leather so sweetly spiced with his aroma and my redemption.

Downstairs I went, tugging and pulling all the way. I towed the portmanteau as far as the rug in the front parlour. No lamp burned in that room, but by the feeble glow of the window, I looked at this odd leather case. I clawed at the object to better understand what it was. With my nose, I pushed it upright, but it fell over. Then, the cover flapped open of its own accord, and papers and prints spilled onto the carpet. I crawled upon those pages and dropped to my belly, grunting to myself in my puggish voice. Around me the house huddled, stilled and shocked.

I saw dark marks upon the spilled pages, forming into pictures pleasing to a faithful dog—it was my Master's work, I knew. A moon in eclipse. A ruined habitation. An orb on fire. Between my paws, a tower threw itself down, sending bricks and timbers tumbling. A paper burned, a skull grinned, and an artist's palette split apart. Images of the end of time and a comfort to a dog in my state of mind.

Long I lay in the dark, panting over my treasure and mourning the man-shaped hollow in the room over my head. I remembered how his deft fingers first lifted me from my littermates, and I felt ashamed to recall how I contracted like a muscle in his hand, sinking my puggish teeth deep into his thumb. In that moment my Master showed his mettle. Where a lesser man might have yelped in pain, flinging me hard against the wall, my Master only laughed and shook his hand free, calling me pugnacious, a fighter like himself. To his human companions he showed off the red print of my teeth in his thumb's skin. He called me his apprentice and the jagged bite my indenture—that division in the paper contracting student to master. Then he took me more firmly in his grip, wrapped me in an ink-stained cloth, and took me home.

From that day on, Master Hogarth kept me well, restraining me from my passion for the street, where horses' hooves and rolling wheels endangered not just my paws and my tail but my whole life. I ate well, dining on table scraps from his hand, and from the sweet-smelling fingers of the Jane we both loved so well. Exercise I took by my Master's side, and wherever he went, I followed. I sat beside him when he sketched with inky lines and washes on sheets of rag paper. I stood by his side when he transferred those designs to the copperplates of his trade. By the tweaking odour of ink, I learned the scent of the presses where the plates transferred pitchy lines to buff sheets. Wet and shining reproductions I saw in abundance, each like its neighbour hanging on the drying line. Fine folk came to view the latest in my Master's print series, to purchase sets of six or eight or twelve images to bind into books or to hang on their walls. Each series told a tale, a modern moral subject—this was the name my Master gave the story-pictures he drew and printed, and which made his name in the world.

Abundant praise the gentry gave my Master, and me also, stroking us and admiring our pluck. Behind our backs they noted our resemblance, our short, upturned noses, our round, curious eyes. When my dog's ears caught such whispers, I lifted my chin as much as a pug can, and I trotted more proudly at my Master's side. I would have doggedly followed him to the afterworld itself, but alas, he passed over the threshold without me. He left me to lie alone on the parlour floor, listening as feet passed, treading upstairs and down.

No one thought to search out a dog. I put my head on my paws and did not know I slept, but when I next raised my snout the window flushed a little, turning a traitorous pink. My Master was dead, but I had light, and I had life, which I did not want then, although I want it now. Distressed, I pushed myself to standing, confused by the printed pages between my close-clipped nails. By the window's glow, I could attend more fully to the other sheets smeared across the parlour rug, a portmanteau's worth of paper. On a nearby page, pale and oblong, I noticed dark marks. Excited, I nosed at the paper, pulling it toward me until I could make out the claw marks of printed words, and then without entirely intending to do so, I began to read.

Indeed, the task is not so difficult as it might seem. Consider how the world is already full of wonders: cellular division, exploding stars, acts of selfless assistance. Compared to these, a literate dog is a modest matter. Truth be told, I've borrowed many a book from your bookshelves, taking down volumes with my teeth, turning pages with the

D. M. Bryan

tip of my tongue. I have as much curiosity as anybody, and learning to read was the best way to scratch that itch. At first, I only gnawed at books as innocently as any infant scholar, but I did not long remain so artless. Soon I learned to settle my paws on either side of the covers, sniffing at the marks that raced across the page. With application, I began to recognize letters, which in turn clustered into words, each attached to an important idea like "sausage" and "beefsteak." With experience, my understanding grew, moving from the concrete to the abstract, just as Mr. John Locke suggests. I went from "meat," to "food," to "good," and hence to "a good," and soon I was able to read whatever I could lay my paws upon. Lounging on the sofa, I devoured novels. Crouched at the desk, I chewed over philosophical volumes. Finding myself standing over scattered pages, I could not help but read what lay beneath my pug's toes.

I scanned several pages quickly, and then returned to the top sheet to read with more care. Bafflement on a pug's face is not easy to recognize due to the wrinkling of an already-puckered brow, but I believe my expression must have been expressive of the confusion that overcame me then. Spewed across the floor of my Master's parlour lay such a variety of documents, I did not know what to think of this strange gift, my portmanteau.

Some of the pages were printed, while others were manuscripts in various hands. I nosed past a frontispiece, and pawed through letters. I found a magistrate's notes, a sinner's confession, and a last will and testament. I counted a number of my Master Hogarth's own prints, including the one on which I had slept, which was his last completed work. But even on this familiar ground, I felt muddled, for the pictures in this portmanteau were all scenes stolen from various tales and did not belong to a single modern moral subject.

I scratched my head with my rearmost leg. The reason for this collection, I could not guess. I had snatched my relic from beneath my Master's very bed, but I hardly knew why.

By that time, my thinking had begun to be troubled by those same urges that so disturbed Gulliver when restrained by the Lilliputians. But Gulliver was large where I was small, and when I turned to the door, I found that someone in the night had shut it tight. Now, the doorknob hung as golden and unattainable as the sun. I pointed my snout and howled for all I was worth, and just as I began to fear the portmanteau papers might serve only to protect the parlour rug, the serving girl heard me and, with a cry of pity, opened the door.

Out in the street, I made water next to a horse's hoof, just as now I might piss on a car's tire. But wherever the century, the sensation never alters—it is always blessed relief.

Now Mary Lewis herself came down and shook her head at what she termed my pitiable cries and lamentations. But she fed me and then took me upstairs again to my Master's bedchamber, where some-one had thrown open the window. Death's brown fug, once so un-bearable to my dog's nose, retreated to the edges of the room, a faint and diminished horror. Now the enormity of my loss threatened to burst apart my heart. The sight of the shrouded, still figure on the bed silenced me, and I curled myself into a fold of the bed-curtains and set my head on my paws. There I was allowed to remain, undisturbed, and how grateful I was that my Master's family took my bereavement no less seriously for all it flowed from a mere pug dog.

The following day, Jane Hogarth herself came up to London, arriving grim and determined but leaning on Mary Lewis even be-fore the girl could shut the hall door behind her. When the gloomy conclusion of my Master's affairs at last allowed us time to return to Chiswick, the leather portmanteau came also. I myself dragged it into the pile to be loaded on the back of the carriage. Sorrowing, distract-ed servants made my deception simple, and I had the satisfaction of observing my case roped to the rest and lashed above hooped wheels. Then I followed Jane into the body of the carriage, both of us climbing into the worn seats—no coach dog I. Jane gave the command, and our London life sank away with the jerk and jangle of the harnessed bays. We clattered westward, the wind rising, and the leaves flapping yellow and black as we passed.

I stayed with Jane for the next twenty-five years, claiming the place beside her as my own. It was the fate of other dogs to be buried in the sombre angle of Chiswick's canted garden, and if she observed that I did not similarly age and fail—well, she was Jane and I was Pugg, and our shared reticence on many matters brought mutual

D. M. Bryan

contentment. In silence we sat in the window seat of the upstairs parlour, watching Middlesex clouds pass west. Then even Jane left me to lie in the ground. Mary Lewis, that faithful cousin, took over the house and kept me also, not much noticing if I were Trump, or Pugg, or some bastard son. Those were overcast days, when the sky sagged like a water-bloated ceiling. Sometimes I wandered away from the house and went down to the grey river to howl. Or I went to the boneyard off Church Street, where I sat on the family tomb and wished to turn to Portland stone. At last, when Mary died and I could stand the house no longer, I left for good, trotting toward Chiswick town, knowing there was no one left to call me home. There I begged for scraps and challenged bigger, milder dogs to fights I could not win. The year was 1808.

In time, I took up residence with a widow who kept for her brother a house on the Devonshire Road. There I lived until I tired of the stink of his feet. The road to London was well marked, and I took it one wet morning, the lines of rain again suiting my mood. In London, I sought out all my Master's old haunts: Covent Garden and Leicester Fields. The city teemed with dangers, but it also contained kind souls in quantity. Every now and again one called to me, told me I looked famished. I was. London had revived my appetite, and I was truly hungry for the first time in this new century. Like the lapdog in Mr. Coventry's *History of Pompey the Little*, I went wherever I was welcomed, ate whatever I was given, answered to whatever name I was called. Many doors opened to me, and many arms. So many new masters, new mistresses, I struggle now to remember their faces, their smells. Some were gruff, while others approached me with caresses and kisses. Some lived in mansions and others in hovels. I dined on roast beef with some, while with others I shared scrag-end soup and turnip tops. But however I lived, I remained at heart a lost dog, always ready to wander away. Each time I wearied of one master, I followed another home. I tailed a parade of hospitable women and men out of that new century and into the next, but in all those years I never again stayed to outlive a master.

In this manner I have trotted on my short, set legs for two hundred years and more. And so, I return to you, my reader, who is also my latest and last master. You sit on your sofa with a well-chewed portmanteau at your feet—that leather companion I've buried and dug up, again and again. Now I am dying and must either pass these papers on or have them vanish forever. They smell of my Master, even after all these years, and I am a faithful Pugg, determined to keep him in the world in any way my dog's body can command.

Long ago, in my Master's day, when new printmaker's shops and bookseller's stalls appeared daily in London's streets; when anybody might put pen to paper and nobody yet knew the rules—then it was that this portmanteau first took shape. In those days, authors wrote as seamstresses make quilts, sampling from whatever was on hand and trading in materials printed for a multitude of markets. The people were hungry to read, and writers served up reheated criminal proceedings, printed confessions, newspaper accounts, true histories, romances, poems serious and satirical, letters, political pamphlets—any kind of writing that might be pressed into service. The contents of my portmanteau share this character with my Master's time, and between its leather covers, you will find a variety of documents, from various hands, for a diversity of purposes. I have put its pages into the best order I can find, but like the time from which it comes, my portmanteau makes variousness its delight.

In these pages, my Master's century takes on new life, and at its heels runs a little ^.^ The first of its borrowings picks the pocket of the prints that made my Master's name: *A Harlot's Progress*. Although sermons and spiritual biographies, sugared by repentance and redemption, sold a treat in those far-off days, the taste for printed stories included reversals and falls as well. In my Master's version, the Harlot no sooner arrives in London than she forgets her Sunday school catechism—and worse is to come. By raiding the notebook of one Justice Gonson, who is the prosecutor of that lady's crimes, my portmanteau makes common cause with my Master's *Harlot* or with Mr. Defoe's *Moll Flanders*.

No less admired by the readers of my Master's time was epistolary fiction, and so my portmanteau sprouts letters in abundance. The most celebrated of epistolary fictions was Mr. Richardson's *Pamela*, which resounds with the immediate scratching of that lady's pen. Mr.

Richardson, himself a printer, asked my Master Hogarth for a pair of frontispieces to illustrate his novel. Alas, my Master drew a pair indeed, but he fixed them to the front of Miss Pamela. Mr. Richardson, appalled by my Master's bad taste, elected to keep his *Pamela* modest. That lady, even today, remains famous for the immediacy of her letter writing. My portmanteau's Mrs. Betty scribbles with an equal passion, but reader, you will meet her yourself—and who can tell how many worlds might be contained within a laundress.

The History of Glossolalia—which appears next in my portmanteau—is a work that baldly names itself a novel. The rise of novels is a question at once vexed, debated, reviled, obscured, considered, theorized, celebrated, argued, avoided, and even forgotten. But what is undoubtedly the case is that the novel rose in my Master's day and borrowed its character from that long-ago time. Novelists, who scarcely knew to term themselves such, again borrowed, copied, emulated whatever they liked best, pillaging continental romances, books of religious instruction, and conduct manuals, as well as the forms already mentioned. In short, novelists pirated whatever set the black ink flowing.

No sooner does *The History of Glossolalia* find its slippered feet than it is interrupted. You will meet the lady who insists on appearing out of turn, but reader, before you make her acquaintance, you should know there was a real Sarah Robinson Scott, the author of *Millenium Hall* and other works. No scholar attributes *The History of Glossolalia* to her, but then that mutable work records nobody's name upon its frontispiece beyond some "respectable lady of mature experience." Scott's known work blurs the critics' line between romance and novel, between fiction and philanthropy, between innovation and conservation—frankly, between a lot of things. Sarah Scott once wrote to her sister, the bluestocking Elizabeth Robinson Montagu, *I should have been born a man and a gardener*, and I have no doubt that Sarah meant it. Many of Sarah's letters to her sister survive still, and in them, she records genteel poverty and illness, charitable projects, and literary ones as well. So yes, there is a real Sarah Scott, but reader, you are unlikely to have heard of her. Why has she chosen my portmanteau to address that deficit? I cannot say. If you like, you may hear her out and make up your own mind.

There were many literary females writing over the course of the eighteenth century, especially in the first half: Mrs. Jane Barker, Mrs. Penelope Aubin, Mrs. Eliza Haywood, or Mrs. Mary Davy. Females in hooped skirts and lace sleeves crawled, swarmed, and hatched their own kind of Grub Street, even if some of them rarely left the front parlour. In fact, the new media of the eighteenth-century produced so many lady novelists, that two-hundred years later a generation of critics and scholars of literature would grow embarrassed by novels like *The History of Glossolalia*. That slender volume's breathlessness and passion, its earnestness and moral rectitude, reddened the cheeks of the gentlemen, and the few ladies allowed to join in. They were all exceedingly eager to establish the seriousness of their new scholarly enterprise, and in their minds, Glossolalia's history led to a shameful line of housewives, charwoman, and shop assistants at the door of the lending library. Ready to the critic's hand was a three-hundred-year feud carried out between those authors writing romances—unlikely tales set in impossible places—and those writers authoring novels— the stories of modern persons confronting everyday problems—and even now, some critics (and bookstores too) preserve this antique debate, separating contemporary fiction from historical romance, or literary novels from fantasy.

With a single rapier cut, the critics shaped the history of novels to suit their own needs, subsiding into a rhapsody on genius, originality, authenticity, and ownership. My Master, who wrote a book of his own called *The Analysis of Beauty*, taught the wisdom of blending variety with regularity. Alas, his ideas were laughed at and then forgotten, as were the patchworkers, the seamstresses, the author of *The History of Glossolalia*, and her sisters. So reader when you reach Glossolalia, treat her with generosity and kindness. She may be stiff as a corset, her history much altered, stitched and threadbare, but her way of telling tales—digressions, stories-within-stories—was loved in her own time and does not deserve to fall to dust in a pug's paws.

My portmanteau's final tale, which concerns the adventures of Messieurs Quire and Gotobed, returns to another of my Master's

D. M. Bryan

prints from *The Idle 'Prentice, Betrayed*. Quire and Gotobed are as ready a pair of thieves as you might ever hope to meet, and they, like my portmanteau itself, steal that picture from my Master, desiring to make something new for themselves. Whether or not they succeed is yours to decide.

The spirit of my Master's age is in these tales. My portmanteau chases an old way of telling stories, following dogleg turnings, skirting the well-plotted path of modern fiction. If you desire a signposted road, well graded, then you must put away my portmanteau. However, if your nose twitches inquisitively at the scent of ink, if you are willing to chew over the contents of a leather cover, then I do not mistake you, my reader.

One final warning. The hundreds of years I have dragged my portmanteau from place to place have made their own alterations—torn pages, wetted pages, vanished pages, impossible pages even. Nothing can age without changing, and these portmanteau papers have been pressed forward through time, the contents seaming like Durham coal. They are not the pages they were, nor are they the pages they will be. You and they must work together to decide what they will become. And this, dear reader, is what you hold in your hand. Poor Pugg's gift. A consolation snatched from death's jaws. A capacious history masquerading as a leather case. A begging question delivered by an inky dog.

Reader, will you begin reading?

The

Justicing
Notebook

of

Sir John Gonson

Including *verbatim* Testimony
from Two Laundresses, witnesses to
the beginning of the end
of William Hogarth's famed *Harlot.*

Being a Work which gives great Light into many Obscure and Controverted Points pertaining to Laundry

Compiled by the EDITOR of the Twenty-four Volumes of LEGAL ETCETERA in Folio

LONDON:
Printed by Mr. Samuel PALMER a little without
St Bartholomew-the-Great
and sold at the Sign of the Tub, Temple Bar

1735.

CHAPTER 2

A printed transcript containing the testimony of
two laundresses respecting evidence of wrongdoing
contained within the first print of Mr. Hogarth's
popular series, *A Harlot's Progress*.

London. 1732.

What is that scribbling fellow doing, Justice Gonson? Each time I open
my mouth he scratches on his page with his quill. When I breathe, he
dips his pen. Watch him there—I believe he's taking down whatever I
say. I don't know I much like having my words locked down in black and
white, but I will tell you what I know, for I've taken an oath to do so.

I've seen that print you call evidence, the one from Mr. Hogarth's
A Harlot's Progress, and it is an astonishing bit of paper, to be sure. He
has drawn us all a grand view of the yard of the Bell, where the York-
London coach arrives with its hopeful cargo of maids in mobcaps.
They're country girls, all of them. Now, some might make a pun on
country, but I won't, and there's no reason for me to make light of those
poor little girls when the world will damn them soon enough.

Justice Gonson, sir, you asked me what I see when I'm out there on
that balcony that sits forever in the shadow of the Bell, where never so
much as a ray of sunshine comes down to dry my poor garments. Still, a
laundress must launder, no matter the weather. The mending I do, and
the washing, and when I'm done I hang it out in the London gloom, and
it waits to dry. The wind brings up the smuts, and sometimes a stocking
falls into the street below where Betty, the girl, must be quick to fetch

it before a horse tries it on (in a manner of speaking). Sometimes an apprentice scoops up that stocking before Betty can get down the stairs and out the door. Then she must beg to get it back, but she'll no more exchange it for a kiss than would I. Our Betty's no milkmaid but a city-bred miss, and she knows how a sweet beginning can quickly go sour. To Hades with you, says our Betty to them apprentices when they run at her, their mouths puckered like pockets. Hose-faced, she calls them, and worse. Betty's not a big girl, but she's foursquare and curved in the right places. Desirable as a chair is Betty, especially to them that's on their feet a deal.

Yes, thank you, I would like a seat. I'm none too steady, to tell a truth. I had a shock when the constables came. I'm an honest woman, as your Honour has had the goodness to say, but in our part of town the constables never bring good news—begging your pardon, gentlemen, but you'll have to avow a truth or tell a lie. Where you come, sorrow comes soon after. But be that as it may, here I am, and you asked me a question, so I'll answer it plain.

I have, as I said before, a view of the Bell's yard that gives me plain sight of the life of this city that finer folk must pay to see, if they see it at all. I mean the hurley-burley of a public house, which is as good as a play for entrances and exits. And as it happens, I'm often in my box seat when that conveyance, the York Coach, with its swollen canvas belly, comes trundling into the yard. I won't say I'm not curious to see the little line of miller's daughters as they come tumbling into the sunlight, a mess of babies, pink cheeked—each one bawling to leave behind some bosom friend made on the journey. A few of those girls have places already, some as maids and some to lend a hand in a lady's kitchen, if they prove quick enough. The lucky ones have a clever mama who has squeezed, out of nothing, the twenty pounds premium for a milliner's apprenticeship. But others have come from the countryside with no more of a plan than they have a map to mark their way through the crooked streets of this city. Those girls I pity, and so does Betty, in her way. Sometimes we lean out over the railings and lay friendly wagers on which ones will be met and by what kind of folk.

"Betty," I say, "I swear that clergyman on the white horse is here to take one of them Yorkshire lambs home to his wife to make a fine

D. M. Bryan

housemaid of her. I see the paper in his hand with Miss Molly's name writ on it."

"Miss Molly's name's not on it," says my Betty.

"Indeed," says I, "what's it say then?"

"I can't see from here. He's got it turned round the wrong way."

"Then you don't know for certain that's not Miss Molly's name scrawled on that scrap."

"No more than you know for sure it is."

And so we argue, while the clergyman strains his eyes to read his paper. He takes so long, I think he must be parsing a tract, not a note, and if so, he surely is one of those Enthusiastic ministers come to preach hellfire to the coach girls and so save their souls. This I put to Betty.

"Never," says Betty, who goes regular to church, and to a regular church too. "Those Enthusiastic gentlemen are too busy saving their own souls to worry over much about misses like these."

"For shame, Betty. They're Christians still."

"Well, the young ladies are, or at least they will be for a little while yet. But hush," says Betty, "who's that fellow coming out of the Bell with his hand in his pocket?"

Justice Gonson, that man in the print, wears a commonplace face, and I know what name some people give him, but I say different. I've seen the man who goes by the notorious name of Charteris, and that so-called gentleman is a great one for taking from the girls the only treasure they bring to town—and I don't mean the few coins they sew into the linings of their gowns. No, that Charteris has a deceitful, cozening face, and the fellow Betty and I saw was none of that. A plump, plum-pudding face he had, with an ample lower lip. He wore the very wig some folk designate as an Episcopal hairpiece. On the basis of phiz and wig alone, I can good as swear that this gentleman was no ravishing colonel but instead a well-meaning person, and an honest one too. As for other people and their idea of what his hand was doing in his pocket, why, their notions are like the gutter beside the street: not worth looking into. For my part, I believe the gentleman was searching for a copper with which to tip the man behind him, who'd provided a pretty piece of information.

And what was that information? Why that must be obvious to anyone with eyes, begging your pardon, sir. The girl, fresh off the wagon, could only be the gentleman's daughter. The long nose, the chin: one face is like a mirror to the other.

I said as much to Betty, who loves to be a little saucy, although she is as good a girl as I ever met.

"That's a book, you're thinking of there," said Betty, "and not the kind of life we watch from the balcony."

"No indeed," said I, for I loved to sauce her back. "The mistake's not mine, Mrs. Betty. Why, you take us for a pair of ladies attending a performance in Lincoln's Inn Fields. You think this is one of Mr. Gay's own plays, stuffed to bursting with female cynics and attended by an audience of whores."

I do beg your pardon once more, Justice Gonson, but you know that sort of work as well as any. For my part, I see no reason why life should be as bad as some authors put about. As you can no doubt guess from my picture of her so far, my Betty takes a different point of view, and she's not shy of expressing it.

"He's a stranger to Miss Molly," she told me. "She no more recognizes that gentleman as her father than she knows the bawd chucking her under the chin as her own mother."

"She's long lost is that Miss Molly," I said. "She won't know him yet, but she's his own true daughter, raised by honest country folk. Happens all the time."

"In stories," said my Betty, scenting my downfall. "Roxana's daughter was long lost in Mr. Defoe's book. That was a story. And wicked Mrs. Flanders was lost and found by her own mother. She claimed it was the truth, but we all know better. Hers was as naughty a story as anyone ever told. Pretty Miss Ardelisa was well and truly lost to the world, if we believe Mrs. Aubin, but Mrs. Aubin does not intend that we do. Now, your Miss Moll's just plain lost," said my Betty, "and she's nobody's daughter—at least nobody like to come out the door of the Bell. No, I see no stories coming true in that yard. All I see is cracked plaster, piles of stone, and a rat like to scurry under Miss Moll's skirts. What do you see, old woman?"

D. M. Bryan

I saw what I chose to see. Sometimes we save ourselves with stories, but I knew better than to say so to Mrs. Betty when she was in that sort of mood.

"I swear," Betty says to me, "the longer I look at that stack of pails there, the more it looks like a gentleman's upright member."

"Betty, I am shocked," says I. "I won't go discussing books with you, if you carry on in that vein."

And no more would I, but I finished hanging my stockings and went back inside, and saw no more of what came of that pretty little Miss and her kind old father.

London's a big city, Justice Gonson, and I've lived here all my days. I didn't always bide in this room by the Bell, and sometimes I've lived in worse places and other times I've lived in better. But for all its size, this city sees us running in shoals. A hake or a haddock swims surrounded by nothing but its own kind, and so it is with Londoners. From Petty-France to Blackwall, from Shoreditch to Southwark, we drift along with those we most resemble. In streets, we pass lordly steps of assembly halls, but we can no more flow up those staircases than can water. We stick to our rightful channels, banked in by those most like us. Hardship parts us and rejoins us, like tributaries of the same river. Fathers and daughters, brothers and sisters must needs keep a watchful eye on any new fish in the stream. Courting is fraught with all manner of peril in our narrow streets. Who knows when family feeling comes garbed as sentimental partiality, or sibling affinity hides beneath robes of love. Sometimes what looks like providence isn't even coincidence. There's wheels within wheels, your honour—we're all taught that—but some of those wheels aren't very big, and the ones holding the likes of us never run very far. Not even the wheels on the York Coach.

As for the girl arriving by that contrivance—to be sure, I don't know. It's none of my business, but I'm willing to bet my cap she's as good as any girl who ever took breath in a romance. If I give her a good father, a mother waiting at home, a brother and sister who wreath her neck with kisses, am I to blame? She's a good girl, I'm sure, and she deserves as much as any girl to be revealed as the child of the Count de Blanchisserie, or the infant lost by Lord and Lady Washingdone. You can be sure of that, Justice Gonson, and I'll say nothing against such fantasies.

I was young when I was read those books, sir, but I like them as well as anything Betty reads me now. Perhaps you've got a different ending ready for that poor country girl—and the way you and your constables are looking at me, I suspect you might—but, sirs, I don't wish you to tell me that story. I don't want to know what goes on at the Bell. I can't help what spills out of the prodigious gut of the York Wagon. And while Betty and I pity those girls standing lost in that grimy yard, there's no story ever wrote that can do justice to what they must feel, as they face into the wind and wonder what will come next.

There now, I've made you a poor repayment for my time resting in this comfortable chair, and the Constables have wasted an hour in coming to fetch me when I had nothing fit for anyone to hear. As recompense, I shall tell you a story of my own, and you may apply it as you wish.

It also starts on my balcony where I was hard at work, hanging out laundry. A gentleman came by and stood for a while, looking at the sign of the Bell with his hands on his plump hips. The York Coach had come and gone, and the yard was empty, save for we two, him on the ground and me in the gods. The gentleman stood so long in the rain, and looked so hard at the signpost, that at last, I began to make him my business. I asked him if he was lost, and I told him if he desired a warm fire or nourishment, he might go through the Inn door and ask the landlord. He'd been gawking so long I thought him simple, but he rapped back at me so quickly that I immediately conceived a very opposite opinion of him.

"Do you know why this signpost boasts a Bell?" he asked, stamping his feet in the mud. Tadpole splotches decorated his stockings and hemmed his greatcoat.

I shook my head so vigorously my cap slipped. "Indeed, sir, I do not," I said, wishing Mrs. Betty was home. She's the bright one, is Bet.

The gentleman hemmed—one long note, in his throat. He looked a bit like a bulldog, with round eyes and a flat nose. "I suppose you know no French," he said.

Again, I shook my head, my hand to my cap for safety's sake.

D. M. Bryan

The man squinted at me. "No matter—no man ever painted a signpost in *your* honour," he said. "Ugly bitch." And then he went away, leaving footprints in the mud.

When Betty came home, she found me by the fire. "He meant Belle," I told her, after I'd recounted what the Bulldog said. "Not Bell. There's far too many Frenchmen in London, not to know that much."

Betty went out in the rain, and she walked in the wet street to find a constable, but when she found him, he told her there'd been no crime. Calling an ugly bitch by its rightful name was no more than using language in the very way God intended, and what's more, the great Mr. Locke agreed with him—or so the constable said. And when Betty suggested they arrest Mr. Locke too, both the constable and the beadle laughed at her, and so she came home.

On second thought, your Honour, Justice Gonson, I don't much care for this story either. It loses something in the telling, and I'm sure it never had much charm to begin with. It ends flat and never gives the satisfaction a body gets when wrong things are put right. That's the problem with stories that contain only truth, and so we prefer those that intermix the plain fact with a little cordial to make it taste the sweeter. Or we cut strong drink with a measure of water, so it's not so heady as to do us damage. However we do it, we always mix romance and true history so the tipple is most to our taste. But begging your pardon, your honour, I've told you two tales, and I can see by your face that neither sits easy with you. And here comes Mrs. Betty to find out why I've been so long away from home. Ask her what you've asked me. Ask Betty, will you, for here she is now, and she knows a deal, she does.

Ask Betty, says my mistress. Fact is, you've fatigued that good lady with your inquiry, gentlemen. Her colour's not right—why did you have to worry her so? You've brought her a wearisome way, and plagued her with questions. She'll say no more for the time being, although I'll warrant there's plenty she could tell you. You wave your printed picture beneath our noses and tap upon faces with your long fingers. What for? That man beneath the constable's well-pared nail has many names around the yard of the Bell Inn. There's a hundred stories about that ferret-faced person with his hand in his pocket. Ask anybody. We all know most of them.

I've washing to do, Mr. Justice. We're women with work waiting and no time to chat with idle constables. But until my mistress breathes a bit more comfortable, I'll tell you what I know. I'll talk as long as she takes to regain her strength, and then you'll call a chair to take her home. These are my terms, gentlemen, and you'd do well to meet them, for it does happen I know a little about the matter at hand. Servants like to bring tittle-tattle along with the worsted stockings—and with the silk ones too. Have you the patience to listen to a little scandal, Mr. Justice Gonson, for the man you're asking about comes with dirt attached.

Once he was a fine gentleman. He had come into the world with a good name and family but very little money of his own, which is so often the case. When the time came for him to take a wife, he looked far and wide for one who might bring him a portion of the size to mend his fortunes, and in time he found just the lady. She was only a young thing, but rich, her father having made his wealth selling the very water God made to sustain us all. The father, having chosen this path through life, could not, alas, be called a good man, and few mourned him when he died. Without friends, he left his daughter all alone in the world, with none to guide her or to discover to her the wicked ways of men. But false advisors aplenty this world contains, and no sooner was the old man dead than many meretricious counsellors began to clamour for the young lady's ear. Each claimed to be worthy of her unalloyed trust alone, but in truth none of them deserved her faith. One after another they disappointed the confidence she placed in them. One lied about the amount of her rents, while another cheated her of the interest on her capital. A third—a Latin tutor—took a pair of diamond earrings from the box where she kept them. Very soon, the young woman discovered that the world held as many ways to be cheated as it held men to cheat her, and in the end she sent them all away and swore she would be the master of her own purse 'til the day she died.

Well, Justice Gonson, you will guess that this lady, Miss G— we might call her, did not keep her vow or else I would have no story to tell to you today, and as you are undoubtedly a canny judge of men, and

D. M. Bryan

maids too, you will have guessed aright. The gentleman of whom you inquire, hearing of the lady's wealth, determined to discover a way to crack open the lady's heart and her strongbox alike. He found himself well suited to this endeavour, for he was still young, neatly formed, and with a noble name.

He made inquiries and soon discovered that Miss G— was paying a long visit to a distant cousin, who was a determined card player with a particular passion for ombre. Accordingly, the gentleman made inquiries of those of his friends who passed their time playing cards, and you'll not be surprised to learn, sir, that the young man knew many of these. Without much trouble, he found a rogue who would introduce him to the house where the cousin also went to play, and as soon as he passed through those doors, he made use of his noble name to engage himself at the cousin's table. In short, sir, the gentleman wasted no time in engaging Miss G—'s relation in a hand of ombre, at which he so charmingly lost that he won from her an immediate invitation to play cards with her on any occasion. The gentleman—he was not a lord for he was only a younger brother, but he was a colonel and so I will call him by that name—accepted the cousin's offer with many bows and fine words, and lost no time insinuating himself into her drawing room. Before long, he found himself fully in her favour, and she soon considered him one of her closest confidants and dearest friends, although in truth they were hardly acquainted at all.

Visiting, as he did, the cousin's house daily, the colonel hoped to catch sight of the young lady, the object of his field manoeuvres, but here he found himself disappointed, for unlike her cousin, Miss G— did not venture at cards and did not risk the contents of her strongbox on games of chance. The colonel admitted that he had suffered a sharp check to his play, but he did not think it sufficient to prove more than an inconvenience, and indeed, in this he was right.

You might ask how I know so much of the tale, Mr. Justice, sir. The truth is I heard it all patchwork, and while it was happening too. I heard one part from the cousin's housemaid, who used to bring that lady's linens in a basket for us to boil up in our pot. I heard a second part from the gentleman's man who brought all his stockings, his neckerchiefs, and his handkerchiefs—about which he was most particular. The third part came from an unexpected person, but more of that in its time.

The colonel rarely endured a setback long, and soon enough he saw his opportunity, for while he was leaving one morning after a full night's entertainment at the card table, he met at the door the virtuous Miss G—, who was just leaving for matins. He immediately swept off his hat, for they were now in the street, and taking the lady's hand, he helped her into a carriage. In the midst of this act of gallantry, he stepped ankle deep into the brown-flowing street and besmirched his finest lawn stockings, and so I came to know of this first meeting, for the gentleman's gentleman told us the tale when he brought us the dirtied garments. "I swear, Mrs. Betty," he said, "it cannot be love that makes my master so careless of his hose, but it might as well be."

The next I knew of the courting came in the shape of an apron stained with claret. This bib was a lovely thing made of a pale green silk and worked with golden threads to form flowers, the like of which have never been seen blooming in any field. The claret formed a rusty stain that ran over one of the pocket openings and dribbled toward the explosion of blossoms that marked the apron's corner. The housemaid who brought it carried nothing else and arrived on a day quite out of her usual time for coming. With the apron spread on the table, she squeezed out a dampish glance at my mistress, asking us in a few words if the pretty piece might be cleaned, for it was a gift her lady valued most particularly. My mistress plucked the apron up and took it to the window, holding the fabric closer to the light. Overhead, the skies hung heavy with rain. The wine stain troubled my mistress—I could read that sad fact as clearly in her face as if she were a broadsheet and I a scholar in a coffeehouse. "What happened, Mrs. Susan, to waste so much wine?" said I to the housemaid, wishing to give my mistress time for her examination.

The housemaid turned her drowning eyes on me. "Oh Lord, Mrs. Betty, 'twas the colonel. He would teach Miss G— to play at ombre, and she would refuse him, and they carried on so until the decanter was overset and my lady doused, and the colonel would laugh despite my lady's dismay. Theirs is not a very proper courtship, and I cannot think why the young lady allows it to continue."

"Shocking," said my mistress, but her heart wasn't in her words. "How long since the spill?"

"Why it happened only last night. And my lady dismissed the colonel as soon as she could make him listen, but I saw him in the street as I came away this morning. He looked very contrite indeed, and he stood by the paling of the house opposite ours. He would have called me over, only I feigned I could not hear him."

"That was very well done," I told Mrs. Susan, and she and I said more in the exchange of a glance.

But my mistress said, "Did you rub it with some salt, my dear? That is the usual physic in a case such as this."

"Alas," said Mrs. Susan, "I would have done so immediately, but my lady would not let me because it is such fine silk and a gift from the same gentleman that ruined it."

My mistress only folded the apron and passed it to me. "Milk," she said, "then wash it, very gentle, in Castile soap with a little fuller's earth. Afterwards, clap it quick between the drying cloths."

To Mrs. Susan, she only smiled a little and offered her a sip of cordial from the special bottle she kept on a shelf above her bed. While I soaked the apron in a little warm milk, Mrs. Susan took some of the sweet drink, and then she took some more. She was very merry when she went home again, promising to call for the apron and, in reply to my particular request, agreeing to add something to the story of the courtship, if there was anything to tell.

"I always try to send them away happy," my mistress told me as we watched Mrs. Susan weave her way across the yard of the Bell, "and if it cannot be one way, why it must be the other."

It was the colonel's gentleman who arrived next, climbing the stairs to our poor room while the apron still dried in its cloths. In his arms he carried a pinned up bundle of regular laundry, which he set on our table with a curt nod to my mistress. When we unpinned his parcel to count each piece before his eyes—a necessary surety with us laundresses—we found, amidst the linen shirts and stocks, a waistcoat made of a tan broadcloth and spotted with a few drops of something like enough to blood to make my mistress pounce like a terrier upon a rat. She shook out the waistcoat, and then she tucked it tight to her nose, taking a mighty sniff.

"There now," I told the colonel's gentleman, "your master has been duelling, and my mistress has discovered him," but the gentleman only smirked, watching that lady as she licked the tip of her finger and touched the stain with a delicacy she did not often show.

"Fie, Betty, hold your tongue," she said to me. "We've had no combat here. The good man's master has employed himself at nothing worse than a spot of writing." She turned to face the gentleman's gentleman and made him a very polite bow, to which he bowed back in a manner every bit as genteel.

Well, I was a bit put out, to tell the truth, to see the two of them bowing like a pair of granddames at a God-daughter's christening, and so I pointed out to them what I thought they ought to have seen from the start. "They may be inky dark," I told them, "those drops, but the stain on your finger is nothing if not the colour of blood."

My mistress bugled a little, which was her way of laughing, and the gentleman's gentlemen gave me a how-do-y'do with his hat, but I held fast to my opinion and crossed my arms firm over my front. "Ink, no matter how red," said my mistress, "smells of ink." And then she passed me the waistcoat with her instructions: "Tallow, very pure, allow it to harden on each spot. Boil the garment and spread to dry."

When the gentleman's gentleman was gone, I did as she directed and found the drops came out, leaving only the faintest of shadow to show where they had been. This, I scraped with a knife, rasping the surface of the affected fibres, until the whole was innocent of any stain. Holding up the waistcoat, I teased her, calling her a witch and telling her she'd be sure of a generous tip when the colonel's gentleman returned. When she heard me, she grew sober-faced and told me she had no expectation of anything extra from that quarter—no indeed, she would not be surprised if the colonel's gentlemen never returned to collect his bundle, and all for want of the few coins to pay us. I was not well pleased at her saying such things, for the labour of cleaning the waistcoat, as well as the stocks and shirts, had been mine, and in truth, I hoped that part of any reward might come to me as well. I could not see what lay behind my mistress' reasoning, and I demanded that she

D. M. Bryan

tell me why she might say such things about a gentleman as rich as the colonel.

"Red ink," she reminded me, "is what financial gentlemen use for the writing down of sums, especially those that must be paid out. If the colonel has been fighting with anyone, Mrs. Betty, it is sure to be with the man who keeps his receipts."

I asked how she knew such a thing, for her understanding to me appeared to extend to matters far beyond the mysteries of her trade, but she only said, as she had on so many other occasions, that "secrets wash out with the linens."

I told her I thought the romance between Miss G— and the colonel was certainly over if his financial matters stood in such a sorry condition. My mistress said nothing to that.

We had no further news of any of the parties for some time. To our surprise, Mrs. Susan did not call for the apron—the piece having turned out very well, the silk quite restored to its former glory—but in her place came an excessively nice person who identified herself as Miss G—'s own lady's maid. She was very exact in her conduct and in her concern for her reputation, and she was equally scrupulous when she came to consider our work. The apron she spread out by the window, examining it by the strength of the light filtering through the yard, for on this day the courtyard was filled with rare beams of sun. At length, the maid approved our work and paid my mistress what she asked, and a little more besides. However, we did not dare ask her to tell us what had come of the matter between the colonel and her lady. Only when she stood ready to depart, poised like a curving mark against our bright doorway, did I have the sauce to ask how fared Mrs. Susan. I hoped, I said, that good person's health did not keep her indoors when the weather was so very fine.

"Mrs. Susan," said the lady's maid, "has been dismissed."

"Indeed," said my mistress, "that is surprising news—and disappointing. She is a particular friend of ours, and a goodly woman besides." I felt a wash of pride at my mistress' loyalty.

"I cannot stay to engage in tittle-tattle," said the lady's maid, but neither did she leave.

"Certainly, it cannot be tittle-tattle," said my mistress, "if you were to do us the kindness of informing us how our friend fares. I cannot guess what might have caused Mrs. Susan's departure from the family, for she has always held Miss G— in the highest esteem."

"Well I might tell a little," said the scrupulous person on the threshold, and she turned and re-entered our poor room.

On account of the water we needed to boil, we always kept a good fire burning, which made the room very warm indeed, but the woman stood before the hearth and baked in her fine clothes. My mistress motioned to me, and I lifted a pile of drying cloths from a chair and offered it to her. At first, she did not seem to understand me, but then she took the seat, dropping down with such a whoosh of skirts that her lappets floated upwards, giving her the look of a rabbit. I thought my mistress might offer her some of the cordial she and Mrs. Susan liked to sample, but she did not. Neither did my mistress sit down beside the lady, but stood waiting for that person to speak.

"You might have guessed from my remarks," the lady's maid began, "that I have some knowledge of the manner in which Mrs. Susan was dismissed. The comings and goings of housemaids are a matter for the housekeeper, but in this case, I am persuaded to take a special interest. Indeed, my own character is such that I hate to see an injustice done."

"An injustice?" I said. "Was Mrs. Susan done an injustice?"

The lady's maid placed her hands together in her lap. "Mrs. Susan overstepped her place," she said, "and involved herself in matters that were not her business."

"What did she do?" said my mistress. "If I may be supposed to be free of the same stain."

"She allowed a stranger to enter her mistress' house—a man quite unknown to that lady."

"But she was discovered?"

"I learned of the matter when she came to fetch my own lady, Miss G—."

"Your lady? Not Mrs. Susan's employer, who is mistress of that house?"

"Miss G— was the lady to whom the gentleman wished to speak."

"What did you do next?"

"I did not like the affair—a stranger unknown to the house, admitted through the wiles of a housemaid to see a young woman with no male relation to protect her. I went to the drawing room and saw the gentleman myself, demanding to know his business with my lady, but he said it was a matter for her ears only."

"So you went to your mistress' cousin, the lady of the house?"

She nodded. "I went immediately and I told her of Mrs. Susan's irregular conduct toward a stranger who would not confess his business. My lady's cousin grew alarmed and came with me to the drawing room. She too examined the stranger, who sat bold-as-you-please in one of her wing chairs."

"And what did he say?"

"Only that it was a private matter between himself and Miss G—."

"Did you not think to summon Miss G— and so make an end of the affair?"

The scrupulous person did not seem capable of immediate speech, and she gazed at my mistress with every appearance of deep thought. At last she said, "My lady was at that moment upstairs, in a private interview with the colonel, and we hoped a marriage contract might be the happy result. Her cousin and I judged it best not to disturb her with idle matters. In short, we sent the gentleman on his way, with a warning not to return."

"But it was precisely on the matter of the marriage contract that the stranger wished to speak with Miss G—."

The scrupulous person looked at my mistress for a moment or two. "How could you possibly know that?"

My mistress only busied herself with the washing. She went to a sideboard where stood a number of bowls and pitchers containing the sundry items required by our trade. She selected a large earthenware jug and brought it closer to her washtub.

"And Mrs. Susan?" I asked.

Miss G—'s maid said, "Mrs. Susan immediately repeated her fault, overstepping her place once again. I caught her at the foot of the stairs where she was making to warn my lady of the gentleman's visit. I pulled her back, and her mistress spoke very sharply to her. Then, sniffing and wiping her nose, Mrs. Susan said some very shocking things about the colonel. My lady's cousin cried out how wicked it was to raise a false report, proving, I think, that she was as much the colonel's advocate as I. Pressed to recant, Mrs. Susan refused, and she was—I blush to own it—dismissed on the spot."

My mistress allowed the faintest look of disapproval to show on her fleshy face. She watched as the excessively scrupulous person, seeking to disguise her discomfort in action, bent to the earthenware container, the better to examine its contents. At last, my mistress said, "You might take care," but already the poor woman had come within smelling distance of the jug, brimming with sharp-smelling urine for whitening. Snapping stiffly like an apron in a breeze, she righted herself. When she turned back to us, her face was wet with tears, and I sincerely hope they were the product of an honest repentance for her treatment of Mrs. Susan.

Whatever the cause, Miss G—'s maid took out a fine linen handkerchief, edged with lace, and daubed at her eyes.

"And now they are married," she said, "and already he spends her money at such a pace my lady grows quite distracted over his love of luxury. Yesterday, she went to see a man, so prudent in the managing of estates as to serve many a rich man as a kind of privy-counsellor. This gentleman told her something very shocking. Acting out of kindness and on the suggestion of some person he would not name, he had already attempted to pay her a visit, wishing to warn her of the colonel's financial improprieties before she took any fatal step. Alas, he was turned away before he could communicate what he knew, and now her money is no longer her own, and so even he is powerless in her cause. My lady returned entirely discouraged and will not leave off weeping."

And here the maid suited her actions to match those of her lady, until droplets tumbled unchecked from her pointed chin, dampening her fichu. "You must believe, I did not know," she said. "He was so handsome, the colonel."

My mistress crossed her arms against her very clean tucker. She stands not much taller than a boy and is grown nearly as broad, and when she places herself in this posture, she shows herself a person to be reckoned with. "You do not need me to tell you what you must do," she said, "but it must be done if you are to have any peace at all."

D. M. Bryan

At this the lady's maid lifted her wet face. She reemployed her kerchief, this time to apply some real order to her features, and then she rose, straightening her dress.

"As to my lady's marriage?" she said.

"As to that, I have no remedy."

Nodding her lace cap, the lady's maid departed without another word, and I hoped she understood the considerate usage she'd had of my mistress, who I thought had been kinder than she deserved. In setting that lady to remedy the wrong she'd done, my mistress had schooled her in the correct method of lifting a blot from a conscience and yet had not asked for so much as a farthing.

The lady's maid proved to be as scrupulous in doing right as she had been in meddling. Mrs. Susan resumed her former station as housemaid in the family where she had been dismissed. The cousin, her mistress, showed her restored servant no prejudice, but rather that chastened lady found every opportunity to seek Mrs. Susan's sage advice. In time, the death of the family's housekeeper—a very aged lady—allowed Mrs. Susan herself to assume the position, in the exercise of which she continues to give her mistress every satisfaction. Her happiness is no more than is due any one of us who has shown ourselves not only without spot or blemish but resistant to both.

As for me, I had one more question. "Mistress," said I, "who do you think advised that prudent financial manager, the rich man's privy-counsellor, to seek out Miss G—?"

"Shush," said my mistress. "And pass me the urine."

But I can see, Justice Gonson, that your constables grow weary of my account of Mrs. Susan and the lady's maid, for while such matters make profitable hearing for servants, I discern that they do not entertain gentlemen whose need for brevity is paramount. You expected my story to concern, not laundresses and housemaids, but the colonel himself.

As for that intemperate person, I know only what all the world knows. The newlyweds set up in a house near to King's Square, where the colonel, in accordance with Mrs. Susan's intelligence of him, proves in every way a great rake. He spends his new wife's fortune at prodigious speed, and poor Miss G— is now styled a fine Lady but with empty pockets. For all her care, she was finally betrayed by her own heart, the loan of which was everything the colonel needed to crack open her strongbox. And even such an excellent laundress as my mistress has no remedy for the complete discolouring he has given to both their names.

Now, I see that my mistress' colour has returned to her, and she breathes evenly again. If you would be so kind as to call for a chair, Justice Gonson, we are ready to go home.

D. M. Bryan

Chapter 3

Letters between Mrs. Betty, in the parish of St. Paul,
and her sister, Mrs. Sadie Nutbrown, who has gone to
live in the country.

Bell Inn Yard off Fryday Street, 1732.

My dearest Sister,

My fingers are sore from washing and can hardly hold a pen, but I
must write. My mistress works hard, and I am always eager to follow
her model. We scrub and scrub, until she tells me, "Mrs. Betty, off you
go now and write a few lines to that sister of yours before she forgets
you." And so I write, although I have scarce the energy to hang out my
thoughts like stockings on a drying line.

Have you forgotten me yet? I have almost forgotten you. How
cruel you are to have married a man who lives in distant Hackney, and
how hard you are to relocate to the country, following that handsome
Arcadian, your bridegroom. I commend your choice of Henry
Nutbrown, who will make a fine husband, but by your new settlement
you have taken yourself beyond the realm of ordinary discourse, and
that is an act I must condemn with all the righteous anger of a sister
left behind. If you needed to marry, I do not understand why you could
not have chosen one of the many dirty fellows who haunt our lane. Any
one of them would have been happy to subsist off the labour of a hard-
working female like you. Indeed, I should take one as my own husband
quick enough—just as soon as I rid myself of this curious disinclination

to marriage, for which I cannot quite account. Although I do remind myself of how, from our earliest infancy, you and I were able to observe repeatedly the follies of a bad union. And as to that, our mother fares not at all well: our father is gone again, and she does not know if she wishes for him to return or to stay away. She asks heaven for both, but God, wise in all things, refuses to decide when she cannot—alas, this is not the subject I intended, and I hoped to write a letter and not a book.

I am writing to you in your newly countrified state so that I might parade before you the many attractions of the town—well, of the city, I suppose, for other than washing the stains from their undergarments, I know little of the inhabitants of those western reaches. Regardless, here is a glimpse of the high life: my mistress and I have been taken up by the constables and brought before the law. Some days past, we were invited to the home of Justice John Gonson, a man of great renown for his very moral campaign, cleansing London's stews. Upon arriving at his handsome home, we were entertained by him in a back parlour filled with dog-eared papers and dusty books. Alas, we were not taken as whores or highwaymen, but rather as witnesses, and so our reputations continue unmade. I told my mistress such a lack of notoriety could only harm our business, but she patted my arm and told me I was subject to such strange fantasies as could only come from books.

"No, mistress," I told her, "the fantasies in books must come from nature first, for even the most unlikely of circumstances must have one foot in experience."

"No experience can teach that it is good business to be taken as a highwayman," she said.

"Unless you would write a book," said I, and she agreed that authorship was a business apart from the others.

But Sadie, you will want to hear more about Justice Gonson. You must imagine a wig, a small pair of eyes, and a ruffle, well-wetted with lashings of his dinner. If you wish a fuller portrait you may see one in Mr. Hogarth's remarkable series pertaining to a harlot, just published. Wiser folk than I have found Mr. Gonson twice in those pictures. They say it is he who arrests the harlot in the third print and who is hanged in a little graffito in the fourth. I myself have not seen the whole series, but I would like to very much. The Justice gave us only a glimpse of one print, which showed a pretty maid emerging from the York wagon, with the signpost for our Bell Inn behind her. Justice Gonson told us that this picture bears investigation and that we might help him get to the bottom of things if we would answer honestly his questions. Now, I hear you asking me what is that bottom for which the Justice delves, and why does he need a pair of laundresses to assist him in his digging. Sister, I do not know. I can only tell you we answered the Justice's inquiries as fully as we could, whereupon he thanked us very genteelly and sent us away in a chair each. Since then, my mistress and I have been all in a lather, but that is our usual condition, and I wonder if I will ever tire of jests about laundry.

Joking aside, I do love to be a laundress, sister. All London comes to our door with their shirts and their socks, and they bring us a great deal more besides. Since our encounter with the Justice, the world comes to tell us that Mr. Gonson's interest in the Harlot's case is far from disinterested. We are told that the gentleman takes to heart the charge that his moral program against harlots does more harm than good. Maids and housekeepers alike whisper that Hogarth's pictures show his Harlot happy and healthy before her incarceration in Bridewell, and her true decline begins with Gonson's entry at her door. Some go so far as to say that the Harlot's death is a charge upon the Justice's bill—that his actions as good as killed the woman.

Those same tongues tell that Justice Gonson would clear his name by refuting the notion that the drawn figures in the prints have real names, which is the very premise that makes London love Mr. Hogarth. I am obliged to think this last is partially true, for when we went before him, Justice Gonson had a dozen questions about one figure amongst the others—the man in the doorway, standing with his hand in his pocket. Did not that man have a face like a hundred other men? Had we not passed dozens just like him on our way to his house? Did we know that Charteris, the rape-master general of England, lies dead and buried—his coffin drawing forth curses and rotting fruit as it passed in the street?

Yes, yes, we said, agreeing with the Justice that Mr. Hogarth's tale must be feigned and all the figures figments. Privately, I wondered why the Justice could not see that the defense of such a bad man as Charteris could do his own name no good, but men are ever thus. In order to prove their innocence, they would come to the assistance of every villain and blackguard within city walls and without. It is a kind of fellow feeling in them, and why they do it, I cannot say.

My mistress agrees that the face in the doorway might belong to one hundred men, but her reasons are not Justice Gonson's. She says she's seen many a spill of fish-sauce on a napkin that seems to have eyes, nose, mouth. Mr. Hogarth's skill at engraving improves upon fish-sauce, but even his most telling detail is no more than ink on a page. Ink might stain a reputation, and it might cause a conscience to bleed, but an impression taken is not the same as the object that made it, and my mistress takes pains to distinguish between the two.

Truly, my mistress does not see as others see, and her way of looking is still novel to me. In order that I might better understand, I have asked her if we might close up our room for a few hours and venture forth into London's streets. I would that we might find a printseller who displays Mr. Hogarth's prints—London so loves his *Harlot* that such a shop should be easy to find—and then my mistress and I might more fully understand the nature of the inquiry in which we have played such an insignificant part.

This proposal my mistress has accepted, and so soon I shall write you the details of our excursion. I am very excited, sister, for although I love to be a laundress, I see vast quantities of washing and very little of the world. I fear one day I will have no conversation beyond how to get up lace and the best method of clear-starching. This last is simple enough: do not let cloths lie in starch; do not use hot water or make your lather with a whisk; do not neglect to use sufficient bluing in your rinse. If you do these things, sister, your muslins will not yellow.

You may see that I am truly your affectionate sister, Elizabeth.

My dearest Sadie,

I shall enclose this letter with my last, for I have written them so close together, a single enclosure will do for both. They are as peas in a pod, and sister-letters to each other.

Just as she promised, my mistress let the fire go out under the pots on our hearth and bade me find my Brunswick jacket. Then, when we were properly arrayed against the day, she closed up our door but did not lock it, for as you know we lodge only and the door has no fastening. Our landlady heard our tread on the stairs and opened her parlour door. When she saw my mistress dressed and ready to go out, she could not restrain an expression of surprise. "La," she said, "has someone died?"

You see, sister, many come up those stairs to bring us washing, and sometimes I run down on errands, but rarely does my mistress set foot in that dank front hall. But my mistress only smiled pleasantly at our landlady, and asked after the health of Mr. Hudson, and all the little Hudsons, a pack of whom looked out from behind their mother's wide skirts. "We're well enough," said our landlady, "but I hope you haven't left that fire untended upstairs, or we'll all be dead when you come back."

My mistress assured her the house was safe, and that she had all that family's linens washed and drying on lines. She added, "The greasy spot in Mr. Hudson's cuff is gone, and the threads restored to themselves." She was right, for I'd removed that stain myself with a coal wrapped in a damp bit of brown paper, the heat doing what no soap could manage. My mistress tipped me a wink of her eye.

"That's well done," said our landlady, "and I thank you kindly. You must rap hard on the door when you return, for the girl says she cannot hear if people tap too politely."

Sadie, you may imagine, with the two of us out together, our landlady had a rare chance to inspect our belongings—and her own as well, for the furniture of that room belongs to her. We should certainly return to whorled fingerprints on our shining copper pots, but Mrs. Hudson's invasion held no fears for us. The woman is honest-minded enough, and the only items in our poor room left unsecured were Mrs.

Hudson's own linens, all neatly drying on the line. Washing those was part of our rent.

My mistress said, "If the girl is hard of hearing, I promise to knock very vigorously—in short, like a footman."

The landlady's pale mouth twisted. "Well, now, your business brings a few of those to the door, don't it?"

"Yes, but they bring no invitations, only soiled breeches," I said.

"Not their own, I hope," said Mrs. Hudson, "for they should wash their own and save their pennies. A clever footman might go somewhere in this world."

"What about your John?" I said, pointing behind her into the darkened parlour, with its half shuttered front window. A boy on a stool looked up. "John might go into service as a footman. Then he could come home of an evening and thunder with his staff on the door."

"He might," said his mother, but she didn't look convinced.

"Is that a book you have there, John?" I asked.

John's eyes flickered, submerged in some deep sensation. "It *is* a book," said his mother with some pride. "He was given it at the school as a prize for his quickness."

My mistress cooed like a pigeon. "Quickness, is it, John? That's a fine quality in a boy."

"Not quickness in running, mind," said our landlady, "but in learning."

We knew, but again we chirruped our pleasure, sparrows now.

"He will read you something, if you like."

Sister, what could we do but watch poor, persecuted John rise from his stool and come to stand beside his mother in the door. His book came before him, its unbound title page a papery shield against the stupidity of laundresses. Can you guess the book, Sadie, for you and I knew it well enough in our day? How often did our child-selves stand like apron-wearing soldiers in ranks before the trustees of the Bread Street Charity School, waiting our turn to be examined? Now, ten years later, I could still join with John, both of us reciting from Isaac Watts' *Divine Songs*:

The Praises of my Tongue
I offer to the Lord,

That I was taught, and learnt so young
To read his holy word.

"How do you know it?" said the boy, when we'd finished together upon that pleasant itch of an un-rhyme. He was as reluctant to admit a laundress might read as he was to demonstrate his own accomplishments.

"John," I said, "do you think I was hatched from an egg?"

The boy blushed, and I heard his sisters laughing from the room behind.

"I won't be a footman," he said.

"Then don't be one," said I and turned away quick enough.

I was sorry to have exposed him to embarrassment. I wished I had not repeated the verse with him, but sister, my tongue does offer praises. I am well aware of those advantages accorded me by Bread Street. My numbers are copperplate, while my mistress must count linens with marks on a tally sheet. Whenever we have a tallowed rush to spare in the evenings, I can read, while she must only listen. Her news is rinsed and rinsed again—it is never fresh—but I can read a broadsheet over a gentleman's shoulder as well as any maid alive.

However, I am forgetting my tale, which I must pick up again at the moment my mistress and I passed out of the Bell's yard and began walking up Fryday Street. And because John and schooling was our theme as we walked, my companion set me to reading the name of every signpost she knew. "Health to the Barley Mow," I read, as we passed by what my mistress calls *The Sign of the Haystack*. "The Arts of Peace," said I, as we moved beyond what she's always named *The Dove and Olive*.

"The Awful Roe," she said, as we passed beneath the last signpost of Fryday Street. "Well," she added, "what think you of my kind of reading, Mrs. Betty?"

I did not understand her at all, and turned back to consider the wooden board. It hung outside a public house, *The World's End*, and showed a painted, flame-spewing globe. I wondered what manner of disaster the anonymous artist anticipated. As I gazed, the signpost creaked a little. A pauper breeze, starved of any real force, blew up Fryday Street. "Row?" said I, "A row of what? How so a row, mistress?"

"Why, roe is round and pale—like the egg in the signpost. Mind you, I've never seen it split like that, with its yoke spilling out. You find it in the innards of a fish—in lengths, long and yellow, like a skein of lamb's wool. Full of bubbles like wash water. Have you never opened a herring, Mrs. Betty?"

I had, but I'd always found fish inside, no froth, no flame. "It's the end of the world, mistress. That's our home there on fire—all of mankind lost in the flame. The signpost shows what the poets call our planet, our terrestrial orb."

"Now you think *I* was hatched from an egg," said my mistress, content in her reading.

We were walking again, leaving behind the inn, whatever its name might be. We reached Cheapside, and as one, we turned right toward the dome of St. Paul's, plump as any breast on Poultry Street. Wide and loud stretched this end of Cheap, filled with the sober coats of men of business and the rough-spun skirts of country girls. Criers swung their wares and lifted their voices, their shoulders balancing full pails of milk or baskets of fish, perhaps full of roe. Wagons and horses sent up spumes of dust, for we'd had no rain for days. At the mouth of the Old Change, we passed a ballad singer making a great noise, although she was so drunk I could not determine the nature of her song. She decanted her notes in a staggering sort of tune that, upon reflection, sister, she must have intended as that familiar melody *Lillibullero*. Over and over again she sang the refrain, or rather bawled it out, as we descended the rest of Cheapside and turned into Pater Noster Row. I felt very sorry for her, for I began to doubt her right in the head, and I was glad to leave her behind.

In Pater Noster Row, the dust settled a little, and the traffic in the street diminished. Now the bookseller's and printseller's shops began in earnest, their windows fanged with pages, so many white teeth. Here we slowed and stopped, standing before this window and that, taking in the sharp-engraved pictures, with their crisp lines. One window displayed a row of characters from Mr. Laroon's *Cryes of the City of London*, and although those pictures are not modern like Mr. Hogarth's, I saw all Cheapside behind the glass: the orange seller with the basket on her head and the gentleman wearing all his hats for sale. Had my mistress and I not walked beside just such a mud-soled woman with braids of onions tipped over her shoulders? We looked for a while, my lady and I, and then we passed by the crowd and left them behind again.

The next window held naught but books, bound already in tan skins and tipped with thin lines of gold across the stitched spines. So many books, some standing shoulder to shoulder, others propped open so that we might see the neat lines of type. Some of them were already old, showing signs of past reading, their pages sliced open and their bindings cracking. I do not care if a book is a little musty, but many of these looked to be the works of divines upon matters theological. We passed on.

The third shop held both prints and books hung, stacked, spread open, the better to invite fine folk to dawdle and then to enter. The bindings seemed fresh and the prints new. This was precisely the kind of shop genteel enough to sell Mr. Hogarth's work, but now that I'd found the right kind of premises, I learned that for a laundress to enter there was a different and more difficult matter. In short, Sadie, I lacked the courage. With my nose pressed to the glass, I attempted to see over the display in order to discover the faces and, more importantly, the disposition of the bookseller and his clerks. A kindly face might encourage me. The sun glanced brightly off panes and pages alike, but behind that, all was gloom.

Sister, I tried, but I could not lift the latch. My jackets and my petticoats are always clean and presentable but, still, I am ever only a washerwoman. You know the few books in my collection: that ragged copy of Mrs. Jane Barker's *Love Intrigues* (the work my mistress loves best); the clean copy of Mrs. Haywood's *Secret Histories* (that she cares for less, even though I read *Fantomina* to her as often as she will allow); and the halved copy of *Moll Flanders* (that she will not suffer me to read to her even though I beg). *Moll* is best loved by you and me, Sadie, and I hope you are happy in your continued enjoyment of the half you took when you went to Hackney. Do you still favour Moll's romance with her Lancashire husband? As for me, I still love to lie abed for the length of a candle stub, feasting on Moll's pocket-cargos of watches, wigs, and good Brussels lace.

But no matter which I praise most—Mrs. Barker, Mrs. Haywood, or Mr. Defoe—not one of these works did I purchase from a bookseller's shop. *Secret Histories* I had from an upstairs maid, who'd had it from the lady's maid, who'd had it from her mistress. *Moll Flanders* I purchased for a copper from a street-peddler in St. Paul's Churchyard. Mrs. Baker's novel, you will remember, came from poor Mrs. Cooke after her eyes went. When a person can acquire such an exhaustive collection of volumes by happenstance and good fortune, why need she ever pass over a bookseller's threshold? So I did not attempt this one, preferring, like so many of us, to run my eyes over the volumes in the window and my tongue over my teeth.

I would be there yet but that my mistress put her hand to the door and, with a slithering of skirts, passed by the jambs and vanished inside. I could do nothing but follow, pulling open the door with little grace and flinging myself in sideways. (Sister, the doorway was very narrow, even for a laundrymaid like myself, who is never elegant in side hoops.) I found my mistress standing before a very surprised-looking gentleman, who sat at a writing desk under the window. He held his wig in his hands, and we must have come upon him just as he was giving his scalp a good scratch. With ill-concealed annoyance, he slammed his wig back on his head so that white dust shot out from behind his ears and drifted downwards.

"Mr. Hogarth's prints of *The Harlot's Progress*," said my mistress, sounding very businesslike indeed, "we should like to see them."

"You should like to see them," echoed the bookselling gentleman, who now rose to his feet. (I never learned, Sadie, if this man were the proprietor or only a clerk left in charge.) My mistress waited— she knew how to outstare a man who was examining her person for social particulars. He finished his scrutiny. "So should half the world. Madam," he said, placing a slight stress on that "madam." Of course, he'd smoked us for what we were, but I suppose a customer is a customer, and I could now see he and we were the only bodies in the shop. I do not suppose we would have discovered the gentleman wigless and dressing his fleabites if business were good.

"Then you do not have that work by Mr. Hogarth—those moral prints so praised by all the world?" said my mistress, looking about her.

The shop was not clean. Shelf after shelf of dusty books rose to the ceiling.

"I have some very nice prints by Mr. Bickham," said the bookseller, although he made no move to show us any.

"Mr. Bickham," said my mistress, "will not do." She spoke as if she knew Mr. Bickham from Adam. Sister, I could not have dared to be so bold, but we were in a shop, not a drawing room, and only my mistress knew how many coins nestled in the purse beneath her skirts.

The bookseller sighed and crossed to a cabinet, low and wide, set with many drawers. Opening one of these, he pulled forth a sheet of paper, larger than a book. This he spread on his sloping desk, which lay near enough the windowpanes that the light fell full upon it. "I must agree with you madam," said he. "Perhaps one of Mr. Vandergucht's then? It is in the spirit of Mr. Hogarth's productions."

My mistress and I, after a moment's hesitation, stepped forward to see. We looked in silence. "It is very amusing. Don Quixote takes the puppets to be Turks," said the gentleman. He was making an explanation, I suppose.

"Yes," said my mistress, "very funny. What a plume that fellow wears."

"The gentleman is Spanish, you see," said the bookseller.

"I see that he is," she replied. "And he has knocked the little puppet theatre quite to pieces."

We all gazed sadly at the ruin of the performance, over which a fellow with a sword was checked by a man, whose massive arms seemed to me the peculiar centre of the work.

"What do you think, my dear?" my mistress asked of me.

I thought it was sufficiently interesting that I longed to know the story behind the scene, but I dared not ask. "It is not Mr. Hogarth, is it," was the most useful thing I could think to say.

The bookseller looked at me appraisingly. "No indeed," he said, "Vandergucht's work is all very well, but here the tableau is stiff and the line constrained. Do you make this purchase for another?"

"Yes," said I.

"No," said my mistress.

"Ah," said the bookseller, touching his finger to his nose and turning again to his cabinet of drawers. Sister, I never really understand what men mean when they do that. You never see a woman tapping her nose like a fool. But already a new print unfurled in front of us. And again we leaned in to see. This page was smaller, so we bent closer to examine the whirl of figures. I saw a pair of buttocks peeping from behind the curtain and a hoard of small figures administering a clyster-pipe as if holding a trumpet to a pair of lips. "This is all I have of Hogarth's, if your master is such a dedicated collector."

Clysters I have given for all manner of stomach aches, as well as to our mother when she was brought to bed with Harry, Samuel, and Small Jacky, but now I could feel the bookseller watching my face with such glittering eyes that I did not know where to put my own. I had no reason to be ashamed; what right had he to expect that sensation to redden my cheeks.

My mistress shook her head and turned away from the print on the desk. "I am sure it's the *Harlot* we wish to see."

"Well," said the bookselling gentleman, lifting the page, "Mr. Hogarth sells them by subscription at a guinea for the six, but you must go to his shop in the Covent Garden for that."

"Oh dear, I cannot walk so far," replied my mistress, saying nothing about the astonishing price. A guinea for six sheets of paper? I fanned myself a little with my hand.

The bookman said, "Do you know the Overtons' shop? It is nearer to here, at the sign of the White Horse."

The White Horse lay close to St. Sepulchre's. I knew the place. I'd been that way many times, although I never liked to take that road, which passed under the shadow of Newgate. I pressed my mistress' arm. "We know it," she said.

The bookseller gently resettled the Hogarth print into its drawer. When it was safely to bed, he turned back to us, saying, "The Overtons have Kirkall's mezzotints for fifteen shillings. They also have a set of their own for six. But that last is not exactly Hogarth's own *Harlot*, and it is on very inferior paper."

He watched us as he spoke. This constant assessment of a customer's purse was surely part of his bookseller's trade, and he must name sums and examine faces, just as my mistress and I had already noted the grime on the pockets of his coat and the unwashed condition of his ruffles. We three sized each other in the space of that shop, coming to our different judgements.

"Well then," he said at last, "if neither the Overtons nor Kirkall will do, you'll want King's copies." Here, his voice took on a plangent tone. "King, that black-hearted villain."

"Is Mr. King not honest then?" my mistress said.

"Honest," said he, making a face, "I'm sure he is honest—that is not his failing. Rather, he is too nice."

"What do you mean?" asked my mistress. "How is he too nice?"

"It's all in the broadsheets, madam. King dares to advertise with Mr. Hogarth's name. He says his prints are "copied from the originals" and baldly adds "by permission," which is a blessing neither Kirkall nor the Overtons possess. The distinction is *too nice*, you see, for King leaves the rest of us somewhat … exposed in this matter of obtaining the artist's agreement to make copies." The gentleman snorted expressively. "And then, to add insult to injury, he sells the whole for a miserly four shillings. I can never compete with such a price, even if I were to set an apprentice to duplicate Hogarth's work."

"Four shillings," I said. Still a fearsome price, sister.

"Only four shillings, my dear, but imagine, Mr. King puts three of Mr. Hogarth's pictures to a page. Three to a page, while the good Mr. Kirkall prints one per page, and he uses green ink. The Bowles brothers' copies are splendid, but now all the world will suppose the Bowles' prints to be inferior to those Mr. King makes *by permission*. It quite makes my head itch."

And astonishingly enough the gentleman lifted his wig again and gave it a good scratch. Indeed, he seemed distracted and had clearly forgotten what kind of company he entertained in that cramped, book-lined room. He rasped at his shaved hairs with his nails and then crammed his wig back on his reddened scalp. "Good God," he said, "selling paper is no business for a man of honour."

I wanted to ask him, sister, if he meant to bemoan a lack of honour in his trade or if he were justifying it, but I did not think the question would receive an honest answer.

"Is business as bad as that?" said my mistress in a kind voice and touching her gloved fingers to his arm.

The bookselling gentleman sighed deeply. "You have no idea, madam," said he.

My mistress, who understood questions of business very well, only winked at me. "Mr. Hogarth's *Harlot* seems to sell very well indeed," she said.

"It is true, a general desire for Mr. Hogarth's recent work spreads like the pox. Alas, securing copies grows as chancy as printing them oneself. No, Mr. Hogarth and Mr. King will soon be the only legal source of that popular work. Did you know, the fellow pushes forward a law so that no honest man can engrave—at his own expense, mind—a popular work for sale? He interferes with every seller's enterprise. With no freedom to copy, men of business such as myself have no way to increase the store of goods and so satisfy a discerning public, such as you yourselves represent. The effect will be a suppression of trade, a rising of prices, and the end to all prosperity. The Overtons and the Bowles brothers will be clapped in Newgate, and I am sure to end up in the Fleet for my debts."

"There, there," said my mistress, but the bookselling gentleman had exhausted his last ounce of vitality and set his arms against the slope of his desk, his head in his hands.

My mistress and I thought it best to take our leave of him then. I would have liked to purchase a book to console him, but my purse forbade what my benevolence urged, and so we departed the shop in silence. Out in the street, the cries of chairmen seeking custom and the feathers of dust from horses' hooves were enough to stun our senses for a moment or two. Hardly had we began to walk back up Pater Noster Row in the direction of home when my mistress stopped me. "Betty," says she, "I feel very well today, and would not be turned away from our purpose so easily. I understand from the sad gentleman we have just left that there are other print shops in the city of London."

"There are, mistress," said I. "In London and in Westminster besides."

"Surely, we needn't go so far as that."

Truth be told, we needn't go any distance at all. An astonishing number of book and printsellers sprouted in the fairy ring of St. Paul's. Paper, bound and unbound, flourished here, quires and folios sprouting in the hallowed soil. But I knew my mistress wanted some more particular intelligence.

"Mistress, I listened carefully to the discourse of the print-selling gentleman. Not far from here is the alley that will put us in the way of the Bowles' print shop—although, I am not certain we will be welcome there. Such august gentlemen may not, I fear, 'grave for laundresses."

"Whether the Bowles make pictures for ladies or laundresses cannot matter much, my dear, if they do not make 'em for a great deal less than four shillings—what a fearsome price that is. But do not fret so, Mrs. Betty, I have a mind to behold the fine goods on offer in the brothers' window. Or if Mr. Hogarth's *Harlot* stands not behind glass, it costs nothing to enter a shop. We may not have so many guineas in our purses, but we can trust to our neat skirts and our clean hands. After all, this is London, Mrs. Betty, where every mercer and hat maker displays his wares for all to see. Even a beggar may gaze for nothing."

"This is indeed London," said I, cheered by her good sense.

Now we were passing through the alley, which stank of urine but which showed a strip of bluing overhead. A few more steps and the white bulge of the cathedral hove into view. In another moment we came upon St. Paul's itself, so like a kitchen sideboard, awaiting only cups and saucers to complete the resemblance. We began to circumnavigate the churchyard until I came upon a name painted upon a wooden signpost. I held up my hand to alert my mistress and together we stood in front of the window.

So it was in the Bowles brothers' glassed-in shop-front that we finally found the whole of the *Harlot*. Not the wanton lady herself but a carefully lettered sign advertising her presence. *Interested parties* were urged to *inquire within*. I read the notice to my mistress, and then we both stood in silence. I looked at the volumes in that window and saw bindings bloody as a calf's liver and pages the yellow of fresh cream. Books to sink your teeth into. Books that might bite back. They lay on a rich cloth that glistened in the sun.

"Velvet," I said.

"Velveteen," said my mistress and opened the door.

Inside their light-filled shop, as wintergreen as the Thames in January, the Bowles brothers entertained such a crowd as could only gather in this fair city. I saw so many persons that I never learned which, if any, of the coated backs belonged to a Bowles. Prints here did not reside in drawers but filled a single wall, hanging rank upon rank and rising to the ceiling. Before this splendid display stood a crowd of black, brown, and blue coats, jostling for space with fine capes of satin and calash-bonnets lined in coloured silk. A curly, long-eared dog sat by his mistress' feet, sniffing cautiously at the white stockings of the gentleman beside her. All else was stiff spines, and sloped shoulders, and wigs rising high. Roaring conversation seemed the order of the day, and the whole place was as loud as a playhouse gallery.

We tucked ourselves in behind this jumble and lifted our eyes heavenward. As we stared, our necks began to ache and our eyes stung at the acrid odour of so many bodies pressed together. Sister, despite our discomfort, my mistress and I pushed forward, until we found ourselves before Mr. Hogarth's print series, a single row on a wall equally busy with framed squares. Those pictures were hung so high on the wall, we recommenced our squinting in an effort to bring the contents closer. The Bowles brothers knew what they were about: like a good bawd they put their *Harlot* on display but left the fullest discovery of her charms to those with a purse full of coins.

The first of the series, the one Justice Gonson flashed at us, I could make out with tolerable ease because I already knew what it contained. The other five prints showed a pleasing array of shades, as balanced as a well-designed brocade. Upon examination, I could make out the person of the harlot in each print, but never her pretty face, which I remembered from before. Nor could I perceive any of the other details that were so discussed in drawing rooms and garrets alike.

"Can you see the figure of Justice Gonson?" my mistress asked me, coming close so that I might hear her.

The din of conversation threatened to drown out my answer. "Is that him, joined to the harlot with a splash of bare page?"

"That cannot be him, for I have heard he appears in the third print."

I counted with my finger and gave that picture a hard stare. "Do I see a figure in the doorway?"

"I see no doorway. Where is the doorway?"

A great deal more of this useless discourse we had, sister, and I will not tire us both with an account of the whole. Suffice it to say that by the end my mistress and I were no wiser than we had been, only buffeted on all sides, our toes stepped upon repeatedly.

"I do not find Mr. Hogarth's work half as improving as claimed," said I to my mistress as we pushed to exit the crowd. "My eyesight is a great deal the worse for having been strained, and my patience has been tried and found wanting."

"Ha ha," said a fellow at my elbow, surprising me more than a little, for such was the babble I did not imagine we might be overheard. Now sister, do not suppose I mistake my transcription of the fellow's speech, for you know the Bread Street school taught us to write plainly and clearly. The person I write of did not laugh; he said, "Ha ha." I thought it odd, for what kind of a man says, "Ha ha" when he means to laugh? Well, I'll tell you what sort of man: he was neither tall nor short, but he wore a tan coat with gilt braid come down in the world. His wig belonged to another and so did his shoes, and yet he assumed an air of importance, as if he were someone in the world. I did not reply to his "Ha ha," but neither did I snub him as I ought to have done—I rather hoped he might be a Bowles brother.

He was not, as you will have foreseen, Sadie—you always were the cleverer one—but he *was* a printseller. Or at least, he sold prints.

"Pardon me, madam," he said before I could object, "but I have within my means a scheme," and here he paused in order to locate the right word, "by which you might *secure* yourself an entirely satisfactory copy of Mr. Hogarth's very moral series of prints."

"You are Mr. Bowles?" said I, undone by his confident way of speaking.

"I am. Not," he said. "But if you would rather do your business with a Bowles." And here he broke off speaking to put his fingers in the air, as if hailing a brother.

"No, no," said I, "I would rather not speak with a Bowles, sir. Pray, put down your hand."

He put down his hand and looked at me seriously. He seemed to have done me a kindness, although I could not have said exactly what. I said, "I fear the price of the prints is not within my means, sir." This day seemed to have been about money in different guises. A golden guinea, fifteen silver shillings, six, or even four tarnished moons floated impossibly in my mind.

"My price," said the man in the tan coat, "is not the Bowles' price. My shop, madam, is just outside. Won't you step this way and see?" And now he gestured at the door, addressing my mistress.

What a very long letter this has become, Sadie, and by now you will have guessed the end of it all. In short, we were tempted and so stepped out of the neat, crowded shop into the street. After all—as my mistress whispered to me—the stranger couldn't very well murder us there, in the shadow of great St. Paul's. We left behind the genteel ladies with their lapdogs, the well-dressed gentlemen in their shining boots, and we followed the man in the tan-coloured coat. Once outside, he led us only a few steps to his shop, but when we got there we found no rooms—only a ragged cloth on the ground, spread with used books.

A boy kept watch over the books but hopped a few cautious steps away when he saw his master approaching. "No, no, no," I said, for how could Hogarth's *Harlot* be spread out upon a length of homespun stuff? It was in just such a manner that I bought our *Moll Flanders* in the days when you still lived with me, sister. Yellow, dog-eared *Moll* made an old book even before we pawed though its ragged pages—newer, crisper goods would never be sold thus. But I was wrong.

The gentleman opened a box that had served as the boy's seat. Inside I spied a pile of pamphlets, unbound and cheaply printed, pages flap-cornered, torn, and creased. One of these third-hand wonders the man in the tan coat had already in his hands. He closed the lid of the box, and seating himself upon it, he motioned us closer, holding out his offering.

Sadie, I was astonished. Having only just left off squinting at the *Harlot* upon the Bowles' wall, I could see at once that she likewise graced the cover of this work. It showed the very same unwise Miss meeting the dissembling Baud in the stableyard of our own Bell Inn. But when I took the bundle of pages into my own hands, I could feel that I held many pages, not six.

"What is this, sir?" I asked, lifting the first page.

Our new companion said, "What is it, she wants to know. Why, it is no more than a very fine emulation of Mr. Hogarth's work, much added to and improved upon. To be sure, it is a privilege to be copied as Mr. Hogarth is."

I scanned the title upon the page: *The Harlot's Progress: Or, the Humours of Drury Lane.* "And the six hudibrastick cantos?" said I, reading the next part out loud, "What's that, when it's at home?"

"That is a superior kind of writing that the gentry and the fine folk like best," said the other. "They all read it," he added, perhaps noting perplexity on my face.

I didn't care about the cantos, which I imagined must be some manner of versification, but saw, writ below, these words: *With a curious Print to each Canto.* Now I had no interest in how poesy dressed itself but wanted only to ruffle the layers, looking for what lay beneath. Between pages eight and nine, I discovered one of the curious prints of the title: a full copy of the Harlot's arrival at the Bell Inn, complete with York Wagon and toppling buckets.

"The picture is the same," said my mistress.

"Why so it is," said I, and continued turning pages. Between leaf twenty-four and twenty-five, I discovered the next print and learned that the oblong of bare page that had so puzzled my mistress and me was a tea table. It connected the harlot with a gentleman, customer to that lady's particular trade. Ten or so pages later, we found Justice Gonson, arriving dimly by the door of a chamber that contains the harlot and her companion.

"'Tis him," said my mistress, very quietly.

I turned back to the bottom of the first printed page, where I saw a price. Two shillings.

I sighed and said, "Now that I see Mr. Hogarth's work," said I, "I do not know that I desire it so very much after all. It does not seem remarkably moral to me, and I do not like this lady's way of life."

You know my method of doing marketing, Sadie, and you will guess at once I have never wanted to make a purchase so badly.

"The verse explains the moral parts—you must read to be improved," said the tan-coated man, with a sour look on his face.

"Verse," I said. "Oh, verse. What am I to do with verse?" I stuck out my hip and stood like a laundress, lacking only the basket of linens to make me one of the *Cryes of the City of London*. But I kept the book in my hands.

The man said, "The prints are graved from the originals. It says so on the front."

"So says Mr. Kirkall and the Overtons," said I, meeting his eye very boldly. "But not everything said is true." Silently, I thanked the Pater Noster Lane bookman for his tutorage.

"Then don't buy," said my opponent. He put out his hands for the book, which I still held. I looked along the churchyard, and the boy came closer and stood near us. He looked fast, and even if I were fleet of foot, my mistress was fat and puffed when she waddled. We would not get far before the boy caught us with our booty.

"The tableau is stiff and the line constrained," said I, a little desperately.

"Ha ha," said the man in the tan-coloured coat. It did not mean the same as before.

"Tuppence," said I. "It's all I have."

Sister, I had rather more than that, but it's not a lie if it's bargaining.

The man attempted but appeared to swallow another ha ha. He waved his hands at my book. "Never," said he. "Give me back my merchandise. You rob me. The price is a shilling."

"A shilling?" said I, pretending to almost swoon away. "I cannot pay that."

"Then don't," said my opponent.

"I do not want the book," said my mistress, "but I will add another tuppence to the price. A foolish act, for I am a poor woman, but I love her dearly." And here she beamed upon me as if she truly were my mother.

In answer, the man held out his hands. I placed the book in them, but I did not let go.

"Another penny then," I said, forcing a tear to my eye. "God knows how I will eat."

The man set his thumbs firmly on the cover of *The Harlot's Progress: Or, the Humours of Drury Lane.* "Sixpence," he said. "Or it is my motherless children who will starve."

A tanner. I was certain we'd found his true price. I looked at my mistress, and she nodded, untying her skirts and taking out a time-blacked coin. I felt the book slide into my hands, even as the man took the money and held it up to check for clipping. Satisfied, he said, "You got a bargain there, you did. If you'd bought that off Mrs. Dod over by Temple-bar you'd have paid the two shillings or be withered at a glance. But she's above doing business with ladies what have white hands and red knuckles, and I'm happy to make everybody a fair price. Now, ladies, I've other items just as delicious as this *Harlot.*"

But we were done with this bit of unexpected marketing and astonished to find ourselves in possession of a *Harlot* of our very own. She was not the clean-limbed lady from the Bowles shop, for she appeared in the first picture tattered and ink-clotted, as if already fallen from grace. Neither did she possess a clean sheet of her own, having been pressed into service her author never foresaw, forced to illustrate needless verse. She emerged between the pages of print, smaller in size and clipped at the edges, like a coin. But even if she were not entirely Hogarth's Harlot, then she was sister to that person, and my mistress and I were well content.

Sadie, how we'd come to part with a sixpence for a set of pictures, I still cannot say, and yet I felt richer for owning them. The whole of the way home, I gibbered like a lady's monkey, shocked and astonished at my boldness. Cheapside passed in a haze of wilting cabbages and country folk bawling for custom. Fryday Street shut out the sliding sun, and within the Bell's yard all was coolness, shadow, and the tang of brewing hops. Soon enough, we had the little book back in our room, but what we did with it there will have to wait for another letter, my dearest Sadie. This one is grown far too long, and if I were to continue I would need more pages. The price of my *Harlot* will bring about a delay in the purchase of writing paper. I will send these sheets now, but you will have to wait for their sequel. Until then, I am your very loving sister,

Elizabeth.

CHAPTER 4

The continued correspondence of Mrs. Betty and her
sister, showing how Mr. Hogarth's *Harlot* leads Betty
into danger.

Bell Inn Yard off Fryday Street, 1732.

Dearest Sadie,

When last I wrote, I warned that you must wait to hear more of
me. I was grown rich in one kind of paper, investing in prints like a
gentleman, but poor in another, having run short of scraps on which to
write. Now that you have this letter in your hands, with so little time
elapsed, you will have guessed that I must have found a supply of good
writing paper. And indeed, I have, for I have made a visit to a printer's
shop—a place I never expected to see with my own eyes. The kind
fellow I met there has sent me such a quantity of pages that I might not
be short of paper this century.

Now sister, you and I will have noticed the edges of this page are a
little soiled. They were crushed by accident when they fell off the back of
an ox cart, and this sad history explains how the printer came to make
me a gift of them. When I saw these pages set aside, I said to the printer
that such sheets, surely, must not be wasted. The man told me, most
respectfully, that they should not be, for they will be used for other
purposes. Spoilt sheets, he said, might find employment as pulled proofs
that check the compositor's accuracy. Or, they are sometimes used to
protect more precious pages before they are bound into quires. Other

times, printers make calculations upon their surfaces, reckoning the size of margins, the number of lines, and the times a sheet might be folded. I praised these economies and told him that a laundress also cares to make soiled things useful again. He said as this was the case, I should myself have some of the paper for my own use. Sister, I have smoothed and wiped this page with a damp cloth, and only a little wrinkling remains to show that it has a past—and truly, sister, which of us cannot say the same?

You must be wondering how I came to be in a printer's shop at all. Will it surprise you to learn I went on account of my bastard copy of *The Harlot's Progress*, with its back-to-front prints? My mistress continues her interest in Justice Gonson, whose hypocrisy killed the Harlot—or so the world says, pressing Mr. Hogarth's prints into evidence. What a powerfully curious woman is my mistress, with a boundless interest in life's persistent oddities. Our summons into Justice Gonson's presence was just such a bit of strangeness, and as I am her acolyte, she has promised to instruct me as faithfully in this matter as in the use of a copper-bottomed pot or fuller's earth.

To begin our investigation, we had no dirty linen, no wine-stained shift, or mud-splattered stocking, only that dearly purchased volume of hudibrastick cantos, the history of which you had in my last letter. We had already seen Gonson's own *Harlot*, held up for us by his clerk when we went before the great man. That was an excellent print, showing very clearly that lady's arrival in the yard of the Bell Inn. Now, the petty-foggers say that reading Mr. Hogarth's pictures aright is a matter of comparing things large and small—in little clauses he suspends great matters. In this way, the artist paints his *Harlot* like a sign-painter makes a sign. Mr. Hogarth splits the lady and turns her into emblems, like so many placards hung before inns. The pale rose pinned to the tucker points to her. The Baud's dangling timepiece points to her. The goose with its neck wrung points to her.

But Gonson's elegant print was not the twin to ours. Based on our careful scrutiny of this latter, *The Harlot's Progress: Or, the Humours of Drury Lane*, we could not have said which small matters conveyed great truths and which were only small matters in fact: blots, drips, slips of the hand, and the like. In our *Harlot*, the graceful clarity of Mr.

Hogarth's line grew muddled and wandered drunkenly. In Gonson's print, a skilled burin delineated most precisely each shade of grey, but in ours, ham-handed grooves overflowed and spilled impenetrability across the page. Our *Harlot* showed herself marked and spoilt, and the ink-stained pages provided as potent an emblem of the wages of sin as anything printed thereupon. Sadie, I cannot convey to you the disappointment I had in my purchase now that I came to examine it at leisure.

"Alas, this is not a stain I can lift," said my mistress, her finger upon the page. "I fear, Mrs. Betty, here is a kind of inkish mould that eats all sense."

"I saw, in Gonson's copy, a mouse near the horse's hooves, but he has scampered from this page."

"Indeed," said my mistress, "he fears the spreading plague of ink."

"That mouse held up a piece of cheese and contemplated the morsel."

"Doubtless finding it as delicious a tidbit as the baud found poor Moll."

"Or perhaps as the man who sold this clotted pamphlet found me."

"Never mind," said my mistress. "We shall read the verse and see then if we are wiser."

Sitting at the table by the window, we bent our capped heads together, and I read aloud. "Oh," said my mistress at the nonsense that attended the clergyman in the first print. "My," she said, at the frank discussion of the Harlot's business. "Dear, dear," she said again when I read aloud the description of the contents of the Harlot's room. When I came to a riddle offered for our puzzlement, she begged me to stop reading—for nothing, she told me, could justify such an excess of vulgarity.

We turned instead to the picture of the Harlot taking tea while Gonson comes to arrest her. "I cannot make out any more here than in the other prints," said I, turning the pamphlet sideways to orient the picture. "This picture is as clotted as the others."

"Do you remember, Mrs. Betty," said my mistress, "in the print the clerk showed us, which side of the page had the door where the Justice entered?"

I thought a while. Because I worked with all manner of embroidered cloths, and some printed ones too, I had a good memory for patterns. "Gonson came from here," I said, pointing to the right-hand side of the page. "But in this print he comes the opposite way. These prints are turned about."

My mistress sat in her accustomed chair with her small nose in the air, sniffing as if she could smell something she did not like. "When you read to me aloud, I see your eyes moving across the page, from here," she said, pointing left, "to here," and she pointed right.

I caught at her meaning. "In this print, if I read the Justice before the Harlot, I imagine him watching her unawares. He is always ready, waiting to catch her out in a moment of weakness."

My mistress sucked her teeth. "But if the print is reversed."

"Why, then I do the Justice a disservice, for it is the Harlot's own behaviour that comes first, necessitating his arrival."

"That is a more generous way of reading the print with respect to the Justice, but perhaps less so in the Harlot's case."

"But which is Mr. Hogarth's intention?" said I. "I cannot tell."

My mistress said, "Do you know Bartholomew's Close, over by the church and the livestock grounds?" I nodded, and you know it too, Sadie, for we used to go as girls to see the puppets and the lithe lass who could put her heels on her head. My mistress said, "There is a printer's shop there, one Mr. Samuel Palmer. I have done washing for his wife, and know him to be a good man. Remember me to him, and ask him if he might tell you which way Mr. Hogarth intended for the Justice to walk."

"When should I go, mistress Veronica?"

"Why, you might go immediately, my dear. Surely, you might trust me to do a little washing on my own."

And so, sister, I put on my cloak and went out into the smoke-blue morning streets. This time I walked towards Aldersgate, following along the bladder of Little Britain and so into Bartholomew Close. After asking passersby for directions several times, I located the house, hard against the church, and I climbed a wide set of wooden stairs to emerge in a long, well-lit room, with a row of paned windows along one side.

Only a day after visiting those places where prints are sold, I found myself standing where prints are made, and if I learn any more about the business, I shall be in a fair way to change my trade. Except that,

D. M. Bryan

as soon as I came into the workshop, I determined to have as little as possible to do with printers. Sadie, their work makes them dirty beyond compare, and a laundress can hardly stand to see one without crying aloud at the trouble of making their cuffs clean. Although, judging by the dress of the printers in that room, I should not soon be put to the trouble. None of the men I saw in that shop appeared likely to employ a laundress, and guessing from the way they gaped at me, they had never so much as seen one before. They were, in short, an impolite set of men, quick to make a body conscious of her disadvantage in appearing before them as a mere female person.

Mr. Palmer himself was courteous enough, although he seemed at first to think I had lost my way, appearing in his shop by accident. But he crossed the long, bright room, silencing the catcalls of his men with a stern look, and offered himself to assist me. I gave him my mistress' name, which he recalled at once with pleasure, and his whole demeanour changed toward me.

"That good woman assisted me once in a matter of great significance to myself," he told me, taking my hand (imprinting it with three dark fingerprints that I struggled to ignore). "Whatever I might do to assist her, I will do immediately."

He spoke with so much warmth that I felt free to unburden myself of the substance of our inquiry, although I was well aware of the oddity of my putting such things to him. I showed him the Harlot's pictures in my pamphlet, and explained how we knew of other prints that ran opposite to ours. I asked him how we might know Mr. Hogarth's intention in designing his *Harlot*. Then, when I was done, I waited for him to frown or even to scold me for the indecorousness of my inquiry. Sister, I do not know Mr. Palmer's former business with my mistress, nor will I guess, but he did not so much as blink at my coming to him with such a matter, and he gave me an answer so material to my question that I could not doubt its veracity.

Leading me to one of the two large presses that filled the long room in which we stood, he commanded the men who laboured there to stop a while so that they might explain to me its secret workings. These men, who only a moment before made free with my reputation, now gave me as respectable a demonstration of their craft as if I might have been the primary projector in some great printing scheme. They bent over the oaken frame, like maids stripping a bed, and unfolded a jointed frame to show me the nest of type inside. "What language is this?" I asked, looking at the letters, strangely familiar but meaningless.

The men smiled their superiority at me, and Mr. Palmer told me it was English, a page of the Bible no less. "And here is the first part of the answer to your question," he said, "for this text is backwards. With much practice, a man can learn to read it."

But, sister, you will remember that lettering backwards has ever been a fault with me, and now I could make out the text of Proverbs 31:26 with ease. "She opens her mouth with wisdom and the teaching of kindness is on her tongue," I read aloud. "What excellent work you do here, Mr. Palmer. I commend you."

"Thank you," said Mr. Palmer, staring at me a little longer than was strictly polite.

At his command, the men took up two padded sticks and spread ink over the lead letters, sitting backwards in their mount. Then they placed a damp sheet of paper into the frame, folded the outer frame to cover the inner and let both down to cover the type. This folded device they shot forward beneath the press itself, which rose up at the end, rather like the headboard of a bed. Connected to the press was a long bar, which one of the men pulled, the muscles of his arms tightening in a manner that somewhat reconciled me to the existence of printers. Then he released the press, and both men moved the frame device forward. Now the second man pulled hard on the bar, bringing the press down with inexorable pressure over a new part of the enfolded page. When they returned the whole to its starting position and opened the folded frames, they could peel back a fully printed sheet. There I saw the verses from *Proverbs* printed in neat columns. With a bow, Mr. Palmer presented this to me. "For correction with proof rather than reproof is itself a kindness," he said, and that, Sadie, was rather more than I deserved.

A moment later he had to take the sheet from me again, for it proved still wet, the ink coming off on my fingers. Mr. Palmer lowered a thin rod suspended by ropes from the beams and added my sheet to a row of others to dry. "Is your mistress still by the Bell Inn?" he asked, and when I nodded, he added, "I shall send it to you there." And then we moved away from the printing press, Mr. Palmer giving his men the command to return to work.

Sister, the rest of the time he and I spoke, those men laboured, placing, folding, pressing, shifting, pressing, unfolding, and hanging. They completed the row of wet prints that followed mine, and they filled the length of the room again. At the other press, a second team exerted themselves, also filling the bright air with drying pages. The room grew fragrant with the tang of ink, the fibrous smell of wet paper, and the sweat of working-men. On the walls were hung examples of their work: printed puffs for patent medications, the frontispieces of sermons, an illustrated handbill for Talbot's menagerie. Under the windows sat long sloped tables, some set with trays and others covered with wooden compartments full of type. Everywhere I looked I saw leaden letters.

Mr. Palmer took me aside and said, "And now I might fully answer your question regarding the intentions of the ingenious Mr. Hogarth." He took up my *Harlot* and opened to the page where Justice Gonson enters.

Pointing at it, he said, "I am sorry to tell you that a worse set of prints I have yet to see. These are certainly not Mr. Hogarth's work, for if he is not as elegant as a Frenchman, he still 'graves with an accomplished line. I know wherein I speak, for I print copperplate engravings in my shop also, and the process is the same. For this reason, my dear, I am certain, your prints are mere copies: crude plates drawn after Mr. Hogarth's own prints, but never touched by his genius."

"A print is not a copy?"

"Of a sort, but Mr. Hogarth's prints are also originals. Your *Harlot* is engraved from his, but what is engraved," Mr. Palmer said, holding out his hands, "is ever reversed when printed," and he slapped one with the other.

"And so Mr. Hogarth means for Justice Gonson to enter from the right," said I.

Mr. Palmer nodded. "And fix his eyes upwards, away from the Harlot."

I looked at my print, and through the inky fog, I could see the lift of the Justice's chin showing the direction of his gaze.

"What does he see?" I asked, unable to make out for myself.

"Well," said Mr. Palmer, "some say he's staring at the witches' hat and broom hung above the bed."

"Broom?" said I. Sister, can anyone be so innocent? My *Harlot's* verse stated very bluntly that that collection of twigs was no broom: "Near there, a Rod of Birch was hang'd/With which full many a Bum was banged." But I did not recite these lines to good Mr. Palmer.

"Well," he said, misunderstanding my exclamation, "even a harlot must sometimes do housework. But others think perhaps the Justice gazes at the paintings on the wall—an image of Abraham putting Isaac to the knife—which causes him to consider his own actions."

"I see no such image."

Mr. Palmer's finger tapped on the upper corner of my print. "It is this area of undistinguished murk."

I squinted hard at nothing, disappointed to miss this improving detail. "What do I see here?" said I, observing a pale shape perched on the taut roof of the bed-curtains.

Still with his finger on the print, Mr. Palmer said, "It is a wig box above the bed belonging to one James Dalton, highwayman."

I bent closer. "I have found out Dalton's name for myself, for it is clearly writ here," said I, showing Mr. Palmer the sloping script upon the box. I felt pleased that my print gave up some secrets. I looked again. "Why, I believe the Justice sees it too, for he fixes his gaze upwards, as if to spy the evidence atop the curtain."

Mr. Palmer nodded. "But observe closely," he said, shifting his finger to the printed bed-curtain itself. "Here, if only we could see it, hangs a lady's cap with lappets, together with a man's wig. And below, what does the little cat do?"

I set myself to consider his question. The white feline sat still as an arrow, its nose pointed to its mistress' skirts. Even in the uncertain lines of my print, I could see how a careful stillness possessed that lady. She, like the print itself, concealed a secret.

"You suggest the Harlot hides a highwayman beneath the bed?"

Mr. Palmer shrugged but added, "Justice Gonson is esteemed a fool wherever I have heard men discuss the *Harlot*."

"I am grateful for the completeness of your knowledge—you see a great deal that was hidden to us."

"Mr. Hogarth's trade touches closely on mine, and his innovations in our business make for much conversation wherever printers gather."

I stared at my page of blotches. "I am robbed of pleasure by my purchase of such a dismal copy."

"Yes, we despise such inferior products as the work of pyrates."

"Pyrates?" said I. Sister, it seemed an odd word to use.

"Aye. They climb aboard of an honest printmaker and plunder him of all his worth."

"An honest laundress as well."

Mr. Palmer smiled. "Mr. Hogarth asks a guinea; you paid a sixpence. My dear, you have shown you are no fool, and you will not despise me for speaking truth. A man—and a woman too—gets what is paid for." No sooner where the words out of his mouth than he regretted them, adding, "But perhaps the improving verse makes up for the vile condition of the printing?" Mr. Palmer turned the page of my *Harlot* and ran his eyes across several lines, and Sadie, I saw him blush.

I moved at once to take the book from him, judging it too ripe for such a good man. At first, I did not think he would give it up, and we engaged in a polite bout of tugging. Sister, I am certain Mr. Palmer wished only to maintain possession for the sake of my moral education, preventing me from possessing a book so contrary to the requirements of modesty. But in case he forgot himself so far as to wish to read further, I maintained my grip upon the *Harlot*'s spine, and in time reclaimed it as my own.

The silence that fell between us then, I filled with rustlings and bustlings, tucking the pamphlet safely beneath my cloak and adjusting the strings of my bonnet. How grateful I am for the business of ladies' dress, which fills many moments that might otherwise prove difficult to navigate. When I judged sufficient time elapsed, I lifted my face again to Mr. Palmer, putting out my fingers and thanking him most profusely on behalf of my mistress and myself. And indeed, we are indebted to that good man, who has been so helpful to us both in all our inquiries.

Dearest Sadie, my re-entry into the close should have been the end of my adventure. I already knew enough of Mr. Hogarth's intentions, and the world's reactions, to return to my mistress and the pleasure of continued conversation over sudsy tubs. But, sister, I made an error, and in doing so, I discovered how easy it is to become lost in London, cast adrift with no kind friends. When I came down the stairs from Mr. Palmer's shop, I came into Bartholomew Close as turned about as my poor printed *Harlot*. Where I should have gone right, I, like the Justice, went left, my eyes fixed upon my own private thoughts. Down a street I cannot name I wandered, knowing not that I had already lost myself, and soon I emerged into the stinking mud of the cattle-ground they call Smithfield. Now I understood my plight, and unable to find the sun overhead, I stupidly mistook my direction again, and thinking my path lay past the sheep pens, I went out of the market that way. I soon reached St. John's Street, where I knew I had gone wrong once more. Oh but Sadie, good fortune did not walk beside me, for I turned myself about, retracing my steps until I came to a meeting of ways, where again I mistook my direction. Now I headed, not east into the city, but west towards Westminster, although I was so lost that I travelled some distance and passed many strange buildings before realizing my sad condition.

I attempted to ask my way, stopping a great bustling woman carrying a prayer book, but she had no time for me and walked directly past as though I were not there. Next, I attempted to inquire of a respectable-looking gentleman, but he imagined I solicited him for lewd purposes, and by the time I stuttered out my disgust at his mistake, I could see only his narrow shoulders and the bow at the end of his queue. At last a toothless person, her hat tied to her wig with several torn twists of Flanders lace, allowed that I was indeed turned about, if Smithfield was the direction I wanted. "Here," she said, "Sharp's Alley will take you down to Chick Lane, which will bring you direct to the sheep pens, if that will help you find your way."

No, I thought, but "Yes," I said, not wishing to reject the assistance I so badly needed, and so I set foot in Sharp's Alley, which of all the wrong steps I had taken thus far was by far my worst.

Now that I have been there, Sadie, I know that Sharp's Alley is a place beyond our ken, belonging to a harder London even than the one that suckled us. It is a labyrinth of trickling brick, far from the cackling commerce of Cheapside. Should you choose to enter there, you must do as I did and summon sufficient courage to start down that

D. M. Bryan

narrow passage, leaving behind light and busy-ness. Bends dexterous and sinister take you past nameless courts, places of shadow even in broad daylight. Meretricious houses in black and white, wearing their wooden stays on their outsides, lean into your path, disguising every crooked twist of the alley. Should you, like me, continue straight where you should have turned south, you will find yourself confronted by a single house, which rises to block your way. The house, as if at bay, faces you with a plastered mask, pieced with diamond-paned windows and toothed with blackened oak. The last century saw the naissance of that dwelling, and this century will surely preside over its demise. It will be dismembered, brick by brick, or perhaps rebuilt, but that terrible pile will never be redeemed.

No one lives here by choice, and if you stand silently in the road before the smokeless chimneys of that house you will hear one reason why. Sister, I heard it: a choked gurgle, like a drowning man might make. Beneath the stones of that street, a river, buried alive, passes with all the malevolence that forgotten waters can exert. The houses that line this blind court grow up like pulpy mushrooms, tracing what once was river stone and silver flow. In past centuries, the alley's old houses backed onto a bank orange and green with boughs of willow. In those days the water flowed past Clerkenwell, where people drank it, finding it pure and dark, liquid salvation. But as the city grew harder, the buildings gathered closer, pushing the river's head down below its own surface. Now the water creeps beneath the packed dirt, dragging with it a noxious air. Thickened odours hang above the street in a fetid mist. Damp heaves the stones and puddles the ground even in dry times, and in the winter the wet swells fingers and toes with chilblains.

The waters themselves do not linger in that place but rush away toward the covered galleries of Fleet Market, where purpose-built kennels convey the roily streams into the ditch itself. Now the Fleet, a thick rope of twisted liquid, slides past the hulk of the Prison and so down to Blackfriars, where the muddy gulp of the Thames swallows it whole. And good riddance, sister, for in its present state the river is unwholesome.

The house is worse, but I did not know its evils then, as I stood lost before its front door. Nor should I have crossed over its threshold if it had not been for the man who addressed me while I wondered what I should do next.

"Please," he said, lifting the flap of a bundle of cloth in his arms, "can you help me, for the child is ill."

I did not wish to look at that bundle. I had seen no children playing in Sharp's Alley, and I was content that there should be none. But the man seemed clean and respectable, dressed in a good coat of brown drugget, and my own sad need of assistance recommended him to me as another equally beset. Unwillingly, I let him come nearer, and he lifted the swaddling beneath my nose, so that I could not help but look at its contents. I feared to see the little one very sick, or even worse, but in fact, Sadie, the cloth held nothing but more cloth. I put out my hand to make sure and found the swaddling empty.

"I see no child," I said, breathing my relief.

But how anxiously the man watched my eyes. How truly he desired my assistance. I could see his need written clearly in the lines of his face.

"Please," said he, again, "can you help me, for the child is ill."

Unwillingly, I put out my hand and felt the bundle again and knew for certain the gentleman's need stemmed from some terrible misapprehension of his mind—and yet his distress was real. Sadie, I did not know what to do. I feared to contradict him a second time, uncertain as to what effect my insistence might have on his disordered thinking.

"I think the child is not as ill as you imagine," I said carefully, letting go my hold on the cloth.

"Please," said the distressed gentleman, "can you help me, for the child is ill."

So I could not help him—his unvarying request pointed to difficulties far beyond my means to address. Yet to turn my back on him seemed equally wrong, and so I determined to assist him at least a little.

I asked him if he lived nearby, and he pointed to the house before us. I looked more closely at its two peaked gables and gaping entry. A grey and creeping mould patchworked the stone front of one side of the house, while sickly mortar limed the brick facing of the other. However, I saw a dim light illuminating the larger of the two windows across the front, and I tried to take heart at the sight of watery figures through the rippled panes. "Come," I said, in what I hoped was a commanding voice, "we must take the child inside."

To my surprise, the man came easily, uttering no sound of protest and gently rocking the empty swaddling as he walked. The great oak door, which I was certain would not open at my touch, swung inwards easily, and together the distressed gentleman and I set foot in the tiled entrance. Ahead of us stretched a passage with massive, carved stairs leading upwards. Where I expected stairs down to the cellar, a trapdoor sat closed and locked with a heavy metal rod. Immediately to my right, a panelled chamber opened into a darker room, lost in obscurity. From this direction, rough voices knocked together, punctuated by the clicking of pewter tankards. At the noise, the gentleman clutched his cloth nothingness closer, and I judged he wished not to proceed in that direction. His wishes matched my own very neatly, for I did not like the stink of ale and the dampness that underlay it. Instead, I led him toward a door at the back.

I knocked and upon hearing a woman's voice, opened the door. I found myself on the threshold of a small, low-ceilinged parlour. A good fire burned in the hearth, and a ruddy light reflected off well-polished wood. I observed a collection of teapots and cups that lined the large sideboard filling one wall. Opposite stood a bed, its curtains neatly closed, and an equally neat woman sat beside a table before the fire, darning thick blue stockings. She evidenced no surprise at our entrance but only set her work upon the table. Rising, she put out a hand to the gentleman who stood behind me. "Please," he said to her, "can you help me, for the child is ill." Then he crossed to her, and she seated him before the fire.

The woman turned to me, speaking as if we were already acquainted. "You must not think less of me if I sometimes let him wander," said she. "I cannot always attend to him when matters press, and as he does not pass beyond those parts where he is well known, he always comes safe home. Where did you find him, if I might know?"

I told her he had only been in the yard in front of the house.

"Ah," she said, "then he was hardly lost at all. In that case, I cannot give you much, you understand, or I shall think myself taken advantage of." Then, she offered me a coin.

I gestured my refusal, and she looked at me crossly. "I will not give you more," she said, the skin of her forehead knotting.

"I think you misunderstand me," said I. "I only wished to assist the gentleman in his distress. I do not require payment for what was intended as an act of kindness."

She looked at me for a moment and then put her coin back into her pocket. Then both of us looked in the gentleman's direction. He sat quietly at the table, his bundle still clutched in his arms. "Please," he said, observing our eyes upon him. He looked first at me and then at her. "Can you help me? The child is ill."

She sighed heavily and crossed her arms upon her chest. "God help me," she said, "I only wish that kindness might help him, but as you see, his condition puts him quite beyond charity."

"Might one not show him the needlessness of his inquiry? It is most pitiable to watch his distress."

"My brother's distress is a fixed impression with him. You might show him its falsity, and he would kindly accept your correction. Then he would begin to collect cloths again, refashioning his waking horror from the very blankets on his bed."

"I am sorry," I said, but for what I hardly knew.

She shook her head. "No," she said, "you mean well enough."

Sadie, I ought to have departed then and there, for I knew I had accomplished everything I could. But still the gentleman's plight expanded like freezing water in my heart, and I had another question I would ask.

I put one hand in the other and wrung them together. "Was there ever such a child?" said I, almost whispering.

I feared my companion might grow angry again, but she only laid her hands on her brother's back. "Such a child?" she said. "There are many," and pressing his shoulder so that he would remain seated, she crossed to a small door I had not noticed before. This she opened and beckoned for me to follow, saying, "You would do a good turn, so let me repay you in kind, and show you something useful for a young maid to see."

A short passage and a second door led to another room, again low of ceiling and dark-panelled in the old-fashioned way. Heavy curtains

D. M. Bryan

shut out all daylight, so that at first all I could see was the good fire burning in the grate. Then, by its flickering light, I made out three ragged women seated at its hearth, each great with child. One sewed a tiny garment from the remains of a torn shift; one stirred a three-legged pot filled with smoking ramps; and the last held a broken-backed book to the flames in order to read by that dim light. At our entrance the women looked up.

"The beds are all full, missus," said the one sewing.

"I'll not share with nobody," said the one cooking. The one reading turned frightened eyes toward me.

I turned to my companion. "You are a midwife?"

"Nature is midwife here," she said, "and her apron is red."

"Lord, missus," said the sewing girl, "how you put our minds at ease."

The cooking girl gave her pot a savage stir and addressed herself to me. "This lady has a terrible way of talking that might put you off—assuming there's any choice in the matter. As for me, I'd rather lie-in with the ladies, rejoicing in clean linen and a paid wink to the Parish. But this is a place where a girl might deliver for nothing, so long as nothing is said."

"That's a hint," said the sewer, giving me an exaggerated wink.

The one reading tucked her book under her arm and scuttled away from the fire. When I followed her with my eyes, the rest of that room slowly revealed itself. A baby wailed weakly, more like a cat than a child. Truckle beds heaped with grey bedding showed like mounds in a graveyard. Under the smell of cooking greens, I detected sweat and the metallic tang of blood. Fouler body stinks rolled off a pot in a half-lit corner. A wet cough sounded from one bed, a dry cough from another. And then I heard my companion hailed by a voice so soft I almost missed it. "Missus," the voice cried.

At the sound, my new acquaintance turned from me and began to move amongst the beds, where there was not room for two to walk abreast. On either side, she stooped, smoothing blankets, but her fingers seemed only to test and not soothe. When she reached the furthest bed, a hand, all bone, plucked at her skirts. She bent down over what at first I took to be a length of rope. Then the mistress of that place put out her arms and raised up the inhabitant of that bed. When the girl was fully on her feet, I could finally make her out—painfully thin and younger than myself, with a torn fragment of blanket over her shoulders and an infant in her arms.

Slowly, she and the lady came toward the fire, approaching, painful step by painful step, even as the two remaining girls drew back. They left their emaciated companion more than enough room before the hearth. There she hunched, the baby hardly stirring, both sucking at warmth and air as though they could never have enough.

"You see what we are," said the sewing girl to me. Her tiny garment lay abandoned in her lap.

The cooking girl gruffly proffered the contents of her saucepan to her deathly sister. "Will you eat some?" she said, but the other only shook her head.

The mistress of that place said to me, "Haven't you seen enough?"

Sister, I could not speak. I left that room, moving like one of the automatons wound up and set running on St. Bartholomew's day. When I re-entered the little parlour, my eye fell upon the gentleman, still with his burden in his arms. As one in a dream—nay, a nightmare—I began to empty my purse upon the table. My companion stopped me at once, pushing back my few coins with such vigour they threatened to fly to the floor.

"Buy her meat," I said. "Fetch her a doctor."

"She has seen a doctor, and meat cannot help," she said. "Did you not notice the public house as you came in? Selling drink is a very good trade, and I need no assistance from anyone. My trade provides those girls with food enough if they want it, and warmth. And if they will wash and dry the linen, they will have a clean bed in which to deliver their child. They do not die here any more often than they die in better places—although why that should be, I cannot tell. The world does damage I cannot mend." And here she looked at her brother.

"The parish—" I said, but she interrupted me.

"You may judge for yourself whether or not parish assistance is an advantage in every case."

Sister, I did judge for myself, and so I said nothing. To be torn from familiar arms and removed to a friendless legal settlement; to be put to the test of naming a father who cannot or ought not be named; to bend

D. M. Bryan

to the rule of the workhouse for three pieces of bread and cheese a day; to have a child taken and fostered in some loveless place—I would not willingly undergo even one of these trials, let alone each of them in turn.

Into this silence came a voice I had almost forgotten. "Please," said the man with the swaddling, "can you help me, for the child is ill."

"Yes, yes," replied his sister, her voice catching. "I am doing what I can." To me she said, "Once he was a man-midwife and made a very good name for himself. We lived west of here, and he attended gentlewomen in their own beds. Even on good streets, he would find the infants abandoned as he walked home in the early hours. I do not know if those small bodies caused him to lose his reason, or if his unreason takes the form dictated by those corpses. It hardly matters. He cannot help himself, and the dead still appear in every part of London."

I would not look at her and started returning my sad pile of coins to my person. "You understand," said my companion, and I felt her eyes close upon me, "I am not without sentiment, but it does no good. One day the overseer of the poor will hear of what I keep behind my parlour door, and then I will lose my ale-house license. On that day, I will be glad to leave this house, for it is built on bones."

Sadie, this time I asked for no explanation, for I wondered if her senses had begun to fray like her brother's. I did not insult her with further offers of assistance, and I made no attempt to praise her—the sharpness of her manner disinclined me even to like her. Instead, I closed my purse and tied it tightly in my pocket.

She smiled at me as I left that room, but never did I see a face more like a mask.

Well, Sadie, now I have told you everything that a long letter can hold. My adventures for that day were not entirely over, but setting down these events upon the page has wearied me, and so I must truncate my account a little. Suffice to say that after some further adventures, I reached home safely and very gladly returned to the bosom of my dear mistress.

Honesty compels me to add that, since my return, I have not been so well as we both might hope. Sister, I did not say so at the beginning of this letter, for now that you have read it, I hope that you will accept its many pages as a sufficient guarantee of returning strength. There has never been, and is not now, any reason for you to feel anxiety on my behalf. I would have said nothing at all, only my mistress urges me not to hide that I have been ill, so that when I tell you I am greatly improved, I might reasonably expect to be believed. And so, I do expect you to believe me, Sadie, and I know you will.

To ease my convalescence, my mistress procured for me another book, a novel, from one of those persons who provide aprons and lappets for regular washing. I am grateful to this lady, a Mrs. Tanner, for her kindness in providing me with a means to entertain and instruct myself while abed. I am not certain if *The History of Glossolalia: Or, Virtues Various* will prove entirely to my liking, but I have only just begun to turn the pages. I have every confidence the tale's chiefest pleasures still lie before me.

Neither have I much time for reading, for I intend to return to work immediately. I can no longer presume upon my mistress' kindness and tender care, both of which she has dispensed generously, with no thought to any result other than my improvement. Now that my body has fully recovered, I am fit to do battle with the only enduring effect of my illness: a curious check to my sensibilities resulting from some trifling details of my return home. Can you imagine that my visit to the house in Sharp's Alley has left me afraid of water? What an absurdity in a laundress. My mistress says I must take a boat ride on the Thames, or the thought of water will forever excite my mind, associating that liquid with those fearful sentiments I felt before. On that noble and open-hearted river, she says, I will find the means to overcome this odd and unexpected check to my livelihood. Sadie, I am certain she is correct, and I will submit to her guidance in this matter, as I do in all things of importance.

But an account of my certain cure must wait for a future sending. For now, I can only assure you of my essential well-being, and that I am, as always, your devoted sister, Elizabeth.

D. M. Bryan

CHAPTER 5

Provides yet another letter to be bundled with the
others, like aprons ready for the washtub. In it, Mrs.
Veronica continues her investigation into the cause of
the Harlot's death.

London, 1732.

Dear Justice Gonson.

You and I have met before, sir, though I doubt you will remember, for I
am a lowly kind of person and hardly worth a second look in the street,
unless 'tis to avoid stepping on me, sir, for I know you are a gentleman.
I am only a poor woman, a laundress, to be exact. Your constables
brought me before you and kindly gave me a chair. It was on the matter
of a harlot that you called for us, sir—the Harlot in Mr. Hogarth's
printed pictures. You asked us about the colonel and the bawd that
chucked the Harlot under her chin. Betty told you, "That's a book you're
thinking of there, and not the kind of life we watch from the window."
Do you remember that, Justice Gonson? Indeed, you must, for my Betty
has a ready wit and most men can recall a jest from out a pretty mouth.
Well, I hope you remember Betty, sir, for she is the reason I write to you
today—or rather, because I have not myself any skill with letters, you
are addressed in the hand of one Mrs. Ezra Tanner, who is a clergyman's
wife and a kind soul, although she bids me not push her to the front of
this letter.

But to my point—alas, my Betty is not well. It sorrows me beyond
all telling to admit that it is so. I have prescribed for her as best I

can—soup is as easily made in a laundry pot as in any other—but that is the extent of my powers, for I am neither physician nor surgeon. I pray soup will suffice, for I have not the coin to bring the medical men into my house, and I do not trust the costly phial, the gleaming lancet. No, my dear poor Betty has been forced to flush, shake, and shiver away the creeping stain of her illness with neither compound nor phial to wash her clean. Still, she fights, Justice Gonson, as only a laundress can. She battles, and her determination, alongside my soup, begins to mend her ragged breathing, her aching head, her bruised limbs. We do see improvements, sir. Her bile, her phlegm, and her blood—if I may be forgiven for mentioning such things in relation to a female person—are not so disordered as they were. Her complexion alters from an ivory silk to a cream-coloured linen, which is to the good. And yet, dear, good Justice Gonson, my Betty is not herself.

What do I mean? I do not know myself, sir, I can only say again and again: she is not the girl she should be. Not the girl she was. She suffers, sir, from a fright of which she will not speak. Her condition makes me think on all manner of physick, and how we might mend what is torn asunder.

You stand accused of a tattered conscience, and do not blame me, Justice Gonson, for stating plain what others most certainly would cover over with ruffles and furbelows. I know you are a justice of the peace and a good man, you need not defend yourself to me. Yet some say the death of Hogarth's Harlot is a charge upon your bill—that your moral program against harlots makes your reputation at the cost of theirs. They say—those that talk—that your ambition killed poor Moll. Or Poll. Or Maria. Or Kate. Or any of the hundred names that printed lady carries.

Now, I hold no love for those who gossip, but when you sent your constables for Miss Betty and me, you obliged us to consider the truth of the matter, sir. That day, I knew nothing of the Harlot or her situation. But you bid me answer for the denizens of the Bell Inn's yard, and I take that charge as sacred under the law. Accordingly, I have made it my business to learn what I can, and now that I know more, my honour as a laundress bids me to lend whatever assistance is mine to give. On this, Mrs. Tanner concedes my point. If I can help, I must.

D. M. Bryan

And what have I learned? Of whores in general I know as much as any virtuous woman. Up and down Cheapside they go, but whether harlots face east or west, they always walk straight at Newgate. These are the strangest of women, for they are very poor, yet they have all the trappings of ladies: silks and laces, a jewel in each ear, a servant to run before them and to push ruffians away from the wall. Good girls, like my poor Betty, must watch them pass and wonder why virtue never earns skirts near as fine as those on Mrs. Hackabout or her sisters. Once, I stood spellbound in the street while a silken lady held forth on the entertainment to which she had just been treated. In a cracked voice, she painted for us a suite of rooms, each with a service of sparkling plate on linen boiled until it dazzled like snow. Those rooms, she said, gleamed with ranks of men, masked, watching white-painted ladies dancing and feasting. Each room opened into another room, until the last, where danced a golden-haired princess in Turkish dress. Now, I have never entered such a series of rooms as stood host to that sinful lady, and while I have seen boiled linen aplenty, I have never seen the heaped plate that stands upon it. The Harlot described candelabra with as many tapers as she had fingers, but only distantly through windows have I seen such a twinkling.

Justice Gonson, as everybody knows, the rewards harlots enjoy never last, and in the end, they are punished—perhaps far more than they deserve. Harlots only play out the world's contradiction, whereas doctors benefit by 'em. For want of a coin, my Betty lies untreated, save for my thin soup, while doctors flock to visit anyone with coin. A harlot may call for a surgeon with his lancet, but a woman of modest means must moulder, fester, boil, and ooze. A poor clergyman's wife must face death, her passage eased only by her husband's prayer. A washerwoman will certainly breathe her last without a medical man to wash her inside-out with clysters.

These are the reflections I entertained while contemplating the meaning of Mr. Hogarth's modern moral subject on his Harlot's progress. It was then that I had an idea, Justice Gonson—a way to set right your sullied name. In short, why do you not moralize doctors, good sir? Why waste your labours on whores, whose situation you only worsen with incarceration in Bridewell? Why not aim for those who come at their gold second-hand, enriching themselves on the innocent sins of country girls? Reform those rapacious mercury-merchants, bidding them to tend to those who need them most, regardless of the rule of gold. Then hear the world sing your praises, dear Justice.

Consider how completely that class of men deserves the name of quack, which suits them so well, they should be a flock of ducks. What is their reputation in both town and city? Why, they always come too late, with physic that never answers. They bring mercury, and lavender oil, and clysters by the carriagefull. They will cup you or bleed you or stare sadly at your suffering—all this they do, and then they depart, but not before you've paid them for your pains. Live or die, you must pay.

Full of these thoughts, I decided to see for myself how doctors are like harlots, easing the body for a palmful of coins. I asked the housekeeper at one of those fine houses where I ply my trade for the name of an excellent doctor, a physician who serves fine folk, not a barber-surgeon that shaves men and bleeds women dry. But, my informant played me a trick, knowing me only a laundress, for she did not send me to the sort of man I sought.

The address, near to the great hospital, fooled me, and I prepared for my visit, first taking the precaution of assuming a costume that was not by rights my own. As a laundress, I have easy access to such a variety of skirts and petticoats that it was only the work of a moment to assemble that combination of garments that might make me a respectable tradeswoman, a prosperous mercer's wife. Accordingly, I dressed me in a satin gown, heavy and glossy. Sleeves I borrowed in quantity, and a fine cloak to cover my head. When I was done, I could not see myself, for I own no glass, but Betty told me I looked the very person of a Mistress Mercer, with one eye for the shop and the other for my own comfort.

"Fie," said I. "A change in dress does all that?"

"It does," said Betty, but with less vivaciousness than before her illness. "Do you have a wish to marry again, mistress?"

I could not contain my astonishment. "Nay," I told Betty, "I do not dress to find myself a husband. You should know me better, child."

"I know so very little," said Betty, her pale face meek.

D. M. Bryan

I hated to see her so, in this blanched state. But I would not lie to her. "Mrs. Betty," I said, "I cannot let you into the secret of my excursion today. An apprentice must remain innocent of some parts of her mistresses' business or else she would be apprenticed no longer."

"I am content to hold my half of my indenture forever, Mrs. Veronica."

"What? Are you also unwilling to marry?"

Justice Gonson, to this raillery she only smiled sadly. Watching her, I hoped I had hit upon some truth more soothing to think of than a disorder in trunk and limb. I remembered me her curious fear of water and of the trips out upon the Thames she'd taken to remedy this distress, so fatal in a laundress. Now, her sad demeanour and bloodless complexion appeared to me in a different light. Was it love that ailed her?

Ah, but the problem vexed me. Such fond suspicions might prove misleading, for I had not myself the skill of diagnosis, and Betty lodges so very close to my heart. Only a doctor might say if a doctor were needed. It was a puzzle.

"I must go as far as St. Bartholomew's, and I will be some time," I said, lifting my hood over my cap. "Do no work, and do not wait on me. Rest yourself."

"But you cannot go on foot." she said.

"Indeed, how else should I go?"

"If you are not you, and I see from your skirts and your cloak that you are not, you must suit your means of travel to your disguise."

I stopped and immediately felt the unfamiliar rustle of fine fabric about my legs. Indeed, such elegant stuff did not belong in the street. "Mud," said I, "should be brushed when dry and removed from silk by the assiduous application—"

"Hush," said my good Betty, adding, "you must choose your chairmen with care."

"A chair, dear Betty?"

"Do not choose any from the Bell, for they will certainly be drunk. You will be set at the transept doors in a heap."

Betty imagined I meant to go to St. Bart's own church. That was well enough—I would not have her guess where I went.

"I shall walk as far as Cheapside, but I will ride from there."

"Have you ready coin, mistress?" said Betty, her hand already upon the opening of her pocket, but I waved her hand away, taking myself to the door. There, I turned and kissed her upon the cheek, which took both of us very much by surprise.

We walk a spiral path, Betty and I, and can only walk together a short time. Her road is new and loops wide, while my way curls tight upon itself. How lucky we are that our different paths ran side-by-side, even for so short a time. One day we must part, Justice Gonson, and that sad foretelling is a stain I cannot remove.

Mrs. Tanner, my scribe, applauds my sensibility, but she says such *pensées*, though fine, prove unwelcome in a letter of business such as I desire to write. She bids me hasten to my purpose, and so we resume our mutual tale.

I sallied forth to the doctor's in a sober chair painted black and with a sashed window that would not lower. The chairmen carried me gently and set me down no little way along a narrow artery, not far from the great hospital. With much deference to my skirt and fine cloak, I was handed out before a dim, shadowed doorway and there the chairmen left me, having first satisfied me that this was indeed the address I sought.

A reeking flight of stairs led me upwards, past the first turn and past the second, to the very top of that undesirable residence. The room alarmed me beyond all measure, for it was poorly lit by a dirty window and decorated with oddities such as I hope never to see again. Wonders there were, but also awful objects whose purpose I could not easily understand. Through the half-open doors of a little closet, I could see bones, pale in the gloom and rotating slightly as if gallows-tied. Above that, some finned creature depended, with its quilted hide and teeth like lace picots. More teeth, these made of metal, distinguished an infernal machine that consisted of many oily parts, gears and screws and a frame—a press or a rack, I could not tell. Bulbous bottles, lettered phials, and snakelike ropes coiled beneath the ceiling, but worse by far was a terrible head, sitting on top of the cabinet. 'Twas a leering, grinning face with wide eyes that looked out at nothing. I could not tell if it was a bust made of stone, or if it was a carved mask, intended for grim masquerades. Perhaps it was what it seemed: a man's skin,

D. M. Bryan

preserved and stuffed with sawdust. At this supposition, I looked away in shame—what kind of man keeps another on display?

My answer stood by a covered table where a further artful arrangement of a book and a skull conveyed the impermanence of life, an odd theme for the decoration of a physician's chambers. The man himself was pinch-jawed, with a peaked wig like the claw of a crab. He saw me and commenced shining his glasses with a filthy cloth and a thumb on one lens. I did not speak, nor did he expect me to. Instead, he clapped his smeared lenses on his nose and circled me once, sniffing, pausing directly behind me, but for what purpose I could not tell. At last he came fully round to his starting point, and resumed his nonchalant posture by the table. "Well, Mrs.," he said at last, croaking genially and commencing to polish his glasses again. "'Tis not the predations of Venus that brings you here to me today. Neither have you the plague."

"Indeed, sir, I think I would know if I suffered either pox or spots."

"You are perhaps over-warm?"

"I am entirely comfortable," said I, although the presence of some waxen death mask glaring at me from behind the doctor ensured the contrary.

"I notice you pant, as if in the throes of some curious passion."

"My want of breath can be easily explained, sir. I am old and fat, and your stairs are steep."

"In that case, I would ask you to show me your lingual organ."

Instead, I showed him my extreme dislike of his request, which in truth I did not understand.

"Fie, 'tis only your tongue, woman. You would show it to me in the street quick enough."

"Only my tongue? Then why not say so?"

"It is but the *lingua franca*. That's Greek to you, I have no doubt."

"You may speak your thieves' cant—I don't care. A doctor's language is only a stew of dead words come up in the world."

"Hah," said the doctor, wiping his nose with the same handkerchief with which he had been polishing his glasses. "Hah, I'm sure. Every trade has its own language. You now, Mother, I'm certain you have your own words for whatever the rest of us need not understand."

Indeed, I have, but I would not have him know the nature of my employment or my disguise was to no purpose. Besides, his overly familiar usage distressed me a great deal.

"Why do you call me Mother?" I said. "You should know I inhabit a very nice set of rooms near the Covent Garden, where every day, on clean linen, I lay out a dinner for my husband, the mercer."

"Madam, said the doctor, lifting the skull from the table and holding it between us as if to ward me off, "I am deep in my studies and unless you require prescribing, I need not think of you at all."

I wanted to go then. His manner, equal parts familiarity and condescension, sickened me, but I would not turn back, having come so far. "Sir," I said, embroidering upon the truth, "I have heard you praised by the highest kind of people as a physician of considerable skill."

The doctor now employed his handkerchief to polish the ridged area over the skull's empty obits. His own eyes shone at my praise, but he only said, "Do not attempt to flatter me, madam. Why, that is no more than my housemaid acknowledges daily at market."

"All London," I said, continuing to embroider, "and perhaps all the world says that no one who implores your aid perishes but that they disobey your prescription. Once a man or woman is under your care, there is no other way to die."

A lobster smile split the man's nose from his chin, and he polished all the harder, saying, "Tut, people do talk, but 'tis true I have a pilule that will make you clear as a newborn babe. It operates by inducing a gentle salivation to restore the freshness of your breath and return to your cheeks the rose that so captivated in the summer of your youth."

I stared at him, until he confessed. "I speak of mercury," he said, and then he struck a sort of orating pose, like a priest in his pulpit, with his body bent forward, one foot advanced and the other knee bent. He raised his left hand, but relaxed his right at his side, the palm turned to me so that he might speak. "Nobel Specifick!" quoth he "Glorious is thy Use."

I did not know what to say, nor indeed where to look while he undertook this performance, so I said, "I do not wish my cheeks to recover the rose of youth. That flower should hang very oddly from such a wizened stem."

"A flash of wit, Mother."

"And again, I do not choose to be addressed by that name."

He gave a roguish grin. "And yet I suspect you will refuse to give me any other, for all your talk of mercers."

I had to admit, he had me there. Mrs. Betty had summoned the mercer's wife from under my satin skirts, but I had not thought to supply that lady with a false appellation, and now invention would not serve me quick enough. Besides, I do not like to lie.

"I have a girl in my care," I said, to get more directly to the point of my visit.

"Ah."

"Think what you will, sir, but she is a good girl, and one I would not lose. She is very low, and suffers mightily from some condition I cannot easily understand."

"Is she below? You may bring her up."

"She is not below. I did not bring her with me. I can tell you whatever you need to know."

The man set down his skull and tucked his handkerchief into some inner pocket of his coat. Setting his glasses on the bridge of his nose he peered at me overtop the wire rim. "Come, come," he said, "the melancholic chambermaid has very few causes—she is with child, surely."

"She is not—no sir, not her."

He nodded. "Well, then, 'tis that other depravation of Venus—she is poxy, no doubt."

I snapped my skirts angrily and slapped away an imaginary speck on the virgin green folds. "She is a good girl and innocent. I would swear it upon my own life."

A point of light flashed on the doctor's lenses as his eyebrows shot up and then down again, but when his glasses were resettled on the bridge of his nose he was quiet. After a moment's thought, he said, "Is she very red or extremely pale?"

"She is pale."

"Do her eyes water excessively? Is there a red tint or a yellow taint to the white? Are they clear, like the ether, or glassy, like a public house window?"

Betty's eyes, I thought, were as they had always been, only sadder. I shook my head.

"Have you observed the movement of her bowels to have a thin, watery consistency or are they well-shaped, holding their form in the bottom of the chamber pot?"

"Sir?"

"These are my methods, madam. An examination of the stools can tell me a great deal. Now, what have you observed?

Mrs. Betty herself emptied the pot each morning from the balcony into the fetid mud of the Bell Inn. Our little efforts vanished under the superior products of the horses, who were hourly in and out of the yard. I shook my head.

The doctor sighed. "But you have felt her pulse, I suppose?" he said. "Have you judged of its number?"

Alas, I did not understand him, and I shook my head. The doctor sighed again and began to come toward me. Confused, I backed away, stepping directly into that infernal contraption, all cogs and levers, until I felt the press of metal through the layers of my skirts. Now I could reverse no further without doing myself some grievous harm. I lifted an arm to defend myself, but could not. The man forestalled me from taking further action by seizing my hand and holding his fingers lightly to the inside of my wrist.

"Now now," he said, "I mean only to give you a demonstration." Reaching into an inner pocket, the doctor drew out a pocket watch, saying, "Verse is composed according to number, but so are ordinary men and women. I intend to publish something on this observation, which I believe to be novel to myself." And then he began to count aloud, staring intently at the face of his little clock.

Dear Justice Gonson, the man's touch disturbed me, and with each new number he spoke aloud, came a whiff of the kippered herring and ale with which he'd broken his fast. I twisted and would have torn myself away, but his hold must have been alchemical. All at once, I felt a pinching pain on my left side, as though a demon sat there, tightening his fingers. Then the doctor, though not the fiendish pain, released me, and the man returned to his place by the table. There, in a single movement, he tucked away his pocket watch and plucked out the

D. M. Bryan

handkerchief, with which he commenced polishing the end of his own nose.

I staggered on the spot, astonished by his behaviour and breathless at his boldness. "What have you done, sir?" said I, checking myself for marks—for evidence of some sybaritic familiarity unknown to a respectable laundress like myself. A chill lay upon me, and my own flesh showed damp.

The doctor replied indistinctly, for his cloth obscured his face and any sense he might be making, and so I spoke again. "Sir, I demand you explain yourself—oh, oh, I must sit down."

His handkerchief returned to its hiding place in the braided coat, and now I could see his visage. Upon the crabby face sat an unexpected expression of compassionate sympathy. At once, the man brought me a chair and urged me into it. Then he said, his voice low and moist, "Your blood, madam, is not in order. It is good you have come to see me, although I am truly sorry at the facts of your case."

"Doctor, sir." I took a deep breath, for to be sure I was strangely disordered by both his actions and now by his countenance. I took my own handkerchief from the pocket I had tied into my borrowed finery, and I mopped my face. It took all my powers to remind him that I did not come on my own behalf. "It is my girl who has the whole of my concern, and I will not be waylaid by some stratagem to sell me a phial or physic for myself." This last came out as a whisper.

"When did your pain begin?"

"My pain?" said I. "You have unleashed some devil, I think."

"Dear dear," said the doctor, bending low over my chair and picking up my wrist again. This time I could not struggle, and I allowed him to set his fingers on my skin as though he were plugging holes in a pipe. "You must not exert yourself," he told me.

Indeed, I could not have moved even if I'd wanted to. His room swam about me, his fishy ornament bleeding into the stuffed head above the closet. The pilasters of his window sprouted seaweed, and the watery light showed me his coat, now blue-green and plated. His touch came again, as gauzy as crayfish whiskers. How very cold I was, and how certain I would die. I began to say the Lord's Prayer.

"Hush, mistress. You must show me your tongue."

Show him my tongue? The terrible fellow. My mouth came open to pray, or set him straight. Or perhaps only to groan, for I never found out. I could not breathe and a lightless tide rose up around my shoulders. Grey lapped the edges of my vision. Through a hole of light, he came at me in a surge of frockcoat and a reek of kippers. Then I tasted a sharp bitterness and felt a tide of spittle between my dry lips. His rubbing fingers, strong and certain, exerted a firm pressure on my jaw. My panic passed its crest and subsided, as I swallowed, gagged. A moment later, I was drinking silken air.

Justice Gonson, I do not know how long I sat, hunched in my chair, panting and sweating. In this position, I remained until, almost insensibly, my agony began to diminish, and, with much time elapsing, I could lift my head. When the tears had fully drained from my eyes, and I was able to look about me again, I found the doctor standing over by his table, with the skull cradled in his hands. Above him, the giant's head and the hanging fish had both returned to their places. The noises of London—cries, clops, shouts, knocks—came audibly through the window. Someone outside was selling carrots and cauliflower at the top of her lungs. New lamb and fresh mint. I took the first easy breath I'd had since I made my way up that man's twisted stairs.

"There now," said the villain himself, fixing me with his wet gaze.

"What did you give me?" I demanded of him, the bitter taste of his physic still numbing my lips. "What vile poison did you force upon me?"

He gave me a surprised look, eyebrows and claw-tipped wig rising alike. "Why," said he, "'tis only Foxglove. I will sell you some if you have not a supply of your own, for it is most efficacious, as every old wife knows. Or, perhaps not *every* old wife." His laughter struck me as cruel, and he soon broke off when I rose from my chair.

"Nay," he said, "continue sitting. You must not rise too soon."

"So you might ply more of your dishonest tricks?"

"What?" said he.

I swayed on my feet, but I would not be distracted from my purpose. I had been badly frightened, and like the foolish old woman he thought me, I determined he should bear the brunt of my unhappiness.

"You are no more than a quack," I said. "My girl, who suffers at a distance, you cannot prescribe for, but in the old body, who visits you in your chamber of horrors, you induce a fit and pretend to cure it so that you might sell me some of your venomous extract—"

"Fairy's Gloves, madam. Virgin's Thimbles. Every countrywoman knows—"

"I am not from the country. I am a city woman through and through."

"More's the pity," said the doctor, dropping his skull near to his foot, where it did not shatter as he clearly feared it might, but rather rolled beneath the table and so was lost to view.

I left him there, Justice Gonson, in that terrible closet hung with grisly trophies, and the last I saw of him was his end indeed. For, having moved myself to the door of that room, I looked back to find him groping beneath the table for his treasure, with only his hindmost parts protruding from beneath the cloth. Sir, Mr. Justice, I longed to put my foot to his sea-coloured trousers, but I dared not, for I did not trust that I would weather the exertion required for such a swift, hard kick as that man merited.

Indeed, I was not entirely recovered from my adventure, for I vomited twice on the stairs on the way down, and thrice in the sedan chair on the way home. I am very sorry to tell you, none of those spontaneous purges landed outside the window, which this time was jammed shut. Instead, I splattered the chair's inner lining—a white silk, which was neither well-chosen nor often laundered. I gave the men good advice for the removal of any stain, including the one I left behind me, but they did not receive my counsel in a manner that pleased any of us. In truth, they were somewhat threatening, and I was obliged to spend another farthing in the form of a tip, making my excursion cost more than intended.

When I reached home, my good Betty was so disturbed by what she termed "my shocking condition" that she forced me to take to my bed, obliging herself to rise from her own. Indeed, Justice Gonson, it is the same bed, but we cannot both convalesce at once. Betty says I have effected the cure I sought, even if my method was not entirely as I might have wished, but I can tell she humours me. Her face is pale and pinched, and I do not like what I see in her eyes.

And now I cannot leave this bed. I cannot lose my trade, sir, for it is my life, and I know not what I would do without its suds and the smell of sunshine on linen. My landlady tells me of an elderly lady, the wife of a country squire, grown to rival the fatness of her husband's cattle, who took a fit like mine and died. First, that lady sweated, and next she grew chilled, and then she cried out that her stays had been fastened past bearing. This last frightened her maid very much for the lady wore no stays, her spell having come by candlelight. The poor girl ran for the master, but when she roused him from the table—for they were a couple who dearly loved to eat and drink—her mistress was already dead, blue and cold upon the floorcloth. And that floorcloth was new, according to my landlady, who does not fully understand how to end an anecdote. But now, Mrs. Tanner urges me to finish my own tale.

Good Mrs. Tanner. I have seen her looking at me with the same expression of compassionate regard I surprised on the face of the quack. Indeed, she presses me on the details of my attack. I tell her again of the fiendish pain, the pretended cure. "'Twas no more than a bit of trickery, designed to part a helpless old woman from her coin," I say.

"And yet," says Mrs. Tanner, "the doctor charged you nothing."

That gives me pause. That makes me think. Could I have been wrong about the man, Justice Gonson—have I been unjust myself?

Now, I hear Mrs. Tanner herself on the stair, speaking too loudly to my landlady. She says I am very damp under her cap and that I gulp at the air like a carp in an ornamental pond. She fears a second attack. Now, she returns and for the good of her soul, I make her write out what else she said, which was, "Call again for Betty. I have loosened the old woman's stays as much as decency allows—oh, I would the girl gets here soon."

I also wish my Betty would return from her errand, for I want the girl beside me. In the meantime, I beg you, sir, to know that I am your fully devoted and most respectful servant, etc. . . .

D. M. Bryan

CHAPTER 6

Mrs. Betty's final letter providing a description of the
manner in which Mrs. Veronica makes her will and
disposes of her worldly goods. A fragment of manuscript:
*The Analysis of Laundry: Written with a View of Fixing
the Fluid Nature of Washing.* How the story ends.

Bell Inn Yard off Fryday Street, 1732.

My dearest Sadie,

How very pleased I was to receive your last letter and the important
confidences it contained. So Mr. Nutbrown is to have an heir to his
vast estates and holdings, or at least, he is to have a daughter, if events
so prove. I am delighted for him and concerned for you. Shall I take
a sisterly tone and prescribe your every move from the receipt of this
letter to the weaning of the child to come? If you agree, I will dictate
the quadrant of the breezes in which you may sit by the window and the
direction of that wind in which you must not so much as open a curtain.
I will forbid you to laugh heartily at a puppet show or to weep over
your parson's sermon—if indeed your parson is capable of producing
such an excess of sentiment (for, certainly, not all have the gift). I will
forbid you from standing beneath a clap of thunder or anywhere near
a church steeple, and at all costs, you must avoid loud bursts of musket
fire, which is only good advice. Sadie, please tell me that I am not wrong
to imagine you, Mr. Nutbrown, and your happy burden to be safe from
perils, real or imaginary. If you will do this, I will consider my sisterly

advice dispensed and will say no more on matters of which I, in truth, know nothing.

My mistress also bids me write to say what pleasure your news gives her. Sadie, although I do not like to write of it, my mistress is much altered, and I am not able to give a very good account of her health by this letter. She has suffered some misadventure, although she has not yet told me everything, and she returned by chair very ill indeed. She has been in bed—oh sister, I weep a little to write those words, harmless though they seem. In any other woman, the phrase, common enough, would mean nothing of import. In the case of my mistress, who laundered late and still rose with the birds, her lying abed shocks me. I will not list here her complaints, for she describes them not at all, and I can only guess at the meaning of her intermittent bouts of nausea and her drooping arm. Although a doctor asks a great deal of coin, I sent the Bell's boy for a good one, but she sent him away. Instead, she lies quietly enough while I do our washing and run our errands. The landlady's daughter sits with her when I am gone, and often as not, my mistress sleeps.

Sadie, I had to leave off writing because my mistress called me away. She saw me scribbling and said I put her in mind of a thing she'd been meaning to do but never before had time. Oh, sister, what do you think she had on her mind? Why, only to write her will.

"Nay," said my mistress when she told me what she would do, "leave off your weeping, my Betty, for you must shape the sentiments on my behalf, and I would not have your fine words obscured. Bring a new sharpened quill and whatever paper you have. A little might do, for I have not much to leave behind me."

Bid me to staunch my tears as she might, I could not entirely control myself as I gathered my pen and my pages. Selecting the best of my empty pages, I came to sit beside her on the bed, my strongbox on my lap in place of a writing desk. I determined me not to wet the page and blot the ink, so I sniffed and dried my eyes with my sleeve. "There there," said my mistress, patting my sleeves with her right hand and threatening to undo the hard work I had undertaken in stopping the flow of my tears. In this condition we began, my mistress dictating to

D. M. Bryan

me the words I include below, so that you might see the kind of woman she is.

I began the proper way by writing *Imprimis*, which is the way all such business must commence.

"Very good," said my mistress, when I showed her what I had done. "It looks very fine to begin with a little Latin, but what means you by it?"

Then, Sadie, I was ashamed at my pretensions and would have crossed out the word, but my mistress only shook her head, a sheen appearing upon her forehead and lips. When I saw what speaking cost her, I made no more fuss, but wrote what she told me.

She said, and I wrote, "In the first place, my soul I leave to the scouring light of heaven, so that it might be as clean as possible. My body I commend to the earth, which lifts stains in its own manner. Whatever share I have of the cloth of common kindness, I would distribute liberally so that it might make good on the promise of its name. My share of rectitude, I leave to those who can measure it out most exactly, and as for my patience, I care little who gets that stained tat—how worn it must be by now. My vice I dispose of to those who would learn most by it, for I have learned little, and my folly I would keep beside me a little longer yet. I feel I have more need of it than I ever did before, now that I am dying."

"Mistress," said I, starting at the word.

"Hush," said she.

We waited a while, she under the heap of patched linens and bleached damask and I with my strongbox in my lap and my bottle of ink upon the windowsill. From out the Bell yard came such sounds—snickers, clinks, bangs, smacks, the tide of drinkers' voices—and smells—dung, shit, ale, smoke—I could not think upon the strangeness of the moment without taking a little comfort at its familiarity too. London afternoon light, long and low, streamed in through the window, for the day had been a fine one, of the sort that did not wish to abide by its proper season. Motes of dust sparkled between me and the glass. I watched them come and go.

At last, my mistress raised her head again and recommenced her will and testament. I wrote what she told me.

"My copper pots, my basins of both sorts, and all my washing apparatus I leave to the person who will follow me in my trade—that's you, Betty, my dear," she added. I nodded and wrote my name after her list of goods.

"My best skirts and stays you must give to them that fit them, for I must be buried in plain wool, as is the law. My laces, both the coarse and fine, are yours, Mrs. Betty, and I hope that you will be married in the latter, for those are a pair of sleeves that would lend elegance to any gown. My lady G— gave them me, and, but for a scorch mark from a candle on the left, which I have almost completely cut away, they will dress a maiden's wrist to the fullest advantage. Your boatman will gape to see you in them, Betty, my dear—I hope I do not guess wrong?"

This speech left her breathless, and it was a few moments before I could put her in the way of knowing an item I hardly yet knew myself— that I had come to admire the boatman who took me rowing on the Thames. He had promised to end my aversion to water, but he had done more than that. In truth, I esteemed him more than any man I'd ever met and would marry him as soon as he found the courage to ask. And now we three know, Sadie, so I exchange you secret for secret.

At the hearing of my sentiments, my mistress let go a sigh and sank back into the bed, and promised me her small fortune for my marriage portion, telling me where I might find it hidden. "And," I said, "you shall inherit my estate, mistress, should I go before you."

"Ha," was all she had to say to that proposition, but I could tell she was pleased by my effort at wit. I waited for her to say more, but she lay in the bed, keeping very silent. I could see the bulk of her rising and falling. So long as she was breathing, I was not afraid, and so I sat a spell longer, still with my ink unstoppered until the press of my box numbed my knees.

I looked around the pottage-coloured room and remembered the moment of my arrival, so many years ago. That day, my mistress inspected me where I stood, half hidden between two tubs and not much taller. The room seemed too large, holding only my mistress and myself, none of my siblings and cousins scurrying between the bed and the table. She kept me too busy to be homesick, and I had so much to learn. As my mistress' custom expanded, more lead vessels and wooden tubs came to crowd the

D. M. Bryan

floor. Jugs and pitchers threatened to unseat the cracked, ceramic Mr. Nobody, that torso-less Dutchman who once had pride of place on the dresser top. Nails and washing lines proliferated, supporting a growing family of shifts, shirts, and stockings. A clothes press arrived, its pursed wooden lips suggesting the correct fold for m'lady's tablecloths. Every time I turned its screw, I heard the creak of wood on wood, and my heart rejoiced at the sound.

Sadie, as I sat beside my sleeping, ailing mistress, I thought of Mr. Palmer's wood and metal machines. I pressed my slippered feet into the wide floorboards, as if I would root myself forever. Through the grain, a furrow showed how we walked, my mistress and I, day after day. Over the years, our feet had made a single way for both of us, from table to dresser, from dresser to tubs, from tubs to balcony, from balcony to bed.

The room grew a little redder. Faint rays of a country sunset pierced the court's jagged rooftops. As the sun westered, the chamber grew darker and smaller, and with the room my mistress shrank, until her squat shape seemed to sink beneath the bedding. When I could not see her loosened belly rising and falling, I could bear it no longer.

"Mistress," said I, and she shifted a little. A moment later, she began to snore.

When only city light lit the room, and I saw all the familiar things by the intermittent flare of lighted links, I stoppered my ink and returned my strongbox to its place beneath the bed. Through the window came the always-roaring sound of the Bell. My fingers deft despite the dark, I unloosed my stays and shrugged off my gown. It fell in a pool at my feet, and I stepped from it like a woman from a bath. Then, in my shift and petticoats, for the night would still be cool, I lay me down beside my mistress and, tugging up the sheets and tired damask, I composed myself to sleep. And sleep I did, sister, drifting all night alongside my mistress, each of us afloat on our own underground river.

I awoke to specks of city birdsong and pigeon-coloured light. Beside me, the bowed curve of my mistress' stomach rose and fell with a delicacy of motion she could not manage in waking life. Not wanting to wake her and occasion a return of her discomfort, I lay perfectly still. Her sleep, I knew could not last for much longer, for this day would soon shape itself into a Sunday. Then, both St. Paul's and the Bow bells would leap up and shout, and in that instant, all of us—those of us numb to our mortality and those of us alive to its touch—would start in our beds and know where we were. I waited, and for a time the bells waited with me, but at last the clamour came, rousing us both.

"Mercy," said my mistress, "is that the time?"

Sister, with the new day pealing about us, I convinced myself my mistress would rally. I set about rising and preparing us both something to eat, stirring up the fire and toasting a little bread and Cheshire cheese by the weak flame. But when I offered my mistress the molten tidbit on the good pewter plate, she would only smile at me and bid me eat it myself. It would do her good, she told me, to see my appetite revive. She said if she could watch me address the bread with vigour, she would feel encouraged and so might, in time, eat also. Sadie, I ate the bread and cheese but every mouthful was like chewing a badly laundered handkerchief, stiff and over-starched.

"You must take yourself to service," said my mistress, as soon as I swallowed the last of our breakfast, but I shook my head. Nothing would convince me to leave her. I could see how she blanched and sweated and hid her pain from me. Instead, I wiped clean the pewter, annoyed that I had dirtied it at all, and took out my papers and inkpot from under the bed and placed them on the table beside the door. Then I did not know what to do with myself and I wished I might work, but we did not wash on Sundays. I stood over the bed and wrung my hands until my lady bid me stop. "Read to me Mrs. Betty," she said, "'twill ease my heart to hear your voice."

Then, I took up *The History of Glossolalia* and read her a little from those pages. However, she soon bid me stop.

"You do not desire that I should read a novel on a Sunday, mistress?" said I.

"I do not desire that you should read that novel," said she and would speak no more of poor *Glossolalia*.

D. M. Bryan

"What would you have me read instead?" I asked, casting my eye over my sad assortment of pages. I did not mention that imitation of Hogarth's *Harlot*, lost in a circumstance I did not like to remember. The other scraps and fragments in our residence seemed ill-suited to our situation. When my mistress did not answer me immediately I had me an idea, and excusing myself for only a moment, I ran down the stairs to rap on the door belonging to our landlady. Mrs. Hudson appeared at my knocking, dressed in her Sunday finery and attended by all her children, each tricked out in fresh ribbons and clean stockings. A line of starched tuckers and neatly pressed aprons, every one from my mistress' hand. *Reflect this Sunday morning on the virtues of new laundered shirts*, I silently bade the children. But then I saw the very boy I wanted.

"John," I said, "may I borrow your prize book? I will take it no further than upstairs, and you might have it of me as soon as you return from church."

I could see immediately by John's face that I might as well announced my intention to take his book to China. His mother looked equally askance. "His prize book?" said she. "His *prize* book?"

I ought not to have used that word.

"Mr. Watt's hymns. Oh John, I would not ask but my mistress cannot go to church, and I would read to her something that might give us both comfort as she is so—"

I bit off what was to come next. My landlady's face gave me to understand that I had already said too much. Mr. Hogarth might draw her face employing only a tiny "o" surmounted by two arches. "I hope," said that lady, stretching her eyebrows even further toward heaven, "I *devoutly* hope, your mistress has not something catching."

"She has no fever, nor any spots," I said. "She has had the smallpox, as have I."

I had not. 'Twas a lie, so help me—I never had it, as well you know, Sadie. The landlady came close to me by the door and peered up into my face.

"You came off most uncommonly well," she said, all but touching my cheek. "Your skin remains very fine."

"Perhaps it was only the cowpox," I said, a little wildly, for no milkmaid was I, and the landlady knew it. "Or perhaps the … soap-pox," I added.

"There's no soap-pox," said John, stating the obvious.

"No indeed, Master John. Oh, he is a clever boy, Missus Hudson. No wonder he took a prize at school." I flattered the child, as his sisters, in a row behind him, rolled their eyes. John, to his credit, looked equally disgusted at my toadying, but his mother, although a modest woman on all other heads, smiled and nodded.

"John," said she, "lend Mrs. Betty your book, for she knows its value, I'm certain." John hesitated, but his mother added in a heavy whisper, "go now boy, for we can cleanse it afterwards with a sprinkling of vinegar," and John went.

Book in hand, I flew back up the stairs, sorry to have left my mistress even for the duration of that short and absurd discourse. I found her sunk very low, responding only when she detected the pressure of my hand.

"Betty," she said. "Oh my dear girl."

Sadie, I dropped a few tears then, thinking perhaps they might fall unnoticed, but my friend opened her eyes and saw the wetness on my cheek. "Read," she said, reaching up to pat the book in my hands.

I sat down beside her on the bed and opened *Divine Songs* at random. I read from Mr. Watts' "Song XXII Against Pride in Clothes:"

Why should our garments (made to hide
Our parents shame) provoke our pride?
The art of dress did ne'er begin,
Till Eve our mother learnt to sin.

"Ah, 'tis as good as a sermon," said my mistress, and her flagging energies appeared to rally a little.

I asked, "Shall I read more?" and when she nodded, I read:

Then will I set my heart to find
Inward adornings of the mind;
Knowledge and virtue, truth and grace,
These are the robes of richest dress.

D. M. Bryan

"'Inward adornings of the mind,' very good," said my mistress, "but if all the world should follow Mr. Watts and learn to dress in such spiritual raiment, how shall an honest laundress earn her living."

"How indeed," said I, for even as a child without a single fine piece of clothing I did not like to be told that I should be wicked if I finally acquired an apron with a bit of lacy trim. It seemed very hard, although I knew I was wrong to think so. "Perhaps there is another verse," I asked my mistress, flipping through John's book.

Sister, I know not if it was Mr. Watt's verse or if something else began to animate my mistress, but she requested that I put away the book and prop her upright, supported by a shabby bolster. The execution of this manoeuvre brought her no little vexation, although she sought to hide from me the full extent to which she suffered. When we were finished, she reclined in relative comfort, with her shoulders and head well supported. Soon the colour returned a little to her cheeks, and she began to breathe more easy. Then it was that she announced her intention to leave to the world more than the will disbursing her worldly goods. "Which," she said, "is a brief enough codicil to life."

She instructed me to fetch my ink and paper again, which I did, and having seated myself again at her side, my strongbox desk in my lap, I began to write as she spoke. She began with her title, which I record exactly as she gave it me: *An Analysis of Laundry. Written with a View of fixing ideas of Goodness, as seen by one who is only a Laundress.* I know now that in naming her work, my mistress anticipates Mr. Hogarth's own work, *The Analysis of Beauty.* There the great artist sought to fix beauty to the operation of a single line, just as my mistress, a laundress like no other, would string beauty upon a single strand of washing.

I, my mistress bade me write, her words sometimes coming in floods and sometimes in painful drops, *consider what lessons might be taken from the practices of laundresses, who have access to so many rungs of the world, from those lofty realms inhabited by persons spotlessly garbed to those lower regions where dwell the indifferently clean. By considering, more minutely than before, the nature of washtubs, drying lines, and clothes presses, in their different combinations, I will raise in the mind the ideas of all the variety of laundry imaginable.*

Here, my mistress broke off and asked that I bring her more water. Tenderly, I held the cup to her lips and she drank. Then I took up my pen. She began to speak again, her voice not strong but determined.

I wrote: Chapter I. Of Repetition.

It may be imagined that the greatest part of a laundress' duty is comprised of daily tasks, repeated for the express purpose of removing every trace of use from the warp and weft of every kind of garment invented for all manner of purposes. The scrubbing of clothes imparts a regular rhythm to our day, so that time itself is measured out in cuffs and ruffs, collars and hems, fronts and backs. We laundresses comprise a kind of clock, the cogs and gears replaced by thick, red arms plunging elbow deep into froth, rising, and plunging again. Each hour passes in woollen minutes, silken seconds. From lengths of bedsheet and tablecloth we twist liquid seasons, entire spans dripping at our feet. And when one day is wrung dry, we begin again. Once again, we set water steaming and scalding, a-dying with bluing or bubbling with soap. With our thick fingers, we sort the thread stockings from those made of worsted. Now we are tipping in the lace lappets, the silk handkerchiefs, the muslin petticoats. Steam leaps up. We poke the mass down to pot's bottom, waiting for it to return, roiling, to the surface. Our hands grow red from repeated immersion. Squeezing, wringing muslins makes our shoulders broad. Each of our movements is practiced and sure, as we lift arms and sheets skywards. We sleep. We rise. We rest. We work. We tuck a dampened strand of hair beneath our caps. We again. We again, again. And again.

Here my mistress broke off her speaking. Her breathing had grown increasingly shallow and from time to time she tightened her fingers around mine. "Oh Betty," she said, gripping my hand, "I would so like to finish this work now that I have begun it."

I hastened to assure her she had no shortage of time in which to dictate her thoughts to me, but I could tell I sought to reassure her on the topic that distressed her more than any other. "Of what," said I, hoping to distract her, "will you speak next, now that you have considered how repetition is a thorough-going characteristic of a Laundress' work?" "Why Betty," said she, weakly waving for me to take up my quill, "I will speak of ..."

D. M. Bryan

Chapter II. Of Constraint.

Under this head, I shall attempt to show what obstacles prevent a laundress from making those garments consigned to her care immaculately clean. Such checks to our pursuit of perfection are several, and they range in severity. The least grave are splatters and splashes, but these still require some show of invention on the laundress' part, for she must set herself to determine the nature of the substance by testing the blemish, employing the system she has devised for this purpose. By sundry means, she must measure its degree of wetness, waxiness, oiliness, greasiness (for these are not the same), dryness, chalkiness, cheesiness, or flakiness, as well as the colour of the stain, the degree to which it enables the passage of light, and the presence of an odour. Also, she must consider the nature of the fabric that hosts the unknown smear: linen, cambric, muslin, lace or edging, Holland shirt, ruffle, or fringe all demand a different treatment. Only once a laundress has fully catalogued the nature of her stain can she employ the means necessary to dispatch it: the precise temperature of the water, the correct use of soap, and all the other parts of her exacting craft. But this is a laundress' art and her joy, or she is no washerwoman.

Constraints of a middling sort are those central to a laundress' practice and comprise all impediments arising from the conditions of her work: the heat; the cold; the constant wet; the indifferent reception by fellow servants upon a laundry day; the confinement to the few steps between vat and hearth; the mistresses' instructions to save soap and coals but never miss a speck of dirt; the sweat of our brow; the blood of our cracked knuckles; the stretch of our day from the earliest hours to candlelight, for our day never ends until the task is complete. These checks upon our well-being are familiar to each of us, they are as water to herring—we swim in their currents and feel them not.

The last genus of constraints are those that threaten to unmake a laundress: the master hiding behind the door; the crafty cadet requesting extra starch; the butler demanding tit-for-tat; the footman in love; the groom with especially grubby breeches; the poetical tutor. Each of these is a danger to a laundry-maid, with her sleeves pushed up and her shift ties loose. The steam, the warmth of the tubs, the presence of a half-washed female, these things bend and shift the light so that a phantom appears in the minds of some men. Her figure hovers over his lady's petticoats—a spectral laundress, *with flowing, dampened locks of hair and skirts lifted on hot currents of wind. When she appears thus, half-nude, posed upon a cake of soap, he can no longer discern that she is only a grubby St. Giles' girl, with a red, running nose and a smear of fuller's earth upon her brow. A laundress must be both quick and wily to defeat a gentleman when this mood is upon him. She must not waste time calling for help or splashing him, but she must run, and run quickly, or ruin is upon her.*

Such scenes are the chiefest of constraints that face a laundress, be she sixteen or sixty, but others still threaten the unwary. Sloth afflicts a few, for not all laundresses love work. Crime tempts others, for some return loads lighter by a length of Flanders lace. Gin calls to many, for the work is long and hard, and the sight of so much water can give a body a tremendous thirst. Decay takes most, for we rot and crumble in the moisture—black mould grows between our fingers. And after decay, comes death, for all laundresses must die, and this is the constraint that brings us renewed vigour. We think on the joys of freshly pressed garments, bright and shining in the sun. Our cleanest scrubbing speaks aloud this sovereign truth: while we wash we live.

Here, again, my mistress broke off speaking, and I would have had her take a bit of ale (for so long had my mistress been about the composition of her *Analysis of Laundry,* Mrs. Hudson and her clutch returned from church, and that good lady no sooner saw my mistress' condition than she sent her youngest for a tankard from the Bell). Alas, my lady would have none of the Bell's wholesome beer, but she closed her eyes and rested a while, her hand upon mine the whole time. I sat beside her on the bed and saw by the light from the window the state of her poor fingers, how wizened and bent they'd become while in the very employ of which she spoke. I stroked them gently and murmured low until I thought she slept again. But I was wrong, for she gave a sudden start, her old eyes opening very wide, and she said, "Come, Mrs. Betty, I must finish what I have begun, for that is a laundress' duty."

"Nay, mistress," said I, pretending to misunderstand in the hope she would rest a while longer, "you shall go nowhere this day, for a cozening grey cloud blows up Cheapside, and I would not have you out in the rain for anything." She knew I did not really expect her to rise and don her cloak, so she smiled a little and let me continue to chide her for suggesting so.

Then she said, "If I must not go outside then I must stay here, while together we complete ... "

Chapter III. Of Variety.

How great a share variety has in producing goodness may be seen in the very repetition that forms the base of all laundry. Consider, if you will, how variety is the product of those forces I note above. Repetition gives a washerwoman the experience necessary for the fullest understanding of her craft, while constraint fixes each woman at her vat, freeing her mind for greater and greater achievement. From these twinned precepts stem all the brilliant variation found strung out on a line of clean clothes: the frock coat of shining midnight hues, free of the shoulder-staining starch that can so mar a gentleman's prospects; the mantua bright as a flower garden, where each stitched lily conceals no spot of veal gravy nor coin of candle wax; the plain blue stockings of an even tone and free from pale streaks, the mark of careless hands. Behold the glory, and remember a washerwoman has restored to each item the colour and the form God intended, which is the good of laundry. A laundress' task is no less than this: to extend that goodness wherever blots, smudges, spills, and stains make washing needful.

A gentleman once told me Aristotle, in Classic times, said something in a similar vein, but in truth, this knowledge has been the laundress' own since time began. I doubt not that Aristotle had it from his own washerwoman, but I believe I have made my point: all goodness comes from laundry, or its like, and that goodness comes in forms as varied as the freshly washed items in a basket awaiting pinning to the line. Laundry teaches love, not of principle, but of variety—of every shape and size and colour and kind. Can I say it simpler, Betty dear?

Here, I shook my head. Despite the broken and halting line of her voice, she could not have spoken more clearly. I understood her exactly.

My mistress continued in a voice so faint I had to bend close to hear her. I wrote: *And as I am a laundress, I understand truth as particular to my employment, but I hold what is true for laundry is true for other trades as well. Alas, I have not been given time to pursue this insight, but I bid you to continue my labours on my behalf. I beg you never to cease to search out variety in this world, which I am now so sorry to leave.*

This last came as little more than a gasp.

Sadie, my mistress' account ends there. I could write no more and, flinging myself upon the floor next to her bed, I upset my bottle of ink. Dark fingers appeared upon the wooden boards. I begged my mistress not to leave me, urging her to consider that my apprenticeship was not complete, that the time of my indenture was not ended. She found my hand and pressed it to her lips. "Mother," I said, for she was this to me and more, Sadie, as well you know. "Mother," I repeated and I felt her kind eyes approve me and saw a pale smile upon her whitened lips.

"Betty," she whispered, "Betty, my darling. 'Tis just like something in a book." And then she closed her eyes, her breathing racked and full of pain.

She did not die then, sister, but lay so for several hours. Mrs. Hudson came to weep over her, as did many of the denizens of the Bell. I could not stop them as they came up the stairs, and they came and went all day. I remember me one very well—a young thing, still wearing the hat she brought from the country. The mark of the city was already upon her, for she had removed her tucker to display her bosom and was certainly drunk. She knelt at the foot of my mistress' bed and lay a hand upon the pale damask. Her head bowed, she swayed a little from side to side, lost in some reverie of her own. When the others left, she remained, although I could not guess the reason why.

At last I wearied of her presence and took up her hand, intending to lead her gently but firmly to the door, but I no sooner saw her muzzy face tilt up toward my own when I remembered all my mistress said in her *Analysis*. I looked backwards at the table where lay her words, and in my own handwriting, each line sloped and blotted in places with my tears. Then, instead of turning the creature out of doors, as I had intended, I knelt beside her, and we waited in that prayerful position for our mistress to be done. And when at last our lady's breathing stopped, and her soul washed softly from this world to the next, the Harlot and I comforted each other, and mingled tears, and we were two variations upon the same weeping girl.

Sadie, I have not buried my mistress yet but will soon. I have not the money to set over her head a stone, but I have in mind a different monument. I would like to take *The Analysis of Laundry*, and perhaps sundry items also, to Mr. Palmer to see if the esteem in which he holds my lady extends to the following kindness: that he might composite her words into pages and print them up as a book.

I wonder if I dare.

My waterman has been to see me. He brings me a gift, which must have cost him dear, Sadie, but which already I treasure second only to him that set it in my hands. A package of papers, well wrapped in a waterproofed cloth, and which, when opened, contains a complete series of those ingenious, much admired prints. These are all Mr. Hogarth's own work and no pale imitation.

Sadie, I spread the first of these across the table and looked hard. Engraved in lines so fine and dark, the yard of our Bell Inn appeared, with its cracked brick walls and muddied ground. And in that familiar court, I found at once the Harlot, and the bawd, and the terrible colonel, and the York coach girls, and the minister on his white horse. With his tools and his ink, Mr. Hogarth set them all in motion, cullies and whores alike, forever progressing, forever trapped.

So engrossed was I in the tale Mr. Hogarth told, I did not notice at first the small figure in the uppermost corner. She has in her hands a pair of second best stockings that she sets out to dry. Absorbed in her work, she pays no heed to the events below. She's no part of the story, and yet there she stands, all because Mr. Hogarth saw her.

Then I was a girl again, rushing heedless home, laden with dirty clothes and fresh news for my mistress.

Sister, I might find comfort yet.

Elizabeth.

The HISTORY of GLOSSOLALIA:

OR, VIRTUES VARIOUS.

A NOVEL

Written by a Respectable Lady
of Mature Experience.

*I shall write on, as long as I stay, though I
should have nothing but sillinesses to write.*
S. RICHARDSON.

LONDON:
Printed and Sold by Thms. GOTOBED & C. QUIRE
at the New Golden Head, near St. Paul's.
MDCCXXXI.

Chapter 7

The History of Glossolalia: Or, Virtues Various.

The Lady's Tale

A novel, containing the following note beneath its cover:
Dearest Sadie, in order to afford you some amusement, I am providing you with the book given me by Mrs. Tanner, which I have finished at last. I say no more of The History of Glossolalia, *except that is a patchwork of tales—a curious volume, full of variety. Affectionate regards from your Elizabeth, who loves you ever.*

London, 1746.

In the great and growing city of London, in the nineteenth year of the reign of King George the second, in a comfortable but plainly furnished room, two women sat, each regarding the other with care and attention. The first, the lady named Sarah, was like her name, compact, with a face as round as a vowel. The second, the lady whose room this was, proved to be a tidy woman of middle years, tall, with a look in her eyes that seemed fixed on some object far distant from the tea-table over which she now superintended. Between them, the fire gave off a light, red and flickering, that lent an expression of warmth to the faces of the two inhabitants, and yet the women were strangers. The peculiar events of their acquaintance curtailed the usual formalities, but in fact Sarah and Glossolalia had known one another for no more than the duration of a short coach ride. Now they sat face to face, while Glossolalia picked up her teacup and looked meditatively at the ochre liquid inside.

"I am," she said to her new companion, "grateful beyond telling for your generous assistance in Mr. Hogarth's painting room. I feel quite restored now that I am once again in my own rooms, but truly, you must think me a weak creature for engaging in a fit of weeping before mere pigment."

"I do not," said Sarah, "for I am myself frequently moved by the artist's ingenious output. I have a volume in which I collect his prints, and I purchase new works whenever I am in funds." And like Glossolalia, she lifted her teacup and saucer with a genteel rattle.

"Still," said that new friend, "I am not much used to crying in public." She sipped. "You and your coach have done me a real kindness."

Said Sarah, "when I discovered you disconsolate before Mr. Hogarth's *Marriage-a-la-mode*, I took it for granted you had a particular reason for your distress. In my experience, dear Glossolalia, no female advances in life without some story to tell, and many of our elder sisters who pass unnoticed in a riffling of skirts are veritable books, should we but choose to turn their pages."

At this long speech, Glossolalia set down her cup with such force she risked chipping the china. "You compare me to a book?" she said, looking intently at her companion's face, as if she also would read something there. "Pray," she added, "do you imagine I am romance or novel?"

"I imagine nothing," said Sarah, "but I have no doubt you have a tale to tell, should you wish to do so.

"The promise of an understanding listener is a temptation indeed, but are you so certain I am worth hearing?"

"Indeed I am. Will you disappoint me, madam?"

"I shall not," said the other, "for the sight of Mr. Hogarth's work has left me eager to confess." And with that, both women settled themselves more comfortably into their chairs.

"My story," said Glossolalia, who was to be the hero of her own tale, "starts in King's Square in London, where I was born. I came into this world the daughter of a rich man who died young, my blessings dilute from my earliest days. My father's wealth came from water, fresh from the countryside but clapped between boards and sent downhill to spend itself in London's sludge. City men punned mightily upon his liquid assets, but he was a solid man too, with large holdings of the rich brown soil that stained the hems of the market women's skirts. I saw such country girls sometime, hawking carrots and cabbages in Covent Garden, and I envied them.

Envy was not my birthright, for I was my father's only heir, and at scarcely twenty-three years of age, I found myself one of the richest women in London. But, I married badly—the same old story—a man some years my junior whose reputation I ignored in preference of his charm and pretty features. His face, I soon learned, masked a rogue and a rake, whose sole interest in my person was my purse. To put it bluntly, madam, he stole from me, and worse, he stole from the daughter I bore him, robbing my girl of that portion of the fortune that would be hers. When I discovered my husband's trespass, I consulted lawyers, who consulted each other, but none could discover a way to remove me from the mire into which I had blundered. My own skirts were cut from silks and stitched in satin, but my hems were as soaked with ordure worse than any countrywoman's. My ruin seemed complete.

Then, one day after attending a service at St. Anne's, my little girl by my side, a lady stopped me in the aisle as I went to pass. Her face and name I knew, and so I greeted her as an acquaintance, though not a friend. "Mrs. E—," I said, taking her hand in mine, "I had not thought to find you here."

But Mrs. E— had no thought for the polite niceties with which one lady greets another. Instead, she leaned forward and demanded, "Are you truly married, then?" Astonished by her urgency as much as her question, I did not know what to answer, but only pushed forward my child, tilting up her face so that my accuser could see I was a married woman, with a daughter besides.

"Yes, yes," said the woman, "I have one too, but did you really go before the parson and swear unto God?"

Dear madam, I do not wish my tale to shock you, but I could not pretend to be unaware of what this lady had done to preserve her own fortune. Neither did I fail to understand how her case touched closely upon my own, so I only nodded. Indeed, I had married the fool and, in doing so, borrowed his motley colours for myself, and for my girl besides. The lady saw in my face that my situation was indeed an unhappy one, and to my astonishment she embraced me with a sisterly tenderness.

"I heard reports," she said, when at last she had expended her ample reserves of compassion. "Tales of your husband roving from bagnio to bagnio, holding entertainments of his own devising. He appears in loose company, always with a glass in hand, his shirt and breeches loosened, and his hat and wig knocked askew. And recently, he has been seen in a very low place indeed, wearing no wig at all, having bared his shaved pate to admonish God for his losses at the gambling table—losses, I am told, he can ill afford."

I turned my head from hers and could not speak. I knew the tales better than anyone, for even my footmen felt free to describe within my hearing their master's wicked peregrinations.

"If the legal case for your marriage is unbreakable, you cannot free yourself as I did," she said. "Your girl will have neither fortune nor a good name to recommend her, while my boy is more fortunate. The boy is heir to my holdings and free from an unworthy father."

I found this hard speech indeed and discovered my tongue at last. "A counterfeit marriage, madam, is a matter for rakes in romances, and not a fit stratagem for ladies. What's more, I would not choose to make my child a bastard."

If I hoped to wound my opponent, who still had her hands laid most tenderly upon mine, I failed. She only gazed at me with more compassion than before. "Mr. Hogarth chooses to paint me in a red dress, but I am no harlot," was all she said. Folding my arm over hers, she led me from the church, my poor girl sticking close by my side and looking up at the lady's face.

We talked together for some time, slowly making our way up Deane Street toward my house in King's Square. In the course of our conversation, Mrs. E— considered my plight from every angle.

However, we did not exhaust the topic on that day, and she began to come regularly to call upon me. On days the sun shone, we went out to walk between the parterres of the square, surrounded by the red faces of houses. On wet days, we sat closeted together in the window seat of my parlour, where drops of rain ran in rivulets down fogged glass. My girl hid in the other seat with the vermillion curtain pulled and drew with her finger in the vapours. She made figures and faces, and my new friend exclaimed at the glass full of wet marks. "You must find a drawing master," she said, "for in time she might learn to paint very prettily."

My husband would have been displeased to know that such a person as Mrs. E— called for me, filling my head with her council, but her visits were kept a secret. The villain rarely returned to the house where I dwelt, having used my money to set himself up in one of his own. Nor did he hear tales of me, as I did of him, for I made every servant in my household swear to never divulge my friendship with that lady. Yes, I considered her my friend by then—the "scandalous" Mrs. Mary E—, whose reputation, tattered by the wrong choice of husband, survived because of her wealth and thanks to those few souls who agreed a woman might act in the cause of her own protection.

Amongst those who took the part of Mrs. E— against the world was the illustrious artist, Mr. William Hogarth. The regard between my friend and the picture maker was an established fact, and neither the artist, nor his wife, seemed to consider that lady's reputation lost. In return, she showed Mr. Hogarth great condescension and extended to him the pleasure of her patronage. On one notable occasion, she and I ventured out together to see her portrait, still drying at the artist's home in Leicester Square. We took tea with Mr. Hogarth, and to my delight, the great artist took up a crayon and rendered me in lightning fast, ochre-coloured strokes. He caught me leaning back in a chair, my arms raised as if sleepy, and smiling slightly at something my friend had said. When he was done, and I said the likeness pleased me, she begged Mr. Hogarth to give me the drawing, which he kindly did. From that day hence, the little scrap of paper has been one of my most treasured possessions. Indeed, its memory must have lodged in Mr. Hogarth's fertile mind, for now he puts it to another use.

As my attachment to my new friend grew, relations with my husband and my financial affairs worsened. Before long, I began to wish I might follow her lead and declare myself no wife, my husband no true father to my daughter. Alas, I had a marriage contract to show that I was indeed an honest woman, the child my husband's hostage, and all three of us no better than paupers. I was forced to give up the house in King's Square and to sell one of the properties in Rutland. I took another house in a less fashionable part of the city and lived there as simply as possible, but to no avail. My husband's bad reputation and debts followed me like uninvited guests that took the best of everything and left misery behind.

In every way, I sought to preserve my privacy, keeping my husband and my friend apart, but this hope proved a vain one. Despite the best efforts of everyone at my new address, the two came face to face at last. My husband, arriving unexpectedly at my door, pushed his way into my front hall and made a great show of shock at finding the "notorious" Mrs. E— under what he termed his roof. Having tried and failed to vent his ill-will in childish name-calling, he seized her arm and threatened to turn her unceremoniously into the street. I interceded, demanding he stop the assault at once, but this only turned his attention to me. He shouted and shook me, pushing me hard against the wall. For a moment I lay, winded, while the marks of his fingers mottled my arms beneath the lace sleeves of my gown,

While he cursed us, I picked myself up and saw that my friend Mary E— had my daughter by the hand. I ran to them, and we three barred ourselves in the parlour, pushing a writing desk in front of the door. On the other side, my husband railed, cursing and calling for me to come out, but after several minutes of this he calmed himself sufficiently to reveal the real cause of his visit. I still had some small sums of money preserved in my own name, and it was for this my husband tracked me down, a hound to my hare.

Now I knew how to rid myself of him, if only for a short time. I used the writing desk to draft a bill of hand, sending it under the door as a flag of surrender. This capitulation pleased him, and he abandoned his siege of the parlour. Still, my friend and I did not dare come out until my girl, standing at the parlour window, announced that her papa had gone away in a sedan chair, wearing a brocade coat he most certainly had not yet paid for.

"You will not see him while the money lasts," said my friend, "but he has discovered you at last, and you will never again be safe in this house. I can think of no better time to put into effect the scheme I have been urging upon you for some time. Quick, while you have some money left."

I understood her, and I agreed, but still I was weak and afraid. I clung to my child and wept, but Mary was determined to save me. Calling for my servant, she bid him bring me my cloak, and warm clothes for the girl too. Then she summoned her carriage, which, for fear of signalling her presence to spying eyes, she always commanded to wait some streets further. At her urging, I had prepared a selection of such items I thought necessary to a long voyage, and now my manservant brought this trunk from its hiding place under the eaves of the house. While Mary settled my child and myself in the compartment of her carriage, my man lashed the trunk to the back of the coach, and a moment later, we were gone, leaving not so much as a smudge on a page.

What happened next I learned only later, in a letter from my lawyer, and it was indeed a lucky chance for me that I did not delay longer. My husband's pleasure at being again in funds did not last long, for he was almost right away surprised by the appearance of bailiffs eager to drag him to Fleet for his debts. Escaping his captors by violence, he returned on foot to my poor house to bang on the door, demanding protection. A crowd collected, listening to him rave and curse, until someone told him I was fled in a carriage. This new information gave my husband the strength to shatter the lock and force his way into the hall. Then, the crowd drew back into the street to watch the light from his lamp move from room to room. Violent crashes told them he found chairs, which he kicked, and walls, which he pummelled. In this manner, he continued until he startled onlookers by flinging open the door and rushing into the street, his wig knocked sideways and a grimace upon his face. I have no doubt he would have set about the neighbours next, knocking them down where they stood, but at this juncture the bailiffs reappeared. As soon as he saw the light of their links, my husband set off down the street, his pursuers close on his heels.

By then, I was long gone, riding safely in my friend's coach to Deptford Reach, where I might secure a passage to Virginia. Upon our arrival, we found an inn where we hid for some days until we located a ship named the Primrose that would take us. Meeting the captain in the public room of the inn, I arranged with him to secure my trunk on board. But now my friend took my hands in hers and urged me not to take the child to sea. Rather, I should leave her safe in England. "The child is a girl," she said, "and we both know how the world exposes us to risks undreamed of by our brothers. If you write your husband that she is in Virginia with you, he will have no cause to suspect I have her in my keeping."

I would not hear my friend, even when the captain joined his voice to hers, urging me to consider the difficulties of the voyage and the perils of the crossing. "This is a time of year for extremes of weather in northern latitudes, and I cannot promise a smooth passage," he told me in his gruff manner, pouring himself another glass of the wine my friend had secured for this comfort. Still, I would not listen. I covered my darling's ears and shook my head.

That evening, as we prepared for sleep at the inn, a wind began to suck at the shutters, and by early morning the miserable river flickered with white spume, like pages turned abruptly. I bid my daughter be brave, but she hid under the sheets and wept. "Mama," she said, worrying the bedclothes between her small fingers, "the Primrose will sink—I know she shall." When I kissed her brow, her flesh heated my chilled lips. I left her there to sleep as best she could and went with Mary to stand at the end of Middle Water Gate.

Under the overhang of a chandlers, we stood and stared at the wet timbers of the Primrose. The ship, all straight lines, rode hard in the middle of the Thames. Yesterday, bumboats beetled back and forth, conveying goods and passengers, but today the ship showed only damp boards, tarnished with rain. "She will not sail today," I told my friend, who had the good sense not to contradict me, but upon our return to the inn, I found a note from the captain waiting for me. The Primrose would indeed depart that day, and a boat would be sent for me at the turning of the tide.

By now I knew for certain my child was ill. Red and damp and so hot to the touch, she watched me as I secured our few garments in a leather portmanteau. The portmanteau was a gift from Mary, one final act of kindness before she'd gone downstairs to order her carriage, for the tide would turn soon. The last thing I packed was Mr. Hogarth's sketch, which I placed carefully between my linens. I did not look to see myself laughing. I could not bear to think that, sorrowful as they were, those days were happier than these.

My daughter saw me fill the leather case, watching with feverish eyes, and when I was done, she asked when we were to leave.

"Soon," I said, but my own voice sounded nearly as weak as hers.

"But," she said, "Papa is come now."

Certain she was worse, I went to her, telling her that papa was miles away in London. She suffered my embrace, complaining that I was wrong and that she could hear his voice. But by then, I could hear him too, barking demands from the parlour below us. I seized my girl and held her for all I was worth, for I had sworn to myself that she would never again be witness to his violence.

To our rescue came Mary, entering the room with a bundle of clothing in her arms. Quickly, she joined me by the bed, wrapping herself in a manservant's coarse cloak. Then, with her finger to her lips, she made signs that I should breech myself in the remaining garments. This I did, although the coat brushed the ground and the hat stank of orris root. Shaking with fear, I went creeping down the back stair, not stopping until I stood across the street, the rain dripping off my portmanteau. Mary came after, carrying my daughter under the cloak.

The plan was risky, and it was our great good fortune the villain remained the whole time in the parlour. Perhaps Mary had arranged for a drink to distract him, and if my husband had been a better man, we should certainly have been caught. On the other hand, if he'd been a better man, we would never have found ourselves sheltering under the overhang of that chandler's shop, waiting for the Primrose's bumboat.

Mary stood beside me with my child's weight in her arms. Tenderly, she drew back the cloak and kissed the girl's forehead. Then she said, "The child is burning—you cannot take her to Virginia with you." I said nothing but watched the beetling shape of the bumboat grow larger in the drizzle. I felt my girl gazing at me from Mary's arms, but I could not look at my daughter's flushed cheeks and over-bright eyes. My decision did not come in words; I only watched the sailors make fast the dinghy, and beckon to us. Then, I bent to my portmanteau, and from between the linens, I removed Mr. Hogarth's drawing. This I placed in in my child's hands with no other wish than that she be good for Mary—that was all the goodbye I could bear.

Next came rough hands and wet boards and a splinter I nursed from the bottom of the boat. Sharp strokes conveyed us in violent lurches through the spume of the wind-threshed river. The side of the Primrose rose, tall and timbered, and I was conveyed to the taffrail, hauled in a kind of sling. I felt sailor's hands touching me through thick canvas, as they banked my ascent like any other cargo. I lay still in my cover, like a side of beef, and came safe to that deck, although they could have dropped me in the Thames, for all I cared.

No sooner was I unwrapped than I looked across the river. Through the rain, I could see that Mary had commanded her carriage to meet her at Middle Water Gate and that both she and my daughter were safe inside. A hand waved to me—perhaps it belonged to Mary or perhaps to my daughter—I could not tell at that distance, and then all was sailors urging me to go below. Above me, curses and the shapes of men filled the air, the latter swinging in ropes arrayed against the dripping sky—a wet web. On the shore, the carriage lurched into movement, and I cried out, slipping on wet boards. Hands clutched at me, lifting me, transporting me along the silvery timbers, until a passage opened and a ladder appeared, which my feet hardly touched.

I was brought winded between dryer walls of wood and hatches overhead, open to the dusk. As I caught my breath, a stench caught me back, an acrid reek that watered my eyes. Through tears, I saw a sailor—a boy really, but with a face already lined—come down the ladder. Under his arm he carried my case, and he beckoned me to follow him down a timber-built hallway. Off this narrow passage opened a series of cells, each made of moveable panels that did not reach even so far as the beams of the deck above. Each had a leather-hinged flap of a door, and the boy took me through one of these. He set my portmanteau on a cot with no linen. Then, without even looking at me, he left me alone. This, then, was to be my cabin.

No one can doubt my state of mind: how I fluctuated between grief for the loss of my child and relief that she was not in that stinking ship with me. Immured in my cabin, I took to my cot, where I lay with my cloak heaped over my head. At last, I fell into a restless sleep, unsettled by events and, soon enough, by the motion of the foul Primrose. When I woke, I could feel the keeling of the ship, but I had no curiosity to see any sight on deck. I rose long enough to use the lidded pot I found under my cot, setting that noisome container in the passage for the crew to empty. I suspected it would wait a long while, but it could do little to further befoul the reeking Primrose. Then, I slept again.

Sustained by the eatables Mary had secured in my portmanteau, I managed to remain hidden for several days, judging the passage of time by the drowned light appearing above the cabin partitions. Some hours we sailed and some hours we hove to, and from time to time I could hear the rattling splash of the anchor. At last, the pitch of my floor grew steeper, and a hand knocked on the wall of my cabin. An almost inaudible voice informed me that if I would see the last of England I must come now, and this announcement grieved me so that I rose unsteadily and made my way to the ladder.

Up on deck, I met the same leathery boy, who seemed in wait for me. By this token, I guessed he was the one who'd knocked and who was now, perhaps, my caretaker. I thanked him for his attention, and he looked at me curiously, before pointing out Gravesend slipping away. I stared at the angled roofs of the houses, a row of nibs writing in smoke, and I tried to take some comfort in the sight. The wind was stiff, and soon all that joined the Primrose to England was the bilge water wake. Then, there was no more England and nothing to see.

It did not take long to discover that in joining the Primrose, I had exchanged one bad situation for another. I had left behind the rake I knew, from whom all of London was my hiding place, for a new rogue, with only the Primrose in which to conceal myself. In short, the captain, in whom I placed my securities and my secrets, and who had seemed all kindness when on shore, proved at sea to be a drunk and a cruel master to his small crew of men. He now instructed me to dine with him, which he did not do as a kindness but as a punishment for my having been fool enough to have trusted him. Twice daily, regardless of the seas or my appetite, I was condemned to join him in the great cabin, where I watched him pour himself cupful after cupful of thick wine.

Nor was any other man on that boat able to protect me, for the captain ruled them all with fear and violence. The first mate, John Jessup, who did most of the work aboard the Primrose, received only curses and grunts as thanks from his captain. Jessup stood always on that part of the quarter deck where I, a woman and a passenger, might not go unless invited, and he did not invite me. He was a capable man, but silent, obedient, and useless.

It was the leather-faced boy who nominated himself my teacher in the matter of shipboard life. He was motivated, I have no doubt, by the hope of a gift of coin upon our arrival in Virginia, and he made his pecuniary interest clear enough. He had great hopes of me, he said, for I was not like other passengers the Primrose had carried. They came with trunks full of planting implements and household goods, and seemed to know all about soils and tobacco crops. They had no use for him, but I, on the other hand, couldn't tell my ass from my elbow, he said, begging my pardon. I did not grant it him, but he took no notice of my coldness, issuing scraps of conversation whenever he could escape the knife-sharp gaze of the first mate.

He named the men to me, and told me something of the Primrose: how her captain had a very warm temper, and how she was a bad boat, and how only desperate men would sail in her. He warned me whenever the captain ordered a flogging, so that I might be safely below, away from what he termed the stings of the cat. Several days out, I asked him his name, which he told me was Jo More. His age he figured to be nineteen, although he was not certain. I thought him considerably younger, but upon closer scrutiny I could see how poverty had cursed him with the prominent forehead of a baby. Like the other sailors, he consumed liberal amounts of rum every day, and whenever he was aloft, I went below. I feared to hear a thud or splash, followed by the cries of the men, but Jo never fell, no matter how often the boatswain's pipe ordered him up the rigging and into the marbled sky.

The rest of the crew was as taciturn as their captain and as frequently drunk. They ran like lurching, purple-nosed automatons, muscled forearms grasping and grabbing sheets and tankards alike. Jo gave me to understand that they sometimes grabbed each other in dark corners, but for my part, I ran no risks. The knowledge that I was the only woman on board disturbed my sleep at night and kept me to my cabin, until lively noises overhead signalled the arrival of morning. In fine weather, I walked the twenty-odd boards that comprised that part of the deck on which I was allowed, and whenever the elements or the language grew rough, I went below. Whether it was these defenses that protected me, or whether I was simply beneath the crew's notice, I cannot say, but when no man offered me any indignity, I began to hope that I might reach Virginia with only the threat of rough seas to make me uneasy.

Regardless, my life aboard the Primrose was miserable. Despite the narrow stretch of decking between us, the mate Jessup never so much as bade me good morning, and the rest of his men followed his lead. Only Jo kept me company, but his duties were constant and he had little leisure to entertain my questions. As for the captain, he produced only monologues at dinner, holding forth on topics that made me blush. At the beginning of meals, he was like to talk of Vaux-hall and the new theatre at Covent Garden, but no sooner had he drunk enough than he turned to White's gambling house or Mother Douglas' loathsome establishment. Across the table, I ate boiled beef and counted the days until we arrived in Virginia. More than anything, I wished myself home again, with Mary and my child.

I discovered the mutiny quite by accident. That was the day some of the men choose the far side of my insubstantial walls for their plotting, and it was the end of any hope I had of reaching Virginia in safety. Although it was only the middle part of the afternoon, I was already gone below to

D. M. Bryan

pass the time in unhappy sleep, when the sound of a conversation next to my ear woke me.

"Is that pale shrew inside?" said a voice I did not at first recognize. A series of knocks on the panels of my cell shocked me into silence.

"You there, missus?" said the same voice, and now I knew the growl belonged to the carpenter, a man named Greensail.

"Not there," said another.

"Knock again," said Greensail. "The way that one sleeps, lazy bitch."

Hearing myself so described wounded my pride, and so I held my tongue, preferring silence to letting on I knew what they thought.

"She'll be up on deck, mooning after England—what's on your mind, Greensail?"

"Well," said Greensail's voice, "like as not it's the same thing you're thinking."

"Might be or might not—who's to say."

"Someone needs to say it."

"You first."

"Let me come at it sideways," said Greensail, "like a parson preaching of Pharaoh. Now Moses had a dream—hell, we've all had 'em. Like Johnson here. Tell them—you dreamed of a knife on a black flag, you said."

I knew the man addressed. Robert Johnson was the boatswain, a man Jo feared more than even Jessup.

"So sharp that knife," said Johnson, "it sliced the canvas I sewed it on."

"That's wicked sharp, Johnson, that is. Just the kind of clean cut we need if we are to make ourselves captains."

"Making captains—is that what this is about?"

A long silence ensued.

"Well, I had a dream too," said another voice, a croak belonging to the cook, who had a scar the size of a shilling on one side of his throat.

"Nay, what's a cook's dream worth?" said Greensail. "You might join us, Abraham, but won't you miss the captain's beefsteak? Cooks grow fat on scraps while the rest of us starve."

Greensail's voice mocked the old man, but Abraham Goss continued as if he hadn't heard. "Three drops of blood on my flag. That's what I dreamed."

"Drops of blood?" said Johnson. "Just three? That's not enough for a proper flag."

"Like he's not enough for a proper man." Johnson and Greensail enjoyed their joke for some time. I lay, not daring to move for fear of discovering myself.

"Wasn't all," said Goss, as soon as he could make himself heard. "In the lower corner I saw a tipped goblet."

"Spilled your wine—you had a nightmare then," said Johnson, to Greensail's evident amusement.

"Wake up sweating, did you, Goss? You was all pothered to soak up that claret with your neckerchief."

"Remember, 'twas only three drops," said Johnson.

"Kissed the deck direct. Licked it up, I'll warrant."

A series of wet salutes made with the mouth completed this repartee, followed by guffaws.

As the conversation degenerated into more insults and rough laughter, I thought to make myself known, as if also awoken from a dream and ignorant of any mention of a knife. Then, a pair of thuds announcing the arrival between decks of more men silenced me.

"Foote, you bastard," cried Greensail, greeting the new arrivals, "we've all had dreams of foretelling. Flags of our own, black and red. Johnson's has a knife on it."

"Flags, is it? And what's yours Greensail? Your sister's underskirts flapping in the breeze?"

"Fuck you, Foote," said Greensail. And then they were all silent so long I could hear the sea beating against the wooden shell in which we floated.

I shut my eyes—a trick I had when the world pressed too hard. I was rewarded with a vision of the depths and one of its monsters, a coil of scaled muscle and rows of teeth. I felt I would rather face that creature than remain another moment on the Primrose, but I continued to cower under my cloak.

At last Foote spoke. He was the gunner and enjoyed no little respect amongst the men. "Happens is," he said, "I dreamed too. A black flag, with a death's head and an hourglass. Silken sheets for hoisting and fair winds always."

A mumbling of satisfied voices greeted his announcement. My limbs trembled as if I were cold. Perhaps I was. But what happened next made me colder.

"What about you?" said Greensail. "Did you dream, young Jo?"

Could I really have imagined a runtish boy my friend?

"I dreamed," said Jo. He did not say what he saw, but he'd said enough.

Long after the conspirators had gone their separate ways, I hid in my cabin. I was too frightened to think, but my greatest fear lay in the possibility the men would discover they had been overheard. What they would do, I did not know, but I sought to disguise my guilty knowledge, acting as though nothing had altered. When evening came, I rose and dressed myself for dinner with the captain, just as I did every night, my fingers doing by rote what they would not do at my command.

Stumbling down the reeking passage to the stern, where the great cabin filled the width of the ship, I found the captain even further advanced in his cups than was his custom. He had one bottle empty on the panelled bulkhead that served him as a sideboard, and another rolled empty at his feet. The bottle in front of him was half full, and he rose unsteadily as I entered and poured me a bumper. I did not refuse his kindness and drained the glass at almost a single swallow. He looked at me approvingly, and poured me another.

This too I lifted to my lips, but as I did so, Abraham Goss entered with a platter and a steaming pie. My hand trembled, and I spilled wine on the stomacher of my gown.

"For shame, my dear," said the captain, but I was thinking of Goss' three drops of blood and set down my glass in haste.

While Goss returned to the galley, the captain divided up the pie and sat down to eat his portion. He swallowed half almost at a bite, and then he looked at my plate, the meat congealing as it grew cold. "You find the seas rough this evening?" he said, and in truth the Primrose listed and rolled somewhat more than I had yet experienced. I shook my head, but the captain only grunted. Then, he emptied one glass, poured himself another, and set to work on the rest of the pie.

When he was done, the captain lit his pipe—for it was his unmannerly habit to smoke while others were still eating, and my dinner sat before me, untouched—and began to tease me for what he termed my distemper. Was it the back and forth motion of the ship that bothered me so, or was it the side-to-side pitching that unsettled my stomach? He had a score of jesting questions, but each time I opened my mouth to confess our shared danger, the confounded cook, Goss, entered the great cabin, with another dish or bottle. Not once did he cast his gaze my way, but his lumpish presence silenced me and set my limbs shivering. I could not help but wonder what he had done to merit that badly sewn patch in his throat.

"That man," I began, when I judged Goss far enough removed from the wooden partition of the great cabin, "has suffered from some past accident." If I could not broach my subject directly, I might instead draw him out on the histories of his men. Perhaps I might inspire him to kinder usage, and we might reach Virginia in safety.

Alas, the captain would not be drawn out. "That fellow," he said, "is a dog and deserves another such cut."

"Was it a cut, then? A knife, perhaps?"

"Knife or no, he's a rogue and understands naught but the roughest of tutors."

"Surely the Bible teaches compassion."

The captain swallowed his wine. "A dog—I told you."

"He has done you some wrong?"

"Other than his cooking, you mean? No, he's nothing to me."

Goss reentered with a dish of pears, purpled and fragrant. "See here," the captain said, sitting up and prodding at the dish with his own knife, "he's opened a bottle of my best Bordeaux on the pretext of stewing some mouldy fruit." Then, the captain kicked out at Goss, aiming for the old man's backside. Goss took the blow on his thigh and, caught off guard, lost his balance on the sloping deck of the Primrose. He fell heavily and did not for some moments seem able to rise.

The captain watched Goss with satisfaction as the old fellow struggled upright and limped wordlessly from the cabin. I did not know

D. M. Bryan

how to reply to this dumb show, but the captain appeared to require no response—perhaps it had not been staged for me. Instead, Goss' tumble put the captain in mind of a new topic, which he broached now.

"Saw a woman founder just like that once, he said to his wine glass, "went down hard on her cunt—"

"Captain."

"—and didn't get up again until the other whores gave her some gin. Then she got up again all right."

I also had risen to my feet.

"She was one of them dancers that contort themselves on the big brass plate. You know the kind."

"I do not, captain."

"Nothing under her shift. Saw her oyster, I did."

His voice followed me into the passage, but mercifully what sense he could still command soon disappeared in the creaking and gurgling that was the Primrose at night.

I found Jo waiting at my cabin door. His eyes were knots in the darkness between the decks. "What do you want of me?" I said.

He did not answer.

I said, "The others might dream, Jo, but never you. You alone on this ship deserve an unbroken sleep."

"But I did dream," he said then, his voice small. "I'm no liar. I dreamed a hempen rope."

"So be it. And on your flag," I asked him, "What did you see? What fearsome weapon? Crossed swords? A red tipped spear?"

"No flag," said Jo. "Just rope."

I pushed past him and went to bed, lugging my wooden cot in front of my door so that none might open it while I slept.

That night, I heard the Primrose's sides groaning from the burden of water that sought to crush her blackened timbers. Yet, the seas pressed us forward too. I whispered to myself, calling myself a fool and wishing I was safe at home. And for wishing that, I called myself a fool again. I slept and woke, then slept and woke again. I had no dreams, and the only flag I envisioned was as white as surrender.

Morning came at last. The below-decks of the Primrose never showed much change in light, but by then I had learned to distinguish between the slow tread of exhausted men changing the watch by night, and the brisker steps of the forenoon crew. When eight bells marked the beginning of the second watch, I dressed myself and lugged my cot away from my door. The stench of the passage seemed worse than ever, and I went quickly up the ladder, toward the square of daylight. I arrived on deck to find Jessup scowling and Jo making signs to me behind the mate's back.

I ignored Jo and pulled the hood of my cloak up over my head. The Primrose was a brig and galley-built, with few hiding places, so I went forward to stand beneath the foresail. The wind blew fresh and clean, and overhead, the canvas belled, taut as a pregnancy. It blew the men's voices over the side of the ship. The boatswain piped and the captain roared, but the words themselves lost shape and substance, thinning and stretching into air. The same wind pushed me sideways into the wooden railing, nestling me in the waisted curve of the balustrade. When I looked down at the sea, I saw foamy waves, a cascade of shells and leaves, French curves and rocaille decoration. I thought of sideboards and chair legs, gilt frames and candlesticks. Out of the wet Atlantic, I built a drawing room.

Jo joined me, peering at the water. "Looks like piss," said he.

I turned from the rail. I had intended to never speak to him again, but now I asked, "How many days now have we been at sea?"

"Since Gravesend? Eight days, now," said Jo. "God be praised, we seemed to have missed stranding ourselves on Ireland."

"And how many more weeks?"

Jo shrugged.

"Please, Jo, you must know."

"I do not," he said, twisting his already twisted face. He seemed to consider. "No longer than it took Noah, if our luck holds, although I've done us no good by saying so."

"Do we put in somewhere on our way? We must touch for water." I dreamed of a new ship pointed west, pointed home—I said as much. "I have money, Jo."

"Gravesend, it was. Depends on the wind now."

"I will speak to the captain."

"You haven't yet."

D. M. Bryan

At this pass, the captain's voice swelled, shouting down the wind. While Jo and I were talking, he'd come up on deck and was striding toward Jessup with an ugly urgency. In the rigging of the Primrose, those who could stopped whatever they were doing and turned to see. Those on deck scrambled to get out of the way of that bulging, purple face.

"God damn you bugger," he shouted at Jessup. "That topgallant is too fucking slant—I told you before."

He was pointing skyward, and I turned to look. I saw the same cradle of rope and flapping canvas that always seemed to divide the sky.

"Dog. I should cut off your ear."

Jessup spoke something the wind tore from his lips. His face had drained of colour—the expression placating.

The captain made no reply but stepped forward to take up a thick end of line that lay coiled under a gun. I saw Jo turn to me, his own mouth open. Then, the captain lashed out at Jessup, drawing a line of red from cheek to jaw, and the mate staggered back and fell. As Jessup went down, the captain flung himself on the fallen man, a rat on cheese, his tail of rope rising again and again.

Silent Jessup began to shriek.

At my arm, Jo fumbled, pulling me toward the hatch and ladder, but I could not go. Without so much as meaning to open my mouth, I heard myself shouting for the captain to stop. All around me, pale faces like thumbprints turned my way. I bade the crew in God's name to stop the man before he murdered Jessup. I've watched enough, I cried. I can see no more. Cowards I called them, and worse, before Jo caught hold of me and made me descend.

Why he bothered, I don't know. The mate's cries oozed through the boards, collecting under the deck, and I prayed for Jessup to stop his noise. And then he stopped, and I realized what my prayers had done.

"He's dead," I said to Jo, who for the first time was in my cabin with me. He sat on my trunk and didn't answer. He was listening as boots beat overhead. Shouts dropped through the timbers. Then, something large was pushed down the hatch and into the passageway. Boots dragged it closer, its heels dragging along the boards. Whimpering came in a thin red trickle along the passage.

Jo's eyes knotted again. "Remember, you begun it," he said. "You bid us stop him. You called us cowards."

"I said no more than a Christian should."

"The captain is God on board—now what do you make of a Christian's duty?"

"God is in heaven."

"Yes," said Jo. "In God's name we end the captain's cruelty, but what is virtue in you is mutiny in us."

"The Primrose has no surgeon for Jessup. Who will save him, if he's not dead yet?"

"Goss can bleed a man, if it comes to that."

Then, Jo got off my trunk and went out into the passage, leaving the door hanging open behind him.

I waited, but nobody came to get me. Darkness in the shape of men flowed past the rectangular opening. I saw Jessup go by, his face grey, supported by a fellow under either arm. Shadows passed without a sideways glance, although I was clearly visible on my cot, with my skirts threaded through my fingers. On deck, the shouting mounted and then died away, and I could not distinguish cries from board-battering surf. I waited for Jo, but when his stunted form passed, he wouldn't look in. More crew went by, and yet more. I could hear them gathering in the great cabin—the rumble of men's voices growing into weather.

All my life I had been afraid: afraid of my father; afraid of my money; afraid of my solitude; afraid of my husband; afraid for my life; afraid for my child. Now, in the floating coffin of the Primrose, for the first time in my life I asked myself what fear had ever won me. In answer, I lit a taper and went out into the passage.

The great cabin glowed tar black in the lamplight. The men had pushed away the captain's table and stood, backs to the door, in a sloping circle around something on the floor. I recognized the mutineers. I saw Greensail the carpenter, Johnson the boatswain, Foote the gunner, and many other crew members I knew by sight, from the proudest able seamen to the most stumbling of the landsmen. I did not see the captain, but in his place his green bottles passed from hand to hand.

I pushed my way between two broad backs and saw that every eye was turned to the floor of that room. Pinned at the centre was a large

D. M. Bryan

sheet of paper with two concentric rings drawn in ink. The names of Jessup, Greensail, Johnson, and Foote appeared at the four points of the compass, and as I watched, other men came forward, taking their turn to sign the curved spaces between. One by one, the men made their name or their mark, and then they drank, the ink and the wine falling in drops upon the page.

The pen came to the man next to me. He took the bottle of ink and dropped to his knees to scratch his name laboriously between two others, and as he did, I took his place in the circle and lamplight fell full upon me. One by one the mutineers saw me, shuffling back until I stood alone, the bilge stained tips of my satin shoes upon the page. The ink ring shone wetly, a circle of mutineers—a body with no head.

"Do you turn pyrate then?" I said to Greensail, whom I took to be the leader, but Jessup answered from under his bandages. Only his right eye showed, and the fleshy stuffing of his lips. Blood stained the linen over his left eye. Blood laced the kerchief around his throat. Blood trimmed the cambric of his shirt.

"We do," he said. "Now, go back to your cabin."

"What will you do with me?"

Jessup shrugged. He blotted the blood from his lips with his sleeve. Red bubbles formed in the corners of his mouth as he spoke. "You are in no danger, but you will be made a hostage."

"I have no one to ransom me."

"I'm sure you will find someone."

"I have no money and less hope. All I have in England belongs to a man who hates me. And I have no friends in Virginia."

"We do not intend to go so far."

"That is my preference also."

Could Jessup smile with those lips?

"I would rather sign your articles," said I.

I thought they would laugh, but the ship creaked in the silence I made.

I said, "Let me sign. Let me take shares. My need is the same as yours." And Jo, standing in the ring of pyrates, turned his back on me.

"She deserves something," said Goss. "She never said aught to the captain. Jo said she heard us talking flags and held her tongue."

I looked again to Jo. Knots, shellacked by lamplight.

"She's almost past breeding," said Greensail. "No point to her. Let her fight with us, if she can."

"A woman sign articles?" said Jessup. Again, a bloody twitch of his lips.

"She wouldn't be the first. There's been others before her." Johnson spoke, and Foote nodded.

"Aye, female pyrates, not lady ones." Jo spat, carefully aiming away from the page of names.

But they all looked to Jessup. He spat too but with less energy, leaning his head between his knees to let the bloody spittle fall from his lips. When he straightened, he daubed at his mouth and nodded. "If you sign," said he, "you'll work, same as the rest."

I nodded. Rough pyrate hands held out the bottle of ink, and I took the pen, dipping the nib. I struggled in my skirts as I bent down to the paper, but I signed my name between two others, and then a ragged cheer went up.

I rose awkwardly to my feet.

"For God's sake, give her some breeches," said Jessup.

Glossolalia paused in her tale. The room had grown chill, and now she called for the girl who kept her company to build up the fire. When the task was done, the lady spoke gently to the child, and put out a hand to straighten the little girl's mob-cap, which had slipped to one side. Then, in the leaping light of the flames, Glossolalia turned anew to Sarah, saying, "madam, you will now understand the cause of my tears when I first gazed upon Mr. Hogarth's *Marriage-a-la-mode*. In innocence, I went with the crowd to view his work, and I did not expect to see myself shown in happier times."

"Your sorrow is only too natural, under the circumstance," said Sarah, "and I confess you bear a resemblance to the paintings' principal female, chiefly in shape of face and generosity of expression. But, forgive me if I cannot see a pyrate queen in the well-mannered person who has kept me company this last hour."

"Whether you see that personage or not," said Glossolalia, "everything happened just as I have related. My story is not edifying, but it is a true history, and the rest can be briefly told, if you wish to hear."

Sarah inclined her head, and Glossolalia resumed her story.

"I dressed myself in breeches," said that lady, "and learned to sleep in a hammock packed head to toe, so many fish in a barrel. My cabin went to Jessup on account of his wounds, which festered and added to the stink of the passageway. When Jessup was dead, Greensail found himself elected pyrate captain, and we soon came upon a merchant sloop, the Triumph, out of Bristol, bound for Boston. When the fighting began, I did not disgrace myself, serving Israel Foote on one of his guns. I had but to take orders—a task for which I had trained my whole life— and no one was neater or quicker when Foote cried, "load the charge." With nimble fingers, I popped the bundle of gunpowder into the barrel, like a bit of biscuit in the mouth of a willing infant. Goss rammed the charge home, and when the fire from the touch hole spat brightly, we ducked as flames belched forth from the gun. A cheer went up when we hit our target, and I mopped out the barrel with a rag on a stick to prepare the next charge. After a few such blasts the sloop lowered its colours, and we had our first prize. Greensail took me in the bumboat with him to negotiate terms with the other captain."

"You?" Sarah asked.

"Who better to intercede than a woman?"

"What did you tell them?"

"That our ships floated above the void, and no country's soil lay beneath our feet. That law began with God, and if we acknowledge God to be just then every man must have an equal right to freedom and a fair portion. That a man had a right to rule his household—whether a kingdom or the meanest hovel in Britain—only to the degree he imitated God's compassion. That the usurpation of that duty by inferior men—whether captains or husbands—invoked that superior law that allowed men to restore whatever order ambition and pride had put asunder. And that if the men aboard could honestly acknowledge their captain free of those failings, we would sail away and leave them in peace, for peace they surely deserved. That's what I told them, and when so addressed, every ship willingly made terms with us, the men coming aboard to sign our articles and join our crew.

Those captains who were liked by their crew survived. Other captains we made governors of their very own islands. The worst their own men put to the sword. A captain's fate made no difference to me. Remember that I had my own tyrant to overthrow, and this I plotted as we cruised for richly laden pinks or shallops heaped with linen. With each victory, I saw sailors saved from cruelty, and I hoped to preserve myself with my share of the takings. I longed to see my daughter, and I believed every packet of powder rammed home, every sword thrust at an enemy, every prize sent to port for ransom brought us closer."

"In your daughter's name you raided and kept the spoils?" said Sarah.

"I returned with no spoils."

"Ah, then you did not benefit from your pyracies."

"Benefit? How should we reckon benefit? When I negotiated terms aboard the Triumph, our crew heard what I said and approved my words. When next I spoke in the Primrose's great cabin, the men listened with greater care than they had before. Before long, they made me their quartermaster. Then came a ship, running in cold waters off the coast of Nova Scotia, first glimpsed across a sheet of shifting foam. I helped to take her, but I never guessed she would be mine. She came on, main and fore and infant mast, mizzen-wrapped. Taking her was butchery, and seas ran wintergreen with streaks of cream where bodies sank. Greensail gave me her command under my own flag. Black ground. White hourglass. I named the snow Ice Queen, and I reckoned her a benefit."

"You had your own ship. Surely now you turned for home."

"Never. I was one of Greensail's men, and I had signed articles. He had a flotilla under his midnight banner, and at his command we took a cruise along the coast of the Americas. Off New York we took two pinks, one of which carried fourteen Negros. I hoped to sell them, but Jo More, that thorn in my side, reminded me of my own fine words, and so I offered the black men shares. I didn't think they'd understand, but to my chagrin they accepted, putting out their hands to me. Then I looked hard at my own crew. Saw Henry Virgin with straw-lashed eyes, flesh pale as gin. Saw Edward Salter, all black and blue. Joseph Philips was red as a lobster, Will Ling a length of sycamore. Jo More stayed small, nutbrown, and impossible to crack. In a port of call, they were useless. When pulling hard, they were worth a fortune. In battle or in a storm, they were worth my life. And so we sailed on, up and down that coast.

Off the Carolinas, we took a sloop, the Barbados. Thomas Read was the master, and she was laden with sugar and rum and more Negros. This time I knew better than to regard men as chattel but set them as a prize crew in the ship that had been their prison. I bid them come raiding with us, which they did, but first I laid the sugar and the rum snug in the Ice Queen's hold.

At an islet off North Carolina, we careened our ships, taking on fresh water and what supplies we could find. Turning north, our superior numbers helped us take a merchant brig, the Probity, fresh from Chesapeake Bay, her hold full of tobacco, twenty-four hogsheads of sugar, one hundred and fifty bags of cocoa, indigo in a barrel, and cotton in bales besides. Other ships we took too. A snow straight out of Bristol delivered us crates of boots, gloves, and pouches made of leather. We found barrels packed with straw and filled with Dutch glass engraved with leaves and fruit, pewter plates, candlesticks, brass ladles, and three-tined serving forks, all bound for Philadelphia.

With so much good fortune, we grew braver and bolder, and the governor of Virginia, hearing of our success, sent out two men of war, the Pearl and the Lime, to take us. The ships flew after our flotilla, laying on so much canvas they glittered in the sun. At last, we'd met our match, and when they drew close enough to loose their guns, they fired the Probity to her waterline. She sank with all on board. That took the heart out of us, to hear those poor men left to choose between burning or drowning. After that, Greensail drove the Primrose as hard as he dared, but an unlucky blast of dismantling shot from the Pearl tore his sails and destroyed his rigging. Then, the Primrose proved as ill-starred as we knew she was, and soon the Pearl boarded her and much was lost. Robert Johnson lost an eye; Israel Foote lost a foot; but Robert Greensail lost his life by trying to save it. The sloop with the Negros out-sailed us all, disappearing over the horizon, and I wished them well.

Caught, we faced the gibbet, but they faced the manacle, the fetter, and the collar, and truly I cannot puzzle out the worse fate.

My end was settled, for the Lime hulled my Ice Queen, and we put off in our launch and our bumboat. I saw my snow founder, her decks subsiding in a ragged rose of blue foam. But harder to bear was Jo More's treachery, for when the sailors from the Lime wrestled us aboard, he would not own me captain, and with looks and signs he made my other men follow suit. In vain, I showed the officers my breeches, my bared teeth, my pyrate tongue. I swore at them and spat at them, but I found myself amongst civilized men once more, and they would no more believe me captain of my Queen than believe a Bedlam lunatic King of England."

Glossolalia looked about the room, at the fire in its grate and the flickering light upon the walls. She appeared to have reached the end of her tale. Her companion watched her carefully for a minute or two before speaking.

"And is that the end?" said Sarah at last. "Forgive me but your tale breaks off rather suddenly, without the satisfaction of some concluding event."

"Indeed," said Glossolalia, "that both is and is not the end. I have myself been waiting some time for the right conclusion to my story, but alas, I have not found it yet. Perhaps I shall one day. Then she bent forward and touched the teapot, which was now cold and empty. The little girl in the mob-cap came forward from her corner and curtseyed, taking the vessel from her. She looked to her mistress, who nodded.

"Will you take more tea?" said Glossolalia to Sarah.

"It is not tea I am wanting," said Sarah, "but adventure. Your story has put me in mind of the romances written when we were both girls. Such works are sorely out of favour now. These days, novels turn out plain and everyday. In place of the glittering Atlantic, they give us the dirty Thames. A horse-ferry must replace the Ice Queen, and the whole pyrate crew performed by a toothless ferry-keeper."

Glossolalia smiled and said, "You have very neatly laundered my tale. That is indeed a different kind of work. I can see you have a knack for novel-writing—shall I trust you to write me the end I'm missing?

But be certain of this: you must include the finding of my lost girl, for without her—"

And then, that lady could speak no more.

The little serving girl in the mob-cap ran for more tea, but what can mere hot water do in such a case? Glossolalia's sorrow was an established fact with her, and no quantity of steeped bohea might suffice to rinse it from her soul.

Sarah did not like to see any once-upon-a-time pirate captain laid low, let alone one she liked so well as Glossolalia, and on such short acquaintance too. At the sight of her new friend's tears, Sarah was moved for a second time to generous commiseration. Her sympathy for the lady was genuine, although in all honesty, she couldn't say if she thought the other woman's tale true in every particular. Nevertheless, Sarah firmly believed there was a marooned corsair in the heart of every woman over forty. One might make a novel of that, she told herself, lending Glossolalia her handkerchief on the grounds that it was drier. And despite her companion's distress, Sarah could not but wonder how she herself might set the scene. In her mind's eye she held her pen, its trimmed nib black as blood. She set that tip to the absorbent page, and the words that blossomed forth honoured her new friend's fighting spirit, regardless of her tear-stained condition.

Then a silence fell over the little room, save for the cackling of the fire.

CHAPTER 8

" … I am, like most Biographers, a little partial to my
hero … "

Sarah Scott's *The History of Sir George Ellison*.

Batheaston, 1762.

Sarah Scott sets down her pen and surveys what she has written.
Inked pages amount to a good morning's work, although as she rereads, she wonders if she has put into the mouths of her characters too
many reflections on the condition of the novel—she must decide later.
Pushing herself away from the table, Sarah gathers up her pages and
tidies them away. Then she takes up the bundle of linen for the girls'
sewing and calls for Meg, the serving woman, to help her. Sarah gives
Meg a rolled, oiled cloth, which fills the woman's arms, spilling over
her elbows and falling almost to her knees. Meg accepts her burden
and says nothing. Sarah approves the woman's silence. No one could
accuse Lady Barbara of volubility, but Sarah values Meg's wordless,
efficient communication. Time with Meg helps staunch the wordy
busyness inside her own head.

The house at Batheaston sits in a green cup, and the garden holds
everything Sarah loves best. Lady Barbara has ordered that the tent
be erected beneath the willows, with a view of the river, and this is
now Sarah's destination. Through the jade peace, she and Meg walk.
Sarah's workbox dangles somewhat awkwardly from her hand. When

she received it as a gift from her father, she was no older than the charity girls whose practical education she now superintends. He meant it as a possession of her own, to take with her when she married. Her new husband would smile fondly to see her bent over her plain sewing. Not her actual husband, of course, but the one Matthew Robinson, her father, imagined on her behalf. Sarah Scott can see a phantasm of that husband's back as he saunters confidently down the path before her. Dark broadcloth stretches taut. Flint-coloured hair. A stone hand to beckon her onwards. Short, clean fingernails.

"Off with you," she says aloud. Meg, who comes behind her, cannot see her mouth and does not know she has spoken. Sarah stops, turns, and smiles her encouragement.

They reach the tent. Inside, a wasp lies on the floor stinging the canvas while it dies. Sarah sets down the pile of cloth and steps on the creature with her shoe. Then she goes outside to wipe her sole clean on the grass. Smoke rises from the farmhouse chimneys. The river folds itself over stones and rattles wetly. Inside the tent, Sarah hears Meg begin first to lay out the oil cloth and then the linen for cutting. As the woman leans forward, the shape of her rear impresses itself against the canvas. There. And there. The tent shakes and its wooden poles sway.

Meg emerges from the mouth of the tent and beckons to Sarah. Inside, the cloths lie unfolded and smoothed. Today, Sarah will inscribe and cut out twelve patterns for pockets for the charity girls to sew. With a smile and a nod, she sends Meg back to the house, and then, stooping to her work, Sarah chalks out the purses, taking up her scissors to cut out each shape. Twelve is a busy number of anything to have to cut so quick, and beyond the mouth of the tent, Sarah can see the shadows moving faster than she can. The girls will soon gather from the tumble-stone cottages or grubby town rooms where they live with their families. How disappointed they'd been that today was not to be bonnets, for the troublemakers among them had put about that they would begin their plain sewing with lipped caps. Sarah told them that pockets would be simpler and just as necessary. "But bonnets," said little Tidy, "will fetch a better price." The troublesome ones were always named Tidy—or Grace. And not because they are Dissenter's daughters, thinks Sarah, but because such is the way of names: a Prudence rarely is and a Patience never. Marys and Margarets behave themselves. And Sarahs—Sarahs are always good girls.

By the time the charity girls arrive, the sun on the tent makes the inside too hot, and Sarah determines they should work outside instead. Tidy is the fourth girl to appear. Already present are two Janes and an Ann. The girls stand neatly in a row, and Tidy brings up the scrag end. By now, Sarah has finished marking and cutting out the work for the girls to sew. She has Jane and Jane and Ann and Tidy come inside the tent, where she bids them to take up the corners so that they might carry the oilcloth out to the shade of a nearby tree.

"But it has no corners," says Tidy, describing a circle in the air with her hand. "It's round as a pie."

"As close as you can to corners then," says Sarah.

"A room has corners," Tidy tells a Jane, "but never this."

"Girls, imagine you are in a room," says Sarah, "Imagine it has corners."

"I can imagine a room," says the other Jane, "It has a huge bed with all the curtains drawn."

"Is there anyone inside?" says Tidy.

"Yes!" says Jane, even as Sarah says, "Girls!"

They all look at her, silently, eyes bright in the half-light of the tent. "Pick up a corner," says Sarah, "I am certain you understand what I mean."

The girls shuffle into formation and each picks up an edge of the oilcloth. They are standing staring at her, waiting for her to tell them what next to do, when Mary enters and stands in the middle of the cloth. "Get out of the room," says Tidy.

"It's not a room," says Mary. "It's only a tent."

"That's not what mistress says," says Tidy.

"Please," says Sarah, "Please, please, please."

In the end, she shoos them all out into the sunshine and drags out the oilcloth herself. Ten minutes later, a passing traveler would have to look carefully to find the twelve little girls and their instructress hidden from the sun. They sit tucked beneath drooping swathes of willow, each girl sewing her pocket with one of the twelve needles Sarah takes from a fish-shaped case from her kit. A skein of unbleached linen thread lies next to her thigh as she sits awkwardly on the ground. How long has it been since she sat in anything other than a chair in a parlour? Her own stiff skirt refuses to lie flat, and the hoops of her petticoat bow out over what should be her lap. How like the tent she is, her every movement provoking an answering shudder from the fabric that comprises her.

One of the two Janes gives her a pocket to inspect, complaining that her thread knots of its own accord, and Sarah squints at the mess in her hands, remembering she has left her eye-glasses in the tent. She gives the tangled sewing back to Jane, telling her it will do her good to fix it herself. "Patience," she tells the child, "is a virtue." Then she sits, not sewing but feeling the little needle-case with the tips of her fingers. She touches the hard-carved edges of its scales. Bone white is the colour of her fish. Lady Barbara has a needle case made of horn, which is darkly variegated, but translucent in places.

"Mistress?" says Tidy, her head bent industriously over her sewing.

"Yes, my dear," says Sarah, "how does your pocket do?"

"I went to Bath with my father on a cart."

Sarah doubts this. Tidy has no father of which she is aware. "How very nice," she says. Her own sewing lies beside her, but without her glasses she can do nothing, and she finds herself curiously unable to rise and fetch them from the tent. Her fingers move on their own, opening the needle case and closing it again.

"I saw some ladies, and they were boxing."

"Oh, I doubt that, Tidy dear. Are you keeping your stitches all the same size?"

"They *were* ladies. My father pushed me through to the front so I could see everything."

"The same size and as close as possible. Even if we can't see the stitches, you'll have the satisfaction of knowing your pocket well made."

"They had a half-crown in each hand, and the first to drop a coin would lose."

Sarah is determined to ignore Tidy's fantastical narration, but the detail of the coins gives her pause. From a distance Sarah has seen boxing matches on the peripheries of the fairs where she sometimes goes to purchase peas and gooseberries. She knows them from the peculiar cries they occasion and by the sight of the crowd, clustering around a rising cloud of dust. Coats, hats, men's backs—who ever would allow a child, a girl, to scramble into the middle of such a scene? Women cannot fight in that manner; proprieties whisper in their ear, make them stop. "Small even stitches make seams secure against hard usage," she says.

"Mine are very neat," says Tidy.

Sarah looks down at the fish between her fingers, which are yellow beside the bone. She hears herself saying, "Are you certain it was a half-crown? Not a shilling piece?"

"Drover told me. He saw."

Sarah looks up. All the girls listen and none work. "Sew," she tells them. "Back to your pockets."

"What's boxing?" says Ann, her hair coming out of her bonnet, each wisp finer than the thread with which she works.

"Smacking," says Tidy, "hitting as hard as you can."

"My sister boxes," says Ann, "and sometimes she boxes me until I cry."

"Girls," says Sarah, but this time the word is more sigh than meaningful speech. Sarah's leg compressed against the boning of her skirt prickles, and her back begins to ache. Also, her head hurts, even in the shade.

Mary sets down her sewing. The two parts of the pocket spread like a butterfly and demonstrate how little work the child has done. "What did they wear?" says Mary. "I would be afraid to box in my ruffles, even though they are already tattered. My sister has promised me hers when she gets new."

Tidy says, "No ruffles. Jackets, all plain. Their petticoats was tucked up into their drawers. They wore their white stockings."

All around Sarah, the girls shake their heads. Margaret clicks her tongue in disgust. "Best stockings," she says, when she finds Sarah looking at her, "are for church." The girls sit neatly on folded legs with their skirts puffed up around them, a field of tiny, creamy mushrooms. Nobody sees their stockings, but Sarah knows their colour. Along with their caps and aprons, she regularly inspects those stockings for neatness and cleanliness, and darning is one of their first lessons in plain sewing. They wear blue stockings, the lot of them—plain, home-spun and dyed dark to hide the dirt. If a girl came in white stockings, Sarah would give her new, just as sober and practical as the others. Sarah keeps her own white stockings in a box at the end of her bed.

"I'm finished, mistress," says the other Jane, holding out her pocket to Sarah. Sarah takes it, and even without her eye-glasses can tell that the stitches are large and uneven, jagged around the edges of the linen form. Jane smiles, her teeth an echo of her needlework.

"And where, Jane," says Sarah, "is the opening?"

"Mistress?" says Jane.

"It's a pocket, child. A pocket. Where does your hand go?"

Jane takes back her sewing and studies it. She has no answer.

"Stop smiling, Tidy. You've not done a good day's work either." Sarah tries to rise to her feet, but her leg has grown so numb it gives her no support. She must lean toward the tree's trunk where a branch of the willow hangs low. Holding the tree, she pulls herself upright until she stands next to the trunk. All around her head, green froth hangs from branches no thicker than the children's arms. At her feet, their voices foam. Her leg prickles as the numbness worsens, and she imagines Tidy's boxers, hands made strong by gleaning or washing or polishing someone else's silver-plate. Each fist on the other's flesh makes the sound of lard slapped against a cut of beef. Inside each palm, the coin, nestles carefully—like an egg in a nest—and then, as each fist finds its mark, it cuts like a knife edge, slicing into the only tender part of a drudge's hand. Each palm, when opened, shows purple marks. Each face shows bruises, fluted like a pie-plate with the imprint of fingers. Sarah shifts her weight, and in her imagining the women shift also, moving side to side as they size up their oppon-ent. Again and again, the fighters move together, swinging their fists so that they make contact with the other's cheeks and shoulders. It wouldn't do to hit directly, with fists clenched, for fear the pain might cause the fingers to release, dropping the precious half-crown. In-stead, she'd hit with the flat of her fist, using the force of the blow to keep the coin in her palm. Sarah looks at her own hand. Thumb in or

D. M. Bryan

out? She tries both before catching herself. She's forty, not ten—she should know better.

"Girls," she says, and this time they all look in her direction. Twelve pairs of eyes, and Sarah has a mad wish to sort them by colour: Margaret in the pale sky, Ann and both Janes between the hedgerows where the fields show dark, and Tidy here under the willow leaves. Instead, Sarah says, "Finish off your threads. Return your needles to me. Tidy, bring me my sewing box."

"Are we finished then, mistress?" says Margaret. She holds out her pocket, seeking Sarah's approval. Ann, both Janes seek to show her their work. She wants to say she is pleased with them, but cannot—will not. The girls must learn not to expect praise; they must discover the satisfaction of the work itself. Whims and dangerous enthusiasms have marred their mothers' lives, and Sarah would replace all that with a quiet satisfaction in their own useful labour.

"We are finished for today," says Sarah. She collects the half-done pockets and the needles, counting each one as she places it in her needle-case.

Lady Barbara sits beside her curtained bed in the back parlour on the ground floor of the farmhouse. As always, she has work in her hands, sewing a shift for the newest of the girls. She shows it to Sarah, holding up the thin cloth to the light from the mullioned window. Across the work, two crossed bars of shadow fall. Sarah takes the work from Lady Barbara and moves closer to the window. Her glasses now sit on her nose where they belong, and Sarah can see the excellence of the stitches. She hands it back to Lady Barbara, who only nods her head as she takes back her work. Sarah thinks of Margaret, of the upturned face, of the need.

Beside Sarah's accustomed chair sits a pile of knitted items: dark stockings, fingerless gloves, men's caps. This is work come from the village—from the old women she and Barbara patronize. A few of the pieces are neatly constructed, with tight seams and the woollen loops exactly sized, but most of the pieces are lumpy and ill-formed. She spreads out a cap so large it might fit two men. She unrolls a pair of stockings as different in disposition as badly matched spouses. She pulls on a glove and counts holes for six fingers. Sarah Scott begins to laugh—she cannot help herself.

Sarah says, "It will be a charitable act indeed to buy these."

Lady Barbara says nothing but sews with a regular motion of the hand, in and out, in and out. Sarah sets the knitting in her lap and lowers her glasses. Beyond her, the farmhouse window shows a quarter of green field and a quarter of blue sky. The other half of the frame features a stone outbuilding. "Doubtless," says Sarah, the rim of her glasses under her fingertips, "the old ladies' eyes betray them. They could knit well enough once."

She remembers the day she and Elizabeth went to the shop in Charing Cross. So many pairs of eyeglasses she tried on, Elizabeth yawning as the young man brought more. "Old," says Sarah Scott's sister, telling the young man his business. "She has old sight by now. You may suit her thus."

The young man politely explains he has all manner of optic glasses and no longer divides his stock into old eyes and young. "See here," and he holds out to Elizabeth the very pair for which Sarah reaches, "the focus of the glass is marked upon the frame."

Elizabeth looks, although Sarah wants to believe she will be unable to see the minute markings. How can a younger sister's eyes fail and an elder sister's function so perfectly?

"Yes," says Elizabeth, examining the inside of the tortoiseshell frame, "I *do* see. How exact everything is these days." She smiles at the young man, and Sarah takes the glasses away from her, trying them on. Instantly, her sister blurs as if plunged underwater, but her own hands leap into view, veined and big-knuckled, the skin so rough she might be scaled.

"These," says Sarah, "I'll take these." But she does not want them.

Once home, Sarah's eyeglasses bring no abatement of the pain that plagues her, but with them on she can sew and read again; she can work at night by candle or lamp-light, decorating fire screens and the lids of lady's toilette boxes. Sarah Scott regards her eyeglasses with an attachment she fears might not be acceptable to God. And yet, she suffers still from her headaches, each arrival foretold by the tightening of the skin of her temples. Sarah massages her head, hoping she is mistaken. To Lady Barbara she says, "Do you suppose it might be an acceptable act of charity to outfit the old ladies with eyeglasses?"

In and out goes Lady Barbara's needle. She sits nearer to the window, Sarah notices, and she sews more slowly by lamplight, but the volume of finished pieces never diminishes. Shifts, petticoats, tuckers for the girls; needlework screens and seat-covers for the house; fine embroidered waistcoats for Sarah's brothers: these are the product of Lady Barbara's needle.

At last, Lady Barbara stops sewing and nods. "Perhaps," says she, "your sister might make a collection among the ladies of her acquaintance—cast-off spectacles, no longer used, might suit the dignity of our old women."

Sarah nods. Picking up the village knitting, she takes the cloth and wraps it all into a bundle to send to Elizabeth in London. Payment for the knitting comes back by a Montagu serving man, with a note of gratitude on behalf of Elizabeth's charitably inclined friends. But then what becomes of the hats and gloves? Are they passed to servants? Given to the parish for distribution to the poor? Will there soon be a beggar on Gin Lane, befuddled by old Mrs. Banforth's mismatched stockings? Sarah binds the package about with string, pulling the cords tight and knotting them fast. The package bulges, confined within a girdle of small, tight half-hitches. Sarah Scott ties one more, pulling hard.

The headache sprouts, grows. Sarah says, "You may have been right about the unwisdom of working outside. I fear I have taken too much sun."

No answer.

"Although, the girls and I sat under a willow."

No answer.

Sarah says, "And the shade was quite complete."

No answer.

"It is still a beautiful day."

The quality of Barbara's silence changes. Then, the rasp of cloth on cloth. Even before Sarah turns back from the window she knows

Lady Barbara has resumed her sewing. The needle dips in and out, with a sharp, piercing regularity. A measured rhythm. A breath. And another. One more.

That evening, Sarah chooses a practical project: a peach-coloured, silk-embroidered gown she must rework into a more suitable shape. The alteration is complicated, for with age she grows stouter, while her gowns keep their girlish figures. Sarah tugs and considers. The fabric of the bodice must be made capacious enough to allow her to pin in the stomacher without unseemly gaps. In this, she is aided by fashion, which dictates that she might narrow her skirts without causing offense. The fabric slides between her fingers, a sickly hue unflattering to her sallowness, but the only calculation that matters is the amount of expansion and contraction, or she will have nothing respectable to wear. She can no longer pay the purchase price of so much brocaded silk, and but for the cost of the fabric, she might be persuaded to abandon the dress altogether. Sarah knows no servant or farm girl might wear fabric so fine. Those ladies of fashion she still knows—her sister's friends—would scorn such an unfashionable stuff as this. No, she must make use of it, slicing peach cloth from the satiny hips to suture to the waist. If only her head didn't hurt so much. She does not begrudge Lady Barbara her fire, even on such a warm evening, but the heat worsens the tightness in the sinews around her eyes, making each temple the seat of a tugging, tearing pain.

Sarah Scott leaves off rubbing her forehead and takes up her workbox. The little bone fish lies on top, and her scissors nestle just below. She will look absurd in rich brocade altered for farmhouse life, but knowledge of her own oddity arrives as a familiar ache. Even in youth, she was never considered a beauty. Her only admirer was a man who never praised her looks or intelligence or wit, and when he'd proposed marriage, she accepted, mistaking his diffidence for respect. On their wedding day, she'd been presentable in this gown, this peach-coloured silk, but upon seeing her in it for the first time, Mr. George Scott, her future husband, said nothing. He merely glanced at

D. M. Bryan

her, as if to satisfy himself that she was present, and then they walked together to the place where the minister waited.

Such a long engagement they had, she and George—and even the wedding service at St. Michael's seemed endless—but at the end lay the prize: a home for herself and for Lady Barbara. The house sat in Leicester Square, near to the Prince of Wales, upon whom George's welfare depended. The furniture and its appointments were all chosen by Sarah, and her choices, she knew, disappointed George. He frowned over her economical cream walls and block-printed cotton curtaining windows and beds. He discussed the excellence of fine deep green with the painter, closeting himself with the paper-hanger's man to find a fabric to exactly match, but in the end, he left to her the final choice in everything.

The day after the wedding, George presented her with a book: a volume filled with prints by the ingenious Mr. Hogarth, who, he showed her out the window, lived at the other end of the square in the house under the Golden Head. Sarah could not make out the door, nor the signpost above, but she promised herself a walk past. The pictures were, her husband hastened to assure her, of a very moral nature and intended entirely for the improvement of those who looked at them. Sarah would take George at his word, and so she flipped past scenes that might make a more innocent woman blush, finding her faith rewarded: each page contained something to her satisfaction.

"Look here," she showed her new husband as they sat together on a settee in the front parlour, "I know this work, *A Harlot's Progress*, for it is very famous and improving in all its details. You see how in every print Mr. Hogarth gives his Harlot the same attendant, so that even in her saddest days she might be accompanied by a faithful friend." She was thinking even then of Barbara.

"You approve the book?"

"I do."

From where she sits, peach silk covering her lap, Sarah can still see the book, sitting in the handsome mahogany bookcase that is the biggest of the furniture pieces she and Lady Barbara take with them from habitation to habitation. She can distinguish the book's tan binding from the identical others by a slight fraying at the spine, the product of repeated inspection. The familiarity of each object hums in her head: the bookcase with its glass doors the girl must clean every week; the chairs featuring her own embroidery on the covers; the round table also made of mahogany; the work-stands and boxes; Lady Barbara's green curtains on the bed; the decorative swags covered with shells and nuts; and on the mantelpiece, the two Meissen figures belonging to Barbara, with the three English copies that are gifts from Sarah.

Apart from the book of Mr. Hogarth's prints, none of the objects that filled the Leicester Square house really belonged to Sarah, for all her careful choosing. When she left that house for good, she took almost nothing with her, and she'd bettered Orpheus, taking no backwards glance. Eyes forward, she walked through the hall without pausing. She passed her brother, Morris Robinson, on his way upstairs to dictate the conditions of the separation from George. She passed another brother, the younger Mathew Robinson, who was detailing to the girl those few items that she and Barbara could not leave without. She passed her father, who ushered her through the door of the coach, then clambered in behind, his expression perplexed and angry. In the seat opposite, she found Barbara, waiting patiently.

As husband and wife, she and George had never, like some couples, gone to sit in each other's dressing rooms of an evening, reading or working on separate projects. On the night that ended her marriage, Sarah made only the smallest alteration in their accustomed practice in seeking him out. She wished to show him the shell-work vase she'd made as a gift—the natural expression of a wife's affection for her husband. Carefully, she carried the vase up the stairs, but even with all her caution a little tawny shell detached itself. *Nucella lapillus*, a common Dog Whelk seashell. She heard it fall upon the wooden tread behind her. From that point, she took tiny, careful steps to the dressing room door, which sat ajar.

As soon as she entered, she recognized her mistake. George was together with a handsome stranger on his sofa, which was a Chippendale, and which she herself had ordered covered in figured green velvet. The two drew apart as she stood there, but she'd seen enough. Later, she imagined herself dropping the fragile vase, stunned by the impropriety before her, but it was not an impropriety—no, it was something more. Instead, she gripped the shell-work urn firmly, apologized for the intrusion, and returned to the room where Lady Barbara sat.

"My husband is indisposed," she said to Barbara, but Barbara came to her and laid her hands upon Sarah's, looking into Sarah's face. When the truth came, her friend's council was quiet, firm, and utterly correct. Together, they wrote her father, so that he would come in the morning with Matthew and Morris. Then they began their vigil.

She cannot recall which gown she had on that night. She trusts it was not the peach-coloured silk, which in those days she wore with ivory ruffles at her elbows, and with lace at her neck and upon her head.

Before she met George, Sarah intended never to wed. She had her reasons: the stain of her brother John's madness; the loss of her sister Elizabeth to Edward Montagu; her own devotion to acts of Christian charity. "I intend to live a very full life," she'd told George, smiling, "and a husband would only get in my way." She hoped he would not think her coy, but in truth, she had a disinclination to marry she could not fully explain, even to herself. George only made her a small bow, as though something had been decided between them. What had they said in silence that day? In his refusal to act the ardent lover, she heard him propose a union of the spirit only, without the need for children or other awkward affections. He was not one to underestimate the claims of friendship. Hadn't he agreed that Lady Barbara should live with them, telling Sarah it was not in his nature to separate those intimates whose highest happiness depended on each other. And in the ten months their household lasted, George Scott proved as good as his word. He showed himself all respectful reserve and attentive disinterest. He never importuned Sarah on any matter—not once. In his way, he'd been exactly the husband she required, delivering on his silent promise. The fault—and the thought distressed Sarah still—lay in her refusal—nay, her inability—to consider that he must have a share in their agreement.

The night she left Leicester Square, George made but one effort to speak with her. He came down the stairs to the room where she and Lady Barbara waited. "I thought we understood one another," he said, looking hard at her. Then he asked to speak with her alone, but Lady Barbara would not leave them, and Sarah—hurt, angry, embarrassed—would not second George's request. Instead, she told him she had sent for her father, that he would come at first light.

"I thought you knew," said George. "I thought—"

"Did you find my shell upon the stair?"

"A shell?"

"From a whelk, of a yellow hue." Sarah pointed to the vase where it sat on a table by the window. "It belongs to the middle section, from a band formed of the same kind."

"No," said George. "I did not see your shell."

Sarah sat. She looked at her fingers, at the pale nail beds flushed with pink. George continued to stand before her, his feet spread, his arms behind his back. He wanted her to say something more, but what? So, Sarah said, "Before our wedding Elizabeth wrote me a letter. My sister warned me not to marry you, but I thought her merely jealous."

Lady Barbara turned now to Sarah, saying, "Hush. No one speaks of these things."

"Sarah," said George. "Please. Nothing of substance has altered between us—not really."

"I said, no one speaks of these things," said Lady Barbara, her eyes now on George Scott.

At her words George sat on a hard-backed chair across from Sarah and said nothing more. For a long time, he regarded them, his mouth twisting, dry as an inkless pen. Lady Barbara knelt by Sarah, leading her in prayer whenever she thought it most needful, and Sarah followed as best she could through the buzzing in her head. The fire burned down to smoking ashes, and no one came to tend it. The servants were all in hiding, and when the room grew chill, Barbara herself rose and poked at the hearth, sending up grey flakes and twists of woollen smoke.

What could George have done, Sarah wondered? What might he have said instead of "I thought you knew?" Should he have begged forgiveness, quoting St. Paul, "I loveth my wife, but I hate my own flesh?" Should he have torn at his waistcoat, at the fine cloth at his neck, rent his garments, gone to the hearth, smeared cinders on his brow? Certainly, he should never have married. He should never have come home with her brother, engaged her in conversation at table, met her eyes with his, taken her to church and made vows before God. He should not have brought her to this house, made a home for herself and Lady Barbara.

He should have found her shell, returned it to her, pressing it into her palm. *Nucella lapillus.* Dog Whelk.

When Matthew Robinson's servant at last rapped hard on the front door, George rose and left the room. Through the gap in the curtains, morning light yellowed the shell vase. It was an ugly and unbalanced object, sideways and misshapen. The settlement returned half of Sarah's portion and provided her with £100 a year, which was as much as George could manage. They would separate but not divorce. Sarah kept her paraphernalia and her clothing, including the peach-coloured silk.

Now, Sarah finds a side seam, using the scissors from her workbox to divide the panels. The thread she removes is also silk, as strong as wire. She cuts and gently splits the fabric, and then she repeats her actions. In this way, she begins to take apart the skirts of the gown, but the fabric is old and behaves in ways she cannot anticipate. Where she cuts away the thread she also sometimes tears the peach-coloured silk, and the more she tries to be careful the more damage she seems to do. At last she drops the silk gown in her lap and lets her hands fall idly at her sides. The fire is too warm on such an evening, and her glasses slide down the slick sides of her nose. She lets them sit there.

She has not seen George Scott in years. She does not know why tonight of all nights her mind runs so continually to thoughts of him, unless it is the peach-coloured silk. Or perhaps this evening's remembrance is of a piece with the other impressions that plague her, that threaten to fill her pages: her smallpox, her sister, her misadventure in the Gardens. Memories flip open then snap closed, with the sharp retort of a book clapped-to. Or the bark of pain in a head.

"I need a different task," she says to Barbara. "These alterations hurt my eyes."

Meg enters, crossing the room to tend the fire. As she passes, Sarah catches her eye, wipes her brow.

The window? glances Meg.

"Yes. Please."

Barbara says, "Tell her she must open it only a little, Sarah." Lady Barbara does not need to look up, her attention directed at her own sewing.

Sarah holds her hands apart: *Only this much.*

Meg opens the window a very little and looks at Sarah for confirmation.

Yes, says Sarah, feeling the snip of evening air unseam the room. Sarah too begins to come apart. Anger seizes its chance and rolls her eyes. Meg laughs conspiratorially, and Barbara looks up at the sound.

Sarah speaks only to Meg, saying, *I can never tell if she's fighting with me. If only I had a coin in each palm, I could be certain then.*

But that's too much eye-talk for Meg to follow. "Mis'ress?" says Meg, out loud, in her rounded voice. Her speech is all river rocks.

"Nothing," says Sarah, clicking and clacking like a pair of scissors. "You may go now." And in a moment, she says to Meg's back, "Thank you."

"She can't—" says Lady Barbara.

"I know," says Sarah. "Don't tell me."

Then they sit, pretending to work, until the clock releases Sarah, and both may go to bed.

In the morning, Barbara feels her forehead and declares Sarah unwell. She sends her to lie down and rest. Instead, Sarah goes outside to work in the kitchen garden. There, under the heat of the sun, Sarah Scott's mind becomes a cabbage, green folds and laborious veins. Her thoughts arch and bend, as she searches with her fingers through the spinach and carrots, finding those places where leaves thin and grow translucent.

Beyond the kitchen garden is a broad flowerbed: rose trees and sweet-briars, pinks, jonquils, hyacinths, primroses, violets, lilies of the valley, polyanthuses, woodbines, and jessamine. The flowers form a girdle, a belt between the house and its accidental visitors. A battleground of pink and yellow, purple and white, where Sarah serves as commander, standing in the dirt with her trowel at her waist. Now she leaves the kitchen garden to review her troops. She can see how the sweet-briar forms a defensive hedge, protection for more delicate pinks, jonquils, and hyacinths. Heliophobic lilies-of-the-valley make their own low shade, throwing a green cover over milky bells. Sun-shy primroses and violets cower alongside. But out in the field, brave woodbines serve out their time, standing alongside a militia of roses, pricks cocked and ready. Sarah imagines the advance, the troops holding the lawn, securing the pasture. When the sun goes down, the flowers will bivouac. Each morning, new buds open, leaves unfurl, and pink sister shelters pink sister.

Overhead, the sun boils. Sarah squints at the river and thinks she sees a woman scrambling up the steep hill. Then, from around the tent, comes William Hogarth's Harlot, wearing a rose pinned to her shawl. Her rose says *pluck me*.

George told Sarah the harlot's dishabille was very moral in nature and intended entirely for the improvement of those who gazed upon those plump shoulders, the rounded mounds below. Sarah gazed, but she was not improved.

George said: I thought you knew. Now comes the Harlot, pleading.

Indoors, Sarah goes looking for paper. Here, her head is cooler, clearer. Shifting a stack of finely ribbed writing paper, she discovers a scribbled note and recognizes her own handwriting. She reads it and recalls that she wrote this scrap in Chilston, while staying with her cousin Callie Best. A draft of a letter to Elizabeth, it says, "My Dear Sister, I have painted an anemony which I brood over with the affection of a Parent, an ugly rose with nothing but maternal love can make me indure to sight of & I am in labour of a tulip which I cannot be deliver'd of till Monday."

In labour of a tulip. An ugly rose. What should she make of her expression of a maternal sentiment in which she must love what she hates, nurture what she longs to destroy? Sarah crumples the note and tosses it on the fire. A quick increase of flame crisps a jonquil into smoke and sends out snapping dandelions that spark and fade.

On the same table, Sarah Robinson Scott finds her own manuscript pages, abandoned where she'd been working on them. She picks up the top page and reads her own sloping script. Sarah clicks her tongue with involuntary disgust. Her headache pinches like an older sister. Yesterday, how delighted she'd been with her work, but today it gives her no pleasure. In the book that Mr. Newbery now sets into print, she peopled her Millenium Hall with as many females as her sister has dresses. To write it, she wrapped herself in Miss Mancel or clapped on Mrs. Morgan. Sometimes she wore Lady Mary Jones or laced up Mrs. Trentham. She is glad to slip them all off now, to return them to her trunk. The book is with Mr. Newbery, and she is tired of invention. Of disguise. She longs to be herself in the world.

In the evening, Sarah puts on her eyeglasses and announces to Lady Barbara that she has found a new project: a grand design for a residence for women, where sister will shelter sister. "I teach our girls to sit and quietly sew," she tells Barbara, "but I would also take us into battle." Sarah ignores the expression she sees cross Lady Barbara's face and announces that she will begin by designing a house for Mr. Hogarth's Harlot.

"I have every reason," says she, "to wish to comfort that lady."

Drawing with homemade ink upon rag paper, Sarah works by daylight, rush light, and firelight. Her back in a snail's hunch, she leaves a shining trail behind her that grows thicker with excitement and thinner with time. When a line dwindles completely, she lifts her pen and dips again. In a Delft dish on the table rests a bundle of cut quills, no longer fletched but trimmed down to the tempered shaft. As each pen cracks or clogs and will no longer make inky divisions,

D. M. Bryan

Sarah exchanges it for one of its sisters in the dish. Then she bends back to her work, marking and labeling rooms.

As designed by Sarah, the Harlot's tiny cottage has a minute entryway with a sitting room to the left and a staircase to the right. Behind the main room is a slope-ceilinged kitchen, with a hearth and a pump in the yard behind. Up the stairs are two cells for sleeping, one whose window gazes forward and one that looks down into the garden. This pleases Sarah, and she lifts her pen a while to dream of the cloud of blue jasmine that explodes over the portico, visible through rippled glass. Dipping her pen again, she adds a vegetable garden with rows of cabbages and carrots, cucumbers in a frame. Then she returns to the cottage, drawing squares and circles. She sets two round chairs before the oblong hearth, one seat for the Harlot and the other for her servant, the frowzy madam of Mr. Hogarth's print. She intends that the women might sit together of an evening, sharing a pipe, or discussing contrition, reformation, and the wonderful workings of providence. How fine that sounds, thinks Sarah. Providence Hall. Penitence House. Magdalene Cottage.

Sarah's pen clogs, and then the tiny dam of ink breaks. A blot forms at nib-tip. A black flower blooms, glossy and irregular. Sarah sniffs, smells gammon reheating in a three-footed pan over a fire. A potage of leeks and potatoes from the garden. Whigs dripping with butter and tasting of cardamom. The ink wicks into her lawn sleeve, stains her wrist. Sarah, pockmarked Sarah, feels elegant.

The next evening, Sarah returns to her drawing, despite the fact that her head is no better. She sees concern marking Lady Barbara's face, but Sarah ignores the chair her friend sets out beside her own. Her quill pens she has carefully prepared, and now she sits at the table where bands of light faint and swoon across the paper. With her pen she makes a margin, scoring her page three inches from the top. From the sideboard, yesterday's drawing watches. Tonight, Sarah will consider her obligation to rakes.

In her book of Mr. Hogarth's prints, she's seen how rakes progress. They hold fluted glasses between long fingers. They set their buckled heels upon a table covered in cards, in dice. Six dots on a die, twelve harlots in a room, ten syllables in Mr. Pope's verse. Sarah hums a line from a lyric she heard somewhere. *Two Harlots for every Rake*, she sings, drawing now, her pen tripping across the parquet page. To the rakes she gives a panelled hallway, with sash windows on left and cell doors on right. A solitary life, as penitential as that the harlots lead— no, more penitential, for the rakes will have no clouds of jasmine. For them, no neat rows of laundry strung in lines. Harlots need to tip back their heads and see sky. Harlots require deep mouthfuls of country between their teeth. Rakes already have had their chests caressed, their ears nipped, their pockets picked. They keep their mouths open when they should close them tight. Sarah Scott thinks.

"Why would rakes come to Sarah's new Hall? Why would they stay?" Sarah asks Lady Barbara, forgetting, just for a moment, their unaccustomed enmity. Lady Barbara has taken up her mending, a nightdress. She shakes her hair, smooth and grey, although her face below is, like Sarah's page, only lightly lined.

"Perhaps they are distempered," says Lady Barbara.

In Sarah's drawing, wet ink scales the page, squares set within squares. She renders shed roofs, workshops for the manufacture of useful items: eatables, useables, saleables. A metal shop, its furnace red-faced and puffing, where rakes heat and beat into plowshares the puncheons and silver platters that once made harlots tipsy. Now, even the swords rakes carried when teasing, rousting, duelling will be re-fashioned into tools for weeding, stooking, threshing. In the furnace's cleansing fire, metals temper and cool.

Rakes break bread at long tables. Sarah draws these, as the rakes wait upon one another. Never speaking except to say *brother, may I offer you more cheese?* Because another shed contains a place where white rounds ripen in wooden racks. Rakes heat milk and drain whey. Dressed in aprons, they squeeze squares of rough cloth and then un-fold the edges to discover milk solids glowing like morning. In their hands, they cup the soft balls of curd, finding them pale and pliable as breasts.

Sarah lifts her pen. Contemplates the cheese.

Without preamble, she tells Lady Barbara what is on her mind, what has been in her head since she set herself to alter the peach-coloured silk.

"You knew," she says. "We *all* knew."

Painfully, Lady Barbara rises and sets aside the stocking she mends, her needle and thread. She walks awkwardly, but when she reaches Sarah her movements are firm and certain. She takes the quill from between trembling fingers. Soothes her with a feather soft stroke, finger to cheek. Banks the fire on her friend's forehead. Trims her like a lamp.

D. M. Bryan

CHAPTER 9

Where I am going I know not, what will become of me,
I am still less able to guess.

Sarah Scott's *The History of Cornelia.*

Batheaston, 1762.

Sarah decides to visit the ingenious Mr. Hogarth, taking him her
drawings to see if he can assist her in finding a suitable engraver for
their reproduction and circulation. For three days she has been hard
at work, despite her churning head and sparks at the corners of her
eyes. Now, a pile of papers sits on the sideboard: her projection, her
scheme, her halls and cottages and sheds and gardens. She recognizes
the oddity, the awkwardness of her preoccupation with her project for
harlots—she has been drawing when she should catechize the girls
or supervise the size of their stitches. Well, Barbara might take up
that task while she is away. Barbara understands the girls better than
she. No, Sarah corrects herself—Barbara better understands her duty.
Sarah understands the girls.

Lady Barbara hears her intentions in silence. Then she says, "You
will only cheapen your drawings if you sell them to the highest bidder."

"I give my books to Mr. Millar, or to the Misters Dodsley, or now
to Mr. Newbery, and he sells them quite openly at the Bible and Sun
in St. Paul's Church-yard. You do not scruple at that."

"That's different," says Barbara.

"I don't see how."

Barbara bends to the work in her hands. Mending again—a fine white stocking this time.

"I know Hogarth's house in London," says Sarah. "I have seen it many times. There is a Golden Head above the door." She does not say George showed it to her, although Barbara knows this very well.

"London is a tiresome journey, and we are neither of us in good health."

"I am very well."

"You complain of your head," says Lady Barbara, "until I am nearly distracted."

"Then you will be pleased if I should take a trip to London without you."

Lady Barbara says nothing.

Sarah says, "Stop sewing will you? Look at me. I am improved. I am quite myself."

Lady Barbara stops sewing and looks directly at her. At night, Sarah can easily bring to mind Meg's face, and the girls' faces come to her often. Her father and her brothers' faces she sees, whether she will or not. Her sister Elizabeth she can evoke from all angles and wearing many expressions. But she cannot fix Lady Barbara's features in her memory.

The object of her scrutiny looks down at her sewing, frowning as if at something awry in her stitchery. With her little silver scissors, she snips the thread and puts the end of the stocking on her hand to shape it. Sarah supposes the mend is in the heel, although she cannot see it from where she sits. Barbara pulls the fabric first one way and then the other, and Sarah knows she is testing the tightness of the little mesh she has constructed. Then Lady Barbara rolls the stocking off her hand and replaces it in her workbox for distribution. Whose stocking is it? Mine, Sarah thinks.

She says, "If my prints sell well, we need not give up this house."

"That has already been decided. We are both healthier in Bath," says Lady Barbara.

"Rooms," says Sarah. "Spinster lodgings."

"You exaggerate our poverty. We will find a very good house, per-haps with a stretch of garden."

"And what of my garden here? Who will take care of my flower roots? What of our beautified chair rail and chimney pieces?"

"Sarah, you should not mind these things."

"But I do."

Lady Barbara has her workbox open and takes out another stock-ing. She threads her needle, slowly and with several failures.

Sarah says, "You did not scruple so when we helped produce Mrs. Pattillo's Cards."

"Those had an educational purpose."

"So do my prints."

"Mr. Richardson was a very respectable man."

"And I suppose Mr. Hogarth is not? He sells by subscription to many excellent people. I do not see any difference between his actions and those Mr. Richardson undertook on behalf of Mrs. Pattillo's geography lessons."

"The mess we had with Mr. Leake," says Lady Barbara as she be-gins to plunge her needle in and out of the fabric.

The charge is unfair. James Leake, a local Bath man, had been Barbara's choice. He bore the name of a character in a pantomime, but there could be no enjoyment of the happy coincidence, for Mr. Leake suffered by it. Damp moistened the walls of his workshop and burst the plaster ceiling. His eyes and nose ran continually; he spat phlegm; and he drank liquor until it spilled from his lips. With kindness and completeness, Mr. Richardson, married to Leake's sister, mopped up after his cheat of a brother-in-law. The cards were printed, but they did not sell well.

"My head pains me," Sarah says, remembering too late that she must not mention her head.

Barbara sews.

"I need fresh air."

Lady Barbara looks up at her.

Once in the farmhouse yard, Sarah walks over to the low stone wall that separates the house from the road. She looks back at the evenly spaced windows. Behind those glowing curtains Barbara sits, trapped. Sarah moves from the road to the gate in the fence that gives onto her garden. Up from the valley floor comes the trickling sound of the river, rocking the roundest stones with invisible fingers. From this viewpoint, she cannot see, although she can scent, her garden that thrives in the blanket of the compost her gardener spreads at the roots. Night blooming honey-suckle and flowering tobacco grow beside the path, where accidental contact intensifies the fragrance. Regularly, she and the man walk between green swells, their feet sinking deep in the gravel. He pinches jasmine between fingers and inhales, while Sarah watches. Jo More came for charity, having heard she would employ a beached sailor, but now he is all gardener. If the fellow were with her, she would walk out between the plants, for the moist darkness is a balm, but something holds her at the gate. Overhead are stars, reminding her of pincushions. She misses the warmth of the fire.

She already has her hand on the door latch when she hears the hollow knocking of horse hooves coming up the road. Turning, she sees, at first, nothing, and then, riding into view, a woman tall on the back of a high-withered draft horse. The woman sits easily on the animal, despite her lack of a saddle, and the reins rest loosely in her hands. Her cloak covers her head, making a kind of cowl and hiding her face. Her easiness on horseback, Sarah realizes with dismay, results from her position astride the horse, skirts bunched up over her knees. Heeled boots, thick with clay, dangle at the widest point of the animal's girth. As horse and rider pass in the night, it is the horse that turns its head and glances at Sarah, giving a low snort. Then the lane narrows and turns, and the woman and her mount disappear into the sound of their own footfalls. A moment later Sarah hears nothing but the Avon's trifling.

Back in the parlour, Meg has stirred up the fire, doubtless at Barbara's call, and has brought out the frame with its crewelwork. Lady Barbara sits before it, laying stitches side-by-side to imitate the variegated green lozenges of vegetation. Sarah stands at her shoulder, watching a silken garden appearing line upon line. In just this way, the close rain of an engraver's burin might fall over Sarah's hall, her cottages, sheds, and gardens, rendering each shape with hatches and cross-hatches. Printed on fine paper, an engraver's lines lie as straight as a crewel worker's stitches, but with what a difference. A print might last forever, while Barbara's work makes only a resting place for a parson's fat bottom. Why the difference between ink and wool? But Sarah knows it is not a matter of material.

Sarah thinks of the woman on horseback. She should have called out, asked her in for something to eat. Such travel at night might mean a breeched birth in one of the farmer's cots, but the plodding pace and the covered head suggest other things as well. And so, Sarah left her hand on the latch and said nothing.

Barbara changes her thread, setting down the skein of leafy green and choosing a length of scarlet for a petal. "The cold air still comes off you," she says. "Will you bring a chair up to the fire?"

"I will not change my mind," says Sarah. "I am determined to go to London."

In reply, Barbara only threads her needle and sets it flashing against the white cloth. Scarlet stitches fill the frame.

Lady Barbara's illness, always with them, worsens. The doctor comes and finds her condition serious, confines his patient to bed, prescribes and bleeds, sends his bill. Sarah reviews the scraps of paper alone at the table, before an unlit fire. The doctor's charges, she suspects, have been shrunk to fit the circumscribed incomes of two decaying gentlewomen. No matter, the bill confirms the necessity of the long discussed, long delayed move to Bath, and the giving up of the Batheaston house. Of Sarah's trip to London, nothing more is said.

The weather changes for the worse, and every morning the charity girls arrive with sodden skirts. Sarah seats them in a row before the fire, where they steam as they sew. They look like a row of small, sad demons pricking their own fingers in eternal punishment. It is in the afternoons that the doctor sometimes comes. In the parlour, he sits and takes tea. He listens to Sarah's descriptions of the spasms that shake her friend, of the pain that comes and stays. He listens and goes, leaving behind instructions. Clysters. Plasters. More bleeding. Can he be as disappointed in his recipes as she is, Sarah wonders. She does not think so. The glint of his coat braid, the crispness of his neck cloth speak to the abiding satisfaction the man takes in himself, and she must bite her tongue as he adjusts his collar in the mirror by the door. In Lady Mary Wortley Montagu's *The Turkish Embassy Letters* Sarah finds the quote she wants: "'Tis in the power of a surgeon to make an ulcer with the help of lancet and plaister, and of a doctor to kill by prescriptions." Perhaps they should be grateful that the doctor does no harm. He comes; he goes; Barbara remains the same.

And yet they must somehow cover his fee.

Their agent in Bath writes to them of a new house, well-appointed and central. Rooms in Bath are an economy—in town, the doctor can come more often and with less trouble to himself. Sight unseen, she and Barbara take the place. The rooms are high ceilinged and bright, the agent says, and Sarah imagines the smell of new wood. She must arrange to have the trim painted. Cream would look very well, or so Sarah writes in letters to her sister and her brothers. Elizabeth writes back to ask if they will have carpet in the sitting room. Elizabeth has carpets both at the Priory and in Hill Street, and she likes them very much. Yes, perhaps a small carpet might provide some cheer, or at least a painted cloth. Sarah measures the bookcase and finds it will not fit. Brother William, who has agreed to assume the remainder of the lease at Batheaston, must suffer to add it to his own domestic appointments, or he can have it chopped and burned in the winter—Sarah will remember not to ask. The books will come to Bath, of course, but they will need a new bookshelf—something less massive and lighter of line. She has printed catalogues from several of the cabinet-makers in Bath and the one in London her sister patronizes. Under the catalogues lie pages of loose paper—her project for harlots, her communication for Mr. Hogarth. Sarah moves the catalogues and tidies the pages. She has not forgotten.

Meg comes out of the back room with a tray, the napkin slightly displaced to show thick slices of bread and butter untouched on a plate. Barbara, who makes the back parlour her sick room, eats very little. Meg passes Sarah but says nothing. If there is nothing to be said, then nothing need be said—Meg understands this better than anyone, and Sarah learns daily from her silences. In Bath, Sarah must find a girl to come daily. Meg will stay in Batheaston to help William and his new bride. Here, in this house, Meg has her own small room, which Sarah has not seen since the day she first showed it to her. She tries to imagine it now. What might Meg own? A brass thimble. A strongbox for her earnings. A brush and a polished piece of mirror.

In the kitchen, the fire spits and pushes eagerly. Meg has filled a small basin with water from the kettle and is washing a cup clean. From the dresser Sarah takes down a teapot, a useful piece out of Mr. Astbury's pottery. It is not new by any means, with an outmoded decoration of creamy sprigs, but Meg has not seen what Sarah is obliged to notice with each fresh visit to Elizabeth: that endless parade of fashionable teapots across the tea tables of the bon ton. Chinese ladies with parasols, blushing country maidens, pink putti.

Patiently Sarah waits for Meg to turn towards her before she proffers the gift. Sarah recognizes in the other something of her own dislike of the pressure of fingers, the brush of a hand. Theirs is a language of looks like nymphs in a poem, their eyes meeting, drooping, lifting. A sigh between them says much. But nothing coquettish survives in the verse they compose, which makes its numbers out of cooking and laundry. Sarah watches Meg's face as she gazes at the teapot in Sarah's hands. "The new kitchen will be smaller," says Sarah when the other's eyes at last meet her own. "I've no room. Perhaps you might find it useful?" Sarah speaks more rapidly than she intends, and before she is done she has turned her head nervously, thoughtlessly. On account of Meg's deafness some of her explanation must slip incomprehensible to the floor between them. Sarah knows this, so she steps closer and pushes the teapot towards Meg, still not touching her. The latter's hands come up, wrapping tentative fingers around the handle and spout. Sarah watches as thought moves like muscle behind Meg's eyes, and then the weight of the fragile vessel lifts fully from her hands.

Sarah nods briskly at Meg. "Keep it safe," she says needlessly and exits the kitchen.

When she enters the back parlour cum sickroom, Lady Barbara is awake, sitting upright with the bed curtains pushed back. Sarah sees a grey day, a boxwood hedge, with a row of trees beyond. Leaves tremble in the wet air, each a tarnished coin. "Darling girl," says Sarah, pulling at the window curtains so that their rings click.

"Leave them," says Lady Barbara. "The light cheers me, despite the cloud. Have you been out? You look flushed."

"I have been nowhere," says Sarah.

"Well, no mind," says Lady Barbara. "We should not complain."

For a moment Sarah is silent. Then she says, "As always, I endeavour to keep my imagination in the sunshine. I have given an old piece of Staffordshire to Meg. The shelves in the Bath rooms are on a more convenient design, but they will not hold as much."

"To Meg?"

"It was only the Astbury sprigged pot. It is not a fashionable piece, and she seemed to receive it with pleasure."

"But had we nothing better?"

"A great deal better, but nothing I judged she would accept."

"Has she bowls to drink from? She cannot be elegant without bowls."

Sarah says nothing, and then: "I had thought you might like to choose the bowls." It is not exactly a lie—the idea is a good one, irrespective of when it occurred to her.

Lady Barbara frowns. "You choose," says she. "I can see I underestimate the intricacies of the situation."

Now the invalid rotates stiffly in an effort to pull her shawl more closely about her. Sarah reaches forward to assist with the fringed edges but finds her hands pushed away.

"What concerns me," says Lady Barbara, losing the corner of her shawl, "is that we inconvenience Meg with a luxury as costly as tea. But I am certain you thought of that."

Sarah had not. On Lady Barbara's cheeks, two circles of red stand out like thumbprints.

D. M. Bryan

"I will give her some bohea from the caddy," Sarah says at last. "Enough to provide a little pleasure from time to time."

"The Congou will make many more cups," says Lady Barbara, "if she is thrifty."

"The Congou then," says Sarah. "A twist in paper."

Sarah puts a hand over her stays and presses. The boning flexes, and between the stiffened sections she feels her own curving ribs. Sarah experiences daily improvements in her own health, the emergency of Barbara's illness a cool compress to her feverish excitement. Or perhaps it is only a change in the direction of the wind that eases her headache and sharpens her appetite. Sarah says, "The doctor promises to bleed you as soon as we reach town."

"Are we to go so soon?" says Barbara.

"Very soon," says Sarah.

The day they depart comes bright and clear. It is harder to leave Batheaston with pale green foam bursting from every stick and tree. Streaks of blue overhead. On the stone of the front step, Sarah finds the curving, silver penmanship of snails. She has intended to walk in the garden one last time before the coach comes, but she finds herself again standing at the gate, unwilling to enter. To distract herself, she turns to the road and watches for the feather of dust announcing Mrs. Riggs' borrowed chariot. In her mind's eye the coach becomes a nib and the road a line in a letter. *Dear Brother, I regret to inform you that I cannot leave Batheaston, for I find I am not a woman at all but a tap-root. Great damage might be done if I am forced from the soil. Perhaps another season might see me safely transplanted, but on this day, I fear, I cannot be removed.*

Her letter done, she notes no dust rising and hopes the coach lies tipped in a ditch, its axle snapped like a stalk. But in this, as in all things, she knows herself destined to be disappointed. After the days of rainy weather, only soft, moist roads run up the steep hillside to the farm. The coach comes upon her suddenly, with no dust, and only a damp rattle to announce its arrival. A moment later, the Batheaston courtyard fills with the reek of horses. Up on his box, the coachman tips his hat. Sarah reenters the house.

Inside, Barbara sits at the foot of the stairs, under the palm-worn newel post. She has been dressed since daybreak, and Meg leans down to wrap her in blankets against the mild dangers of the day. Beside them, a pair of trunks, a large basket containing items needful for the journey. Everything else will go by ox cart to the new house. Now, Sarah mounts the stairs and takes from an empty room the leather portmanteau containing her drawings.

Lady Barbara watches as Sarah descends, case in hand, but says nothing and struggles to her feet. Upright, she sways, her boneless dress flapping, for she can no longer bear the discomfort of female buttressing. Flushed and guilty, Sarah comes forward to take her arm, while Meg gathers the bag of necessaries and the leather portmanteau.

Unexpectedly, a small figure comes in from outside. Sarah stops, the girl's name on her lips, but before she can speak, Tidy catches her eyes, and then curtsies, exactly as taught.

"No more school," says Sarah, for the girls cannot come so far as Bath for lessons. She has repeatedly informed the girls of the fact.

"Not here for school," says Tidy. "I'm come to assist Meg. She promised a tuppence if I'm more help than hindrance."

Meg's raucous laugh surprises Sarah, but Tidy, eager to prove her worth, begins to tug at one of the trunks. Lighter than it appears, the trunk comes forward rather suddenly, and she stumbles toward Sarah, leaving behind a long scratch in the floorboard. Sarah looks at the floorboard showing a white steak of bare wood. Her eyes travel to the newel post, palm-worn and finger-stained. She glances through the open front door for a final time, and there is the coachman to hand them to their seats.

Sarah attends to Lady Barbara, helping her into the chariot's forward-facing bench. The coachman assists, and Sarah feels herself lifted, then deposited, half on the leather and half on Barbara's skirts. She shifts and tugs and settles what seems like yards of fabric before both she and Barbara are comfortably seated, side-by-side. Sarah leans out the open door, finding Meg standing on the threshold of the farmhouse. Beside her, Tidy imitates the older woman's posture, arms crossed and feet apart.

"Tidy," Sarah calls, and the girl steps forward. But Sarah has nothing more in her mouth except for the root of her tongue. She stares at the child, unable to look at the grey gables. The empty windows.

Lady Barbara speaks from her other side, her voice lost in the creaking of coach-wood. Sarah turns, catching at the words. "The key," says Barbara more distinctly.

Detaching the key from the enamelled equipage at her waist, Sarah leans down and beckons Meg forward. Meg takes the key with care, attaching it to the plainer device around her own thicker waist. With a self-conscious gesture she smooths the iron against the fullness of her bottle-green skirts, and then looks seriously up at Sarah. Sarah nods.

The sun has risen fully, burning off the last of the fog. Those plants closest to the house show points of pink and blue, white and violet. Sarah leans across Lady Barbara to open the louvered window. Now she can see all of her garden, sparkling with green sunlight. The coachman closes the other door, and the vehicle dips and quivers as he loads the trunks. Then, as the man takes his seat, the giant wheels roll to and fro in the gravel, the horses stepping like dancers. Sarah turns back to the window on the house side. Meg and Tidy wait by the door.

Too soon, says Sarah to Meg. *Call me back.*

Meg waves from the doorstep.

Tidy daubs her nose with her apron, and with a start Sarah realizes the child is weeping. A voice, Sarah's own, says, "is that a clean apron, Tidy? Where is your handkerchief?" but of course Tidy cannot hear her from inside the vehicle. Sarah wills Meg to place a hand on Tidy's shoulders, but Meg reads lips, not minds. She keeps her red-knuckled hands folded over her skirts, the key dangling beside them.

Sarah turns to Barbara. "Will you wave goodbye?" she asks, leaning back in the seat they share. Barbara shakes her head and knocks with surprising firmness on the wooden wall of the coach.

They roll through the yard, saluted by roses with their chins held high, by jonquils with leaves gleaming like muskets, and by drooping woodbines at the gate.

Sarah reaches over and snaps shut the louvers.

CHAPTER 10

The History of Glossolalia: Or, Virtues Various.

The Tale of the Breeched Girl & the Laundress' Tale.

London, 1746.

Glossolalia, whose history this is, sometimes eased those episodes of sadness to which she was given with excursions that put her in mind of her former life as a pirate captain. Ladies such as herself— solitary women of mature years, under the necessity of a respectable reputation—had little occasion for heroism, but on the night in question, she longed to take to the water, even if it was only the Thames. She had, on short acquaintance, joined a party determined to visit the gardens of Vaux-Hall, which lay across that sedate river, but no sooner had she set foot in the waterman's boat than Glossolalia knew that she had mistaken her companions. They were silly and giddy, clutching each other in the bottom of the boat. In short, Glossolalia's new associates quickly grew tedious to her, and as soon as she set foot on the Southwark stair, she determined to set out alone and damn respectability.

The theatrical illumination of the Vaux-Hall oil lamps, a distracting, yellow-green spell, gave Glossolalia her chance, and she slipped away unremarked. Her slippered feet crunched knowingly upon the gravel path. At first, she hurried, glancing over her shoulder lest someone observe her flight, but seeing she was not hailed and bid to return, Glossolalia came to a halt and stood for moment to breathe in the moist, warm air.

The garden stretched about her, its central grove of lime and elm branching upwards into a verdant ceiling. At the heart of this fine clearing, an elegant edifice of wood and stone supported an orchestra on its second story, and the whole of the garden sounded with a pretty air played on stringed instruments. Around three sides of the grove ran the low colonnade that formed alcoves for fashionable parties, but Glossolalia instead stood upon one of the gravelled alleys that led deep into Vaux-Hall gardens. These pleasant paths ran to and fro in the leafy maze, everywhere doubling back, so that strollers might surprise themselves under green linden trees.

For perhaps half an hour, Glossolalia walked along grey-pebbled lanes, enjoying the forest cool. Wherever she could, she avoided meeting anyone, but as she went deeper into the gardens, she was overtaken by a pair of young women. The girls swished past in a rustle of skirts, their arms linked and their heads together. In a silk mantua, the first was as pink and white as an apple blossom, while the other wore a blue-trimmed hat upon her high hair. As they passed Glossolalia, they begin to sing a popular air, commencing with more vigour than art, and turning their heads to look behind, where two fellows trailed after.

The girls sang, "Think how hard my condition and pity my case."

"I pity you, pretty misses," called out the first fellow in his sober blue coat, brushing past Glossolalia without a sideways glance.

"Think how hard my condition," said his friend, who was less sober.

The women giggled and fanned fans. Reaching a break in the row of trees, they turned, and both parties went down a passage where Glossolalia could see the screening bulk of bushes and not much more.

"The Dark Walk," said Glossolalia, for what took place in that part of the gardens was well-enough known to all. "I am fortunate not to have taken that path in error."

But the lady was entirely mistaken. The Dark Walk lay, in truth, already beneath her leather slippers. Innocently, Glossolalia continued with her stroll, but she soon began to perceive several new sets of figures approaching. As they drew closer, she saw a stout, short man accompanied by a fat-bellied pug dog. Both man and dog puffed as they came upon her, but the man found sufficient breath to call lustily behind him. "Pugg," he cried, waving a walking stick, "pick up your feet, you handsome fellow. Come along smartly." For a moment, Glossolalia thought she recognized the red-faced fellow, but he passed by her so brusquely she did not think he could be the person she remembered.

And already her attention was turning to a rather more splendid sight—a courting couple in all their finery. First came the gentleman, a locust-waisted beau with a flaring coat-skirt. He held tightly to the arm of his lady, her court skirts wide as a butterfly's wings. These exalted figures passed in a wash of orange scent that lingered, and behind them scuttled their drab chaperon, beetling her brow.

With their passage Glossolalia found herself well and truly alone. The gravelled walkway continued before her, with stone urns appearing at intervals, like so many divisions on a draftsman's rule. In places, trees parted like bed-curtains, revealing a blue-black sky and stars brighter than those in London. Night had come on, and only faint strains of music reminded her of the other inhabitants of the garden still circulating under gilding lamplight. Soon, she came to a forking of paths, and she took one but had gone down it only a score of steps before she decided against it. The gloomy, glaucous light gave her a chill sensation. A break in the distant music of the grove left, in its absence, a silence as deep as a hole. She did not understand how she could have so quickly and so completely put herself beyond the comforting circulation of other persons. The pirate captain she had once been seemed very far from her now—a thought that did not much improve that lady's happiness.

With a shiver Glossolalia returned to the crossroad, and took the other path, which she liked no better than the first but which soon widened a little, causing her to take heart. In this new direction, Glossolalia travelled briskly, one ear cocked for the resumption of the garden's orchestra, or even the laughter of some couple, intent on amorous discourse. It was with relief then that she turned a corner of the pathway and beheld, some distance away, a further widening of the gravel into a little square.

Glossolalia had already taken a few steps toward the square—which was bordered by a high boxwood hedge—when she noticed, hanging above that leafy barrier, a soft smudge—no more than a fingerprint on the night. She squinted and took it to be one of the stone busts that trim Vaux-Hall's greenery. Stepping lightly, the lady made her way forward, but as she drew closer, the stone head surprised her by moving.

Vexed, Glossolalia stopped, but the statue had already seen her, swivelling in her direction. Next, it revealed itself to be a speaking sort of statue, crying out in an odd, braying voice: "Now gentlemen, hold off. Here comes a lady." It gave an affected laugh, before clapping on a three-cornered hat.

Glossolalia did not know what to make of this apparition and stood amazed.

Then, another voice, a bass to the head's counter-tenor, said, "Nay, bitch—there's no one."

"Really," said the head, "I do see a lady."

"Pull the other," said the bodiless bass voice.

Said the head, "She's coming this way."

The bass voice sighed audibly. "Have a look, will you?" it said. "See if anyone's coming."

"Look yourself," said a third voice. "I'm nobody's footman."

Astonished, Glossolalia took the simple expedient of stepping off the gravelled path and into the garden. So thick was the undergrowth in this part of Vaux-Hall, she at once found herself immersed in a tangle of branch and bush. As quick as she could, she put the slender trunk of an elm between herself and the loquacious stone head.

"She's just now stepped behind a tree," said the same head.

Said the bass voice, "No doubt she's got urgent business there. Now, sweetheart, why don't you sit yourself down on that bench, and keep me company?"

"I'm happy enough standing, thank you. You see, I've rather a large party with me, and they're not far away. They'll be here immediately."

"Sit down, sweetheart."

"I don't want to sit down." The voice was rising in pitch, and Glossolalia was now certain it belonged to a young woman, regardless of the hat.

"That's a shame, that is." It was the third voice speaking, an oily baritone.

"Here now, I'll sit beside you." The bass voice again.

"I like your stockings." The oily baritone.

"Don't touch me." The statue, still valiantly attempting to disguise her sex.

Behind the elm, Glossolalia reunited with her pirate captain. At once, she began groping in the underbrush until she found a dead branch, both thick and stout. Stripping off the twigs and leaves, she clasped the branch firmly, and swung it to and fro to feel its weight. Satisfied with her improvised cudgel, she stepped out from the underbrush and crunched her way up the path, pushing up her fine lace ruffles. By the time she turned the boxwood corner and entered the square, Glossolalia's blood was thoroughly up. She had not time to tie up her gown so that she might not stumble and go down in a ballooning of skirts, but she swept them aside with her hand as she strode.

The night had darkened so completely that she could not at first see the three figures clustered around the little bench, but as she came on she heard a slap and a rip, and she made out a slight figure tussling with two much larger assailants. Glossolalia hefted her stick, but instead of applying it to the backs of the attackers, she took the thick end in her hand and leaned upon it. Then, in a tremulous but carrying voice, she cried out: "Oh, naughty girl. Are you bothering the young men again?"

She was a pirate captain still, but pirates employ subterfuge as surely as they use violence.

At the sound of her voice, the two villains stepped apart, releasing the young woman, who slipped off the bench and spilled onto the gravel.

"On your feet, foolish child," said Glossolalia, stepping forward, leaning hard on her improvised cane. Reaching the young woman, she poked with her stick, finding the breeches untorn, the face unmarked, but the girl herself stunned and slow to respond.

The men—for whatever their station in life, the avenging Glossolalia refused to think of such persons as gentlemen—had gone no further than the edge of the square. Now they watched Glossolalia uncertainly.

"Has she harmed you at all, my dear sirs?" cried that lady. "It is a shock to find her once again with her breeches down—she knows full well that passing on her distemper will never rid her of it, no matter what that quack doctor says." And the lady peered at each man in turn, seeking for a face beneath the shadow of a hat. But the two were already stepping back, moving away from the two women. Then, Glossolalia said, "Indeed, get you gone, sirs. Her father and brothers come up close behind me, and will want to know your names." And as if on cue, high notes of laughter floated across the garden—the distant sound of merriment. Hearing the sound, the men turned tail and began to make off in the opposite direction, and a moment later, only the fall of stones on the pathway told where they had gone.

"Quick," said Glossolalia to the young woman, "we must rejoin the crowd at the grove. My plan was embroidered according to an improvised design. Those villains may return when they have had a moment to consider the looseness of my stitching." Glossolalia did not know if the girl would take in her words, but the latter rose sluggishly. Standing, the young woman was tall, her person more neo-classical than rococo. One smallpox scar disordered an eyebrow, while another twisted her lip. The plump flesh of her cheeks was pitted with them. She might have carried off her boy-disguise if her nose had been less pert and her round eyes a better match for a queued wig. Her hat was gone, and as Glossolalia could not see one lying on the scuffed gravel, she gave it up for lost. "We go this way," she said, seizing the girl by the arm and pulling her down a path opposite to that taken by the rogues.

The girl said nothing but followed with at least a show of willingness, and by the time they found the first of the illuminating lamps, she no longer tripped and stumbled. Following the light, the women moved along the pathway and in time found themselves returned to the grove at the heart of the garden. They emerged into golden light, rich with sapphire gowns and scarlet coats, and here, where the stone pineapples grew, the girl stopped and begged a moment to catch her breath. Glossolalia took the young person's hand in her own and led her to a bench not far from an oil lamp. There, the girl, dropped down and cried with the silent heaves of a body unused to tears. Glossolalia let her alone. Indeed, that lady found she herself was shaking, despite the warmth of the evening. The elm branch she still clenched tightly in her hand, and now she flung it away, sending it back into the bush with a crash and a quivering of leaves. Then all was still.

By now, the girl was more measured in her distress. She had dried her eyes and begun to put her disordered costume to rights, and by the light of the little oil lamp, Glossolalia could see that the breeches and coat were well cut, although not of a recent style. The wig, still askew on her head, contained a share of elm twigs and lime leaves, but Glossolalia did not do as she wished and put up her hand to set the floured strands to rights. Instead, she sat silently and waited for the other to recover. Her patience received its reward when at last the girl began to speak, thanking Glossolalia warmly and apologizing at some length.

Glossolalia held up a hand. "Please," she said. "Consider I was myself alone upon the path. And I have not youth as an excuse."

"Still," said the young woman, "I remain sensible of your bravery."

"Ah," said Glossolalia. "Bravery." And then she considered what else she might add, but found herself without any sentiments whatsoever on that topic. At last she said, "A boy's disguise is one of the pleasantest I know. The costume affords us women a taste of freedom we might not experience by other means."

The young woman rubbed her eyes. "Is that then how I look? A girl at a masquerade?"

Glossolalia said nothing.

"I had hoped to conceal, not flaunt my sex."

Glossolalia said, "That is not so easily done. You make a very pretty Rosalind, although tonight we have both seen how Vaux-Hall is no forest of Arden, my dear, for all its charm."

Considering Glossolalia's words, the girl said, "I should have disguised myself as a clergyman, for a clergyman's cassock is like to a petticoat and licenses him to betray a little femininity without censure. If I had dressed as a clergyman those brutes on the Dark Walk must have been obliged to treat me with as much decorum as if I had been a woman. Although, now I think on matters, I *am* a woman, and they treated me with very little decorum at all." The girl paused, thinking on the problem, concluding only with a shake of her head. Then she said, "Either way, I could not lay hands upon a cassock. We have no clergyman in my family—although my sister thinks our brother William might make one in time."

"The breeches are his then?"

"The breeches belong to Charles, but he is gone to sea, and so I borrowed them. The coat is also one of his."

"And the wig? Did he not take his wig to sea?"

The girl chewed at her lip. "The wig is my father's." She now removed this object, revealing a smooth coil of brown hair tightly wound into a knot on her head. She held the wig on her lap and picked leaves from its white bristles. "My father has a very large head," the girl said at last. "The wig is not a good fit. I hoped, perhaps, my hair might hold it in place, but it slipped repeatedly. I have been ridiculous." She seemed like she might cry again.

"Oh, my dear," said Glossolalia, feeling for her handkerchief. "We are all ridiculous. We all have tales we might tell against ourselves."

"Tales," said the young woman. "Well, I have a pretty one now."

"You are safe," said Glossolalia, "and now that you are somewhat recovered, we must add the *finis* to the tale. Doubtless, your brothers and father circulate about the gardens, worried about your well-being. Shall we find them and return you home?"

At this the girl wiped her nose with her ruffled sleeve, although she still held Glossolalia's handkerchief in her free hand. "Perhaps," she said, "I might join your party?"

"My party," said Glossolalia, and she began to laugh.

In the end, they agreed to walk together to the boats at the Vaux-Hall dock, hoping to pass as mother and son, or aunt and nephew. Then Glossolalia did take the wig, and placing it on the other woman's head, arranged matters so that the smooth, brown hair was covered better than before.

Glossolalia said, "If we are to be travelling companions, what shall I call you?"

"Sarah Robinson," said the girl, and then appeared to regret her honesty.

"Perhaps I should give you a boy's name, since you are still in disguise. William?" said Glossolalia, "Charles?"

"Morris is my favourite brother."

"Morris, then," said Glossolalia.

They rose, and Morris took Glossolalia's elbow. As they took the wide boulevard that led out of the garden, Glossolalia turned to her companion and said, "I know the end of this tale, but I wonder if an account of its beginning would divert us both on our return journey, which otherwise must be long and filled with awkward silence?"

"Certainly," said Morris, "I owe you that much. I shall start with my birth."

"That far back?"

"We have a considerable distance to travel."

Glossolalia assented, and so Morris began: "I was born the younger of two sisters in a family of brothers. My father and mother, desiring to send none of us away to school, had all of us instructed at home and by the same competent tutors. My sister and I thrived on this regime, and we proved as quick as my brothers. More than any other branch of knowledge, our family excelled in rhetoric and argumentation, and across the dining table, it was our pleasure to debate the issues of the day: the necessity of the Witchcraft Act, the efficacy of the Gin Act, and, of course, the wisdom of the Licensing Act. My father used to jest that he had spawned nothing but parliamentarians, and he encouraged his daughters to hold forth as vigorously as any of his sons. We called my mother "The Speaker," and she moderated our discourses lest we grow too hot and lose our tempers. In such a household, I grew up happy and content with everything and everybody.

Alas that time did not stop and freeze me in place, but seasons and people shift and change. My sister, whom I loved better than I loved myself, grew weary of our pea-pod closeness. She shook off husk and tendril, and let a friend carry her into glittering society. Without her, I grew fervid. Before long, I erupted all over with marks, red and painful, and my lips burned with lesions. They gave me water to drink, said prayers, covered the mirrors in all the rooms, and when my sister returned to me, they would not let her into the house. She was young and still lovely to look at, while I had scabs on my face, my trunk, my limbs, and always beneath my fingernails when I scratched. My sister wrote to me of the lilies of the field, and how I might yet be glad to toil or spin. She would flower while I became as useful as an apple with pitted cheeks. I crumpled her letter. I expected never again to be happy.

Alone, I took walks over frozen stubble-fields, but my sister's letters did not stop. She met and married a man who made gold out of friable black rock. He put diamonds around her neck, which pleased her. He gave her houses with stairs and beds and curtains and cooks and chairs and bedpans. He gave her a park in the country and a coach in town. She leased half her heart to him but preserved the rest for her own purposes, and he was content with the exchange.

My brothers one by one went to Cambridge or to sea; my father read the broadsheets from London; my mother prepared to die. I watched the sun rise over the oak at the edge of the lawn and set behind the outbuildings where we kept the chickens. In summer, the arc resembled a slice of peach, but in winter, it shrank to a shivering bite.

At home, my mother rallied, then complained of the stone, then rallied again. She obtained a squirrel she liked to call her "pretty fellow" and her "little love." When the French offered to invade, she refused to decamp and so secured the crown for King George. Again, she took to her bed, and this time she died. No sooner was she buried than my father packed up his papers and moved to London. He said living in the country was like sleeping with open eyes.

I did not know what I should do. The house was my mother's and my eldest brother Matthew her heir. He loved politicking and pamphleteering—his work both brilliant and strange. His beard he kept at a Biblical length, and he bathed only in the sea—our house was a three-hour walk from that body of water. He did not tell me I must leave, but I wrote my sister almost at once. *Come*, she wrote back. *Bring all your things.*

In Berkshire, where my sister settled, I had a bed and a place to leave my gowns, but I did not have a home. My sister sparkled in her setting, but without letters between us, I did not know how to say to her what I needed to say. Without my pen, I was dumb and dull—what a disappointment I was to the both of us. Before long, my father wrote me and said, *Come—leave your things with your sister.* And even though I knew I should not, I went to him in Tunbridge.

D. M. Bryan

As soon as I arrived, he left me for the races at Canterbury, and I found I must serve as my own chaperone. He did not understand the proprieties that whispered in my ear. I hid indoors, drawing the bells of blue Penstemons with a little camera obscura. At length, my father returned and embarrassed me again with his free speech to a merry widow—this one named Nun, which seemed a satirical jest on nature's part. I wrote my sister of my father's wit, of which I'd had my fill. But when he returned to London, it was he who refused my company and not the reverse. I asked him where I should go, but he only stared back at me.

"Chin up," said my father and pulled tight the strap on my portmanteau.

This time, when the proprieties breathed coolly in my ear I would not listen. I wrote a letter to my sister, telling her I was to go to Chilston to stay with cousin Callie. Then, I took myself to London. Young and unaccompanied, my sex made me conspicuous in the coach, and upon arrival I was cheated by two hard men for a harder seat in a sedan chair. My sister had a new townhouse on Hill Street, empty save for the painters and plasterers, but the house was ready enough for me. Past the decorator at the door, I breezed, asking how the wainscoting did— the man knew me. Up two flights of stairs I went, and into one of the bedrooms at the back. It contained a new sofa protected by a length of linen cloth. There, I sat and wondered what I should do next.

I looked about me. Stacked in the corner was a bed frame, and between the windows sat a pier table with a workman's clay pipe sitting cold upon it. Near the door, a crate held clothes belonging to my younger brother, Charles, who had gone to sea, and to William and Jack whom my sister sent to school. Under a pair of folded breeches, lay the wig I now wear upon my head, although I do not know how it came to join the rest, for as I have said before, it is my father's. For a long time, I sat on the sofa with this wig in my lap and wondered at families: how they are composed and to what purpose. In time, the clattering of workmen died away, and when the uncovered windows went dark, I knew they were gone home to the scent of gammon and onions. I realized how easily I had strayed beyond anyone's particular care—but why should that condition have surprised me."

Glossolalia stopped Morris there, putting her hand out to signal silence. Already, they had followed the dusty road that returned the nymphs and shepherds of Vaux-Hall back to the river-crossing. "Am I to understand that you intend to return to an empty, half-furnished house," said Glossolalia, "and that you have no one waiting to receive you in warmth and safety?"

"I cannot return even to my sister's house, for when the workmen left, they set keyed locks, proof against both entrances and exits."

"Then how did you escape?"

The two began to walk down to the Vaux-Hall stairs where the watermen plied their trade. Morris said, "When I finally heard what the wig had to tell me, I went, like a fool, out a window casement. I wore Charles' breeches and stockings, William's coat, and Jack's shirt. As for my stays and hoops, I stuffed those under the linen sofa cover."

"Do you then intend to return through the window?"

Morris shook the wig. "It is too far over my head."

Glossolalia had no response to this. She was haggling with a waterman in his skiff. They soon came to terms, and Glossolalia stood expectantly until Morris remembered to hand her into the little craft.

On the way back to London, the river's current was with them and made the man's work easy, so he lit a pipe and smoked as he plied his oars. Morris and Glossolalia sat in the stern and looked out over the waters. Morris looked behind at the faint flickers of Vaux-Hall, while Glossolalia looked ahead at London, heaped like a smoldering mound of bone.

Once they were well away on the water, and some distance from any other boat, Morris turned away from a scrutiny of the vanishing gardens and said, "I jumped from the window because I heard voices in the street and feared discovery. I imagined if I were taken as a burglar, I might be clapped in Newgate and hung as a thief. I thought the judge would suppose I had broken a lock to gain entry, and I knew what that meant in law. When first I put on boy's clothes, I feared I might not be convincing, but as I straddled that window casement and contemplated discovery—well, then I feared the opposite. That thought made me jump and kept me company in my mad rush down St. James, toward the

Whitehall Stairs. My actions were not an intention—they were the very opposite."

And now Morris removed the wig and sat bare-headed in the river breeze, which picked up the loose strands of long brown hair and showed them to the stars. Glossolalia glanced at the boatman, but the same breeze made contented flags of the smoke from his pipe as he puffed. He pulled on his oars, keeping the stem of his pipe between his teeth and his gaze fixed on the horizon.

"I am not so stupid," said Morris, "as to confuse romance with life. I know I am not a boy and that any careful inspection of my costume would confirm my imposture. But I have seven brothers, and I hoped I might successfully play one, as if on stage. I have been to the theatre and have seen it done."

"Rosalind again," said Glossolalia.

"My assailants did not appear to know the play," said Morris. "They did not court but followed me until I grew afraid. Then I could no longer control my manner of walking, and my squeaking way of speaking would have shamed a *castrati*. Poor Rosalind was never so served."

Glossolalia pulled up her cloak to cover her head, for they had neared the middle of the river, and here the breeze sharpened into a wind. The Thames waves also wore white shawls over their glossy faces. "Are you not cold?" Glossolalia asked Morris.

Morris shook her head. "I am angry," she said. "But I must put off anger like I must put off breeches. Neither suits me."

Glossolalia looked out over the water, watching the churn of the currents. At last she said, "I once heard tell of a woman who commanded an attack in Trepassi Harbour—a Bristol Galley boarded and taken. The lady acted coolly, taking not a single life, so that no one could say of her what they said of the pyrate Roberts: that he grew to love mischief for its own sake."

"And what is the moral?"

"No moral. She did it for silver teapots and some fine creamware tureens, shaped like melons."

"When I was attacked in the garden," said Morris, "I should have swung my feet and hit with my fists, but propriety told me I was still in petticoats. Propriety asked me what I was doing there so far from my father and brothers—why had I gone where I had no right to go?"

"It wasn't your fault," said Glossolalia.

"Wasn't it?" said Morris, pulling at her shirt collar. "I hate these clothes." She threw the wig into the river Thames, where it floated like a slick of paint. In a moment or two, a wave tossed it on its side, and the wig slipped beneath the surface.

"A fine catch in the morning," said Glossolalia, and Morris began to laugh.

"I want," said the girl, "but one firm friend, who will stand at my side in all things."

"You have a sister."

"And yet I want another."

"I want," said Glossolalia, "to recover what I have lost."

"And what is that?"

Glossolalia frowned. "The subject of another tale," she said. "But I believe I can serve as your friend, at least for a little while longer. As soon as we land, I will take you in a coach to your sister's house to recover your own costume. There must be some caretaker who will open the door to us."

"Very likely," said Morris. "But I cannot present myself at Hill Street dressed as I am. If any person from her staff should tattle, I would not like to face Elizabeth's questions."

"Like as not, I can help with that," said the boatman. His voice startled them both, for they'd forgotten him completely. He'd taken his pipe from his mouth and held his oars dripping above the waves. For the first time, Glossolalia and Morris really looked at the man. He was a fellow of middle years, dressed in his own hair, the loose shirt, and kerchief of his kind. Now, he relit his pipe and spoke through teeth clenched around the stem. "My wife is by trade a laundress, and she serves many fine folk. She can certainly provide the loan of suitable garments, so long as you ensure their careful usage and prompt return. Many times, she's done the same for others when they need to dress as fits their station but haven't the means. She's a kind soul, my wife."

Glossolalia and Morris took little urging to fall in with this plan, for it was a good one, and they soon reached the city side of the river.

D. M. Bryan

The minute they disembarked at the stair, the boatman tied up his craft and whistled for his son. The boy, a child of no more than eight, appeared with a torch in his hand, prepared to lead the way through the dark streets. If the child was surprised to see his father accompanied by two ladies—one dressed as a wigless gentleman—he gave no sign, and walked with his parent's hand in his until the party reached the low front door of a Thames-side cottage.

Inside, Glossolalia found firelight illuminating a small parlour, with smoke-darkened beams and whitewashed walls. A worn sideboard held stoneware plates and bowls, and over the mantle stood the ceramic figure of Mr. Nobody, his head joined directly to his legs. At the back of the room, a flight of stairs led upwards, most certainly to a pair of low-ceilinged rooms. Beside the stairs, a door opened onto a small shanty, built onto the back of the dwelling. This held the rounded pots of a laundress' trade and rack upon rack of drying cloth, and the whole cottage smelled equally of Thames water and of soap.

Glossolalia could see Morris looking about her with interest. Had she ever been in a house as low as this one?

Now, the waterman's wife came forward. She was not the stout, coarse person Glossolalia expected but a very pretty soul of five and thirty who showed herself at once capable of both discretion and efficiency. Betty, for so she was named, made a neat curtsy to her unexpected guests, evidencing no surprise at Morris' costume. She only set about sharing out the warm broth intended for her husband. Glossolalia protested at this diminishment of the man's supper, but both Betty and her waterman refused to hear. "It's cold out on that water this time of year," said Betty, "and anyone who comes off it needs something to warm the bones."

Glossolalia, noticing how weary Morris looked, acquiesced, and soon Betty had seated the two women in chairs before the hearth.

When the boatman explained to his wife what was needed, she disappeared into the room behind the stairs. When she emerged, she had the necessary garments draped over her arm: a linen shift, a hooped petticoat, boned stays, a pale silk skirt, a gown of brown satin, a lace apron, a tucker, and ruffles for the sleeves. Betty set her load down on the table and went back to her laundry. When she returned, she held in one hand a cap to cover Morris' hair and in the other a straw hat trimmed with cloth roses. She said, "These things belong to a young lady about your size, who won't call for them this week and maybe not the next one either. She's a mercer's daughter and is never short of something to wear."

"Thank you," said Morris, speaking very softly.

"Your thanks are very welcome," said Betty.

Glossolalia took her purse from her pocket, and Morris already had some coins in her hand, but Betty would take neither. Then Morris was sent upstairs with her arms full of clothes, having refused all offers of help. "I have unfrocked myself," said Morris, "and now I must do penance." Dressing did not take her long however, and when she came down the stairs, Glossolalia smiled to see how little the gown and tucker altered Morris.

The girl joined them all by the fire, but now the assembled company recognized they had arrived at a difficulty, for the evening had advanced very far, and it was grown too late to rouse the caretaker at sister Elizabeth's Hill street house.

"Nay," said the waterman, who was enjoying the rest of the soup, "We must all stay put until morning."

"But we cannot put you to so much trouble," said Glossolalia, who knew that small cottage held few rooms and fewer beds. Besides, the size of Betty's family, which included her husband and son, now swelled to include a girl of about twelve and a baby in a Moses basket, who needed nursing.

The waterman relit his pipe, using a straw held to the flame. Leaning back, he looked proudly at his wife. "Happens," said he, "my Betty can spin a tale to while away a handful of hours on a cold evening."

Again, Glossolalia protested at the trouble caused, and again her objections were waved away. Indeed, the boy and the girl quite begged their mother for a story, and Glossolalia saw at once that this was a settled way of life with them—the fireside, the ring of faces, the familiar tale.

"Give us the one about pale man, Mama," said the girl.

"Yes, do—give us that one," echoed her brother.

D. M. Bryan

"Will that not be too frightening for you?" said his mother, settling the baby on one breast. "Last time I told it, you would not sleep in your cot for a week, but bothered your father and me, and woke the baby."

"I did not," said the boy, glancing quickly at the visitors.

"Tell it," said the girl. "It is your best."

"My best?"

"Well, I like it best," said the girl, lifting her chin.

"Very well, said her mother, "I will tell you all about the pale man. My tale begins with a house, ramshackle and ill-kept. It stood in an alley that was made like an eel, with a cloaca at one end and a mouth at the other. The teeth, I had met already in the form of the mistress of that house, who bit me hard in that part I call my conscience. I had just bid that cruel person farewell—although in truth I did not know if she *should* fare well, and certainly, she did not expect to do so—when I found myself in the front hall, which smelled of liquor and rising damp. Distantly, I could hear voices, raucous laughter reminding me of what I was—an unaccompanied young woman. I was overdue for heading home, but, as I turned to leave that gothic pile, I heard a great creak and saw I could proceed no further.

In the very floorboards before me, a crack appeared, gaping wide. In another instant, a trapdoor opened, and someone was rising to block my way. The figure that stood there looked more shadow than man, dressed head-to-toe in an ink-coloured coat, with a hat that brimmed his face. He stood in my way, like an unpleasant thought. His hands vanished in the ruffles of the coat that overhung them, but he held up an arm and the motion of the cloth urged me down the stairs that now opened in the floor between us.

"I'm not going down there," said I. And then: "Out of my way."

At the sound of my voice, the figure lifted his head. In the poor light of the hallway, I saw a face of stretched linen, with eyes like holes. At first, it seemed to have no mouth. Then, one opened, small as a plughole in a basin, and the voice was only a man's.

"You do not need to be afraid of me," he said.

"I am not afraid," I lied, "but I am expected at home and already late."

"Mistress," said the pale man, "descend with me." And my dears, it was not a question.

Said I, "It would be no end of foolish to climb down into the cellar with a gentleman I do not know. I am no actress or orange-seller, but rather a laundress, and that is a name that means what it says. If you give me your ruffles, sir, I will wash and starch them for you, neat as you please, but I will not step down those stairs with you—not for one hundred golden guineas."

"Your help," he told me, "is needed below," and that gave me pause. You see, I had already tried to help once in that house and had been repulsed, denied the satisfying view of myself as a benefactress. Beneath my cloak, I carried a copy of Mr. Hogarth's *Harlot*, and that work was a powerful spur to my conscience. I did not trust the man who blocked my way, but I had seen the character of that house and well believed it might contain a soul in distress.

"Who lies below?" said I. "What can I do?"

"You are good," said the pale man. Indeed, he almost moaned. "You are all goodness."

I was not. But I wished to be. And in the end, it was that desire that proved irresistible. Chiding myself for a lack of courage, I made my decision. I descended those stairs, and my companion followed, blotting out all light from above.

At the bottom, I found a layer of dampness seeping through the leather soles of my shoes. "How wet it is," I said.

"You must go forward," he urged me, and afraid of him in the dark, I went on.

I moved along a passage a foot or two but stopped when no light or doorway appeared. A feathery touch between my shoulders made me continue, but a step later, the floor dropped, and water lapped my shoes. "I can go no further," said I.

But the pale man had an explanation. "The Fleet runs beneath us. At this time of year, the hallway floods. Take but another step or two, and all will be well."

I walked on and found only more water. My long skirts sucked at the wetness. My cloak soaked up its share of river water, adding to my discomfort.

"I will go back," I said, my voice a panicked, flapping thing.

"A little further. They lie below."

D. M. Bryan

"Who?" said I. "I can do no good down here. Let me go up again."
All the dim mustiness of the hallway over my head now seemed to me
the brightest summer's day.

Glossolalia, who had been watching Morris carefully, now
interrupted Betty. The girl, in her borrowed dress, looked cold although
the fire burned brightly and the room grew overwarm. No doubt the
effects of her experience with the Vaux-Hall villains plagued her still.

"I fear, said Glossolalia, "that the tale is too frightening for one of
my mature years—perhaps we must find another."

"Oh no," said Betty's little son. "The story is at its worst now—you
will suffer more if you don't hear it out."

"Please," Morris said, "I should like to know the rest."

"If the company wishes to continue, Mrs. Betty," said Glossolalia,
"I shall not stand in our way. But might I beg the further loan of a shawl
for my young friend? She shivers a little in her borrowed finery."

"Allow me," cried Betty's daughter, jumping up and returning with a
woollen mantle, which Morris accepted gratefully.

Then Betty continued. "Every time the pale figure spoke in the
dark, his voice teased me with its ordinariness—a man might be
standing there, and then the nature of my peril would be clear.

The pale man said, "The darkness frightens you?"

"Is there not a lamp or candle you might light? If I could but see
where I am."

"You should not mind so much," he said, and glancing behind me, I
could just perceive his outline, a pale seam stitched in shadow. "We are
born of darkness and wet." And again, I felt something soft and damp
pushing me forward.

I moved away from his touch, finding only deeper water in my way.
Then, I reached out and felt the walls around me. When I encountered
wet, splintering wood, I knew I stood on the threshold of some room. As
soon as I entered, a current caught at my skirts, dragging me sideways,
and I took small, staggering steps, like a drunken duchess. Then, the
floor dropped again, and this time the water reached my knees.

I cried aloud and tried to go back, but I could hardly move my legs,
the burden of my skirts deadweight against the current. The Fleet that
ran beneath that house had risen high enough to reach the cellar, and

now I foundered in its hold. The more I struggled, the deeper I went, until I felt the water about my thighs.

Then, I stopped struggling and tried to see where I was. A kind of blue-black light rose up from the water, and I could observe a pelt-like sheen upon the surface, as if muscles roiled and coiled beneath. Above, rose the four walls, of which excavated recesses filled three sides. In some of the bays I saw wrapped shapes—tapered bundles of linen and silk, some long, some tiny. I suspected what these were, for the woman upstairs had no churchyard for her burials. The fourth wall contained only the brick arch of a sewer, wide and tall as a man. The current moved toward that low opening, and indigo light trickled from it.

"This place has many uses," said the voice, coming from the passage door. "The Fleet has always been a baptismal font," he said. I heard him and shivered. I could only just feel my feet, unsteady on the gritty floor.

"You've tricked me—there is no one here I can help," said I, unwilling to look again at those bundles. Fingers of cold pierced each layer of my own costume, so that I was chilled to my neck. If anyone had been baptized in this place, it was a deadly sacrament.

"Only yourself," said the other, his voice now low to the water. I imagined him, snakelike, coming closer.

"Help me," I said. "Help me or be damned, for I will escape you in death."

"Nay," said the voice, very near my elbow. "I tell you that you will live. No murder in this house."

"You forget—I know who is mistress here." I thought of the woman upstairs and her peculiar carelessness in everything.

"Nature is mistress here," said the pale man, "And it is to me she gives the harlots' children. I take an arm—a bone in my grasp—settle the child on its back, and tug it into the current."

"And then?" said I.

"I let it go."

I stood with my head bowed and my jaw convulsed. I waited for the pale man to seize me and pull me below those nightmare waters, but his sucking touch never came. I listened for his voice, but I heard nothing save the lapping of waves on stone walls. I asked him why he did not complete what he had begun, but my own words echoed on water.

D. M. Bryan

My apron floated, seafoam lace. I could no longer control my shaking, and now the water began to embrace me. Soon, I could no more distinguish water from cold than cold from comfort. I began to sink into the numbness of the liquid in which I was trapped, my clothes billowing around me. I had no hope to swim, but neither could I remain to die of cold. When the water reached my neck, the weight of my sodden costume lifted from my shoulders, and I rolled on my back and felt the current take hold. I was drifting toward the brick arch. A shimmering spot of light led the way, like an underwater moon. Bone scraped and cut my stockings, and my head went under the water. My breath exploded into silver bubbles, as other shapes swirled around me, dark against the pale water. The river was very deep now, and as I sank, the Fleet filled with silk ruffles, with petticoats, with linen shifts. With gowns. With swimming arms. With heads and hair.

Freed from my cloak, Mr. Hogarth's print floated away. I felt the *Harlot* leave me. Then, I felt no more.

My dears, I cannot pretend I died in that place, for here I sit, alive and well. They pulled me out where the Fleet crosses under Chick Lane. There is a bridge there, and a woman washing her garments in that foul water saw me floating with my face upwards towards sun and air. She waded in to grab me by my hair and pull me ashore. A crowd gathered, and a sailor stepped forward who knew how to push the water out and the sense back in. When I sputtered and spat, sitting up at last, a pug-dog jumped up and licked at my face, welcoming me back to the daylight.

"You are quite the biggest fish, we have pulled on to shore," said the washerwoman, when she saw I was alive.

My throat ached, and I was still retching water, but I somehow asked her if she meant there were others.

"Indeed, there are. My son Moses is one, and he is such a good boy—a gift straight from heaven."

I spat out more water in my surprise. "Surely heaven didn't sink him in the Fleet?"

"Oh hush," said the washerwoman, "He's no whore's whelp—if that's what you mean." And with that, she turned her back, leaving me lying on the cold bank.

I walked home, my lungs aching and my clothing such a mess that my mistress herself could not put it to rights. She nursed me with all the skill she had, but when I finally revealed to her that I could no longer bear the thought of water, she took me, on a blue-sky day, to the shores of the Thames. There she set me into the care of a waterman, whom she knew to be a good man, and if his gentle nature did not reconcile me to water after our first voyage upon the waves, it softened my disappointment in having to undertake a second."

"And that is our father," explained the boy, beaming at Glossolalia. "So the story has a happy ending."

"Indeed," said that lady.

"And look," said Betty's girl, who had again jumped to her feet, "here is the *Harlot* our father gave our mother to replace the one she lost in the river." And the girl held out a large package of waterproofed cloth, which she set on Morris' lap.

When Morris opened the flaps, she found a set of Mr. Hogarth's much-admired pictures. These she leafed through with many expressions of admiration, for the prints were very good and must have cost the waterman many a cold Thames crossing. Returning to one of the prints, Morris said, "I cannot approve the danger you took in your adventure, but I understand how Mr. Hogarth's illustrations moved you to charitable action. They also remind me to be more generous, for recent experience teaches me it is easier to fall than I knew."

Betty passed her sleeping infant to his father and got up to better see the print Morris indicated. It was the one in which the still-innocent Harlot arrives in London and none are there to save her from ruin. Betty nodded, but said nothing, only kissing her finger and letting it hover over a small figure at the back of the print. If Morris noticed the curious gesture she made no comment but passed the package to Glossolalia, so that she too might enjoy the waterman's gift.

For her part, Glossolalia lingered over the print in which the Harlot's son sits alone beneath his mother's coffin. "This picture holds a message for me also," she said. "I could do more to assist others. I have dwelt too long on my own sorrows." And then she smiled, for she had made a resolution in her own heart.

"Thank you for entertaining us so well with your tale," said Morris, "and as for Mr. Hogarth, why he must be the finest artist in all the world. I should like to meet him one day."

Mrs. Betty's family took great pleasure in seeing their guests so entertained by the very things that brought them so much joy. As for Glossolalia and Morris, their taste for adventure, slaked by experience and by Mrs. Betty's tale, left them content to end their own in the parlour of that happy house—at least, until curiosity pricked them again.

CHAPTER 11

Curiosity now prompted us to walk on; the nearer we
came to the house, the greater we found the profusion
of flowers which ornamented every field.

Sarah Scott's *A Description of Millenium Hall.*

Bath, 1762.

From the back bedroom of Edgar's Buildings on Bath's George Street,
Sarah can see how the whole of her new garden fits into a single pane
of window glass. She has lied by the most recent post, telling brother
William this plot is a hundred feet long. She told him the area is not so
large as to entail expense but big enough to bring her pleasure. Now,
looking down from above, she knows the opposite is true. Enriched
town soil is expensive, producing only sad roses, haunted by weedy
convolvulus. One day, perhaps, she will learn to love this patch of soil,
but at present the length of red-brown clay leaves her as dissatisfied
as the other aspects of her life in Bath. Every day, their new home
uncrates itself around Lady Barbara and herself, items appearing as
needed—a chair to drop into, a bed for sinking down upon. A cup
for tea, the saucer sliding into place, just in time for the clink. Even
so, each object arrives precisely placed and subtly wrong, as if drawn
from the wrong angle. And then there is this garden. Through the
window, Sarah takes one more look at the meagre, townish stretch of

clay that is hers to tend. How she misses the man More, who digs and plants and spreads the cow shit for brother William now.

In her pocket she has a letter from Mr. Newbery, who is publishing the novel she wrote in hope of saving Batheaston—too late now. Any money earned must pay for the expenses incurred in the move. Mr. Newbery writes to say the process of printing *Millenium Hall* is well underway, and the book will be ready soon. He expects the work to be well received and has prepared it for the public with diligence. The finished volume, he tells her, will contain a fine frontispiece, and he has sent her a proof of the print. Two gentlemen stand in graceful attitudes along an avenue of oaks. In the distance, stands that honest and entirely imaginary edifice, Millenium Hall. Sarah will approve his choice of frontispiece—Mr. Newbery is certain of that.

Sarah wonders what right John Newbery, for all his goodness, has to be so sure of her opinion. In fact, he has a knack for misinterpreting her sentiments. The very words she commits to ink seem to slide about on the page while in the post-carriage to London. By the time Mr. Newbery opens her letters they have achieved a new form. He challenges her prefaces and her conceits, remarking they are too delicate for a reading public. He says *delicate*, but he means *obscure*—Sarah knows this. Lady Barbara's view is that Mr. Newberry knows his business as well as any man alive. Mr. Newbery, says Lady Barbara, is all kindness and strategy.

Sarah, who would rather *Millenium Hall* not sell at all than have it sell through stratagem, says only: "My dear, we two speak of nothing but Mr. John Newbery or the doctor. As we are resourceful women, do you not think we can light upon some other topic than the opinions of men, no matter how well founded?" And what did she and Barbara speak of next? Sarah cannot remember. Brother William most likely. Or the excessive speed of Mrs. Rigg's coachman.

The move to Bath has vastly improved Lady Barbara's health. The doctor still comes, bringing with him his clysters and his purgatives, his bleeding cups and his bottled tinctures, but his conversation is jovial, general—he takes tea with them both. Sarah Scott writes letters to sister Elizabeth, describing the improvements in her friend's health. She shapes the words in shining ink, and they dry into truth.

She writes, *Lady Barbara now sits with the window open. Across George Street, new buildings go up, and she follows each erection with careful attention. She rallies—she recovers. Believe me Ever most affectl[y] Y[rs]. Your most affectionate Sister and Obedient Serv[t]. Every Y[rs.] S.S.*

The import of her own words is clear enough to Sarah: if she is to go to London to see Mr. Hogarth, the time is now, and her most recent letter to her sister communicates her desire to visit. Elizabeth, who encourages her, replies to say that Hill Street, as always, is at Sarah's disposal. Edward Montagu is at Sandleford Priory, which is his usual habit at this time of year, but she, Elizabeth, will remain in town to greet her sister. As for Sarah's intention to hire a post-chaise or, heavens above, go by public conveyance, she must promise that she will undertake to do neither. One of Edward's agents is to be carried from Bristol to London on some matter of business, and if Sarah does not mind the man's company, he has agreed to break his journey in Bath so that she might have the convenience of the Montagu coach.

And so, Sarah will at last make her trip London. She will carry the leather portmanteau containing her drawings and little else, for she keeps a gown and other necessaries at Hill Street. And if the age of the garment means she will not be of the latest fashion, she doubts the few visits she intends to pay will demand anything *a la mode*. As for Montagu's man—a former Turkey merchant by Elizabeth's account—Sarah is not opposed to a fabulous tale or two to accompany the rolling changes beyond the coach window. She hopes he might amuse her with stories of Adrianople and the court of the Sultan. Such a romantic locale, dignified by proximity to Homer and Virgil, must hold at least one or two anecdotes suitable for her ears.

Perhaps she will find some inspiration there. Recently, her pen holds her close to home—Vauxhall, Clerkenwell. Her tales nestle like Chinese boxes, but each grows smaller and more noisesome than the one before, and Sarah would rather sink her fingers knuckle deep in good loam.

Through the back window of Edgar's Buildings, Sarah casts one last disgusted look at the sterile plot that is now hers. Then, she leaves the bedroom and goes into the front parlour, where she finds Lady Barbara, keeping her vigil at the window. On the polished table lie

Sarah's pens, her inks, her little knife for trimming each nib. A brass candlestick with a tallow candle, neatly snuffed and trimmed. A pile of books. Pages in Sarah's own handwriting.

Sarah crosses to the table, and at her approach, Lady Barbara looks up. She presses her fingers together and says, "I am tired of the street, and I hate to be idle—will you read to me?"

Sarah is glad of the suggestion, taking her seat at the table with no small measure of relief. She and Barbara have not been so companionable as late—Barbara's illness and their removal from Batheaston have interrupted all comfortable routines. The doctor forbids Barbara to sew, lest it tire her head, and the new girl makes a stingy fire and is late with their meals. Sarah misses Meg but does not say so. Neither does she speak of the garden, and Barbara has not mentioned the trip to London. It is as if they have decided all this between them—but they have not.

"What were we reading last?" says Sarah, a little shocked that she cannot remember.

Barbara says, "I would like to hear something new – perhaps from the manuscript you have been working on?"

"Certainly," says Sarah, taking her eyeglasses from her pocket. Barbara knows every page of *Millenium Hall*, having reviewed each word. On occasion, she has had to put its own author straight on some event of forgotten significance. Sarah rifles the pile before her and finds the pages she is looking for—if Barbara wishes something new from her pen, she shall have it. Adjusting her eyeglasses on her nose, Sarah reads: "Do you know the horse-ferry that runs between Lambeth and Westminster?"

"A horse-ferry?" says Barbara, immediately. "Is that not a rather low subject for your pen?"

"Mr. Newbery tells me Mr. Oliver Goldsmith has written a sentimental novel that combines both the high and the low, and that it is a work of genius—Mr. Newbery's nephew intends to bring it out very soon."

"Mr. Newbery says this of Mr. Goldsmith? I must confess, I am a little surprised."

"Nevertheless, he has given me an idea for a satire on a romance of my own—Mr. Goldsmith, that is. Not Mr. Newbery."

"A satire?" says Barbara. "Surely you are mistaken."

"I do not know how I might be mistaken about the product of my own pen. You must give me fair hearing," says Sarah, rattling her pages.

Barbara inclines her head, indicating that Sarah might resume.

"Do you know the horse-ferry—"

"Yes yes," says Barbara, turning toward the window.

Sarah skips ahead. "Then know this," she reads, "The person who runs it is a kind of pyrate queen, ropey-faced and tidal as the river. I once heard of a couple who wished to cross the Thames from Southwark to London. How they found themselves in Lambeth without proper conveyance is nobody's business but their own, but without a boat, the muddy Thames might as well be as wide at the Atlantic. As soon as the couple entered the ferrywoman's ramshackle hut, they made their requirements known. At first, she greeted them in a friendly manner, but as soon as she discovered they had no horse, her warmth receded and left a stony shore behind. "No horse?" she said, opening her eyes as wide as they would go—which was still a kind of smoke-stung squint. "This is a horse-ferry I run here."

"It is no matter, madam," said the gentleman. "Our money is good."

"It's not the health of your coin that concerns me," said the river dame, "but rather how I will tally the accounts. See, there's one price for a man and a horse, and another for a horse and a chaise. That includes the man, you see. And, then, there's a price for a coach and two horses, which includes the driver and all the fine folk that ride inside. Now, you seem like gentlepeople, and no sooner did I clap eyes on you than I told myself you was the coach-and-two-horses kind. But now I hear you have no horses at all."

Sarah looks up, but Barbara only stares out the window, and so she continues: "Alas," said the gentlewoman, "our coach met with a terrible accident and is upturned in the road, one wheel broken. Worse, both horses have run away."

The Ferry-keeper came closer and looked at the lady's face with some care. "No," she said, "that's Vaux-Hall dirt, that is, and a bit of grass is lodged behind your ear. It wasn't the road what tumbled you. I can't be fooled so easily as that."

"Nay," said the gentleman, "you mistake our condition—"

Now Lady Barbara is twisting her fingers in her lap. The motion is a discouraging one, and Sarah stumbles in her reading. She takes a breath and begins again: "Nay," said the gentleman, "you mistake our condition. We met with highwaymen and were robbed of everything but the fee for the ferry. We had to flee for our very lives through field and byre—the grass behind the lady's ear is proof."

"Oh no," said the river-woman, shaking her head, "there's no highwayman this side of the Thames—at least, there is, but I happen to know he's drinking tonight at the King's Head. Him and all his gang."

"Are you in jest?" said the gentlewoman, who had seen Mr. Gay's *The Beggar's Opera* more than once.

Now Lady Barbara sighs, audibly and purposefully. Sarah stops reading.

"Is that the end?" says Barbara. "Are you finished? That seems a very unsatisfying conclusion."

"I am convinced," says Sarah, "that my narrative is not to your taste."

"Not entirely," says Barbara, with admirable evasion. Then, she looks directly at Sarah. "Does your female person have a name? You continually call her 'the lady' or 'the gentlewoman.' Without some particular designation, she seems the merest stick."

"She is called Glossolalia," says Sarah, and then: "No, wait—that is *not* her name."

"Your audience thanks you. Glossolalia—what a mouthful."

Sarah stares at her friend. Barbara's face is pale. Her hair parts severely beneath her lace cap. Her eyes shine as though lit with a taper. She is, Sarah notes, very angry.

"The dialogue seems a satire on travel," says Barbara. "A warning against, perhaps. But, I wonder how it ends. Which is the sign of a clever author, is it not? That we cannot guess the ending."

D. M. Bryan

Sarah folds her pages in two. "I should not have read this aloud," she says. "It is not the comic tale I intended."

"A comic tale?" says Barbara. "It has not had that effect on me."

"Your strength returns," says Sarah. "And I am glad."

And Sarah is glad. She counts too much on Lady Barbara's patient counsel. Barbara cannot always be Sarah's conscience and must sometimes be allowed to be bad-tempered on her own account. Just as Sarah must be allowed to box back.

"I shall need my strength," says Barbara. "I only hope it lasts."

"You cannot alter my decision, dear," says Sarah. "I am quite decided to go."

"Then I must be content," says Barbara, sounding anything but. She turns back to the window, as though to a better friend.

Sarah leans back in her chair and shuts her eyes. The arrangements have been made. Tomorrow, early in the morning, the coach with its Montagu markings will stop in George Street. At that hour, light will enter the Edgar-Row kitchen in ashen flakes. In the road, wagons and other conveyances will pass with a knocking of hooves and a sticking of wheels. With a key of bright iron, she will seal Barbara into the Bath house, with only the half-trained girl for company. An invalid's cruel entombment, but then long partnerships are built on confinement—one heart locked within another. For this, she has given up Batheaston.

No, it is as Barbara says—they must both be content. Nothing will prevent Sarah leaving for London tomorrow, carrying only her leather portmanteau. In the meanwhile, she is not fit company for anyone. Rising, she leaves Lady Barbara in full possession of the parlour.

She and Edward Montagu's Turkey merchant, Sarah Scott considers, might as well be made of different substances. She, plants stalks, bruised, aged into an essence both delicate and subtly spoilt. He, wires, levers, gears. She glances at him in the jolting carriage, trying to take the measure of him and to shame him into looking away. Finding he will allow her to do neither, she turns to stare though the louvered window, taking refuge in the sight of the town. Block after block of terraced row houses, yellowed and chambered as sponges. What was Elizabeth thinking in imagining such a man to be a fitting companion for a long carriage ride?

Almost certainly Montagu himself had suggested the arrangement, thinking more of convenience than of propriety, but Elizabeth had surely agreed, recommending it to Sarah as suitable in every respect. Sarah thinks of the woman her sister has become, with coal dust on her silk shoes, the plans for new colliery outbuildings under her fingers. She walks beside Montagu and his engineers, her wide hem sweeping the dirt.

Now, Sarah holds a folded note, passed from Elizabeth through the conduit of this man across from her. She opens it again and rereads. This time it is more of her sister's business—the particulars of some minor alterations Elizabeth is having made to Sarah's unfashionable Hill Street gowns. Sarah will not, thanks to Elizabeth, be allowed to make a countrified figure after all. The Turkey merchant watches her as she makes much of Elizabeth's few lines. He is well dressed and yet not a gentleman. He is, perhaps, not even entirely English. Thinks Sarah Scott.

What is her evidence for such unchristian speculation? Upon her entry to the carriage he met her eye. He grinned at her. His address was improper … jocular. And avuncular, even though he is very much younger than she. He'd patronized her. "Here you are," he said, pulling her into the carriage, laughing when she collapsed inwards, giving way under pressure like the rotten spot on a marrow. "All right there?" he asked, pulling her from the floor. An unpleasantly forthright concern for her person, and yet she cannot fault his kindness. She cannot rightly think what she faults.

Now, they have ridden for some minutes in silence, carriage-jostled, knee-to-knee like wrestlers taking stock of one another. Their acquaintance suffers an embarrassing adolescence. How to behave, she wonders. How to make the correct address, employing which forms? What tone of voice? Who should begin?

Can he really be a Turkey merchant? He seems too young to have voyaged so far.

Sarah Scott recalls that she is a woman of character, not without resources, equal to all social difficulties, even those without precedent. She unfolds the folded note, and pretends to read something of importance written therein, although Elizabeth has included nothing beyond the disposition of the green silk and the yellow. Sarah concludes this dumbshow and looks up, finally speaking. She says, "I understand my brother Montagu recommends you unreservedly as a person of honour. You are, my sister writes, entrusted with matters of great importance to himself." Also, gifted with the burden of his awkward, ugly sister-in-law, she does not say.

The Turkey merchant bows.

Sarah coughs slightly and regrets the mannerism as fussy. She coughs again. "I am afraid my sister has not chosen to convenience me with your name."

"Mr. Achmet-Beg," says the Turkey merchant, bowing again.

"Indeed," says Sarah, for he is, as she feared, more Turkey than merchant. She can think of nothing that might safely cushion this severest jolt. They sit in silence.

From Bath to London is more than a hundred miles. Beginning, as they have, at the first light, they must travel until the dying rays of the day. At intervals, the horses must be watered, fed, rested, changed. Their own fast must be broken and, later, a midday meal obtained from some suitable public house. Sarah cannot eat from a kerchief like a serving girl. At nightfall, they must trust the driver atop the carriage to choose a reputable inn, with two rooms appropriate to their divergent social positions. In short, two long days and one night lie before them.

Sarah folds her note and transfers it to the intimacy of an inside pocket, even as her companion shifts his gaze outside the window. At last, thinks Sarah.

Mr. Achmet-Beg, she notices, has a leather portmanteau much like her own. Filled with urgent notes in closely spaced, masculine handwriting, she imagines. Strong downward strokes detailing schemes and expansions. Perhaps a diagram or two. A plan, like those she carries with her. Rooms, halls, buildings, paths, roads, trees, gardens. Nay, collieries, sheds, wheels, chimneys, pumps carefully delineated and cross-hatched to appear as real on the page as they would be set against Northumberland's wizened crags. In the margin, she envisions a doodle. A Michaelmas daisy blooming from a heap of slag.

No, Sarah decides. A man of business carries nothing but sums, carefully entered, inked in red and black. Expenditures and income. Profit. Bound books of columns, purpose-printed.

Might Mr. Achmet-Beg explain these mysteries to her? Her printers—Mr. Newbery, like the Dodsleys before him or Mr. Richardson in his time—send her little in the way of figures. She sold Mr. Newbery her *Hall* for a price of thirty guineas that, if reckoned by the number of days she took in the writing of it, seems fair to her. But she knows Mr. Newbery, who spreads much joy beneath the sign of the Bible and Sun, close to the milky dome of St. Paul's, is rumoured to be a rich man as well as a kind one. If her *Hall* should sell well, at the cost of three shillings, Mr. Newbery might expect to see some profit after he has sold—how many copies? Sarah tabulates. Two hundred books? No no, he has other costs as well. Paper, ink. Sarah shakes her head. Calculating in a coach makes her eyes sting.

"Are you quite well, madam," asks Mr. Achmet-Beg, who returns his eyes from the window to Sarah on the padded bench across from him.

"I am well enough, sir," she says, stiffly. Then regrets the coldness of her tone. They have scarcely left the outskirts of Bath, and through the window the rising sun touches olive hills and turns them to butter. They must travel a long way together. "I am a sufferer sometimes of the head-ache," she says, although she is sensible she should not mention such a personal frailty. Her companion is not embarrassed, but a furrow of polite concern appears between his eyes. These are very brown.

They are moving through the countryside, at a pace that is brisk without excessive speed. Mr. Montagu keeps very good horses. Perhaps I should say so, thinks Sarah Scott. Horses are a subject on which a man may discourse knowledgeably but not improperly. Might she not express a polite interest in questions of driving fine horses, of saddlery, of the best way to settle a tanner's bill for a bellows she has

D. M. Bryan

purchased for the Bath house? If she might draw Mr. Achmet-Beg out on such subjects—subjects that must certainly be doubly beloved of him as man and *homme d'affaires*. Then might she not turn the topic to other forms of reckoning? Without mentioning her *Hall* directly, she might learn which costs a printer might account for and where, and in what order?

"Mr. Montagu keeps excellent horses, or so I am told," says Sarah, flushed by her daring, but she knows all the world understands the Turks to be vastly fine horsemen. English lords introduce their Arab stallions to their own brood mares to improve the breed—and Sarah Scott resolves to think no further in this direction.

"Are they good horses?" says her companion, his fingers flexing upon his worsted knee. "I confess myself glad to hear it, for I know little of horses beyond the number of their legs."

"I must express my surprise, Mr. Achmet-Beg, for I imagined your countrymen uniformly expert upon this head."

"My countrymen, madam?"

Sarah sees very genuine confusion in his eyes.

"The Turks, sir, are known to be very fine riders and as much connoisseurs in that way as an Italian knows paintings."

"The Turks?"

"Have I erred, sir? Perhaps I am mistaken? Your surname, Mr. Achmet-Beg, suggests you descend, at least on your father's side, from that excellent people."

"What did you call me? Achmet-Beg?" And Sarah's companion, as though to prove himself as English as a bell-tower, claps out a high, nervous peal of laughter.

"You are not Mr. Achmet-Beg?"

"Lord, no. Gotobed is my name." Enunciating each syllable so that she might not be taken in a second time by the jutting of his vowels, the swallowing of his consonants. Why had she not before noticed London on his breath? The gurgle of the Thames in his throat?

Now Mr. Gotobed cannot stop talking. At first, he celebrates the comedy of her misapprehension, laughing and professing himself delighted to have his name so mistaken. Then, apologizing, lest he make too much of a lady's honest error, he makes himself speak seriously.

Her mistake is most understandable, he tells her, for in London no man's history need be known to any but himself. That city is the whole world's crossroad and a glory, where a man might reinvent himself, if he has the need. He is not, he confesses, a Turkey merchant, but only a pretender to the title of trader. He thought once of going east to trade for cotton, but he got no further than Brest. There he found himself deceived in the soundness of the scheme and came away no richer than before. He was, he told her, no better a judge of ships and captains than he was of horses.

"But my sister was most exact on this point. I was to travel with a Turkey merchant and an agent for Mr. Montagu."

"I am more usually a print-setter, madam."

Sarah says nothing but is glad she did not quiz him on her own business concerns. What if the man had guessed her purpose. Printers, pressmen, and booksellers alike form a cabal. Suppose word passed from tongue to tongue that Sarah Scott suspects herself the victim of sharp-practices by honest Mr. John Newbery—what would the world think of her then?

"Shall I explain myself?" says Mr. Gotobed.

"If you can, sir. I should be most happy. I should not like to think my sister misled."

"Never," says her companion, striking the side of the carriage with his hand. "Oh, I should not wish—" and he breaks off, too confused to continue.

Soon, however, Mr. Gotobed recovers himself sufficiently to ask, "Have you seen, madam, the announcements of the good Dr. James' extraordinary Fever Powder?"

Sarah is more jostled by this change of subject than by the coach, and she wonders if the man might be a little mad. "I have," she says, speaking with care. And she has. From sachets and endpapers, from broadsheets and periodicals, she knows the illustrated advertisement of the tumbled man awaiting his Good Samaritan. She doubts the nostrum has the same power for good as an act of charity, but her skepticism has never prevented her from taking an interest in the printed picture. In Dr. James' advertisement the invalid is gaunt, the

Samaritan but a pinprick on the road, and the frame a distressing mélange of curlicues and French curves.

"I have myself inked and pulled many copies of that ingenious advertisement," says Gotobed, leaning forward. "Dr. James makes a prodigious number of claims, but set in a fine typeface, they appear convincing, even to me, and I know how the trick is done."

"Print has that magical capacity," says Sarah.

"Would it surprise you to learn Dr. James' Fever Powder does not, in strict point of fact, belong to Dr. James, but rather to the man listed only as his agent?"

If Sarah is surprised, it is only to find Mr. Newbery appearing in the conversation despite her inclination to keep him at a distance, for she knows full well, it is he who is listed as Dr. James' representative on every bottle.

"And," says Gotobed, waving a finger in the air, "I know as a fact that the substance the patent so boldly asserts on the page is not the same as that in the sachet. Yes, indeed, and the contents themselves alter materially from purchase to purchase."

The carriage rocks gently from side to side while Sarah considers what she might say. "If that is true, sir, the claims made upon the bottle appear very deficient," she says at last.

"Deficient, madam. Yes, the very word. The medicine, in short, is worthless, and every Doctor knows it. But, for all its deficiency, Dr. James' Fever Powder *can* cure patients—that is, when it does not kill them. Men and women alike return to health, having swallowed the contents of those famous sachets. Given the impotency of the powder, do you not wonder that this should be the case, madam?

Sarah, who has a paper of Dr. James' wonderful powder at home, with which she takes pains to dose Lady Barbara whenever the Doctor's remedies fail, does wonder. She allows her brows to rise quizzically.

Mr. Gotobed hastens to supply her with an answer. "The powders work," he says, "entirely on account of the advertisements that fill the backs of the broadsheets and gazettes that circulate from coffee house to coffee house. The readers have confidence in whatever they read, madam, and belief accomplishes what Dr. James' vile concoction cannot. My point is, good Mrs. Scott, if I might call you that?" He pauses while a reluctant Sarah nods. "The point is this, patient, kind Mrs. Scott. Upon my introduction to your valuable relations, I only wished to represent myself a Turkey merchant in the same way that Dr. James' Fever Powder shows itself a valuable medicament. Do you take my meaning, or am I too obscure?"

"You are not obscure in meaning, sir. Let me see if I understand you. You went before my brother, representing yourself as the very man he hoped to find, and you intended, by dint of his wishing, to become that man."

"You understand me very well, madam. I puffed—I advertised myself as something better than I am, for I can be a printer no longer. I am sick to death of ink and lead. Of damp paper. Of so little in my pocket."

"And so, you are now employed as Mr. Montagu's agent?"

Mr. Gotobed does not appear to comprehend Sarah's question. No, Sarah corrects herself—the man does not seem aware she has even asked a question. He stares at her, all self-satisfaction, head nodding and smile broad as the landscape through which they sweep. Thin bands of sun cross the interior of the coach, and lie like strips on Sarah's lap. She looks again at her companion, at his agreeable dark eyes. The man has lied to Edward and Elizabeth Montagu. Sarah finds she does not mind so much as she might—as much as she should. Surely, she should mind.

"Such misrepresentation is not quite right of you, sir."

"No, I am ashamed of myself."

Then why is the man still grinning?

And somehow, this performance, safe inside the confessional of the coach, makes friends of Mr. Gotobed and Sarah. They travel together cheerfully now, accustomed to the swaying of the coach. The public houses and tollgates of Box, of Chippenham and Calne, occur as a predictable change in rhythm, like the chorus to a song. At Beckhampton, the coach slows first to a banging walk and then to a jiggling halt. Sarah gathers her skirts to her, for they are to eat their midday meal at the Waggon and Horses. She feels, rather than sees, the coachman clambering down, and then, there he is, opening the door and presenting a gloved hand. He sets Sarah down beside

D. M. Bryan

a gabled building of grey fieldstone and greyer thatch. The yard is sprigged with straw and bejewelled with Minorcas, so black they shine like emeralds. Sarah is heartened by the crimson combs and white ear patches. The farmyard reminds her of Batheaston.

Mr. Gotobed stands beside her in the yard. She turns to him. "I should not mind, Mr. Gotobed," she says, "if we women were encouraged to imitate those Minorcan fowl in our dress, for I believe they look very well in their feathers."

Alas, Mr. Gotobed has stepped in the leavings of another coach's horse and cannot answer, for he must occupy himself with scraping the substance from his boot. When he at last dislodges the disobliging mass of half-digested hay, a serving girl appears to lead the two of them into a furnished parlour. Under the smoke-lowered ceiling, by the light of the leaded window, Sarah seats herself at the polished table pleasantly placed before the hearth. She likes this inn very much, from the fresh rushes on the floor, to the cracked Mr. Nobody on the mantle. Some of the plates are pewter and some are earthenware— but all speak to her of the countryside. She turns in pleasure to Mr. Gotobed, who sits beside her.

"It stinks," says that person, before sharply exhaling. "It stinks even inside."

The man, Sarah discovers, has hardly been beyond the fogged skirts of London, and now that he sticks his head from out under those layers, he does not like what he sees. The gammon he orders reeks of sweat, the bread tastes of chaff. He finds fault with the rustic bench on which he settles his thin quarters, and then he condemns the stalks that keep his besmirched foot from the clean flags. The girl, he tells Sarah, cannot be English, so odd is her dialect, and he must repeat each word she speaks as though translating to an invisible foreigner. Only the ale seems to him palatable, and this he consumes without benefit of anything solid until Sarah fears he will come off the rustic bench and settle among the reeds he so despises.

Back in the coach, they ride in silence for many miles, Sarah pressing her face almost into the louvers to admire the changing of the country. The frame of the carriage window converts land into landscape—a succession of vantages and light effects. Hedgerows mark perspective, arriving together at the crucial point between the fall of this hill and the rise of the next. Moisture breaks up distant views into distinct brushwork. Meanwhile, Mr. Gotobed sleeps off the effects of his lunch.

At Marlborough, the coachman halts to rest the horses. Mr. Gotobed wakes and excuses himself. The carriage jostles as the horses spread their legs, and the sound of pissing, equine and human, fills the air. Sarah uses the pot beneath the seat, arranging her skirts and her expression with equal care. When she is done, she opens the door and tips the content into the mud beside the front wheel. The liquid sinks neatly into the rut. By the rear wheels, a wide pool of animal urine steams and overflows the grooved ground. Sarah returns the pot beneath the seat and closes the carriage door tightly. Her companion knocks at the other door, but before she will admit him, she pries the cork from the small vial of lavender oil she carries in a pocket and dowses her kerchief.

"Does your head ache?" he asks her as he takes his seat.

He is more solicitous than properly polite, but she nods regardless.

Unbidden, a memory returns to Sarah. When she was a child, her brother Robert had a book—a collection of scrap pages, to be more exact—called *The Progress of a Harlot*, which amused him very much. Secretly, Sarah borrowed it, taking it from its hiding place beneath his bedclothes, wishing to show off her daring to Elizabeth. Neither sister liked to touch brother Robert's belongings, for he was a little piratical even then, long before he went to sea and died in foreign lands. But on that day, Sarah dared, and she stole the pages, rolling them in her hand and covering all with her skirt. In the open air of the garden, with breezes further tattering the pages, she pored over the ink-clotted print, struggling to understand. She read, imagining hoarse male voices, battered and low, or barking with laughter. She puzzled over the meaning, feeling rather than comprehending what lay beneath the words—some ugly leviathan swimming below the surface. Flushed and unhappy, Sarah returned Robert's book to its hiding place. She never told Elizabeth she had taken it, for she hoped to forget such books existed.

D. M. Bryan

Now, thirty years later, in a coach in Marlborough, Sarah's memory returns to her an entire passage from Robert's pages—a long jest concerning noxious bodily effusions unloosed in a stagecoach. A gentleman passes off the unpleasant odour on each of his female travelling companions. Now, Sarah discovers herself smiling at the jest. The long-submerged leviathan swims into view, trout-like and disappointing.

Sarah suspects the Bath Road encourages allegory, for after Marlborough comes the steepest part, a check to tired travelers and horses alike. Ahead of Hungerford, comes the hamlet of Halfway, named like something out of Bunyan. Halfway amuses Mr. Gotobed with its absurd tollhouse—tiny but castle-shaped, with a crenelated roofline. To Sarah, he ridicules the ambition of its architect in designing a building so above its station. She wants to ask him how he, a printer-cum-Turkey merchant, dares censure another man's presumption, but, of course, she cannot. Instead, she watches the sun drop behind the Halfway tollhouse, red rays streaming from beneath a thick bolster of cloud.

Sarah and Mr. Gotobed sit in silence while the coach jostles them a mile or so further to Speen, where each finds accommodation to suit in a new-built inn. Under the elegant, fanned transom and up the stairway, Mr. Gotobed mounts higher than Sarah, climbing past the grand balustrade, to where only spare, wooden banisters mark the passage of his boots. Sarah sleeps but poorly and awakes in the morning to an indifferent breakfast, taken in a high-ceiling but damp room. A fire burns distantly, and the light through the sashed windows is green with rain. Afterwards, Sarah waits with her portmanteau inside the inn's door.

Mr. Gotobed, whom she does not see at breakfast, joins her there, crushing against her skirts in the narrow passage. Finding himself thus incommoding her, he sets down his portmanteau and takes to the rain, plashing in the puddles. When he stops and stares intently for a moment or two at the front of the Inn, Sarah realizes he scrutinizes the sign that swings audibly over the door. From the shelter of the porch, she calls to him, asking him what he sees.

"The signpost," says Gotobed, peering upwards. "I understand the foremost animal to be a hare, but the resemblance is not convincing. The creature is strangely split lipped, snaggle toothed." Gotobed continues to walk to and fro while Sarah watches him. "The two shapes on the left are clearly hounds," he says.

He himself is more pup than hound, she appraises, and then turns away from his restlessness. She applies her fingers to her neck, every squeeze revealing the damage done by a slumping feather ticking. The place is new but indifferently cared for, and already the flaking paint of the door lies like moss on the wet stone step.

When their coach pulls around from the back of the inn, Mr. Gotobed helps the coachman pass both bags into the interior. Their driver pays the same respectful attention he showed them the previous day, but his face is a husk, and before they set forth they hear him retching against the side of the carriage. He has taken the coachman's customary prerogative to refresh himself alongside his horses, and this morning he pays for the privilege. When the coach joins the Bath road, resuming its jostling, jolting pace, the man overhead groans so loud they hear him. Mr. Gotobed's face forms into an empathetic mirror, and Sarah wonders whether he knows what he does.

Past Thatchum, Sarah grows restless, the countryside no more than a wide sky of needles. Closing the louvers, she collapses the world into the finely joined boards of the coach. Her companion's brown glance falls on hers from time to time, and she takes this as an invitation to question him more closely about his visit to Sandleford. In the close confines of the coach, they continue as friends, although they must emerge as distant acquaintances at the end. Did he see much of her sister and brother's house at Sandleford, she asks. Elizabeth has newly painted the stairs—did he happen to notice the colour? The plasters in the drawing room are much admired—did he see them? Sarah warms to her topic, telling him how Elizabeth desires to remake the house along more gothic lines—Mr. Walpole setting the fashion, of course—but Mr. Montagu will not suffer to have such alterations made—what says Mr. Gotobed to the matter?

Mr. Gotobed says nothing of the gothic and only a little of the plasters—he did not see them but wishes he had. He speaks more freely of a rabbit pie he was served, which he found delicious. He thought Mrs. Montagu a most admirable woman and was very honoured to meet her, having read about her literary salons in the newspapers. To his eyes, she seemed in tolerable health, although he admits to Sarah he is not a good judge of such matters. Of Mr. Montagu, he has firmer opinions. Mr. Montagu is most exceptionally capable in managing his collieries and lands. He is a gentleman who works hard to improve his holdings and collects his rents assiduously. With his own eyes, Mr. Gotobed saw the panelled chamber where he works, where sits a vast desk, covered in papers—so many papers. Papers of tremendous importance, Mr. Montagu told him. Papers that carry his orders from one end of England to another, from north to south, from Sandleford to London, and from London back into the west. Mr. Gotobed delights in the thought he might do Mr. Montagu a kindness by carrying those orders, by transporting some modest portion of those valuable papers. This is a task of which Mr. Gotobed hopes to be found worthy.

"I know little enough of that," says Sarah.

He asks her how she likes Bath, and she finds herself telling him the truth. She admits she is lonely, and that the last attack on her dear friend's health frightened her very much. She even mentions Barbara's spasms ... fits ... She does not know how to name them to him. Indeed, she should not try, she understands from the embarrassed redness that lies like paint upon Mr. Gotobed's cheek. "The doctor comes repeatedly to examine my friend, but he accomplishes little. She has pains in her limbs, in her teeth, in all her parts," she says, a little cruelly, while Mr. Gotobed stares at the closed louvers, as if at a view.

They pass Arkham. They pass Belbury. They water the horses and the coachman in Puntfield, at the Drunken Weasel, where the thatch in the roof is black with rot. Mr. Gotobed snaps open the window and droplets freckle his face. Voices, drenched and sodden, shake themselves off, preparing to fight. "Like dogs," says Mr. Gotobed, watching.

Berkshire flows past in streaks of watery ore, jade and silver, emerald and peridot. On one side, a copse of saplings, and on the other, a grouping of cattle on a green ground, couchant. Clouds part and hint blue. Light thickens and thins. The louvers blur.

Sarah wakes to the sound of Mr. Gotobed's foot tapping repeatedly against the side of his leather portmanteau. How he must feel the cramp in his legs, poor man. She sits upright, tasting the staleness of her own mouth. Her cap sits sideways and she works to right it, tucking in loosened hair. Stays press against unguarded regions, and Sarah puts a hand to her ribs, uncertain how to fix her garments. Mr. Gotobed releases her from her uncertainty, studying the ceiling while she tugs, rotates, replaces, pats, smooths. That the result is not entirely satisfactory she sees in her companion's smile, which flashes as quick as the shadow of a coach under unsettled skies.

Again, they speak. "Do you have a wife, Mr. Gotobed?" she asks him, thinking the question, for all its impropriety, best aired.

"I have a sweetheart," he says, eyes fixed on some stain to his coat sleeve.

"Ah," says Sarah. Mr. Gotobed, she reminds herself, is very young. Any engagement must necessarily be long, but in time, she hopes he will find happiness. Her imagination summons up a sentimental print: a neat front parlour, a pleasant fire, the girl with her narrow waist and pink cheeks.

"You smile," said Mr. Gotobed.

"Do I?" Then she says, "Is it not a spinster's duty to rejoice in the happiness of others?"

But then, Sarah reminds herself, she is not a spinster—not really.

The stain on the man's sleeve absorbs his attention. He plucks at it, taking between his two fingers a pinch of broadcloth. Sarah watches him closely. "Is there some obstacle to your union?" she asks.

Mr. Gotobed gives her an astonished look. Then he nods, glumly.

"Mr. Gotobed, in my limited experience, every union entails obstacles—but a willing heart is the only true necessity."

Mr. Gotobed begins to scrape his sleeve with a thumbnail. Twice he rasps the rough cloth before abandoning all. He presses himself back into the corner of the carriage, crossing his arms but turning his full attention upon Sarah. "Many difficulties," he says, "might be overcome by a willing heart, yes, but not all." He nods at her, catches her eye.

D. M. Bryan

Sarah thinks she understands—Mr. Gotobed prefers not to speak of the nature of his distress, but Sarah might guess. "Let me see," she says. "The lady is too low for you?"

"Not too low," says Mr. Gotobed.

"She is too high?"

Mr. Gotobed shakes his head glumly. "Both and neither at all."

"You riddle with me, sir."

A hard-facetted laugh. A surprising laugh—she had not imagined him capable of much bitterness.

"Your sweetheart's father—"

"Dead."

"Her mother—"

"Most willing."

"You lack sufficient standing in the eyes of the world."

"I do. But my love would have me regardless."

"She loves another."

"There is only me."

"She marries another."

"Nay. My sweetheart marries no one."

"She will not marry then," says Sarah, very quietly indeed.

"On some days."

Sarah says nothing.

"Do you imagine you are done guessing, madam?" He tries for a smile.

"Not every woman wishes to marry, sir," says Sarah, as gently as she can.

"But will you not guess why."

Sarah will not guess any longer. She shakes her head.

"I cannot marry my true love," says Mr. Gotobed "because my darling won't give up—"

But now, with a heave as vast as the sigh of a disappointed lover, the coach ceases its forward momentum and slides sideways. Sarah and Mr. Gotobed are thrown equally into a confusion of limbs and intentions. For a moment, one louvered window fills entirely with weeping sky, while the opposite door swings open, revealing a bed of rutted grit. Through the open door, Sarah, Mr. Gotobed, and both leather portmanteaus tumble directly into the mud of the Great Bath Road. Then, motion ceases, and all is wet dirt, darkness, and the press of bodies.

For an instant, Sarah lies dazed. Then she is thrashing upright, twisting her limbs away from the weight of Mr. Gotobed's legs and pushing at the wet pouf of her gown. Mr. Gotobed scrambles away, as eager to separate from her as she is from him. Freed, she crawls out from under the tilted coach, inching leglessly in her wet skirts. When she reaches firmer footing, her companion is there to haul her upright. She notices his mouth moving as he makes utterances she has not time to comprehend. Then she is fully standing, and he is still speaking. He tells her to seek shelter, and Sarah turns to see the coach, canted as handwriting.

Gotobed stumbles toward the upright horses, as Sarah thanks God that she is to be spared the screaming of dying animals. The two bays stamp and shiver, their leather traces hanging in slack loops, trailing off into mud. Sarah sees Gotobed reach the first horse, laying one hand on a matted rump, but his actions are tentative. He fumbles for harness straps, urging the horses forward, but they stamp and snort, and they will not pull in one direction. The bays step and shift under his hands, but without confidence or understanding. He has not underestimated his lack of horsemanship, Sarah thinks.

Their plight continues to reveal itself. One coach wheel, huge and metal rimmed, sticks fast in a well-watered rut of remarkable depth.

Sarah looks for and finds the coachman sprawled only a few feet away, calling weakly for assistance. She scrapes rather than scoops up her hems and goes to him, but she cannot discern injury from intoxication. Unable to do more than pull him into a seated position, she watches as he settles his head on his arms and curses.

"Jesus Christ," says the coachman, speaking into the hollow of himself. "Jesus Christ—I flew."

"Get up," shouts Gotobed at the cursing coachman. "Help me, God-damn you."

"God-damn yourself," says the coachman, lifting his head. "I'm broken all over—I tell you. I came off my seat. I flew, you bastard, I flew."

Gotobed again attempts to make the horses pull but only succeeds in making one animal step sideways into the other. Hoof claps on hoof. The second horse half-rears, bugling in alarm. The coach rocks violently but never budges, and Gotobed disappears between the plunging bays. Sarah knows he is there only by his voice—raised and blaspheming. The horses come to a standstill, snorting, expelling clots of snot, and Gotobed backs out from between them, wiping his hands on his breeches. He looks at Sarah, but doesn't speak. The coach is hopelessly mired.

The sharp drizzle changes angle, and the wind picks up. Sarah's skirts cling coldly, wrapping her legs in layers of wet cotton, wool, and silk. She watches as Mr. Gotobed retrieves their portmanteaus from where they have fallen in the mud. He takes up one and tucks it beneath his arm, but when he lifts the second, it yawns open, unfastened. White pages flick from its mouth. The wind grabs each sheet, lifting them over Gotobed's head and out across the fields. Stunned, the poor man stands stock still, while page after page pours forth. Sarah too is transfixed by this vision of butterflies, wings white-green under cloud. The next moment, she returns to herself, snatching up her muddy hems and running at the wheeling sheets. She catches some. Gotobed stops others at their source, scooping them to the breast of his coat, grabbing for more with his free hand. But still they blow, catching in the short grass before careening wetly toward the next clump. Cattle watch, blazes shaped like hourglasses.

How many moments pass before Sarah thinks to check the sheets of paper themselves, seeking to distinguish between familiar and strange, hers or his? Whose papers cling wetly on her hand? Whose is the loss? The first few pages she looks at have nothing writ on them. She turns them over and finds nothing on the verso. These, she thinks, belong to her, for she carried in her portmanteau not only her drawings but also blank sheets, tucked in between to protect her fragile ink lines. She discards several blank pages before holding one up to the light. Nothing but fibres, grey with water. She lets fall the page, and for an instant, wonders if the rain has washed away her harlot's house, her rake's workshop. The gardens, cross-hatched? An ink-gravelled pathway between beds of herbs? Black petals running like rain? Is all her work gone—laundered clean?

Mr. Gotobed takes her elbow, but she fights him, striking him hard upon the forearm. She shoves him, taking him unawares so that he slips down into the mud. When he rises, a piece of paper clings to his thigh. A blank page, showing only a filthy, pristine surface. Gotobed removes it, while Sarah stares at him, unable to believe her misfortune.

"These are my papers—the letters I carried for Edward Montagu—these are your brother's papers," he says, holding out the page. The paper droops, wraps around his hand. Under the tawny mud is pale nothing.

"Mine," says Sarah. "A projection. A proposition, if you will. A proposal for a man who knows the business. All washed away."

Gotobed shakes his head. "It was my portmanteau that came open," he says. "Yours was hardly wetted. I have returned it to the coach to keep dry."

"You found my portmanteau?"

Mr. Gotobed nods.

"But these cannot be Edward Montagu's papers," says Sarah, looking at their damp faces in confusion. "There is nothing writ upon them."

Mr. Gotobed scrapes the soaking page from his hand and drops it into the mud. Buried in the ooze is the root structure of the grass. Soon, these pale fuses will explode into tufts of green sparks, but now they smolder imperceptibly in the rain. Mr. Gotobed puts out his foot and grinds all, plant and page alike, into a thready, pulpy mass.

"It is an old trick," he tells Sarah. "I've been made into bait—a snare for the dishonest. Montagu gave me to understand I transported bills of hand. He gave instructions to all his servants that I was to be accommodated in every particular on account of the significance of what I carried. At the time, I wondered at the trust he showed his household, and his lack of caution with a stranger, but he acted by design, no doubt. There are highwaymen on this road, at Maidenhead Thicket, and closer in, just before Hounslow. If any of those should receive regular intelligence from his household." He shrugs.

D. M. Bryan

Sarah tries to speak but cannot. She has begun to be very cold in the wet and the wind.

Mr. Gotobed continues. "They quarrelled, he and your sister, when she decided that you would join me. He refused to send the coach to Bath, but your sister went behind his back."

Sarah hears Elizabeth reasonably insisting. Montagu overruling her, unwilling to expose his grubby plan and lose his decoy. Then Elizabeth countermanding her husband, giving new instructions in Edward's name that Sarah would be accommodated after all.

"I do not like commercial dealings, Mr. Gotobed," says Sarah Scott, shivering. Together, they beginning to walk back to the crooked carriage. Sarah says, "Commerce makes men dishonest. You have a good heart, Mr. Gotobed—can you not do without business?"

Gotobed turns his head to stare at her, tripping over an errant piece of landscape.

At the scene of the accident, a group has gathered. Wagons, coaches, buggies are pulled up in both directions. Two women crouch beside the coachman, lifting his limbs and chaffing his hands. In the road, several burly men rock the carriage back and forth, while a countrywoman, a girl really, sits on one of the two horses, skirts hiked over her knees. She kicks her toes alternately into the horses' ribs to make them pull together. Sarah remembers another barebacked rider and dismisses the thought that the sight was a premonition. Superstition and nonsense, but still she offers up a hope that other girl reached her destination in safety.

Mr. Gotobed removes his greatcoat and offers it to Sarah. The garment drips and reeks, so she refuses.

The coachman sways to his feet, to good-natured cries from those around him. When he sees Sarah, he returns the bottle to a reaching hand.

"That wheel," he says, coming toward Sarah, "that wheel was always buggered."

But now the coach, which the burly men and the girl with the horses have been causing to move forward and back, makes a great sucking sound and rolls free of the muddy hole in which it was stuck. The wheel stands again on firm ground, as round and right as a cheese.

Sarah turns to Mr. Gotobed and says, "I will not travel another inch with this driver. It is his inattention that caused us to overturn."

"Begging your pardon, missus," says the driver, employing a fine irony, "but I don't see how you on the insides of the coach might know what happened on its outsides."

"I know your eyes," says Sarah, "were fixed on the bottom of a bottle."

Mr. Gotobed hastens to step between the two. "But how will you get to London? What will you do?" he asks Sarah. "I know not where we are."

"What will *you* do, Mr. Gotobed? Do you intend to continue playing hare for Mr. Montagu? He knows the role of the fox better than you ever will."

Mr. Gotobed makes no answer.

Sarah goes over to the horse girl, who has clambered down and is fixing her skirts. From a deep pocket, Sarah removes a coin and tucks it into her hand. The girl thanks her. Another coin, put into the hand of a wagon driver, secures her place on that conveyance. He is leaving this minute and will soon pass an excellent coaching inn, both warm and dry. On the morrow, she might take the post-chaise safe into London.

Finding Mr. Gotobed already returned to the body of the Montagu carriage, Sarah conveys what she has learned, but he only hands her down her portmanteau. The leather has darkened with rain, but the wet disorders only the surface of the case. Inside, Gotobed assures her, all is dry and secure. Sarah reaches up and proffers her hand to the man. He does not press it to his lips but shakes it.

"I wish you would come with me, Mr. Gotobed. Your company," she says, speaking boldly, "has been a comfort to me."

"I must finish out my journey in the same way it began," says Mr. Gotobed. "I have not the luxury of distrusting my employer." And Sarah understands he has found his answer.

The coachman, who is climbing heavily back up to his seat sees her standing at the window. "You there, missus," he calls down from on high. "Get back, if you don't intend to ride with us."

"You can be sure I shall speak with Mr. Montagu, your employer," says Sarah.

"Get back."

She remains where she is. To Mr. Gotobed she says, "I know not how, but be happy—your sweetheart and yourself."

Gotobed gives her a twisting smile.

And now the coachman lifts his reins, and the horses shift in preparation. One expels noisome air from under its tail. "Out of the road," shouts the coachman, and as Sarah steps back, the coach begins to move, stiffly at first, and then more and more easily. She waves to Mr. Gotobed, but the louvers on that side are caked shut with mud, and, anyway, she hardly knows the man.

The coaching inn is as the wagon driver described: warm and dry. Sarah has the luxury of a room to herself. She removes her still-damp clothing, her stays, shift, petticoat, and skirts, and sets them all to steam on a line before the fire. She lies down on the bed, beneath a woollen blanket, and studies the shape of her own body. Her feet she pushes from under the tatted fringe, and she spreads her toes. She holds up her hand and tilts it. Her limbs, her appendages have not changed. Her face, when she touches brow and nose, cheekbones and chin, feels the same. But still.

Her leather portmanteau lies beside her on the bed. Its condition, after the accident, is more disordered than she expected. No, *disordered* is not the exact word. Some other operation has taken place. The contents of that portmanteau have altered, just as her chest, waist, hips, legs no longer feel entirely her own. Unmoored from Batheaston, from Bath itself, from Barbara, she feels both herself and an entirely different woman. Under the scratchy inn blanket, beneath its brown and hairy surface, she closes her eyes. "A tale then," she says, beginning to write herself into one more shape.

THE
LIFE
AND
TIMES
OF
CASS QUIRE,
GENTLEMAN.

The First Edition

LONDON:

Printed for T. BAKEWELL and are to be sold at his
Shop over against *Little Britain Street*

1762.

[Price Six-pence]

CHAPTER 12

THE LIFE AND TIMES OF CASS QUIRE, GENTLEMAN.

Acquaints the reader with Cass Quire, an orphan and
sometime printer's boy, who is also a thief.

London, 1746.

A tale? Well then, I confess to taking the print, but in my defense, it
was always meant to be mine. Mr. Hogarth drew it and hung it high
in the window of Mr. T^ho. Bakewell's shop. I heard its rustling call and
recognized the sound. There are many signposts in London, for ale
shops and silversmiths and mercers' stores, but this was a sign for me. I
did no more than took what was mine. Nobody else understands that
picture like I do, and when the final judgment comes, that will be the
one theft that leaves no stain on my soul.

Upon my entrance to that shop, providence emptied the room
of clerks. Usually, Mr. T^ho. Bakewell has three men in his employ,
bastards in buttons with wigs askew—I know and hate each of them.
Let us call them Messieurs Dash, Quibble, and Blotpage, but these are
feigned names to protect the innocent and guilty alike. But, instead of
these villains, Bakewell's shop on the day in question held only rows of
books and the rolling balls of dust beneath the clerks' tall desks. In the
window hung Mr. Hogarth's print, twisting slightly in invitation.

Who am I? My true name is known to nobody. Feigned names I have by ream and bale. I pull them on and off like stockings. I have as many names as I can spit out, and then, while constables bite their pens at the spelling, I twist free. Away I run, down the street and through some door my pursuer never noticed before. There, the constable must stop, rattle the latch, and ask permission to enter. By the time the old body who lives there hears him calling, I am long gone, having fought past her skirts to leap from a window. Mind, I'm not always so lucky. Sometimes the latch is locked, and I must find another door. Sometimes a ratepayer's hand takes my shoulder, and I must writhe and twist, a scrap in a pan. Once, I was hid in a cupboard until the constable passed, but that was a counterfeit kindness and the worst of all larks.

But I lose my story. These tales are nothing but graved flourishes to the design of my life, which I would rather give you straight and unembellished.

My best name I chose myself, and I never heard another like it. I took it from what the French engravers name the papers on the top and bottom of a printer's ream, the spoilt pages smoothed flat to protect the others. Cass Quire. The printers use those pages for scrap, marking them with notations, little wet squiggles with pens or dry ones with their bent twigs of charcoal. They sometimes write up their bills on them too, which boys like me take to the booksellers. The booksellers, like that Mr. T^{ho.} Bakewell, frown over those scraps of paper. Then they shake their floured curls and send me away with no something for my trouble. No something is a nothing in my book.

Mr. T^{ho.} Bakewell has given me many a nothing, and his treatment of me certainly eased my conscience, as I entered his shop. Providence, having cleared the room of clerks, now showed me how I could cross the dusty floor and put one foot on the ledge where Mr. Bakewell's best books lay open to an illustrated page. Easing myself upwards, I found I could climb high enough to take the corner of that print and pull gently until it came unstuck from the glass, where Dash or Quibble or maybe Blotpage had fixed it. And this I did because the paper was already mine—as I think I have said. Then, I walked from Bakewell's as calmly as one who had regular custom there.

As soon as I was in the street, I fashioned the paper into something resembling a tube and strode about with the air of one who cares not where he goes. My mind was settled on the morality of my action, but I was a little troubled about what I would say if someone should stop me, for the constables of this world love to question boys like myself. Accordingly, I said to myself that if anyone should ask, I would say I was Sir R—'s boy who was taking home a print my master had purchased and wished delivered poste-haste. Content with this story, I continued walking until I was well away from the bookseller's shop. Then, I began to look about me for a place where I might go to fully examine what I had in my hand, and which was now beginning to absorb the moisture from my fingers, so tightly did I clutch my prize. It was while I was thus occupied that I heard someone call my name.

Many know me as Cass Quire, but few are fool enough to use that name in the street where anyone might hear. At first, so incensed was I at this bold behavior, I did not choose to answer but continued walking without altering my pace in the smallest degree. However, after hearing myself repeatedly hailed, I let my feet slow until the person caught up. Then I saw who it was that was calling me.

I knew the man but slightly, or possibly I should say I hardly knew the boy, although there was hair on his chin and he stood a head taller than I. He matched his stride to mind, nimbly picking his way around the refuse in the street. He gave me the wall, but did not open any business with me, preferring to keep company in silence. For my part, I kept walking as though I had a destination in mind, but I took the precaution of tucking my precious page behind my back, where I hoped it was out of his sight.

After we had walked for half a block, his silence began to make me itch. Then, I asked where he was walking, thinking to free myself from his company by choosing a different place as my destination. But, the devil said he had no end in mind and was merely taking pleasure in the sights available in fine weather. Alas, I had no answer for this and could take no pleasure in any sight, except for that of my picture, which was a joy his company prevented. Accordingly, I walked a little further with him, and then, choosing some serendipitous street, I told him our ways must part, and I bid him farewell.

"It is too soon to tell me good day," said he, "for I also must turn here."

I exclaimed aloud at my good fortune in finding myself able to continue in his company, but inwardly I cursed my luck.

We walked a little way further before I tried again, choosing another street, darker and danker than the one before. Once again, I took my leave.

"But hold," he told me. "We must not part ways yet, for my path also lies down this alley."

My new exclamation of surprise did not sound as pleased as I intended it should, but I mastered my displeasure and walked on with him. Our alley widened into a small courtyard, and we passed by an inn in silence. I hoped he might suggest going in, so that I might decline his offer and escape his company, but he walked mildly by the place, hardly sparing it a glance. Not even the painted Miss, who hailed us from the shelter of its doorway, attracted his attention. When the alley narrowed again, I looked crossways at my persistent companion and took his measure more carefully.

I had already noticed that he was tall, but now I saw that he was also thin. He had a hollowness of cheek that suggested his start in life had been as hungry as my own, but I knew his lot had improved since those lean days. He was now apprentice to a printer and very like to end his indenture before the year was up. It was in the shop where he conned his trade that I first made his acquaintance, for I had sometimes employment there, earning a few honest coins as a pressman's dog. He knew me only as Cass Quire, but I knew him by his real name— Gotobed. What his Christian name was, only his mother knew. He was that sort of boy.

The alley narrowed again, a constricted gulp, wet and uncertain in its end. A dim doorway appeared to my left. I stopped before it and tried the latch. To my joy, it lifted and a crack opened around the door. Turning to Mr. Gotobed, I told him I was now at my journey's end, that I had enjoyed the happy company of his person, but that now I must take my leave. Then I wished him a very good day.

"Nay," cried the infernal Gotobed. "You must not bid me take my leave yet, for this door is the very one that I also hoped to find."

"That is impossible, Mr. Gotobed," I said. "You told me you took your leisure and walked according to pleasure."

"And yet," said Gotobed, "this is where pleasure took me."

Angry and a little alarmed, I looked about and recognized where I was. We had come as far as Duck Lane, and I could see the great light and dust of Smithfield at the far end. I wanted to sprint away from the infernal Mr. Gotobed, but I was afraid to leg it, for my companion had the well-shaped calves of a fast runner.

"Alas," said I, closing the door. "I have mistaken the place." Never was I more aware of how high-pitched and boyish my voice sounded.

"It is an easy error to make. One door is so much like another." And he gave me a satirical smile I did not like.

I did not know what to say next, but he did. "We will continue in each other's company," said he. "Which way will you go, Mr. Quire?"

So it was that Mr. Gotobed and I began to walk again, this time toward Smithfield market. We followed the sour, grassy smell of livestock, and no sooner did we step out of the dimness of the lane than sunlight and the stink of cows assaulted our senses. As one body, we stopped, Mr. Gotobed and I. Dazzled, I shifted my precious paper to one hand to better wipe my face with my sleeve. When I was done, dampness discoloured the cambric.

Gotobed appeared not to have noticed and stood gazing about him through eyes narrowed to slits. The glinting sunlight showed up the bristles on his upper lip and on the point of his chin. Now, he seemed to me more man than boy, as if he'd grown in the time we walked together. This fresh observation of him, not to mention the many groups of idlers who drifted across the marketing ground, reminded me to hide my purloined print, which I tucked again behind my back. The very paper felt so enticing to my fingers, its surface rough and fibrous—how I longed to examine the page alone.

"Where to next, Mr. Quire?" said my companion, much to my dissatisfaction.

I looked up and saw the cupola of St. Paul's, thinly sketched against the torn edges of the sky. I said a quick prayer. "Mr. Gotobed," said I, "why are you following me?" His game was now obvious, even to its dupe. "Is there something I can do for you?"

He nodded—happily, I thought. He had reason to be pleased. He had caught me fairly, but why he wanted me I could not tell. His game was obvious, but his reasons were not.

Hidden away, I had any number of fine watches that could be Mr. Gotobed's, should he but say the word. I also had a silver locket, a small collection of gentlemen's wedding rings, a piece of lace, and two snuffboxes. He need only put out his hand, and any of these treasures might be his—indeed, any of them could be his, for all I knew.

I said, "I have in my keeping a few odds and ends of value—name your prize, and it shall be yours."

Then, Mr. Gotobed nodded and, without the slightest hint of his intention, took the rolled-up paper I held hidden behind my back. I hardly resisted, so shocked was I.

"No sir," I said. "Not that. Give it back." To my horror I was beginning to cry. A tear of rage dripped from my chin, blotting my neck-cloth.

"There there, Mr. Quire," said Gotobed, quite gently, holding out his handkerchief.

I would not take it and again pressed my sleeve into service.

Gotobed returned his kerchief to a pocket. Then, he unfurled my page and held it up in the light. As I gazed upwards, my eyes scrubbed and burning, I could see the verso of the drawing. Its mottled patches of light and shade concealed a pattern I could remember but not entirely discern.

"I am interested in this," said Gotobed. "One of Mr. Hogarth's I perceive, but not a print I believe I have ever heard advertised. Its subject is obscure to me."

Not to me, but I would not give him the satisfaction.

"Who asked you to steal this?"

I shook my head, insulted to the very quick. "I am no thief," I said. I always say this, adding to my sins that of untruthfulness.

"Come, Mr. Quire," said Gotobed. "I do not believe you. You are a thief, but what you are not, I think, is a connoisseur of furniture prints. How came you to steal this?"

I should have held my tongue, but instead I cursed him to the best of my abilities, and my abilities are considerable. When I stopped, I knew I'd earned a cuff to the head. Instead, I received a cold, even smile. How weary I was of this tall boy and his undeserved mastery over me. How angry I was at my size and my tears. I wished to make him as afraid of me as I was of him, and it was at this exact moment that a stratagem presented itself that, if I were careful, could get my print back again.

I began by pretending to sigh and weep some more, wiping my eyes on my sleeves in a very showy fashion. At last, I said, "Mr. Gotobed, you have the right of it. I did indeed help myself to that print from out of Mr. T^ho. Bakewell's window. I am a thief, and if your desire is to condemn me to eternal damnation, you have enough evidence to take me to Newgate and all the way to the gallows."

At this speech, Gotobed looked up from the print, which he examined still, and peered at me with the same interested expression. "I have not the slightest desire," said he, "to lead any soul to perdition." Then he furled the print tightly and commenced tapping himself on the thigh with the reformed tube.

This casual treatment of my page set my teeth on edge, and involuntarily I put out a hand to stop him. "Please, you must not do that, sir."

Gotobed stopped and arched an eyebrow.

I had forgot my stratagem. I returned to my point. "You must not ask again upon whose orders I stole that print," I said and waited.

"I had no thought to do so," said Gotobed. "You're no peach, Quire—why, any man can see that."

I continued to wait.

Gotobed looked around. Smithfield was both empty and crowded, it not being a market day. Groups of men pooled together and then trickled away, carving a solitary path through the mud. St. Paul's dome brightened. The breeze lightly touched my curls.

"All right, Quire," he said at last. "Let's play. Upon whose orders did you steal that print?"

"He met me in a coffee shop, but he offered me no name. He said it was enough to know that he loved his country."

"His country?"

"Perhaps he said kingdom."

Mr. Gotobed's other eyebrow rose. "Well then," he said.

"The price he offered me," I said lowering my voice even further, "was an awful lot for a simple theft."

"Which can only suggest—" said Gotobed, breaking off judiciously.

I nodded, as if to confirm his suspicion, whatever it might be— some political conspiracy, I hoped. The age was ripe with 'em. "What's more," said I, "someone took great care to ensure that Mr. T^ho. Bakewell and all his clerks removed themselves from the front of the shop just as I came down the street."

"A significant detail," said Gotobed.

"Given the arrangements made, sir, I would not like to report the print has fallen into the wrong hands."

"My hands, *exempli gratia*."

"Just as you say, sir."

Mr. Gotobed appeared to be thinking, which was an action I did not wish him to undertake. "Secrets," I said, quite in a rush, "fearful secrets embedded into the print. In this manner, I believe, they communicate."

"They? But surely you can't suspect Mr. Hogarth of any wrongdoing?" Mr. Gotobed had seized the tale between his teeth and run on before me, the dog.

"Oh my, no. Not Mr. Hogarth."

"Then who? The printers, perhaps?"

"The printers in on it?" I warmed to the idea, but as Mr. Gotobed's face folded into an angular smile, I recalled to mind his trade. "Oh no, an absurd thought, sir. As you well know. The guild—not possible."

"I fail to understand why not," said my companion. "A printer might be as wicked as the next man."

My turn to gaze upon him. I did not trust his tone. I feared my tale was missing its mark. That Mr. Gotobed was no lover of intrigue. That my voice wavered and quavered. The square grew brighter and hotter. The odour of cow shit rose heavenward.

"Really Mr. Gotobed," I said, sounding uncertain, even to myself, "how can you explain the fact that no one was in Mr. Bakewell's shop— where did they disappear to, all the clerks at once?"

"You mean Dash, Quibble, and Blotpage?"

I had not realized Gotobed knew them.

"Those bastards," he said.

He knew them.

"Mr. Quire, sir," said Gotobed, "I will confess I followed you on a whim. When I saw you inside Bakewell's, up and down in the window like a monkey on a lady's shoulder, you interested me strangely."

"A monkey?" I prided myself on the naturalness of my actions. I'd seen a gibbon once, all line and no grace.

"Sir, I intended no offense. But the vision of you in Mr. Bakewell's window startled me. You appeared like the answer to some question I did not know to ask."

Was the man's face flushed? I sniffed his person as surreptitiously as I could. But his eyes shone clear and no acrid vapours hung about his mouse-coloured coat and breeches.

"The dexterousness with which you secured this print and the casual authority with which you left the scene of your crime has won you an admirer in me, sir."

"Then give me my paper back."

Gotobed considered. "I am afraid you will run away, and while I could catch you, I do not wish to chase you."

"Upon my word of honour, I will not run."

Mr. Gotobed's laughter caused a passing soldier to turn his head. I spat.

"Again, I fear I have insulted your finer feelings, Mr. Quire."

My finest feeling told me to set off across Smithfield and disappear into the thick press of skirt and leg, and I would have done so but for my print clutched in Gotobed's fist.

"Why this single print? Would not a complete set of subjects earn more?"

I examined the stain on my sleeve. I felt the urgent need to see the paper again.

"I expect no profit," I told Gotobed. "The print is mine."

"Was yours," said Gotobed.

I cursed Gotobed wildly, and hit out. This time, he stepped forward, holding me so that my paper came next to my face. I could smell the ink. With one arm, Gotobed pinioned me, setting his mouth at my ear. He sent hot and ticklish breath upon my cheek, telling me to calm myself, to not draw attention to ourselves, lest we both lose the print.

By way of reply, I let my knees go limp, and then as we sank toward the dirty ground of Smithfield market, I shot upwards, bringing my crown into contact with Mr. Gotobed's chin. Mr. Gotobed staggered and released me. I took a step backwards and watched him reeling in circles, hand to his nose, the print still held carefully above my head. When he could stand upright again, vermillion droplets spotted his neckerchief. "You bloody little bugger," he said and came at me, attempting to push me down into the mud and cow shit of Smithfield.

I evaded him with some difficulty, aware that I'd begun to cry again. The tears, even angry ones, had to stop. Seeing them, Gotobed cursed me roundly and let me go. Then he began to employ on himself the handkerchief he'd once offered me. Angrily, he blotted away a rosette of blood, then turned an angry and slightly swollen eye on me. "Bugger you," he offered again.

"It's not yours."

His only answer was to turn on the heel of his shoe, and begin to stalk away down Duck Lane. After a moment, I ran after. I had no choice. "Please," I said, trotting along beside him. Truly, his legs stretched a great deal further than mine. I attempted to get in front of him, but he quickened his pace and I tripped. After that, I did not demean myself by nipping like a pug dog, but grabbed his coat and made every effort to hang on.

Gotobed stopped and put his head down close to mine. "Let go," he said. "Or I will really hurt you." He shook me for good measure.

"Please, sir," said I, all stratagem exhausted. And perhaps he heard something in my voice for he let go of my collar. "Keep the print," I said. "It is mine by rights, but perhaps we might both keep some share in it."

"What do you mean, share it?" he said. "It is entirely mine because it is entirely in my hand—that is entirely the case, little Mr. Quire."

"I have a proposal to make, if you will listen." I was thinking as hard as I could. The thought of losing that print was a cramp in my gut. Worse than hunger, was that pain.

"You have nothing to treat with, you little gibbet-bird."

"I do, sir, I do. But you must listen. Hear what I have to say, in all fairness."

Gotobed scratched his head under his wig. "Fairness," he said, as if to himself. Then he dragged me under an overhanging window, where we were out of the heaviest flow of foot-traffic. "You have until Great St. Bart's sounds," said he.

Over the stone dwellings of Duck Street, the church tower showed its face. The hands of the clock were almost clapped to. I had not a moment to waste. And yet, I had no scheme in mind.

I stood, staring at the fellow, at his thin shanks and stained sleeves. And then, as if in a tale, a project entire leapt into my mind, a stratagem so complete it might have been Heaven sent—nay, it must have been Heaven sent.

I smiled at the inky devil and made my proposal.

Chapter 13

The Life and Times of Cass Quire,
Gentleman.

Which gives the nature of the scheme Cass enters with
Mr. Gotobed, but also provides some cautionary notes
on the comportment of young people who have nobody
but themselves in the world.

London, 1746.

I had no way of knowing the proposal I was about to make would end in
the slicing of my print down the middle. Had I known, would I, like the
true mother in King Solomon's judgement, have let Mr. Gotobed keep
the picture for himself? I cannot say—all I knew was that Mr. Gotobed
had the advantage of me, and I must act quick if I were to explain my
stratagem.

"Have you seen George Bickham's sorry copy of Hogarth's *Harlot*?"
I asked Gotobed. "I recently stole a copy from a shop in Mays House in
Covent Garden—do you know the work?"

Gotobed's only answer was to look at the clock in the nearby church
tower. It showed the little share of time he had given me to explain myself.

"Are you aware, Mr. Gotobed, that Mr. Hogarth's *Harlot* sells for 2s
6d, while Bickham's asks only 6d for his vile imitation?"

Of course, I'd paid nothing at all. Still, Mr. Bickham's ugly
rendering of a bare breasted harlot and her vomiting sister cost me peace

of mind. My own mother might have been one of those women. I knew little of her beyond her name, and the cheapness of Mr. Bickham's line, combined with the ugliness of his sentiment, left me feeling very low indeed.

"Well," I continued, "I can tell you that Mr. Bickham's rendering is very stiff, and his composition is flaccid. He copies Mr. Hogarth, as so many inferior artists do. Now, as to the print you hold there. It is most definitely one of that ingenious artist's original works, although I have not seen him approach this subject matter before. Still, every detail carries the stamp of his inimitable style."

Mr. Gotobed appeared to be listening despite himself, and when I was finished, he said, "For a thief, you have a knowledgeable way of talking of pictures."

"Whenever I am in the street," I said, "I make the printseller's window my school. It is free to look and cheap to learn. Mr. Hogarth is my constant study, and I know all his work by heart. I promise this print is a new production, never before seen by a public hungry for more."

"Someone," said Gotobed, who as a printer's apprentice was equipped to reconstruct the crime, "has taken this precious page from Mr. Hogarth's printery—snatched it up from the horse where it lay drying."

"It will be missed," I said, glancing over my shoulder, so that no one should overhear us, there in Duck Street.

"Bakewell took a chance displaying it in his window."

I agreed. The bookseller had indeed risked the ire of Mr. Hogarth—a man who did not easily give up his cause when roused. I put my finger to the bottom of the page where nothing was written. The print did not yet give the artist's name, nor did it say, as his prints always did, *Published according to an Act of Parliament*.

Gotobed saw my gesture. "But is there no law without the words?" he asked me. We looked at one another. In truth, neither of us knew, but we shared the superstitious reverence, common to all apprentices, journeymen, and even pressboys, for Mr. Hogarth's legal amendment.

Now Gotobed unfurled the print, shifting a little so that we both might look. We were still tucked under a window overhang, out of the way of any passersby. He extended one long leg, so that I might not easily snatch the print and run from him. Hemming and hawing a little over the page, he finally said, "This is a trial-pull only. He's testing the composition and the balance of the tones before he finishes the work. Only the central design is complete. Look here."

We bent over the page and Gotobed drew my attention to the rectangular frame around the image that stood empty and waiting adornment. At the top we could make out a few light strokes of the burin running horizontally, interrupted by one or two short vertical lines that carved up the spaces between.

"Bricks," I said, understanding at last what the marks would become—a frame constructed to fool the viewer's eye, making the print look as if it is already hung on a wall. "And more embellishment there," I told Gotobed, pointing with my dirty nail. "Like on a monument. And here, at the bottom, a cartouche. Like on a silver cup."

Gotobed was nodding. He picked up the page and found the words on the back: *Tom Idle Betrayed by his Whore*. "Here he's written the title for the top. And in the cartouche, he'll print some improving verse, no doubt."

I nodded. We both knew the genre. "Blessed are the weak," I said, noting, not for the first time, poor Tom's peril.

My companion laughed. "Meek," said he.

"He's meek enough too."

"'Tis a series," said Gotobed. "Like the *Harlot* and the *Rake*. Each print is a little part of the tale. There must be others."

"Eight," said I, the verses leaping unbidden into my mind. "One, Tom is born, poor in spirit and in all things besides. Two, Tom loses his mother and would mourn her as much as is in his power. Three we have before us—the weak are ever meek, for they know themselves faulty and easily imposed upon."

I waited for Gotobed to correct me, for we both knew what I should have been saying if I gave the verses in their proper form, but he held his peace, and so I continued. "Four, Tom is hungry and thirsty and would be righteous, even as he takes a silver spoon from a tavern. Five, he is merciful, for he holds his tongue when the constables come, even though he could take others with him. Six, he is pure of heart, praying in Newgate with as clear a conscience as ever was had by a man in his sorry state. Seven, he makes his peace with his whore, for she comes to explain her choice, and he understands. Eight—"

"Eight," said Gotobed, "he hangs on the Tyburn tree, and blessed are those who are persecuted for righteousness' sake, for theirs is the kingdom of Heaven."

"That is the final verse exactly," I said.

"It will not sell. Your theology is peculiar to thieves."

"My exegesis is as good as any man's."

"Agreed. But still such a series will not sell—not without Mr. Hogarth's design, his cleverness with the tale, his choice of the one hundred tiny details that give us all so much pleasure in the reading."

"Give me some paper, and I'll show you," said I.

Gotobed was a poor man but also a printer's apprentice. He had paper. More surprising, he appeared willing to give me a chance to prove myself. He gestured to me to follow him, and after a little hesitation, I did. After all, he still held my print.

Together, we went down Little Britain and into Aldersgate. Passing through an alley even more intestinal than Duck Lane, we slid out the bottom of Red Cross Street. At the entrance to a gin shop, we stepped over a pair of women lying in the street, one propped up against the other. The younger of the two, a yellowing cap on her head, flickered an eye at Gotobed. When he ignored her, she stuck out her stockinged leg for me, but I skipped around her torn slipper and came safe into Grub Street.

Gotobed's chamber lay through a grimy portal and up a set of piss-reeking stairs. We climbed, passing walls crudely marked with ships and gibbets. A person my own age came down the stairwell toward us. She carried a roaring baby in her arms, a sibling or perhaps her own child. Perhaps both. The baby raged, wriggling, maggot-like in its swaddling, until we climbed past it and its anger. On the next landing, we stopped at a door that had Gotobed's name scrawled beside it. He was a Th^{ms}— now, I knew his Christian name, although I did not feel the better for it. The room beyond the door held eight floorboards, a table, a truckle bed in an alcove behind a torn curtain, and a fireplace both cold and bare. On the mantle sat a teapot.

Gotobed kept scraps of paper in a wooden cupboard that hung upon his wall, and brought one to me, along with a pressed piece of charcoal of the sort some printers' masters use to make notations.

To prove myself, I drew Tom in Newgate, on his knees in an oblong of light. I adapted but did not copy elements of Mr. Hogarth's compositions. Tom's purity of heart, I put in his face, taking pains to reproduce the fleshy oval and cap of dense curls from the original. When I finished Tom's expression, Gotobed gave me a small sigh of contentment.

"You have him exact," he said. "It's a fair copy."

"I emulate, not copy," I told him, bending back over the shading of the larger cross that fell across the floor of Tom's cell and over the shoulder of his coat.

"But he would never be alone in Newgate," Gotobed said when I had finished Tom's figure, and so I added two rogues dicing in the murky background, and also a man and a rat fighting over a scrap of bread. By the door, I drew a gaoler taking a bribe from a poor woman to improve the care of her cadaverous husband, whose ring was being slyly removed from his finger by a boy as like to myself as a boy could be. I made each of these into a group that was a story in its own right, but I made sure of the balance of light and dark. I held in my mind the massing of figures and shapes, teasing the whole into a curving line that delighted the eye.

Gotobed approved my picture with an even more intense pleasure than I had thought to occasion. He termed me the cleverest fellow he'd ever met and wasted as one whose employment consisted in snatching watches from pockets. "What is your history?" he asked me. "You must have once been an engraver's apprentice to draw with such ease. Can you 'grave—oh tell me you can work the burin with the same facility."

Alas, I was no apprentice, and I could not engrave, but Gotobed did not remain downcast for long. "Never mind," he said, "I know engravers aplenty, but you must draw the rest in the way I tell you, so that when we print—"

I stopped him there, excited beyond measure by what he had just said. The engraver's art was religion to me, and I longed to see the trick done. I told Gotobed I would do the drawings, but I must be allowed to watch the engraver grave the plate. I had never before imagined the chance might be mine—to sit at the elbow of a master and watch him work, to understand his tools and learn his technique. I feared Gotobed would think me foolish, but he agreed without appearing to think at all of the importance of the thing he granted. I went to thank him, but thought better when I saw that he was utterly preoccupied with calculations, bits and pieces of which tumbled from his lips.

"You say Hogarth sells for two shillings a piece?" he said.

"Two shillings and six pence."

"We must not be greedy—two shillings it is. Now, we may multiply that by as many booksellers as will agree to our terms. And how many in London?" he asked.

"Booksellers?" Truly I had no idea. More appeared every week.

"Purchasers," he said. "Buyers. Customers. How many people in London?" He began to laugh. Truly, it was an impossible number. He might well have asked how many stars in the sky or fish in the sea.

"Hogarth will advertise," said Gotobed. "He always does, and when he does we must be ready with our prints, for we must at once convert them to gold and vanish like the magician Fawkes."

Mr. Hogarth's willingness to advertise was well known but so was his hatred of those who would sell copies of his prints. I said so.

"Ah," said, Gotobed, "but these—my clever little man—are not copies but rather are emulations—as you yourself so righteously showed. His engraver's act leaves untouched those of us who would honour his intentions with designs of our own."

"But we use his tale, his title."

"What title," said Gotobed, "Tom Idle?" Why that's my name and your name too, I'll warrant."

"The story—"

"Is written ten times over and sold at every hanging since Judas." And upon this dark omen, which he appeared neither to recognize nor understand, he seized my hand and shook it vigorously. I was still unsettled in my mind when he took a knife from someplace he had secreted it, and mutilated the print, slicing a zigzag line down the middle.

D. M. Bryan

Gotobed might as well have slashed a knife through my own pale chest. The paper curled up around the jagged cut. It cleaved Hogarth's picture—Tom's betrayal in a low tavern—in twain. When I had a moment to recover myself, I sprang to the table and without so much as examining my fingers for dirty smuts, I tried to rejoin what had been sundered.

The first cut ran along a low overhanging beam of the ceiling, and from thence reversed to separate Tom, the idle apprentice, from his even wickeder companion, a fence dealing in stolen goods. As if in an act of charity, Gotobed's cut separated the fence from Tom Idle's company, even as Tom made his criminal exchange. In Tom's upturned hat are fob-watches and snuffboxes like to the ones that so often came, as if of their own accord, into my own hand. The fence's face was more like a skull than flesh and blood, but even thus it was a visage with more life to it than all of Bickham's posed, drawn dolls. The cutline continued, taking with it Tom Idle's hands, as befits a thief, and the well-formed calf of his leg. I mourned this calf most particularly, for its curved line was beauty itself in accord with Mr. Hogarth's discourse on the matter—which I had not read but had heard discussed in the coffee shops. No matter, Tom's leg was cleaved in twain.

"Are you mad?" I cried, examining the damage from every angle.

At first, Gotobed looked surprised, but then he consented to explain himself. "By the line of this cut," said he, reaching over me to spread apart the severed halves of the print, "we are indentured to each other. The uniqueness of this cut makes the picture both key and lock." And with this he pushed the portions together so that the cut almost vanished and the print appeared whole again. Then he rolled up and handed me my half. "This is our contract," he said solemnly, and I might have argued if I hadn't been so distressed at the fragmentary nature of what he pushed into my hand. Some of this must have shown on my face, for Gotobed himself looked down at what remained, and he shook his head. "It was necessary," he said, both of us watching as the remaining paper curled in on itself, forming into a nautilus.

"It was not," I said. "You might trust me without it, you know."

To this, Gotobed made no reply, and I began to fuss with my tube.

True, thieves are not considered the most honest companions—and I had never given the fellow any reason to find me honest. On the other hand, Gotobed might have kept Mr. Hogarth's proof all to himself, but instead, he gave us each half of our common stock to keep for ourselves. I could see some fairness in his choice, but his action appeared all impulse—more a boy than a man. I wondered, not for the last time, why I should trust Mr. Gotobed.

I opened my share of the picture. I had the half with the young woman in the kerchief, caught in the middle of betraying poor Tom. She holds one hand out for the money and points to Tom with the other. She must hate Tom a great deal, I thought, wondering what he might have done to deserve such enmity. I looked between them, comparing their faces and their strong, full bodies, until I realized the truth: she was as like Tom as if she were himself in skirts.

Tom's death by hanging upon the Tyburn tree was a certainty, for I'd heard of it in a pamphlet called "A Full and True Account of ye Ghost of T^{ho}. Idle." This work was written for the improvement of those of us who made our living just as Tom did, and so was circulated widely and very cheaply indeed. Those of us who could were often importuned to read it aloud by those who could not, for that amusing confession was a great favourite with all.

And perhaps it was the cruelty of the world, where trust and goodness are a luxury, that made me forgive Mr. Gotobed his slicing of my print. Or, perhaps it was the certainty of punishment that rendered me careless, but I did pardon the man. I tucked my truncated print under my arm, and then, again, I took his hand to shake on our bargain.

Mr. Gotobed and I parted ways. He promised to send word to me at a nearby coffee house when he had secured the engraver he sought, and so I waited upon that exciting event. A day passed. I went out in to the street and tended to my business. When, after a second day, I did not hear from him, I went out again, but I was not of such good heart this time.

Before I say more, I must explain first where I live, for a young man adrift in London must always have accommodation on his mind. A room in an inn or a respectable house is best, but if these are beyond his means—as certainly they exceeded mine—he must still secure himself a place each night that is out of the wind and rain. For a boy truly down on his luck, the street must suffice, and if he is quick, he might claim for himself a foot or two of dry ground under the arch of a Fleet footbridge or below the vaults of St. John's Gate. But, as soon as a bit of coin comes a fellow's way, he will rent a bed by the night in St. Giles, although "bed" is a grand word for a shared sack of straw. At night the floors of those flop-houses run so thick with bedbugs they crunch under the feet of anyone using the pot in the corner. The street is cleaner and sometimes safer. No, what a boy of fluctuating means needs most is a bolt-hole that affords security and some privacy, and above all, is easy on his purse. Luckily, for boys and girls with a little craft and dexterity, such places exist that keep us all safely out of Bridewell.

Of course, no bolt-hole in London is without its landlord or landlady, and in my case, it was the latter. She kept all clean and respectable, although, to be sure, she was neither, and I called her Mother, although, God save me, she was not that either. All of us under her care were tender in years, but none of us were whores, neither of the male nor the female kind. She would not let us ply that trade, and those she caught in the bagnios or in the gin shops, she turned away, weeping and wiping at her eyes with a yellowed piece of Flanders lace. Her advice to those of us under her protection was to take on nothing but proper work, such as thieving or coining, and to let alone the trade that ended in disease and death. She warned us to do our business far away from home, keeping the constables from her door, and to deliver up whatever we could, as regular as possible, for her to sell on our behalf. I did my best to oblige, and she repaid my industry by providing me with that most unlikely thing of all: a little London room of my own. It was the merest box, but I did not mind, for when I shut its plank door, I was alone.

Mother's house had once been a fine dwelling, the residence of a merchant whose wealth allowed him to build generous chambers on every floor. My room, such as it was, had been fashioned from one of these, divided from the rest by partitions of lath and plaster. In one particular place where the wall crumbled, I dug with my fingers to make a shallow hiding place. Over this hole, I pinned Mr. Bickham's ugly picture, and in this secret cupboard I placed whatever of value I had

D. M. Bryan

about me: the watches, handkerchiefs, and snuffboxes that I did not yet wish to tender to Mother. Here, I also kept the small bag of coins that was my own, and now half Mr. Hogarth's bifurcated print found a hiding place.

With Mr. Gotobed's absence stretching into a third day, I stumped down the many stairs to Mother's parlour in a truly discontented state. My sham family had been called to account for itself, and the room held a number of infants in a variety of borrowed dress, sitting cross-legged around the false smile of Mother's skirts. I was the last to arrive, and, as one of the favourites, I took for myself a chair between the window and the fire. The small girl I unseated scuttled away, finding herself a new place against a leg of the sideboard. It did me good to see her anger.

Mother was one of those who was especially fond of Tom Idle's Christian repentance upon the gallows, and she often read aloud from that broadsheet. Tonight, she propped this very page before her, listing in a slightly slurring voice all of Tom's crimes: spurning his master's advice, reading novels, and the like. "But of course," Mother said, "Tom was lost forever when he commenced gaming," and she mimed the shaking of dice.

We, her listeners, nodded a little nervously. She often accused us of gambling away some of what we had earned. Then she would pinch our arms and demand the truth, claiming that she knew if we held anything back.

Now Mother said, "I cannot abide a gambler, and neither do I like a drinker," and we agreed with her, to a man—even those of us who were girls. We knew that visiting a public house for purposes other than stealing a silver tankard was sufficient to condemn a fellow to perdition.

The declaration appeared to have tired Mother, who was leaning back in her chair, looking up at the stained ceiling of the parlour. She rested her eyes there, clearly seeking wisdom in the direction of God's own abode.

"Didn't Tom go sometimes to the playhouse?" tried one of us, an ineffectual thief with a cough, whose lack of skill condemned him to sleep on a bench in the kitchen. "Them girls on the stage can snatch your soul—isn't that right, Mother?"

Mother did not bother to answer him.

"Don't be daft," said another, a tall cutpurse about to mature past all usefulness to the company. "You will lose your purse, not your soul, at the playhouse."

I thought Mother might say that a man could lose both, and his time in the bargain, but she continued to contemplate the heavens, breathing deeply and regularly.

A young coiner spoke next—his voice uncertain, for he'd not been in that house long—and asked how Tom Idle could be already a true sinner when he had not yet become a highwayman and taken gentlemen's gold at the point of a pistol. "For robbery's worse than gaming or drink," he reasoned.

At this, a sigh went up, for all of us children longed to be highwaymen, and we lounged on the floor or in our chairs with as much swagger as we could manage. We were pupils in an infant's school of crime, and the highwayman was the highest calling we could imagine. We could not aspire to be a lord, nor his steward, and not even his clergyman. Having no money for an apprenticeship, we could not aspire at all but to the glorious career of an outlaw and brigand.

I saw myself engraved in a guinea print, riding the road to Bath, stealing jewels from the ladies' necks. Armed robbery on the King's highway had to be the point past which a man might never go to heaven, for how could a fellow truly repent *that* taste of glory.

The broadsheet slipped from our Protectress' fingers, making the swish-swish of a robber's ghost. We all jumped, from the nervous coiner, to the cutpurse in the corner. Mother herself awoke and sat upright, her eyes blinking to find us still there, gathered at her feet. "What are you all doing here?" she said, shooing us from that room. "Get out. Go. Earn your living, for that's the way to reach heaven."

All around me, my family scrambled to their feet.

Like the others, I went out to work, although my heart was not in my labours. I soon found myself in the streets near to Bartholomew's, half hoping, half fearing to see Gotobed again. I began to think I would walk as far as Covent Garden to see if lights burned in Mr. Hogarth's rooms behind the Golden Head. But that was a long walk, and before I could turn my feet that way, I came across the girl I'd turned out of the favoured chair in Mother's parlour.

The child stood in the street outside Great St. Bartholomew's and she was singing with her feet spread and her hands clasped in front of her. Two men stood by, and lewd sallies flew between the lines of her song. A fellow in a mustard greatcoat splashed with mud gave her a wink and a leer. "Come on, darling, shut your mouth, or open it for a more useful purpose," said he. But she made no reply, only ending one song and beginning another. She was younger than I, although I was not certain how many birthdays I'd had—with no one to mark them, I'd begun to lose count.

I stepped in between the two men to make a crowd, and I caught her round, fishy eye. All men love a press of people, and seeing three of us standing shoulder to shoulder, others began to gather. In the small knot of newly arrived onlookers, I spied a country drover, his sales complete and coins distending the deep leather pocket tied to his waist—he sauntered up to see and stayed to listen. Joining him was a brace of rakes, their bag-wigs dangling down their backs. A thin person, dressed all in inky hues, hung behind us, like a coat one of the company put off to dry. A clerk, I guessed, or an author—he looked hungry enough to be learned. He stayed too, although from his careful glances at the company, left and right, I could soon tell he was wise as well as educated. In time, came the figure I waited for: the tall cutpurse almost grown past use. He scowled at me, thinking me moving in on his game, but I put my hand to my own pocket, drew out a farthing, and threw it at the girl's feet.

"Sing us another," I shouted, for she'd come to the end of her song and had paused to draw breath.

The rakes beside me patted their soft palms to indicate their approval of the girl's efforts, or my generosity perhaps, while the drover shouted, "Yes, lass, sing one for me," and reached into his own purse. As he threw the copper he let the bag of coins hang for a moment from his hand. The cutpurse and I noticed this most particularly, but so, I thought, did the corpse-like fellow behind us, who stepped out of the oblongs of light cast by a pair of church doors. I half turned so that I might see him better, but already he'd vanished into the night. Then the singer burst into song, throwing apart her arms to distract attention from the cutpurse, who was making good on his name. The quick gleam of lamplight on knife blade was only visible to one who expected it, and I knew the drover's money to be now in the hand of the cutpurse.

Now, the girl broke off singing and cried as loud as she could. "For shame, sir," she said, and she spun away from the cutpurse to stare hard at a fellow in a bubble of apron, who stood close beside her. To a man, we turned to examine this person so addressed, and the cutpurse slipped swiftly toward the blot of darkness beyond the church doors.

"Only a coward would pinch a maid in a crowd," said the girl, still playing her part.

"I didn't touch ye," said the fellow in the apron.

"Pinched in the crowd?" said the man in the mustard coat. "Why, you must pinch her upon the arse." And he followed this witticism with more winking and leering.

Now came the part of the game I did not expect, for the corpse-like man stepped out of the shadow to take the cutpurse, a trout rising for a fly. Nobody saw but I, and I was the only witness to the briefest of struggles. Soft, white appendages covered the boy's mouth and held him. But by now both figures were sunk in the gloom of the narrow lane that leads off Cloth Street, and I could see no more. I heard rather than saw a body fall to the cobbles, but perhaps fear only conjured the sound out of silence.

While I stood, shocked, the drover discovered his loss and, after seizing a flailing fop, thought better of his choice, knocking down the little Miss in his effort to take me. Astonished at this sudden turn, I made to flee but even as I did, I found myself treading on air. I was hoist off my feet by his countryman's arm. His face swung into mine, and I sneezed as hoppy fumes found their way up my nose.

"You stole my gold, wee man," he bawled at me as I shook my head so that my neck cracked. I told him I took nothing and that he might search me, but that I would prove as good as my word. And search me he did, somehow, holding me with one hand and squeezing every inch of my person with the other. He pawed and pinched until, at last, his stupid face assumed an expression of surprise, and he shoved me so that I fell hard against the rough stones of the church. We exchanged a look, we two, but he had nothing more to say to me.

D. M. Bryan

By then, the girl was long gone, as were the fops who'd cut so fine a figure in their braided coats. An apron showed white in a distant pool of lamplight and then passed beyond.

But, nothing can happen in London without a crowd, and a new one gathered around the drover and myself: three ruffians in coats, a tattered man on crutches, and a spongy-faced porter lifting a dog by its tail.

"A wrong one is he?" said the porter when he saw me looking at him, and he set down his animal so that it ran in circles around his legs, shrieking and yelping. The porter leaned down close until I could see the dark veins in his nose. "I'll set my dog on you for a thief," he said.

"I'm not a thief," I said, attempting to rise, but a crutch swung round and pushed me back down. "Tell them," I begged the drover. "Tell them I'm an honest boy."

The drover wiped his mouth with the back of his hand. "To tell it true," he said, "I don't know what he is."

"There's your thief," I said, pointing into the darkness of the lane behind my accusers, right at the spot where the cutpurse had fallen, but the men only laughed at what they termed my ploy and drew in closer around me.

In a book, someone would have come from the church—a priest concerned at the sound of my cries or a warden of the church ready to do a poor boy a kindness—but no one came, and so hard hands gripped me and shoved me to my feet. They made me walk down Cloth Fair, which I knew better than they, so I felt every stumble and every stagger they took on the way to Smithfield, and for a short while I began to hope that the effort might prove too much exertion for ones such as these. A few gave up my persecution—one ruffian was sucked into a dim gin shop and another tumbled into a brighter, noisier tavern—but in time I found myself kicked and scraped the short distance to the cattle-ground. There, under the inspiration of the bright stars, they began to test the depths and various foulness of the miry ponds of liquid that dotted the place. At last they found one of a suitable depth so that they might lie me flat with my face at the deepest part, whereupon they commenced to repeatedly plunge my nose and mouth into the vileness. Mud choked me and plastered over my eyes. At least, I told myself it was mud, plain dirt, although the rankness of its odour suggested some other substance plugged my nostrils and was gritty between my teeth.

I screamed. I cried. I begged them to not dunk me again, and I protested my innocence until one of them lifted me dripping from the mire and hissed in my ear, "Confess and we'll stop." This I did as soon as I could find breath, and, after a few more dunkings, my persecutors grew tired of my protestations and stopped. Then, they dropped me on my side, while I coughed and vomited up a gallon of the finest cowshit Smithfield had to offer.

"Are you properly shrive then?" one of them demanded of me, when I was done. I blinked my eyes until I could see him. His calf and foot hung bent and shrivelled behind. A wooden post was bound to the thigh of that leg, and he had two crutches tucked under each arm. So equipped, he moved with great facility. He swung a crutch now and knocked me painfully on the chest. "Have you learned your lesson then, boy?"

I nodded. Whatever the lesson, I felt I could honestly be said to have learned it.

The little dog, who still kept faith with the company, came now and licked my face, his paws upon my bruised chest. The dog's master checked my pocket and came away with my own purse, empty even of the farthing I'd thrown to my sister-in-crime. I shuddered in one of the cruel breezes that sprang up in the openness of the cattle-ground. The dog's master regarded me with disgust and threw me back my empty purse.

"Not a penny richer," said he, "for all your thieving. Remember, boy, the wages of sin will never make you better than the rest."

"It will make him worse," added another, "for at least our coats is clean." They laughed, each in a different register.

The man on crutches said, "He's just lucky we chose not to call upon the constables," which was as true an utterance as might ever be made. I nodded, and the fellow grinned at me before cracking me hard on the side of the head with a crutch. My ear so burst with noise—or perhaps it was pain—I almost lay me down in the mire again.

"He has confessed. Be easy with him, brother," said the porter, calling his dog to his side.

D. M. Bryan

The remaining ruffian leant forward and offered me his hand to pull me from the pool where I half lay, half sat. I feigned not to see his thin fingers and began to struggle on my own to rise to my feet, but my head hurt beyond measure, and I had to pause to vomit again. When I was done, I wiped my mouth with the sleeve of my reeking coat, and finding the ruffian's hand still extended, I seized it, not entirely remembering to whom it belonged. I found myself pulled to my feet, and held in place until I could stand on my own again. When he let me go, I staggered but managed to steady myself, using the man's ugly features to show me which way was up. He'd taken a step backwards, and already his figure had begun to fold back into the night. I saw his eyes, liquid in the starlight, and, below them, the ghost of his smile, and then he turned away and left me alone, his coat flapping in the Smithfield breeze.

They were all done with me, the men. Already, I could see the porter's back diminishing in the direction of the hospital, his animal at his heels. The man on crutches was little more than a wooden tattoo in the dark, beating the way back toward St. Bart's. I began to walk myself, a drunken sort of stumble that sent me reeling from gaping doorway to knuckle-scraping wall, and I continued in this state for some minutes. As I lurched through the streets leading off the square, I noticed heads turned toward me, but nobody thought a gin-dizzy child worth robbing. Shadows barred my way, only to fall back again, allowing me to continue, though in an uncertain direction.

How I found my way back to my bolt-hole in my confused state, I hardly know. I know only that when I found myself in the doorway of Mother's crooked house, I sat on the stone step and wept. Then I roused myself and knocked. No one came. I knocked again. I sat back down on the step and wept some more, until, at last, I remembered to try the latch of the door and felt it give way under the pressure of my hand.

Upstairs, in the safety of my room, I stripped down to my shirt, leaving behind my mud and dung-covered breeches, waistcoat, and coat lying on the floor. Then I slipped me beneath the blanket of my bed, for I had no linens. I regretted the filigreed pattern of dirt my filth-stiffened curls left wherever I lay my head, but I had not the strength of will or of body to so much as wash my face. I awoke from time to time, from cold or pain in my belly, but I could no more light my fire than I could eat the bit of bread and cheese stored on the mantle. Indeed, I had the severest trouble telling the time of day

My room had no window, the strange result of its having been formed, as I think I have said, from the division of a larger chamber. Each resulting cell retained some feature suggestive of its grander past, which is how it came to pass that my bolt-hole featured a mantelpiece that was both unusually large and unnecessarily elegant. This magnificent item had old-fashioned curves that now, in my illness, made me think I was at sea. Sick fancy set me in a ship that rose and fell at the whim of the pain in my head. In the faint daylight that filtered in through gaps in the dividing wall, I watched as the prow of this boat broke waves into droplets, sending up sprays of bell-shaped blossoms. At night I shook and shivered in the sea air, feeling the roaring of a great tide press hard against the bones of my head. The heaving of the wooden boards of my floor made me sick, and I first filled my chamber pot, before vomiting bile into the ashes of my extinguished fire.

The first morning of my illness, Mother came to see why I had not descended to break my fast with my criminal kindred. I awoke to find her bent low and sniffing at the heap of mud-stained clothing that were my only garments. She kicked them aside with the toe of her slipper, causing a cloud of dust to bloom from their folds. "Quire, child," she said, rubbing her nose with the back of her hand, "I don't suffer my young gentlemen to drink. You know that well enough."

I groaned from my bed by way of an answer, desiring to explain, but when I looked a second time, Mother had taken on a foggy appearance, her bulging outline bleeding wetly. "The sea air," I told her as best I could, "eats all things. You are not safe."

She loomed over me now, her face shimmering from beneath the waves. Her lips parted and silver bubbles hung between us. "—in London, fool," she said, as she surfaced. She gulped, drawing breath into her lungs. Lacy foam covered her breast and crested over her head.

I warned her, "The deep shall enfold you," but Mother only slipped back beneath the swell, the inky stain of her skirts spreading as she sank. I stood alone beside the Thames, watching the rising ribbon of water—a shining strip stitched with a hundred masts. Ships at anchor, tarnished and soft with rain. I looked for a ship to bear me away, but

D. M. Bryan

no little craft plied the span of water between deck and dock. And so, the storm took me. In my panic, I could find neither candle nor chamber pot. Hunched with pain, I arose and urinated in a corner of my cabin. The pitching caught me off balance and I fell hard against rough boards. Then I crawled back toward my bed. The blanket, stiff as it was, comforted me as I drew it up beneath my chin.

When next I awoke, the grey dim light of another day filled the chamber—although I did not know that then. Rain fell on the roof, and damp patches appeared in the plaster of my wall. I saw there a map of continents unvisited and vast lands of exposed brick. I watched the sea around my doorway, until that plank opened into the hallway. In came the small girl from the street—the singer—and with her she brought a dirty napkin. She pulled a chair beside my bed and sat in it, opening the napkin and setting a roll upon each knee. She sat for a while, silent and staring about her and wrinkling her nose. She was perhaps nine or ten years old—the same age I'd been when I'd first come under Mother's desultory care.

"Hullo," I said in a voice made of sand. I was clemmed with hunger, and the drumming on the roof hurt my head very much.

"I saw them take you," she said at last, and looked very hard at me. When I didn't answer she gave me a roll, which I ate in tiny bites, chewing carefully because of the pain. The girl spoke again. "You came back," she said looking aggrieved, "but where's our Nat?"

"Nat's at the bottom of the Thames. A storm—" but even as I said the words, I knew I spoke a dream—or something akin. "I don't know where Nat is." After a moment, I said, "Who's Nat?"

"You know Nat. When I sing he—" and she made a motion with her hand as if she cut something with a knife.

The cutpurse. I never bothered much with finding out what my family called themselves, for few stayed with us long. Some changed their names daily, and some found other families and never wanted us to know them again. Some vanished into Bridewell where, even if I knew them when they went in, I took care to not know them when they came out again. The girls in particular I ignored, for most who passed through that house became whores, despite Mother's warnings. A singer on her own had no trade whatsoever, and so I didn't want to tell her what I'd seen: Nat dropping in the dark like a ham cut from a beam.

The child got up and found me a cup full of stale water. I drank it and had the second roll from off her skinny knee. "Nat's like to be gone awhile," I told her, my mouth full of bread. "He had some business come up."

"How would you know such a thing?" she said at last. "He'd not tell you of any business without telling me first. I know he wouldn't. Why, you hardly know us."

There was nothing for it but to be honest and open with the child. "I saw a man—at least, I think he was."

She stared without a word. I looked at the ceiling where straw poked through the damp plaster.

"He was made of clothes," said I. "Like he was naught but a suit. A coat both thick and glossy."

"A religious?"

"More like a clerk or a scribbler from up Grub Street." I thought of Gotobed. "That's all I know. That's all I want to say. I saw a man, and don't look for Nat to be coming home."

She made no reply, but one of her herring eyes began to be rimmed with a tear. It grew fatter and fatter until some mysterious barrier broke along its salty perimeter, and it sank into a wet line down her pale cheek. The other eye remained perfectly dry.

I turned my back on her. I felt too sick to witness her sorrow, too tired to watch her wrestle.

In time, the girl slipped softly down from my chair and closed my door behind her. Despite myself, I wondered if I knew her name, and I thought I must have heard it before. Moll? Poll? But she hardly mattered, for I did not like girls and had no need to know one.

I wanted rest. I lay under my blanket and waited for sleep to swallow me whole. My nausea had eased a little with the bread and with water, and while I felt more hungry than I had before the rolls, exhaustion kept me from going in search of more to eat and drink. I tried to shut my eyes, but my lids seemed painted open like the wax dolls at Bartholomew Fair. I could no more sink back into darkness than I could stop running pictures through my head.

In that state of mind, St. Bartholomew himself appeared to me, standing perched on his pedestal and holding the large bladed knife they'd used to skin him. 'Twas a butcher's blade, and the saint held it upright and at his side like a soldier with a musket. He'd go marching with it by his side into the day of final judgment, but on that day, I knew I would have nothing in my hands with which I might defend myself. The entire store of my small cupboard would avail me nothing, for my Judge would not take the fine cambric handkerchief, nor the snuffbox with its enamelled lid. What cared He for my small bag of coins or the golden rings? He'd look into my heart, and what would he find there? He'd find a secret cupboard as bare as any in London. I was no more than a thief—or worse—and now I was dying.

The grey light in my room had grown intolerably bright. My eyes stung but still I could not close them, staring at the broken plaster and the beams, furred with years of smoke. The reek of my room grew intolerable, and I was ashamed of the wet patch in the corner. I would that I had thrown down a little ash and swept away my shame. Now, my room opened to me like one of Mr. Hogarth's prints, full of emblems that might be read and understood. The overfull chamber pot. The empty cup upon the table. Bickham's picture on the wall. The gutted fire. My own thin torso, crouching, my face uplifted. My hands stretch out in a supplication as clean as a sheet of fine linen paper.

Oh hear these words, O Lord.

I did know the child's name—it was Dorothy. I'd known all along, and Nathaniel, her brother. She was still a child and did not understand the risk that attended her, never further away than the hem of her skirts. That danger was a little dog now, a pug that nipped at her ankles. She'd consent to let it tease, laughing at its mock growls. In time, a bite would close on her hand, but by then it would be a bigger dog, its sunken face watchful and patient. When she grew hungry, it would lead her into Tom King's coffee house, and then it would bar the door, showing its teeth if she tried to go before her time. A borrowed dress, it would bring her, and it would pad after her when she took her gentlemen upstairs. If she wept, it would comfort her. If she had children, it would howl. And when she grew ill, it would live on. I should have shown her that dog, drawing its likeness upon the walls of my room with a bit of charcoal. *Doll, meet the dog,* I should have told her, sketching its round head and trim ears. *Beware.* I tried to call her back, speaking her name aloud. Doll. Dorothy.

Truly, I was ill. I thrashed so in my bed that my blanket sprang from me and caught between my legs. In haste, I pulled up the blanket and down my shirt. I sat up, fearful that someone had come, but no one had heard me. I was alone.

My mother wore a scarlet dress, and she was dead. I was alone.

I knew I'd slept when I woke again, my head fully clear at last. I could sit up, but I was weak for want of food, and I was still that way when Mother entered. "Phew," she said, when she had satisfied herself that I was not a corpse. "It smells very poorly in here. I could send up my girl if you had something to pay her with." It was one of Mother's rules that we saw to our own needs, for her servants had better things to do than tend to infants. I nodded weakly, for I could also smell the pissoir-reek that rose from my hearth and from other parts of my room as well.

"I can pay," I told Mother. "Bid her come up."

Mother nodded, pleased by this, and no sooner had she left my chamber than one of her servants came up to me with a piece of beef, a heel of bread, and a jug of well-watered wine. While I ate, the woman swept the hearth and built a fire. I bid her scatter clean ash in the corner of my room, which she did, and it served to improve the odour somewhat. While she worked, I quizzed her on the whereabouts of Dorothy—a task complicated by the number of children in the house.

"Which one is she?" said the maid. "Is she crippled in the arm?" but I could not remember that she was. "No?" said the woman. "Then tell me if she be fair or dark, tall or short. Is she a pretty one? Has she quick fingers? Does she—" and here she winked at me, "take gentlemen on the side? Oh, you look so shocked, little sir, but they all flout Mother's rules, and the sweetest ones more so than all the rest, for they have most opportunity and are least suspected."

I thought Dorothy still innocent, but neither would I argue the point. "She sings," I told her, "while her brother picks pockets."

The woman took out her fire-steel. A small, pale flame danced and spread, burning bright. "There's many as fit that bill," she said, rising and brushing off her apron. "Choosing out one from the rest is like to finding a particular sparrow in a whole flock. Mayhap God can do it, but 'tis more than I can manage. Your ear's all covered in blood, small sir, if you don't mind me saying."

I put my hand to my ear and found it crusted and twice its natural size. My head still hurt and speaking made the pain worse. I asked her to fetch me some warmed water from the kitchen, rising while she was gone to find a coin to pay her. When I gave it her, she took the token gladly but kept it in her hand, begging my pardon but saying she put nothing in her pockets on account of all the thieves that lived in that house.

When she had stumped down the stairs, I washed my head, paying particular attention to my ear, which bled feathers of rust into the basin of water. Afterward, I had nothing clean with which to wrap my head, until I found me a Monmouth cap I'd bought from a sailor to keep my head warm on winter nights. It was made for a man and too large for me, coming down over my ears, but stuffed with a worsted wool stocking, it made a tolerable bandage. My neck, my arms and my legs, I washed as well as I could. Then, I regarded my clothes on the floor, but I could not imagine how I should clean these, for a good laundress was beyond my means. Layers of dried mud and shit covered both breeches and coat, and also coated the row of buttons. I was very proud of these buttons, for they were made of pewter, with a death's head pattern, and I thought them very fine. I had stolen twelve dozen from a draper's shop, and my effort pleased Mother so exceedingly she had allowed me to keep six of them for myself. Now, they had lost their lustre, and I had nothing else to put on, so I went back to bed, still in the shirt I'd been dunked in. The garment had dried under the blanket with me, and most of the filth had rubbed off, settling in the creases of my mattress. We were old friends, that dirt and I, and so I curled up in its middle and went back to sleep.

It was in this condition that Gotobed found me. On the third day after we shook on our deal, he'd gone to the coffee house where he'd promised to wait, and when I did not at length appear, he began to ask after me. In time, he came to Mother's door, where he was firmly told that no such person as Cass Quire lived there—a reply that was no more than routine in the business that was that lady's. Luckily for me,

Gotobed understood at once what Mother was, and knew he had come to the right place. He knocked again, and this time demanded Mother herself, and after submitting to the servant's careful examination of his person, and following the transfer of a farthing from his pocket to hers, he found himself admitted to the ground floor parlour where Mother sat at an escritoire, pretending to write.

Mother demanded at once to know Gotobed's business, and he told her he looked for a young person who lived there, and that he came on a matter of no very great importance save to young men such as himself and Mr. Quire. At this Mother set down the pen she held dripping over an empty page. "Mr. Gotobed," said Mother, for my new friend confessed she had forced his name from him the moment he entered her parlour, "the gentleman you seek is at church—my boarders go very regular. I myself make sure they do." All this Gotobed told me later, when we had leisure to speak of such things, and I sat open-mouthed to hear Mother tell such a falsehood. I knew that I lied often and well, but Mother was a master.

"Mr. Quire does not strike me as a regular churchgoer," said Gotobed. "Are you certain?"

Then she told him, I was ill and very likely had the smallpox, and if he had anything for me, he might vouch it her for safekeeping. "Anything at all," she said. "It will not go astray, sir, should it be worth ever so much."

Gotobed commended her generosity, but said, in truth, he had nothing of value to leave with her.

"Then I do not know him, sir," said Mother. "I mistook the gentleman's name. I am truly very sorry."

"So he is not upstairs and taken to his bed?"

"He is not." And with that Mother took up her quill and blotted the page further, while Gotobed found himself taken by the elbow and led gently from the room by the very person who'd shown him in.

On the landing, Mr. Gotobed stopped and turned about. He went back into the parlour, where he found Mother waiting for him. Taking another, larger coin from his pocket, he set it over the blot in Mother's account book, and in this way Mr. Gotobed, at last, found me.

To me, Gotobed arrived like a ministering angel. He came in, leaving the door open behind him, and whatever remained of the sickroom miasma rushed out. I snatched up my blankets and drew them to my chin, even as he entered and immediately tripped over my discarded coat and breeches.

"What's the matter with you, Quire," he said just as soon as he'd righted himself and his eyes could adjust to the light cast from the few embers of my fire. He hung back from the bed. "Your vile landlady said you are poxed."

"Pox? No indeed," and I turned my head enough to show him my ear. "A man split it with his crutch, and ever since I have been distempered."

"I see only a cap, and under it a dirty stocking. Are you sure you have no vesicles. Why do you cover your chest?"

"I'm cold. Let me show you my injury." I pulled off my Monmouth, removed the blood-clotted linen, and brought my ear as close to Gotobed's nose as I dared. Gotobed looked on, but made no move to examine my wound more nearly.

"Your face is clear enough," he said at last. "Let me see your hands." Willingly, I held out my palms, which were clear of blisters and, after my ablutions, almost clean.

"Well, a mere blow to the head would not distemper me," he said, putting his hands on his hips. "Come, dress yourself, for I have found us an engraver and a printer, and you have wasted too much of my time already."

I willingly forgave this boastful way of talking, and I made to examine him on his arrangements. "Have you acquired the right paper?" I asked. "Each sheet must be fine pressed with only a little tooth, and it must be of a size with the plate."

"I am a printer's apprentice," said Gotobed, rolling his eyes, "I have the paper."

"Do you have charcoal?"

Gotobed said nothing to this but showed me the whites of his eyes again.

"It should be linden charcoal, for that wood burns the purest. And do you have crayons of white chalk? I must have that. And a camel's hair pencil? Do you know how to find such a thing? You printers do your reckoning with anything that will make a mark, but that won't do for me. And also crows-quill pens, well-shaped. You must give me those."

"I will give you nothing unless you get out of bed. Your ear is not bleeding and the wound looks dry enough. Here." He plucked my coat from the floorboards. It no longer dripped with puddle-water, but it still smelled very foul, and no sooner had he lifted the garment than Gotobed dropped it again, stepping back from the noxious bouquet that blossomed at his feet.

"They put me in a pool of shit at the Smithfield market," said I.

"Who did?—but never mind," said Gotobed, "Do you have any other coat?"

"Do you?"

We were at a stalemate.

In the end, Gotobed sallied forth into the street and bought me an old coat from a stall that sold such things, and when the goodbody who sold it him turned to retrieve the fine stockings that might just do, he stole me a pair of breeches as well. The stockings, he decided, alas, would not do, but he paid the woman with less haggling than was usual with him, which was, he told me, how he squared his conscience in matters like these.

"Damn your conscience," I said, "I still have no stockings," for I was quickly pulling up the breeches, while he illustrated just how the goodbody turned her back. The breeches were too large, but not by much. I stuffed in my shirt and reached for the coat.

"That shirt is very dirty," said Gotobed.

"Did you steal me a clean one?"

"I did not," he said, grinning.

I pulled on the coat, wishing it were not cut in the newer, more open fashion. I said so.

"Worse and worse," said Gotobed, "I understand that breeches are worn more tightly this year, while yours are—"

"Mine are slipping down around my arse." I gave them a tug. "And I have no waistcoat—you should have bought me a waistcoat."

"You did not wear one when we first met."

"You have a good memory."

D. M. Bryan

Gotobed bowed facetiously, although I meant the compliment. I took up my old stockings and shook them out, examining the extent of the bloodstain on the one I'd used as a bandage. Then I pulled them both on and buttoned my breeches over top. Together, Gotobed and I examined my legs. The stain was extensive and the effect was—as my companion said—more Banquo's ghost than Sir Fopling Flutter.

"It matters not," I said, pulling down my Monmouth over my damaged ear. "When we are rich, I'll buy ten suits, and everyone will have a vest and a clean set of white stockings to accompany it."

"And when we are rich," said Gotobed, "I'll return to the goodbody the price of your breeches."

This he said with no trace of a smile, and I guessed he had not yet salved his conscience, no matter what he told me. Such qualms seemed too nice in a man so rough, and I stared at him in some surprise. For this, I earned a scowl.

Shrugging, I dismissed all consideration of his contradictory nature, following him willingly from my bolt-hole and into the street. Finally, we were embarked on our scheme together, Mr. Gotobed and I, and so together we went forth.

CHAPTER 14

THE LIFE AND TIMES OF CASS QUIRE, GENTLEMAN.

Contains the sequel to Cass' projection with Mr.
Gotobed. Much is written on the nature of engraving
and printing. A gentleman mentions Mr. Hogarth's
view of pyrates.

London, 1746.

The workshop filled the top floor of a ramshackle building very near
to St. Bart's the Greater—that place where Doll sang and Nathaniel
vanished. We entered through a door off St. Bartholomew's Close,
making our way up two flights of steps until we emerged in a long, stone
chamber that ran the length of the three houses abutting the church.
Windows, intermittently placed and made of buckled squares of glass,
let in the light, although not for us, for we came as thieves at night.
Once, these premises held a respectable printer's firm begun by Mr.
Samuel Palmer, who was reckoned a good man, but Palmer had died
a year or so before. Now a pair of letter founders, brothers surnamed
James, paid the rates on the building and intended to expand their
foundry to fill Palmer's old premises. But they hadn't done so yet, and
in the meanwhile the presses sat unused and waiting. With nothing but
empty floors below, the workshop's situation could not have been better
suited to our purposes.

Gotobed, as he showed us around, grew expansive, swigging from a bottle and leading us through the long room. To see him, anyone might have thought he had purchased the workshop rather than forced an entry. He set down his candle, wiped dust off the presses, found out the chases, and showed me the ink balls. He'd thought of everything, he told us, while we listened.

There were two of us dogging Gotobed's heels that night—myself and the copper-engraver newly brought into our scheme. On first acquaintance, I cared little for the fellow, and I liked him less with every approving nod he gave to Gotobed's arrangements. He treated me with blond conviviality and wrung my hand heartily, but cold looks were all I could return. My behaviour distressed Gotobed, and as soon as the subject of my enmity stepped out to take the air, Gotobed demanded that I tell him what I had against Prosper, for such was the fellow's absurd name.

Prosper was one of those apprentice engravers who had travelled across the channel with his master to exchange fancy French work for good English money. That exchange I did not like, and I told Gotobed so. "We have English engravers as good as any in France," I said.

Gotobed had given me the drawing materials I demanded, and I was now beginning to draw the pictures that were my part in the bargain. In soft lead, I began to outline a dog struggling with a man over a bone. The dog formed a detail in the first of the eight false Hogarths.

Gotobed shrugged. "The French are our masters in all things pertaining to elegance of line," he said. "But Quire, in all seriousness, our scheme—we are not working on behalf of English art."

"Mr. Hogarth is an Englishman who engraves his own plates."

"Prosper says that is not always the case, that Hogarth worked with Monsieur Ravenet on his *Marriage a-la mode*, and others of his countrymen besides.

"Prosper is a fool."

"Is it his religion you object to? Are you a bigot, Mr. Quire?"

On my page, the dog began to snarl with a vigour that surprised even me. He looked as though he might tear off the arm of the man grasping the disputed bone.

"I care no more about his religion than I do his wig."

"Prosper does not wear a wig."

"Exactly so." I left off drawing for a moment to think of Prosper's head, so much did the subject irritate me. I waved my lead in the air, saying, "I do not know which offends me more—that the man pays a barber to shave so much of his hair, or that he pomades what's left into that pointed beak."

"I think his hat shapes it thus," said Gotobed, but his heart had gone out of our discussion. I saw him glance at the stairwell, overprinted with shadow. Then he looked at the silent presses filling the workshop.

In truth, I knew we must have Prosper—or someone exactly like him. Each of the eight drawings I drew required inscribing, in reverse, on its own copperplate. This was Prosper's task, which he would carry out well enough, *if* he were the trustworthy member of our party Gotobed believed. If not, he would steal my designs and take them for his own, selling us to the constables in the bargain. Then, my next sketch would be on a cell wall. Or worse, his skill at engraving would disappoint, and he would render my work as stiff and lifeless as Mr. Bickham's—God save us from that betrayal.

"He has been a very long time," I said, setting to work again with my crayon.

"A man must have his diversions. Not everyone is as well entertained with paper and lead as you."

"He must be fully diverted by now."

"Honestly, I don't understand this fit of pique—you were the one on fire to meet an engraver and observe his skill. I must ask you again, my dear Mr. Quire, to set aside whatever differences you have with Prosper and welcome him as a partner in our enterprise."

Why, I might have asked, is he already "Prosper" and I still your "dear Mr. Quire?" but instead I said, "What does it matter what I think of him, so long as we both carry out our separate tasks?" Then I renewed my grip on my crayon and began to draw again.

From under my fingers came a small figure of a girl, her chin lifted and her bonnet set straight. On her apron I drew a parish badge, and in her hand I put a small fluted glass, which a companion was teaching her to lift to her lips. I recognized Doll and saw that already she was drinking gin. The folds of her dress I filled in with lines of an even firmness, pressing hard against a shudder in my hands.

Gotobed came to stand by my shoulder, leaning down over the small table at which I worked. He'd given up the quarrel and was watching me work. "Really, Quire," he said, speaking softly, "such a character might be one of Hogarth's own."

I did not—I could not—meet his eye, but laboured over the dress until I had quite ruined the fall of the apron.

It was while we were thus, silent together and feeling little need for further discourse, that the sound of footfalls on the long wooden staircase announced Prosper's return. Instinctively, I put a protective arm over my page, although why I did not wish him to see my work I could not have said. When he reached us, he bent forward, placing his hands on his knees. He was breathing hard, panting like a dog. "I had," he said, his peculiar English made even more incomprehensible by his gasps, "to run very ... very quick."

Gotobed was all aflutter, patting him on the back as if to ease the passage of English air into those Gallic lungs. As Prosper pulled off his brown greatcoat I continued to draw, filling in a section of house I had roughed out earlier. I knew the details mattered less than the design, but I would not leave even the shape of the stones to another. While I worked, Prosper's story emerged.

He had, he said, exited our secret workshop, seeking only a breath of fresh air. As he came into the close, his appearance startled two men lurking in a doorway. Immediately they saw him, they ran, and he—oh, brave soul, French you know—ran after, following them through the close, splashing along New Street and from thence into Aldersgate, where he lost them.

"What?" said I. "Lost them in Aldersgate? Why the street's as wide as your mother's—"

"Quire," said Gotobed.

Prosper said, "They turned, just before an inn. I did not see the sign."

St. George's. No signpost. No need. Everyone knows it—well, almost everyone.

I said, "Did they turn down Maidenhead? Or did they take to Nettleton's Court? If it was Nettleton's, you had them like hens in a bag."

Prosper shrugged with unnecessary vigour, so like a Frenchman. His blue waistcoat flashed. I eyed the silver-bullion and tinsel buttons.

"Quire." Gotobed watched my face, his own an emblem of warning.

"Quire," I mimicked and went back to the facing of my building.

Gotobed and Prosper put their heads together and discussed what the fleeing men might portend. Prosper fretted and dithered, but Gotobed dismissed his fears. "Beadles and constables," he said, "never run," and I thought he had the right of it. Watchmen would have come to the door and rapped smartly with the ends of their cudgels, and when they discovered us inside, they'd have rapped on our heads just as smartly. No, Prosper's lurkers were doubtless a pair of gin-drinkers finding shelter from the rain. Or perhaps they were the kind of man who preferred the companionship of a fellow in a wet place to the dry bones of a girl in a stew.

Soon enough, and this usually happens when I draw, I forgot my companions. I forgot the long room, squared with night, and I forgot my complaining belly. I forgot the presses, which were usually unforgettable, dominating the room like ships at sea, rigged with flags of paper. All around that frame, the ghosts of print-men worked like common tars, shifting pages from press bed to the drying racks high overhead. Sometimes those phantom pages stirred, as a breeze from nowhere sent a surf-like whispering along the length of the building. Once, I lifted my head and found myself lost in clear water, gazing up into pale currents, but then the black marks of my crayon anchored me to my drawing again.

I drew a street, a set of verticals and horizontal strokes. At the top, I drew a banded box—a slice of London, a linear width of weather. Into the white page, I scumbled clouds with my crayon held sideways, rubbing away the smell of the tobacco from Prosper's thin-stemmed pipe. I saw only my leaden London street, its houses and churches and businesses stacked like empty boxes while its citizens stood framed in doorways: a lord with a face like a pinch; a drover in a broad-brimmed hat; a lady whose shift hung torn as a wet rose. These figures, I had to my satisfaction.

In their midst, and at the point to which all the action tended, I drew a Tom Idle to match the one in Mr. Hogarth's print, only now

Tom found himself worse off than before. I drew him searching for a drink in a street lined with geneva-sellers. A smudge encircled Tom's eyes, and a single curved line traced the sad decline of his ribs to his belly.

"You tell us a story," said Prosper in my ear.

He undid all my forgetting in an instant. "Of course I tell a fucking story," I said.

Prosper either didn't understand or wasn't offended by the vulgarity of my speech. I prepared to repeat myself for his more complete edification, but he put out his finger and seemed to feel the air above my drawing.

"Here, don't touch that page."

"I don't," said Prosper. "I don't touch."

Gotobed came over from where he'd been sitting, and Prosper told him Tom's story, pointing out each moment with elaborate care. Prosper said, "I look at this street where he," pointing at Tom, "looks through the window at the fine silver," pointing to a tiny, drawn spoon, "and she," pointing at a fine lady, "sees what's in his heart, and he," gesturing at a constable, "observes Tom and the lady." And so Prosper continued, while I watched.

That morning, in a street of lifting grays, we parted company but promised to meet again the following evening. My way lay toward Cloth Fair and the market, where I hoped an hour's picking of pockets would forestall Mother's imprecations at an empty-handed return. Gotobed and Prosper turned up the close together, walking side-by-side on their long legs like a team of spiders. They intended to break their fast nearby and hole up to sleep, before returning to the workshop. Then, Prosper would begin to engrave my first completed sketch.

They did not ask me to join them at breakfast, and neither did I ask if I might. I still hated Prosper—I hated his crested head and his silky waistcoat—but he'd read my story back to me, properly compositing my sketch in his thickened English. Prosper followed the marks my crayon left like another man might follow Fielding's silvery phrases, or Mr. Richardson's more stolid typeset—like a fellow might follow Mr. Hogarth himself, weaving with his eyes until loose ends connected. I still hated Prosper, I really did, but I'd come to a decision: I'd give him a chance with his burin and plate. I'd see if he could a second time translate my drawing, this time line-by-line into copper. Then Gotobed could test the plate's inky truth on a clean white sheet. And if the work measured up—if Prosper passed—then I might consider us a partnership of three.

Three thieves—an artist, an engraver, and a printer—to imitate one inimitable genius.

I turned to look, but the others were already gone.

The following evening, I waited for my fellow schemers in the darkened close, slipping into a doorway at the passage of every yellow lantern and link. In between times, a chalky moonlight shifted along the street, whitening the line of cottages. Down cellar steps, sheltered beneath a bay window, drinkers settled in for their first sleep, grumbling over a candle's sorry warmth. I wrapped myself tightly in my coat, and set to shivering as the evening deepened to slate. Then, from a square of blackness, I saw coming toward me two pale forms, pressed and silent. As they drew nearer, I stepped out of my sheltering arch, and both greeted me with handclasps, the warmth of palms masquerading as speech.

As soon as we entered the workroom, Gotobed began lighting tapers—two this time, one for me and one for Prosper. From under his coat, Prosper drew a bulky bundle, well wrapped in stained canvas. From this, he removed a tight roll of paper and peeled off a single sheet, thin as the skin of an onion. He gave me the page and bade me copy my drawing onto its opaque surface. He said, "Trace only the—how do you say it? The *contour?*"

"The outline," said I, looking instead at the opened canvas bundle and the copperplates therein, red-gold peeping from sackcloth. I looked as another might squint at a breast.

"No detail," said Prosper. "You do not make a drawing here."

"I know," I said, but I did not—I wanted to learn with every fibre of my being.

While I traced my drawing's outline onto the onion-paper, Prosper selected a plate, tipping it this way and that before the candle, as if looking in a red mirror. Then, he rolled up his sleeves and unwound a kind of canvas belt, turning out a collection of small hand-tools, each fashioned of metal and wood. The canvas itself he transformed into a heavy apron to cover his shirt, refastening the ties around his neck and waist. A foggy cube turned out to be wax, which he melted over the copperplate, rubbing it against the metal to form a thin surface layer.

When I had traced an outline of my drawing onto the onion skin, I gave it to Prosper. He nodded his approval and pressed it, face down, into the waxed copperplate. Then, he began to retrace my lines with a tipped tool. I leaned forward, and when Prosper saw me looking, he turned in my direction, so that I might see more completely. He followed each of my lines, pressing on the paper, and when he was done, I could see that he'd left a faint impression in the wax-dulled surface of the copper.

Next, Prosper put his tools in order, laying them in a row and picking up the first, a kind of metal stylus, with which he began to incise directly into the plate. This time, when he held up the copper sheet, I could clearly make out a street lined with figures, but to me it seemed a crude thing, more like graffiti than an engraved plate. Prosper laughed at the eyebrow I raised at him, and said to Gotobed, "The little Protestant—he has no faith."

From the line of tools, Prosper chose a new one. Unlike the incising tool, which was metal rounded to a tip, this was a thin rod, squared and filed, so that three of the edges ended in a dangerous-looking point. He gave it to me and named it: a burin. Next, he took out a bag filled with sand, which was a mystery to me, until he set it in front of him and gently placed the copper-sheet over top. Taking the burin between his fingers, he set it against one of the lightly scored outlines and began to rotate the plate on its sandbag base. A thin burr of copper snaked from the tip of the tool, until the burin reached the end of the line, and Prosper took up another tool to snap off the burr, brushing it away.

Then he picked up the burin again and repeated the process, each time pushing the plate gently. "See here, faithless boy," said Prosper, "the plate moves, not the burin. That way all my strokes are curved and elegant—proper French lines with none of your English stiffness."

"Ha," said I, although I could not dispute his claim. He had transformed the marks copied from my tracing into arcing parabolas of gold. Their beauty excited me, but I had witnessed nothing as yet. Only when Prosper finished my outline, and began to work freehand to fill out the incised contours, did I understand just how much grace lay coiled in his long digits. Working from my crayon drawing, he translated my sketched details into cross-hatching that shimmered as the plate slowly spun. Candlelight caught in the red-yellow webs. Slowly, slowly, my scene emerged, luminescent and glorious.

I could not watch the whole time of course. Gotobed needed me to continue working on the designs of the other prints. So, with a little reluctance, I sat me down before a second candle and began to rough in another moment from poor Tom's life. In truth, I did not mind so much as all that. Now that I had seen a little of what engraving was, I wished to discover if I could adapt my drawings to better suit Prosper's art. Soon I lost myself in the attempt, laying in light and shadow according to my new understanding.

Dimly, I felt Gotobed stalking between Prosper and myself, his movement a mark in the corner of my eye. Once, I looked up to see a smile tweak his face, and I knew that we pleased him, we two. Accordingly, I scowled in his direction so that that grin might grow less certain, and I was happy to see his expression falter and then fail. He stopped pacing and came to lean over my page, and there he stood for a long time, watching me work.

This night, I drew Tom stopped by a pair of constables. For the officer's faces, I pyrated familiar, hated phizzes, and I set the scene in the laneway that lay behind Mother's rows of windows. In life, I had never seen a constable force his way into that reeking passage, but as soon as I began to sketch, I saw that laneway as no more than a contrast of darks and lights. Using the cross-hatches I had seen Prosper work into his copperplate, I rendered the shadows massy and rough. Then, I surveyed my work, pleased with the effect, and saw at once how I might play the white flare of the constables' links against the black of a wall. In this way, I could isolate Tom in the silence of an honest thief. Happy with my conceit, I lifted my crayon and returned to the page.

So occupied, we worked until the glass in the windows turned as opaque as onion-paper. In the morning's light, Prosper set down his burin and looked around him as though dazed. I busied myself making a last addition. In one corner, as if on the lane wall, I drew a little scrawl, the merest graffiti of a man on his back in a bed, his nose like a sail over water.

Prosper, came over to see my picture, and he laughed when he found the tiny rebus. "Ah Gotobed. This boy has immortalized you in art."

Gotobed came at once, and when he saw the scrawl, demanded I remove it. I shook my head. "Master Hogarth includes the like," said I.

"Take it out."

I put my hands on either side of the page, letting my crayon fall from my fingers. "You flatter yourself that someone will read it aright," I said. "You are beyond obscure, Gotobed."

"Take the damned thing out."

I looked at Prosper, who only winked at me. I shook my head at Gotobed.

"If you won't, I will," and Gotobed took up my crayon, making a heavy amendment to my page. When he was done the rebus had vanished, and my design was unbalanced.

Too angry to speak, I pushed away from the table, rolling up my page as I went.

I was making to rush into the pale splash of the morning, never to return, when Prosper stopped me. With his hand out, he gestured for me to give him my design, quietly saying, "Never mind, little Quire, I will put back in what he removes."

I looked at him.

"You study to draw like a Frenchman. When I engrave this one, I will change very little."

"Is that supposed to be a compliment?" I said, but I put my roll of paper into his hand.

Then I glared over my shoulder at Gotobed, but I saw only his coated back.

That morning, I did not have the heart to pick a pocket or snatch a pewter tankard, even though I saw one disregarded, sitting on a table in a yard. Instead, I walked home through woe-gray streets, stepping over clouds reflected in puddles of piss. I stole a pie, or else I might not have eaten at all, and then I went home to my bolt-hole.

Outside that respectable house, two men stood in the street, deep in conversation. I did not like the look of them, but they soon parted ways. Even so, I watched from a distance to make sure they were gone. Then I climbed the step to Mother's front door and went in.

Gaining the hallway, I removed my shoes and commenced tiptoeing up the stairs. I did not wish to draw any attention to myself, for more than anything else, I feared an invitation to visit Mother in her parlour. It was her habit to tax us her share of our gleanings as soon as we came home, sorting wheat from chaff. At first, I crept along in perfect silence, but then a creaky tread set up an alarm, just outside her door. Immediately, I heard her stir inside her room. Worse, she hailed me by name. How she knew it was me, I cannot guess. Sometimes she seemed downright supernatural, did Mother. For a moment, I considered fleeing that place, but in truth, I had nowhere to go, so I went in.

I found her reclining on a sofa, her eyes hidden behind a cloth. "Dear child," she said, sighing. "I've been so ill. I've had to take a little of Dr. James' powder."

"Have you a fever then, Mother," said I, coming no closer than the rug.

"No, not a fever," she said, lifting one edge of her cloth and peering out at me. "'Tis a queasy kind of illness. I am so out of sorts, I cannot think clearly." She lowered her cloth.

Then, without rising from the sofa, she put out her hand for me to fill with gold.

I felt in my pocket, and to my horror found I had nothing beyond a few coppers and the half-eaten pie. I had never before failed to bring her home a fistful of guineas or the same in fine goods, and I did not know how to excuse my poverty.

"Quire," said Mother, snapping her fingers. "What do you have for me?"

In desperation, I took out the pennies and stared at them lying hopelessly on my palm. I closed my fingers, and felt their edges sharp against tender flesh. I wished I knew some trick to make them multiply, pennies to pounds, but I was a thief, not a magician.

"I've had very poor pickings today," I said.

"Pickings," said Mother. "The word turns my stomach."

I reached for a lie, but found nothing in my tired head. "In truth," said I, "I have only a few pence."

"False boy," said Mother, and she belched. She sat up, taking the cloth away from her eyes. "Come nearer," she said.

I stepped up to the sofa on which she sat. Close up, she did look ill, bloated, with cheeks as striated as a marbled side of beef.

"Quire," she said, "what do you conceal in your grubby fist?"

I shook my head. I was ashamed to show her what I had there.

"This is disobedience," said Mother.

Again, I shook my head.

"Quire. Give me your hand."

I gave her my hand and she pulled it close. Under her very nose, I release my fist and showed her the coppers, but also the crust of my pie, bits of gristle still clinging.

What Mother said next was indistinct, lost in the emetic effect of Dr. James' fever powder. Engraved, she might have served as an advertisement for the astonishing purgative potency of that substance. I yanked away and ran, bumping into the servant as she entered the room, basin in hand.

I hid away in my bolt-hole, fearing the noise of footsteps on the stairs behind me. But none came. Mother's indisposition seemed to suspend the usual order of that place, and servants in the hall below came and went without calling so much as my name. I waited fearfully, but then, hearing nothing alarming, I went to stand at the top of the stairs.

Some moments later, I saw coming up from below, a girl I knew slightly, a thief who specialized in wig-snatching to order. "Heigh-ho," she said, when she saw me. "Why do you stand there like an old suit of armour?"

"What news of Mother?" I said.

"Why, she is drunk again," said the girl, "but thinks she is ill. The doctor is coming so we must make ourselves scarce. Have you some need of her?"

I shook my head. My indiscretion, such as it was, did not seem to have produced any lasting effect.

"Have you seen Doll?" I asked on a whim.

"What do you offer?" she asked.

I pressed the scrap of pie into her palm.

"Doll who?" she said, inspecting the crust, and that was all she had to say.

Back in my room, my grate was cold, and my truckle bed grey with filth, but my secret cupboard remained secret. I climbed under my blanket and went to sleep.

That evening, I went to work on my third drawing for the partnership, and, not wishing to pass by Mother's parlour again, I exited over the tiles, freeing myself by the very back exit I included in my second picture. For the newest design, I went back to the beginning of our tale and decided to draw Tom's birth in a workhouse. For this, I had to use my imagination, for I had never been in such a place.

Gotobed came over to where I worked, looking down upon my drawing. I was still angry over his rude treatment of my rebus, and now we served each other civilly enough but with a stiffness too. We were partners in business only—I would not disturb myself chasing after his good regard.

I set to work on the dimensions of the lying-in ward, which I intended to be wide and airy, with windows at one end, very like those in this workroom.

Gotobed startled me with his growl. "Where in hell is that?" he said. "Do you prepare to draw a lord mayor's banquet?"

I was so surprised, I let go my crayon, and it rolled onto the floor. I chased it under the compositor's table, from which vantage point I could see Gotobed's coarse stockings and his worn shoes. One buckle had lost its purchase on the latchet and was sliding sideways. The fellow shifted irritably from foot to foot, and a hole showed in the heel, passing through leather and wool to reveal something pale inside.

Then the shoe vanished, and Gotobed's face appeared, inverted and about to lose its wig. He clapped a hand to his head. "Do not hide from me, Quire," he said.

I came up again, my crayon between my fingers.

"Idiot," said Gotobed. He meant me—there was no one else.

I would not reply, but sat myself again at my page and stared hard at the scene I'd begun sketching.

"Don't be so offended," he said to me. "I only meant your work is not so good as usual."

A bit of soot filled my eye, and I wiped it hard. "You bring us such cheap candles," I said. "I can hardly see to work."

"Prosper has no such difficulties." We could both hear the soft clicks of Prosper employing his tools, putting down his burin to take up his scraper. He had not yet finished graving the first plate, for engraving is more laborious than sketching.

I said, "Candlelight answers well enough for putting grooves in copper."

"You grow expert in Prosper's line of work."

"And you in mine."

We had duelled to a draw, and so we sat without moving, each of us looking down upon my page. Before I could find some pretext for further abusing my foe, Gotobed addressed me in a low voice. His words flowed from him in an unsteady fashion, as though he would rather not speak at all. He said, "My sister had her start in one of Matthew Marryott's houses, the one in St. Giles, which was the worst of them all. They had no place for women lying-in, so they put my mother with those who were too sick to work. I visited her there, saw her cared for only by other paupers, earning their keep. If you would draw a workhouse ward, you should show a cramped room, crowded with beds. Show Tom's mother crying out. Show the toothless nurses busy at another bed, helping someone to die."

At his words, the picture drew itself in my head. I looked up at him, and silently Gotobed handed me a new sheet of paper. This, I set before me and focused inwardly upon it. I could still hear his voice, even though he no longer spoke. It told me the dying man sat bolt upright, his features a mask of agony. I outlined the man's eyes and mouth, but I did not mark his papery skin with my crayon, intending that Prosper not work this area with his burin tip. In their sober dresses, the nurses ringed round, like velvet around a button of bone. In the women's hands, candles cast a penumbra that divided the room. On the far side, I drew Tom's mother, labouring in her own frail shell of light. As Mr. Hogarth had done, I envisioned a window filled with moonlight, muntin and rail casting a shadow. Crossed bars fell across the blankets that covered the mother's writhing form.

"Better," said Gotobed, and he moved away.

I finished that sketch before daylight and went away as I had before, bemused by tones and shapes imprinted on the insides of my lids. London seemed a page and I a caricature flickering across its surface. I ate; I stole; I slept; and I planned my return to the abandoned workshop where my pages had all the depth and variety my waking hours lacked.

The next night, no one met me at the door of the old printer's premises, but when I tried, I found it open. At the top of the stairs, the nighttime workroom lay revealed in candle flickers and pools of light. Gotobed was not there, and Prosper worked alone, still graving the first plate. His yellow head bent industriously over the copper, and everything about him shone. Bright streaks of reddish light flickered on his chin and forehead as he glanced up at me. I did not inquire about our absent partner, but Prosper told me regardless. Gotobed, weary of waiting for the plate to be finished, had done as his name promised and gone back to his room for whatever sleep could be found there. He would come again in the morning to see what had been accomplished overnight.

I drew for a while, working on Tom's mother's funeral, but I could not find the right picture in my head, and in time I put down my crayon. I wished now I had asked Gotobed to tell me more about his mother, reasoning that a fuller account of his life's story might help me find a shape for her. I had seen his Grub Street room for myself, and it held no clues to any family life. Gotobed seemed as alone as I.

Lacking inspiration, I put down my lead. For a time, I watched Prosper engraving, but after three day's repetition, his careful furrowing of the copperplate proved a familiar miracle, and as the workroom grew colder, I pulled my coat around me and curled up under his neatly shod French feet.

The light and the clicking of tools awoke me. Prosper had finished the plate and was gathering up his metal implements for the day, neatly wrapping them in his apron. Gotobed leaned against one of the presses with that tweaking smile upon his lips. I found myself glad to see him, although I said nothing. Indeed, I had nothing to say but only rubbed my face to clear it of possible dirt, for the floor of a print shop can never make a clean bed.

That morning, all three of us went to a low sort of place to break our fast together. We had ale and some stale bread, and a bit of cheese as well, but we were too early and too poor for a better repast. I sat between Gotobed and Prosper, laughing at their jokes, and when we parted ways, I stole a gentleman's pocket-watch in full good-cheer and took it home to Mother.

When Prosper finished the engraving and declared it ready to print, the time came, at last, for Gotobed to shine. For some time, he had been footling with one of the presses, scraping it and cleaning its surfaces. He contrived to fill a tub with water, in which he soaked that folding tray that is the tympan. This, he set into the frame of the press, cushioning it all around with folded cloth. Into the workroom, he brought ink, sealed inside a small stoneware pot. He scraped some of the thick black paste out onto a stone block and used a brayer, a flat metal tool, to pull it across the surface, thinning it repeatedly so that he removed imperfections. His physical energy, a distraction from the beginning, intensified, so that we were all of us in a state of high excitement when Prosper put the finished sheet of shining copper into his eager hands.

I knew the ink must be spread on the plate, but I could not help a little start when Gotobed began to thickly apply the paste to its beautiful surface. He looked at me then and spread the blanket of ink, thicker and blacker. Pressing with a padded piece of wood, he ground the pigment into the incised metal as hard as he could. When he was done, all the golden light was extinguished under a sticky, dirty coat.

Prosper watched these preparations, his elbows folded and a pipe between his teeth. Gotobed gestured at the fellow with his brayer, saying to me, "He knows better than to be bothered by the sight of ink on his beautiful copper plate. Why, he's the very picture of … of … what the devil are you a picture of, you Frenchman?"

"*Insouciance*," said Prosper, speaking around the pipe-stem.

"Exactly that. Now if I was to get a bit of ink on his fine blue waistcoat, he'd lose his studied composure in an instant. Shall I?"

He was asking me, making as if to flip black paste from his metal implement onto Prosper's coat. Prosper didn't so much as stir, but Gotobed himself already showed some ink on his sleeves. I wondered that he didn't wear an apron like Prosper. I said nothing, but Gotobed saw me looking at his soiled ruffles. "Printers are always dirty men," he said, lowering his brayer, "and women too in some shops."

"Never," said I.

"I've seen it," said Gotobed. But now he'd picked up a cloth and had begun to rub the ink off the copper plate.

I leaned forward. "Won't it all come off," said I.

"Nay," said Gotobed, "it's lodged in the grooves. That's why I pushed so hard."

He polished much of the ink off, and then he took up a different, cleaner cloth and polished again. Finally, he rubbed with his hands. "To get the last of the ink," he said, "you need the grease from your palms." And he held them up, black and shiny. Glorious.

The rest I knew, for I was a pressboy, when I wasn't a thief. On those occasions, I had to work at a furious speed, meeting the pace the pressmen set. Compared to that, Gotobed's pace was serene. He placed the inked plate against the press stone, closed the protective frisket over the soaked page I'd placed on the tympan, and gently set the whole under the platen. He made both pulls himself, accepting help only to shift the carriage, and he rested after each. Prosper and I stood back and watched, for this was Gotobed's art.

When freed at last from the press, the finished print seemed to me astonishing. Gotobed leaned over its damp, glossy surface, muttering about unevenness of tone, while Prosper took his pipe from his mouth to inspect the quality of his lines. Each declared himself disappointed with his own part, but I could not fault this product of our mutual labours. I kissed it, tasting the wet ink upon my lips and smudging the minute lines of an innocent, cross-hatched cloud. Gotobed slapped me on the back of my head for my importunity, but the blow was not a hard one, and I knew my co-conspirators were as pleased as I.

We were in business, but our work had only begun. Gotobed began to circulate around the lower sort of print shops, offering what he hinted was a small run of a new series of modern moral subjects, released before their time by the esteemed Mr. Hogarth to try the market. I do not know if anyone believed Mr. Hogarth's part in the tale, but when they saw the sample copy they were convinced that Gotobed had prints sufficiently like the artist's own to merit interest.

As an added inducement, if any were needed, Prosper had added at the bottom of the plate, the man's own formula: *Designed and Engrav'd by Wm Hogarth; Published according to Act of Parliament.* The words worked like a magician's enchantment on printsellers, inflaming their desire for our product, and the spell was especially potent over those who had never themselves been able to secure legitimate copies of the artist's work. And there were many of these, for Mr. Hogarth tightly controlled who might sell his prints. Soon, we were hard pressed to know how we would satisfy demand.

I quickly finished more of the drawing, and begged Prosper to set me to work on some unimportant corner of a copperplate. At first, he only laughed at me, but I practiced with a burin on a scrap of metal until I could produce tolerably straight lines, evenly spaced. Then Gotobed told the Frenchman that he might give me a chance. Better, said Gotobed, I should learn correct technique from Prosper than appear one evening with a burin in my eye. And so, Prosper set me to work on the underside of ceiling beams and empty patches of ground, although we all agreed the quality of the engraving suffered wherever I substituted.

"Never mind, little Quire," said Prosper. "You will not likely have another chance to make such a mess." He was speaking kindly, I suppose.

Gotobed no longer worked leisurely but pulled and pulled until his coat came off and his shirt grew as damp as the pages he printed. Prosper protested that eight prints were too many and that the most he might engrave in time was six. Bitterly I complained. Mr. Hogarth's purloined print contained a small decorative device in its frame, clearly intended to include one of the Beatitudes.

"And there are eight of those," I said.

"I think we might combine a few," said Gotobed, exhibiting the carelessness in religion typical of an Englishman.

Prosper flipped through my sketches. "I do not like the seventh drawing," he said. "This thin girl is Tom's lover? Why does her face look so wet? Is she drunk? I do not understand."

"Tom makes his peace with her," I told him, but he did not listen.

"She has no breasts to speak of," said Gotobed. "And her fanny is flat as a press stone."

"I think," said Prosper, "Monsieur Quire knows not very much about women, he draws such an unsatisfying one."

Gotobed said, "Let us get rid of her and add her verse alongside the design for plate six. That drawing, Tom in Newgate, is much better."

I did not care for this decision at all, but they overruled me. Then, they further combined the first and second images, Gotobed asking, "If Tom's mother takes only a single print to pup *and* die, might it not be considered an economy?" In the end, they reduced the number of images to six.

"Why not four," said I. "Or two?"

"But I have already engraved three," said Prosper, having failed to puzzle out the sarcasm. "We are half-way done."

"There are six *Harlots*," said Gotobed, and that settled the matter.

With all six drawings finished, Prosper and I worked together to complete the remaining three plates. Gotobed inked and printed, inked and printed. He pulled like a man in a frenzy, working night after night and forgoing his daytime employment, so that he might have the strength to continue. When we had finished engraving the last plate, Prosper and I set up a second press and began to print also.

Now I could teach the Frenchman something, for he knew even less of printing than I. However, my grasp of the niceties of operating the big press did not satisfy Gotobed, and he lifted a page right off the frame to show me my poor workmanship. He pointed to where the ink was not strong and dark, and where whites looked as grey as Clerkenwell pump water.

I made to discard the disgraced pull.

"What in the devil's name are you doing?" said Gotobed, stopping me with an inky hand he no longer had time to wipe.

"It's not good enough," said I.

"It is good enough," said Gotobed. "Dry it with the rest."

And then, one day, we were done. It was bright morning, but we'd long ago forgotten to sneak like thieves in our workroom. The stubs of guttering candles littered every surface, as did cheese rinds and bread crusts. In holes lined with chewed paper nested a generation of rats who'd known us from earliest infancy. We, like they, were established denizens of the place.

In front of us, on my drawing table, was piled a sufficient quantity of the series to take to the printsellers. We were dirty, and exhausted, and poorer than ever.

"How do you know we will not be cheated?" said I, watching Gotobed, who carried a rustling bundle of pages under his arm.

"I will not be cozened," said Gotobed, and watching his face I believed him.

I returned to my bolt-hold and tried to return to my accustomed way of life. Mother, long recovered of her distemper, found me in my little room. She demanded I either return to my former good behaviour or she herself would call the constables on me. I did not doubt her, and I got busy robbing innocent souls in the street. I went from crowded market to busy thoroughfare, helping myself to whatever I could find, and if Mother did not make a handsome profit from all the silk handkerchiefs or fine shagreen cases I brought her, she had only her own lack of ingenuity to fault. Soon enough, I had her meek and mild, and I found myself restored to her questionable favours.

With work in the print shop momentarily halted, I had time on my hands. I spent much of it in my chamber, my secret cupboard open and my drawings spread for review: the stiff Bickham, the half Hogarth, and a little page I'd had since childhood, from whence I took all my infant love of a crayon scrape. How I missed Samuel Palmer's cast-off workshop and my labours there. I imagined it, equally empty by grey day and indigo night, haunted by three ghosts: the first bent over a page, the second a plate, and the third a press. One evening, I walked as far as the close and tried the door, but I found it still secured with the lock placed by Gotobed. I took this as a surety on our return, and I did not waste my time in waiting. Instead, my wandering took me as far as St. Giles, although I knew the pockets were not so full in that quarter.

We had agreed—Gotobed, Prosper, and I— that after the passage of a week we would do the round of the print shops together. We would collect our earnings in each other's company, so that each of us could be certain we had our fair share. On the day appointed—a morning when the rain seemed never to stop—I went to meet the other two at the agreed-upon inn. I had not seen Prosper since our last day in the workshop, but Gotobed had come sometimes to visit me in my hidey-hole, where he leaned up against the wall with his arms and his legs crossed, saying very little at all. He'd grown thinner while he'd worked the press, and he seemed oddly breakable as he watched me from his vantage point. Now, as I entered the steaming public room, Gotobed's was the first face I saw, and catching him fresh in this way, surrounded by strangers and a blur of yeasty warmth, I thought I saw poor Tom standing in his place. In that moment, I thought of the rebus, and I was glad Prosper had not restored the little graffiti to the laneway wall. And then there was Prosper himself, who greeted me with a Gallic salute to both cheeks.

We three shook hands, and ordered ale, and after we drank we went out into the thick October air. Along wet streets we walked, passing wet men in wet coats, all struggling over wet flags, between wet walls. A carriage passed and spattered coins of dirt on everyone alike. As we walked, I began to think the weather worked a change in my two companions. The cool autumn air helped to dissipate the warmth of the workroom, as summer must give way to fall. The last week had only added to Gotobed's rakish gauntness, and he had added to his equipage with a stout oak staff. He seemed a penknife honed to razor sharp, and I found myself quiet before him.

Our destination was the neighbourhood of St. Paul's, where Gotobed had left our prints with some of the booksellers and print shops that make that their address. Soon, we came in sight of a set of stalls lining Avemary Lane. Putting out a hand to stop us, Gotobed pointed at a row of people, droop-arsed and ham-hocked, sheltering from the rain beneath the projecting roof of one of the shops. "There," he said, "you see the good effects of our work."

"I see the good effects of the rain," said I. Wet weather didn't improve a bookseller's business, but it did contain it under his roof.

Gotobed shook his head. "I have been observing the same thing every day since our prints were hung up to be sold—people are talking. Go closer, if you don't believe me."

Prosper and I edged closer, standing next to a small knot of citizens waiting out of the weather. All six of our prints hung at the back of the stall, and it did not take long for us to hear that they were already the subject of conversation. A mackerel-seller, fringe of fish at his waist, was examining one closely. He rubbed his eyes and looked again, nudging his neighbour.

"I'll be damned," said the mackerel-seller, pointing at a face in the crowd I'd drawn. "If that ain't the bastard what short-changed me last week. Why, I recognize his phiz—that Hogarth has netted him exactly."

His neighbour, who happened to be a Quaker, sober in black, did not appear to welcome the fishy elbow of the mackerel-seller. But, he smiled beatifically and said, "I am sorry to think that perdition may indeed be your lot, for I know that fellow in that picture. He no longer lives in London but has removed himself to Woodford for the betterment of his soul."

"Betterment of his arse," said the mackerel-seller. "I say I know that phiz, and it's no more in Woodford than I am."

"Peace be yours, friend," said the Quaker, "for I have no reason to fight with you. Indeed, I am only sorry that you are so mistaken in your views."

"Well, ain't you a canting sort of fellow," said the mackerel-seller, laying a hand on a fish as another man might reach for his sword.

The printseller, who had been following the dispute with interest, now stepped between the men. "Why, you shall each take the prints home today," said the printseller. "Why quarrel here when you can be right in the comfort of your own front parlour. I ask only two shillings six for the entire set—a very reasonable price indeed."

The Quaker pinched his nose. "Two and six?" he said. "What price truth?" And with that, he exited into the rain, brown mud plashing his black costume.

"How about you then?" said the printseller to the mackerel-man. "Two shillings six is a very good price. Will you buy?"

"I might at that," said the man, "if I sell a few more fish afore they rot in the rain."

"I'll buy," said a tall lady. She wore an old-fashioned headdress that stretched almost to the ceiling of the stall. "Will you deliver me a set in Soho square?"

The printseller agreed, closing the sale and releasing the lady into the rain.

Gotobed joined us, and the print-man, recognizing him at once, took him by the hand and shook it. "These pictures, sir—well, you see how they sell."

"I am glad to know it," said Gotobed.

"I could sell as many again, if you have them?"

"Perhaps," said Gotobed, leaning upon his staff. "But first we must be paid for those you have already sold."

"Ah," said the printseller, his face instantly guarded. "As to that, I can pay you what I have, but you see I extend a little credit to gentlewomen and some others with whom I have long done business."

Gotobed said nothing, only looked at his stout cudgel as if wondering at its presence in his hand. The mackerel-man, who had been following the exchange with round, wet eyes, vanished into the watery weather. With a little more room under the bookseller's roof, Prosper sat himself upon the stall's counter. Reaching under his backside to locate a book, he held it in his hand as if reading, but he watched the merchant carefully.

"Might I show you my receipt book?" said the printseller. "I am certain you will be satisfied with my manner of accounting for each set, for I am an honest man." This last came as a sort of plea.

"I know so, sir," said Gotobed, tapping his staff against the tip of his shoe. He leaned in over the merchant as the man brought out a leather ledger, filled with closely ruled, spidery lines of ink. Then, the merchant and Gotobed conferred awhile in soft voices, and at the end of this exchange a small bag was slid over the counter. Gotobed dropped the little purse into his coat pocket.

Seeing him use his pockets so, I went over to him and stood on my toes to whisper in his ear. "Keep your fingers tight about the bag until we come safe home," said I.

"What's that," said Gotobed, very audibly. "Do you warn me of pickpockets, Mr. Quire?"

At this, Prosper laughed at this and threw me the book he was pretending to read. I caught it and returned it to the printseller with a scowl. Then, we three stepped back into the rain, even as another row of customers pushed past to squint at the prints.

The next shop we came to was entirely indoors, and I felt glad of that, but otherwise the scene played itself out with little variation. And the next went the same: Gotobed and his cudgel, a clerk and a ledger, a soft, sliding bag of coins.

In the last place we visited, the seller paid up like the rest, but he accompanied the chinking of silver with a kind of curtain-lecture. He said our price was too steep and cut into his margins. He would buy again, and happily, but at a lower cost.

Gotobed frowned at him, and I did not like the look.

"To tell the truth, gentlemen," said the printseller, and he lay some stress upon this last word, as though he had some doubts about the matter, "I am astonished at your monopoly on this latest of Mr. Hogarth's series. Perhaps I shall make inquiries into the nature of your agreement with that honest artist, for he is not so very hard to find, and his view on piracy well-known."

I heard this with a kind of creeping coldness, for I had always before me Mr. Hogarth's *Publish'd according to Act of Parliament*. I did not care that my own pilfering of watches merited the gallows, but I did not want to disappoint Mr. Hogarth.

Gotobed had an answer ready. "By all means," said he, "ask your questions, but remember, you will first need to explain to Mr. Hogarth your own part in the matter."

"I have nothing to prove—my name is very well respected," said the printseller. He was a stout man and handsome in a red-faced way. "I am trusted in this business—who are you again?" Then, he eyed the three of us to show that we were nobodies.

"My name is as good as any man's," said Gotobed.

"You, sir, are a damned pyrate and that French fop a dirty cat and mice."

I saw Gotobed pale, and the angry look on his face settled into something fixed and ugly. Quick as thought, he swung his cudgel, even as Prosper put up his hand to stop him. The oak staff swerved to miss Prosper but in doing so knocked over a stack of unbound tomes. A moment later, we stood on a floor strewn with paper.

"Get out," said the bookseller, his face redder than ever. "Get the hell out of my shop before I call the authorities."

Gotobed's expression threatened more violence, but he turned from that place and left, the little bell over the door jingling discordantly.

As soon as we were out of the shop, I placed myself at Gotobed's elbow, but Prosper was already on his other side. Prosper said, "You must give him his price. He's right—we cannot fight back."

Gotobed said nothing to this, only walked very quickly, splashing though puddles.

"Cat and mice?" said I, struggling to keep up. "That fellow curses very stupidly—he is the vastest sort of fool."

"Little Quire," Prosper said. "This is business. *Tais-toi*."

Gotobed bent his head against the rain. "Shut up, both of you," he said. "Cass, I am aching with cold and have a coat heavy with money. We might at least go where the last can repair the first."

And at this, Gotobed strode away, leaving the two of us alone.

The wet was washing away the day, leeching light from the sky and the glass of windows. In shops and houses, lamps began to glow. We emerged from the mouth of a lane, and then we were in the churchyard of St. Paul's. All day, the dome had hovered over our shoulder, but like a home-truth, the closer we got, the harder it was to see. Now, it stood in front of us, bulbous and hard, a bowl in the sky. "There," said Gotobed, and he set off, making for the steps, almost at a run.

Prosper could keep up, but I fell behind. When I found them again, they had passed through the doors and stood on the chequer floor, candlelight blooming from wrought-iron candelabra, tall as soldiers. I had never been inside St. Paul's before, and I did not like it now. Incense prickled my nose, and an iciness seeped up through the flags and into my wet soles.

Gotobed made for a side aisle, where he slid into a pew as if on to an ale-shop bench. Prosper paused and genuflected as he crossed the apse, while I scrambled after. Even before we sat down, Gotobed was pulling handfuls of crowns, nobles, and marks out of his pocket, forming them in glittering piles on the pew beside him. Deftly, he sorted each crown and each shilling, down to the pennies. Then he formed three hoards, explaining how he carefully weighted each to reflect the nature of our contribution. He had a little more than Prosper because he had communicated with the printsellers, and Prosper had a little more than me because engraving was more labour than drawing. With so many coins on view, nobody disputed his reckoning, and we watched him work in silence. When Gotobed was done, he shoved a pile toward each of us, and I held in my hands a full two pounds in ready money.

I had never had so much as that before, and was quite dazzled. What was I to do with so many shillings and half-crowns? I scarcely knew, but after a little thought, I drew up in my head the following bill.

D. M. Bryan

	L.S.D.
For a first month's lodging in a safer house than Mother's ———	1 0 0
For a supper of bread and beer to celebrate the success	
of our scheme ———	0 8 0
A maid-servant attending ———	0 1 0 0
Tobacco and a fire ———	0 7 0

Having made my calculations, I quickly determined I had, without any effort, already run myself five shillings into debt. Accordingly, I set about keeping my money safe. Holding the coins in a fold in my coat, I rolled down the tops of my stockings and dropped the most valuable inside. Cold as tears, they sank around my ankles, settling against the arches of my feet. They would raise blisters I knew, but they would be safe. The smaller coins, I secreted about myself, in pockets under my breeches and in slits in my coat, for I had a number of hiding places that I used in my trade.

Gotobed and Prosper watched me, making jokes of the care I took, but I paid them no heed. They had each secured the wealth in a bag tied at the waist and hid beneath coat flaps. It would take me no longer than a blink to snip the cord of each and make away with all their money. But that was an action I would never take. In the time we'd worked together, drawing, engraving, printing our Tom Idle, we had been anything but idle ourselves, and out of that shared effort, we had made something that was more than the sum of six sheets of paper. I could no more betray them, lifting their bags of money than I could—well, I could not betray them. That was all.

I could see they needed watching over. In particular, I saw Gotobed continued in no very wise mood, and the feel of money around his middle would unsteady him further. He needed securing, did Gotobed. Like all poor men, he did not truly believe wealth was his to hold. Tonight, he must give some of it away or lose faith in the man he knew himself to be. Tomorrow, he would be sorry, but tonight he must be unwise.

On the steps of St. Paul's, I stopped and looked about me. With the cathedral's hulk at my back, I had a view of the sky, and the cloud tucked about the city's ears. Now, as I gazed, a gash appeared overhead, jagged as a knife cut, and through it, I could see a point of light or two. A drover once told me how, in the countryside, the stars show bright as flung silver, but not here—not in London. Nay, in London we are lucky for a celestial glint, a wink, a sly peep. Still, a star is a star and ripe for wishing. I closed my eyes and moved my lips, and the thing was done.

I was a thief. I worked alone. I had no need of partners. And yet, tonight, I wished to keep my friends safe beside me. I would watch out for them—yes, I would.

CHAPTER 15

THE LIFE AND TIMES OF CASS QUIRE, GENTLEMAN.

In which Gotobed contemplates how to spend his earnings, and Cass experiences a downturn in his fortunes.

London, 1746.

I failed. Of course I did.

The Sign of the Grapes lay at the end of a narrow passage, so urine-tart it made my eyes water. As we stepped through the door, I was pleased to leave behind the wet night, but no sooner had we entered that low place than I began to wish myself outside again. At least the rain was clean, while the serving-girl who greeted us at the door was not. She smelled of cooking grease and sweat, and she had a blue-green bruise upon her cheek. I eyed her up and down, letting her see my disapproval, but to my surprise she returned my stare and bettered me a sniff. Then, she stuck her pert nose in the air, and I became newly aware of the stink of Smithfield that still perfumed my greatcoat. My hand flew to my head and found the caterpillar scar on my healing ear. We were at a stalemate, the girl and I.

But she knew Gotobed, and now she expressed herself very glad to see him, fawning over his person in a way that made me sick. Worse, the unhappy fellow played along, showing me a side of him I had not seen before. At Gotobed's bidding, the girl conducted us up a short flight of stairs and into a smoke-stained chamber. There, she invited us to take our ease, pushing away Gotobed's inky paws. Freed from his fingers in her skirts, she vanished—upon what mission I dreaded to guess—and we ranged ourselves before a brassy fire of bright-glowing embers.

I put my feet to the warmth, my clanking stockings beginning to steam. Looking about, I saw at first glance a richly appointed room, but nothing stood up to scrutiny. Many Italian paintings covered the walls, but the gilt frames were only cheaply painted wood, and the fine-seeming landscapes only dashed together with a thick brush. The pair of backless sofas flanking the walls showed many worn patches, and the oak table at the center of the room had lost its sheen. Only a red curtain hanging on one wall held any lustre, and as I looked, I saw its rich folds twitch and part. From behind that disguised doorway came a craven person, both wigless and bald. After bowing and showing us his toothless condition, the man set down a cracked bowl of punch on the table, and made away behind the same curtain.

From the appearance of the punch, Gotobed made clear he was set on celebration. He lifted his bowl and drank off a bumper to Prosper and me in turn. Next, he made Prosper do the same, and then, nothing would do but that I raise my bowl and propose a toast.

"To the coin left in the morning," said I, holding my stemless goblet in the air and sipping a little of the rank concoction. Prosper drank his with the pursed lips of a Frenchman tasting English flip, but Gotobed threw the contents down his throat with such a show of willing that I feared he might swallow his glass.

"A very good toast, Quire," he said to me, shaking the red curtain on the wall, and calling for girls.

Girls came. Three. One apiece. Each was dressed in a silk gown that did not fit, but whether it was the lack of proper petticoats that made them so loose or the meagre proportions of the females, I had no means to ask. The first girl had dark hair and a blue mantua; the second was blond in mustard yellow; and the third was a mousy person wearing green silk too fine for her, or for the shabby chamber in which she stood. With my thief's eye, I accounted it stolen, for this was the sort of place that kept a good fence busy. The girls set immediately upon Prosper and Gotobed, the one in blue seizing the latter, while the one in yellow

D. M. Bryan

smiled slyly at the Frenchman. That left the mousy one for me, but she took one look and began to complain.

"Oh no," she said, "I'll not have the boy. He'll only cry and then refuse to pay. Look, he's got no hair on his chin."

"Ha—she has you there, Quire," said Gotobed, settling Blue on his lap.

"Happens I don't care for her either," I said as loud as I could.

"Care has little to do with it," said Prosper. Mustard sat balanced on his knee, but he did not look pleased.

My girl stood by the chair where I sat, but she did not approach. "Why don't you go home to mother," said she, returning to her theme. "You're not old enough. And you look damp. Run along now."

"I'm as old as you," which was no more than the truth.

"It's different for girls," said my mousy companion, and she crossed her arms over her invisible chest. I thought of Doll and looked away.

I turned to Gotobed for help, but there was none to be had from that quarter. The gentleman had grown busy with his hands again, rummaging in the front of Blue's gown like he'd lost something there. He had a distant look in his eyes that made the small quantity of punch I'd drunk sit less easily in my gut than I liked.

"Attention, Madame," said Prosper. Despite Mustard's arms about his neck, he was still sitting upright at the table, the china punch bowl before him. "He is only a boy, but a boy who is possessed of many, many *sous*."

"You need only feel his stockings to know that," said Gotobed, a little indistinctly, for his mouth was busy upon Blue's slightly dirty neck.

Mouse appeared to look more favourably upon my rights as her beau. At least, she perched herself at my side and poured the party another bumper of drink in our fly-specked bowls.

Prosper, sitting across from me, resumed grimly sipping, more like an English *biftek* than a continental gentleman. "I do not like this drink," he said after several swallows. "It is too … *acide*. It is lime?" He sniffed at his cup. "No, vinegar, I think."

But, he continued swigging with a set, unhappy expression.

"Ain't you going to drink your physic then?" said Mouse to me.

I wanted to object, but could not think of any wording that did not sound petulant, half-grown, unbreeched to my own ear, so I drank my sour dregs.

"Slow down," said Mouse.

Mustard said to Prosper. "'Ello monsieur. Comment za va?" and then she took a turn with the long ladle of the punch-bowl.

"I don't want any more," said I, but Mustard ignored me, tipping the ladle until each cup brimmed over with sticky, brown liquid, and rivulets ran down the sides. Little circles of damp formed on the table. We would pay for our refreshment by the bowl, I guessed, and as long as that vessel emptied, the destination of the punch mattered little.

Mustard caught the ruffles of one sleeve in the spilled liquid, and she daubed at it with an already dirty handkerchief. "We catch it if we mark the good linens," said she, finding my eyes upon her. "Rumfusian is the devil to lift from so fine a weave as this."

"It's not Rumfusian," said Mouse.

"Fuck you," said Mustard. "The gentlemen know what I mean."

Squeals and a short shriek came from Gotobed's partner, as he bodily lifted and carried her off to one of those backless couches that lay against the wall—how uncomfortably like beds they were. Sprawled together, Blue and Gotobed began to teasingly slap and tickle each other. Items of clothing fell off, as if by accident. A kerchief and Gotobed's hat lay already on the ground, and I saw how Prosper's unhappy eyes flickered over these items, disregarded on the grimy floorboards. He turned to Mustard.

"Madame," he said to that lady, "take care with your sleeve. You must not press the liquid into the fabric because you leave *des taches*. Employ a little salt, if you have any."

Mustard looked properly grateful at this advice, but she said she had no salt.

"None?" said Prosper.

"Not on me," said the lady.

"*Hélas*," he said, shrugging.

"Monsieur," said Mouse, lowering her eyelashes in Prosper's direction, "will you tell me what the ladies wear at Paris?"

"They wear sailor's slops and wigs of Peruvian camel," said I, and Mouse stuck out her tongue.

From the divan, Gotobed lifted his head from Blue's sprawling bosoms—she was at least well provided in this respect. "Gentlemen, have you never been to a brothel?" said he. "Are you really so ignorant as to suppose you are expected to sit at the table and discuss the *mode* with the ladies—Christ. Prosper, be a man and touch her bubbies."

Prosper mumbled something I didn't catch.

"What?" Said Gotobed. "Don't talk your gibberish to me. Grab the bitch, you French fuck. And as for you, Quire, anyone can see you are still quite a little boy after all. If you sit in the corner with your eyes closed, I'll buy you a nice syllabub for a treat when I'm done." And then he looked down at Blue's blue-veined chest and began nibbling at her, as though she were a piece of stilton.

I had promised myself to take care of Gotobed—to keep him safe. He was, at this moment, no less my friend than when I stood on the steps of St. Paul's and named him such, but I cannot own I liked him very much. In truth, I had almost begun to hate him a little.

The punch glass before me on the table stood empty, only the damp rings to show where I replaced it after each sip. My head spun. I burped and tasted vomit. Mouse sat beside me, her hands tucked beneath her thighs, shoulders hunched in her voluminous gown. She twisted away her head and did not look at me, but I could see her bone-ribbed chest, flat as my own. If I put my fingers in the neck of her gown, like I might slip them into the pocket of my greatcoat, what would it avail either of us? I thought for a moment or two I might try. And then I knew I would not.

I put my shoe on the seat, making a regrettable, dampish mark, and took out a coin from my stocking. This I passed to Mouse, who gaped at it.

"What's this," said she. "What do you want?"

"Is it too much?" said I. "I have left some mud on the chair." I pointed to the stain.

"But you have not begun—you need not pay me *now*."

I did not know what to say. I longed for the night and the rain, for silence and the cleansing cold.

Mouse was turning the coin over in her fingers, the surprised look still upon her face. In a slow, thoughtful tone of voice, she said, "What about the punch? That's paid separately."

This seemed merely grasping to me, and I wanted to take my coin back. I said, "But I have already overpaid you. Strictly speaking, the punch was all I received."

"Whose fault is that?" said Mouse.

"Shut up, you bawling infants," said Gotobed, his face reddened and devilish from the divan. The skirts of Blue's gown were higgledy-piggledy and all I could see of the girl was her face, which slowly rotated in our direction. Once, in a coffeehouse, I overheard two men speaking of the Earl of Shaftesbury, who believed that a virtuous man operated from a spirit of complete disinterest. If so, Shaftesbury might have found his ideal here, in this brothel. Blue's face said all—she had no share in whatever Gotobed did to her. I applauded her virtue.

Mouse had made my coin vanish as if never in the world and again hunched in her chair, as though she did not know what to do next. I thought the time right to make a dignified departure—rising to my feet, throwing back my chair, and delivering a short sermon on the wrongness of our actions—but just as I steeled myself to begin, Prosper arose and stole my thunder.

"French fuck?" said Prosper, decanting Mustard from his lap. He had a long fuse, he did, but at last he went off like a firework. His rush-bottomed chair hit the floor with a clatter, and he rose to his feet. Pointing a finger, he began to curse Gotobed in a stream of French syllables. Then, he took a deep breath and switched to English, so that we might better understand what he had to say. "I cannot stay here any longer," he told us. "I do not like this place. That is a terrible drink," and he pointed at the punch bowl. "These are terrible girls." This time he did not point, but we all knew who he meant.

"Hoity-toity," said Mustard, retired to the far side of the table. "I don't care for you neither, Frenchie," and she drank down Prosper's untouched punch.

Gotobed emerged from the froth of Blue's skirts, a sailor from the waves. His coat had joined his hat on the floor, and his linen shirt was

D. M. Bryan

untucked at the waist. He looked at Prosper. "What the hell?" said he. "I mean, *what* the hell?"

Prosper's pointer finger returned to circle the air in Gotobed's direction.

"I think he means you're terrible too," said Mustard, helpfully.

"You do this thing out in the open," Prosper said, finding his tongue, "like pugs in the street."

Gotobed hooted in assumed astonishment. "A timid Frenchman," said he. "Who would have guessed?"

"And *such* a filthy room."

"It's a side-street bagnio," said his opponent, his surprise now genuine. "Of course, it's dirty. If you'd only take out your pizzle, Prosper, you'd forgive it soon enough."

Prosper spoke again in French, but his meaning was clear. He would not take out his pizzle—he valued his pizzle far too much to expose it to the dreaded English affliction, to syphilis, to a dose of the clap. He named this disease in our native tongue, and was well enough understood by all.

"Well, thanks very much," said Blue, sitting up and gathering her garments to her.

Gotobed swung a long leg over and sat square of the sofa. "Perhaps, said Gotobed, suddenly stuttering and ugly, "that printseller had the right of it—you are one of those Ganymedes who cares not for girls."

Prosper broke with us then. He spat once, hitting Gotobed's cheek, and again on the floorboards, leaving little wet marks in the grime, and then, with a clatter of his buckled shoes on the planks, he was gone. We heard his footfalls all the way to the bottom of the stairs.

"Damn," said Gotobed, wiping his face with his sleeve.

"Well," said Mustard, "now who will pay me?"

"Shut up," said Gotobed, but his voice frayed as he said it. He went to the door and looked after Prosper. His untucked breeches slid halfway down his white thighs, exposing grey linen, but he did not seem to notice. He looked around for me, and when he saw me standing, he said, "There you are, Cass—you will not leave me."

God help me, I did, although I do not know for whose sake I went. All the way down the stairs, I seemed to see Gotobed's face before me, for I had never before seen a man look so lost.

Outside, the rain-washed night hung clean as laundry. I touched the scoured cobbles with my feet and took off running. As I went, I listened behind me, straining to catch Gotobed's following feet, or his voice urging me back, but I neither heard nor saw anyone. Only the moon peeped down at me, round and silver as a sixpence. Down the street and around the corner, lighted windows marked my way, and in them, I saw London tableaus, illustrations in a black and golden book. I saw a man in a doorway, covered in lather, tipping his chin to the ceiling, as a barber tugged his nose to shave his lip. Through a pointed opening, I glimpsed a family at prayer. Down an alley, an open casement held a handsome whore in a neat black cap. She smiled and waved me in, but I knew she was in jest. To her eyes, I was only a boy, and I did not disagree.

I took off again, turning my feet toward Mother's. Soon, I came into a bending lane of houses, dark walls with white, moonlit edges. My shoulders brushing bricks, I raced along, but with speed came a sweet pain, spreading through my chest, and soon I could no longer breathe with ease. Neither could I ignore the weight of my wages, clanking in my stocking. I jangled as I came to a halt, tumbling myself into a gloomy cranny, bent double, gulping air.

All around me, night stuck fast, and fleeting shadows ran wetly along the brick walls. Cats padded and rats scurried. But even here, London's poor tucked themselves out of the weather beneath the corseted overhang of leaning houses. A gaunt figure hurried past, wrapped in a cloak. A ragged woman with a bundle crept by me with a distrustful glance. An elderly gent stumped past, followed by a curly-tailed dog. The little animal stopped before me and barked shrilly.

"What's that?" cried the gentleman, turning to his dog. "Curse you, Trump. You must shit soon, or we will wait forever," and the two of them trotted away.

I thought to repeat this sally to Gotobed, and then I remembered.

But even as my heart broke, I saw my friend—it was indisputably him, handsome in the glow of a tavern window. He saw me directly,

D. M. Bryan

though I was still half in the shadows, and he cried out, a little brokenly and a little drunkenly. "Cass," he said, stepping towards me. "Can you forgive me?" And then he reached me, and my imagination failed. Gotobed turned to a puff of air and blew away on a night breeze.

In a crack between rooftops, the moon reappeared—now a clipped sixpence behind a disk of cloud. I remembered the boy, Nat, lost outside St. Barth's flinty church, and Doll's weighty sorrow, and yet here I crouched, a jingling fool, abandoned in the road. At the thought, I began to cry. First, droplets of water slipped from my eyes, but then snotty tears, big as buttons, filled my mouth with salt.

We had fallen out, we three. Our partnership was dissolved. Gotobed would never see me again. I would never see him, and never stretched a span too long.

It was work to find my way back to the bagnio. In the end, I followed the cup of St. Paul's to the one crooked alley that smelled worse than the others. After that, the grape-laden signpost showed me the way. I knocked, expecting the serving girl who answered before, but it was Mustard who opened the door. Close up, she stood a foot above me. Her face showed very pale and, between stained lips, her teeth parted in something like a smile.

"Go on," said she. "You're back for your penny's worth." Her laugh ended in a cough.

I peered behind her in the hopes of seeing boots descending from that upstairs room. The hall candle flickered, but it was only the draft from the door. I said, "The gentleman upstairs—"

"Long gone," said Mustard. "Paid for all of you and left."

She wrapped her arms around her as she spoke, as the night chill crept through the open door. She craned her head a little and looked out into the street. "Faith," she said, "what season is it now?"

I stared.

"It's a simple enough question."

"Autumn, madam. The leaves on the trees are the colour of your gown."

Mustard looked down at the skirt of her mantua and then gave me a sharpish nod before stepping back a pace to shut me out.

Mother's lay in darkness, and at this late hour no servant would rise to unfasten the lock, but a barred door was no impediment in that place. Moving to the rear of the dwelling, I climbed to the top of the wall, over the tiled roof, and through the window that always stood open, no matter the weather. Inside, I found a floor filled with sleeping children, curled up under shared blankets, on whatever spare bit of ticking they could scavenge. The moon showed through the glass, and as I crept on tiptoes, I peered into each face I passed, finding more than one glittering eye upon my own. Each time I found a wakeful child, I bent and breathed a name into its ear, until I found one who silently pointed to a spot near the door.

Doll lay by herself, hardly covered by a tattered shawl and an old rug. When I shook her shoulder, her eyes flickered apart so quickly I doubted if she'd ever been asleep. At night, after the fires burned down, the house grew chill, and the air, icy as a wintergreen wave, rolled through that window left ajar. In cold seasons, sleep came in close-fisted, parsimonious portions. It was no house for a friendless child—no place to live alone.

"Come," I said to Doll, "you'll be warmer with me."

She rose up with a practiced quiet. Noiselessness is any young criminal's first and best lesson, and once learnt, it is never forgotten. In my room, the air was warmer, although the fire showed only cold ashes. I had a truckle bed, straw ticking, and a better blanket. Doll had her shawl and rug. If we curled up together, Doll and I, we might sleep in tolerable warmth. I gestured for her to lie down, and she only hesitated a moment before crawling beneath the welcoming layers. Next, I sat myself beside her to slip off my shoes and roll off my stockings, making a kind of bag for my coins. I still had many of the larger pieces hidden in my coat and breeches. Then, I lay me down to sleep, my coat beneath my head, and my stocking beneath my coat.

Doll stiffened as I settled myself, but I didn't care. I had no designs on her, whatever she might imagine.

We did not sleep for long. Just before dawn came a pounding on the door that set the housemaids shrieking. Doll was out of bed at once. Overhead, childish footsteps thumped, rattling the ceiling so that plaster fell.

A man's voice down below demanded to know what kind of house this was, but he wouldn't have asked, if he hadn't already known. Mother paid good money to avoid that very question, and the house rang with her objections. Recriminations rose and fell, like a warrior's axe. She called after the men to go, to stop, to pass no further, but the constables were too many for her. The stairs thrummed with boots.

Doll scrambled in the unfamiliar dimness of my little cell. She reached the door but returned for her shawl. Frantically, she dug for it in the mess of blankets. Pushing past her, I sprang in my bare feet to where Bickham's print covered over my hiding place. I tore the ugly image away and snatched up the folded page I kept there, tucking it into the lining of my coat. Mr. Hogarth's half print, with its irregular indenture cut, lay there also and I placed this into my pocket. Then, snatching up my shoes and holding my coin-laden stocking, I grabbed Doll's hand, and together we ran out to the landing.

Our preparations were our downfall. We were already too late. A constable stood on the floor above, blocking our passage to the room with the open window. Downstairs, the way looked clear, but as soon as we crept to the landing, we spied more constables milling in and out of the rooms below. Mother, a candle in her hand, stood half in, half out the front parlour, turning this way and that, swearing at the officers. Unpinned from her stays, she seemed looser and somehow softer—I do not mean kinder. She'd grown indistinct at the edges, cloudlike, but with all the diffuse malevolence of a thunderhead. Curses flew, striking hard against whatever target she could find. When she saw Doll and me peeking down the stairs she crackled angrily, shocking us back to my room. We pulled closed the door behind us and stood a moment in the dark.

"She might have kept quiet," said Doll. She adjusted her shawl, and its tattered length ran over her shoulders to pool at her feet. "She always tells us to do so."

"Never mind," said I, as footsteps stopped before my door. I seized the handle, pulling it closed with all my strength, and Doll lent her sparrow's weight to mine. Then, the metal bar was wrenched from our fingers, and the door came suddenly open.

The two constables who entered wasted no time. Without any address, the first struck me, and the other snatched at Doll. The girl ran as far as she could in that tiny room, but a few paces were all a grown man required in any direction, and he soon snatched at her, catching her up. As she struggled, the shawl came loose, sliding to the floor, threatening to trip the constable reaching for her. He kicked it away, and hefted her into the air, so that her petticoats flipped up and her stocking legs kicked free. Over his shoulder her face showed damp, white hair clinging to her skull.

I hit the man holding her with my stocking-cosh as hard as I could, landing a blow on his thigh. He grunted, reeling, almost dropping his burden. As he righted himself, Doll shrieking and hammering him on the back, his partner tore my weapon from my hands. With his other hand, he grabbed me by my coat and held me fast.

In truth, it would have been easy enough to twist myself out of that garment and sprint away, except that I would not willingly leave my coat behind. Instead, I had to watch as my gaoler held up the stocking, the lamp-lit folds of his stupid face opening in surprise.

"It's chockablock with silver," he said, while the coins jingled in their woollen cover. I spat at him, and he shook me by my collar.

"Here," said the one holding Doll, "half that's mine."

"Half?" said my assailant.

"We split it even—that's fair."

"What's fair is finders-keepers."

"I got a black and blue lump that says different."

"Keep your damned voice down or the others will hear."

With his foot, Doll's captor pushed closed the door to our cell.

I knew what ought to happen next—even in my neglected state, I'd heard a fairy tale or two. Our captors would begin to quarrel over

D. M. Bryan

the treasure, and in their greed, would come to blows, destroying each other. Doll and I would creep out into the morning light, unscathed, our pockets filled with gold.

But my stocking held little gold. Mostly it contained copper farthings and pennies, leavened with a few crown coins. And our captors were true born Englishmen, pragmatical and phlegmatic. With a free hand, the constable carrying Doll held open a flap in his coat, while the other poured in a generous dollop of tinkling metal. Then, without taking his hot, heavy hand from my collar, my gaoler tucked the rest, still in its stocking, under the cord that held his trousers up. He patted the bulge under his coat and bent down to me, his kippered breath in my face. "What else you got, you little sneak?" He said. When he searched my pockets he found my half Hogarth and looked it over. A moment later, the print joined Doll's shawl, crumpled on the floor.

I lost my faith in stories then—at least in the kind with happy endings. And I hardly cared when we were made to walk downstairs and stand with the remnants of Mother's household. That lady herself sat, a prisoner of her sofa, while her parlour brimmed with black coats. As we passed, she looked our way, and gnashed her teeth, a terror to the last. Even more than was usual, the weeping of children filled that house.

In time, we would discover our destination. It was a façade of white stone, a blank visage with a gaping mouth—a place called Bridewell. Who I met there and what happened next, you must wait to discover.

CHAPTER 16

I could not expect you should find any Amusement in my Narrations, if I did not keep alive a little Curiosity. Suspense is the Soul of a Story, without which it grows dead and lifeless.

Sarah Scott's *A Journey Through Every Stage of Life.*

London, 1762.

Sarah reaches her destination. A façade of honeyed stone, a neat visage with a gleaming front door—the house in Hill Street. How pretty the place looks from outside, a slice of pound cake, but inside the story is different. Inside, greasy smells from the kitchen, damp from the cellars, paint from all Elizabeth's renovations, combine to leave her queasy, headachy, sorry she has come.

"Do you like them, Pea?" says Elizabeth. She sits across from Sarah in her newly decorated dressing room and gestures at the furniture—the very chairs in which they sit. "I think the gold is perhaps too much?"

"No no," Sarah says faintly, unable to look at the glinting fabric, the gilded spindles. A cup of tea hovers between her fingers, and she wills it to remain there. Elizabeth has put some acid-patterned cover on the floor that puts tears in her eyes. "Everything is perfectly lovely," she says, focusing on her sister's set mouth.

Complaint to Elizabeth on the matter of Mr. Gotobed proves impossible. Elizabeth allows to Sarah that Mr. Montagu, Edward, disappoints his wife more than he can ever sadden his sister-in-law. His affairs, great and small, fill the dressing room one flight below them, but the man himself, as always, declines to be in London. When Sarah seeks to draw her sister out on the subject of her coachman, Elizabeth evades with descriptions of Montagu's conversation. "He brings me nothing but sums," says Elizabeth.

And diamonds, thinks Sarah catching the flash at her sister's elegant neck. At forty-three, Elizabeth achieves a sleekness unavailable to Sarah. The look of her sister's lace fichu and high velvet band make Sarah's own neck itch, and she jiggles her cup in her hand so that she might lay a soothing finger upon her skin.

The blankets in the inn where she lay last night were hairy and heavy. She rarely sleeps well, and the novel, which she jots on pages shuffled in her portmanteau, kept her more than usually awake. Still, when Elizabeth scolds her for leaving the coach on the Bath road, for enduring a dirty bed, and for arriving in this pressed and folded condition, Sarah protests. She is not a letter and cannot be creased in transit. Fields green her soul, and the lowing of cattle is a psalm to those who have ears to hear it. Waving her teacup, she tries to describe the fortifying sheen of Minorcan hens and new grass in the rain.

Elizabeth claps her hands in pleasure, and for a second Sarah is fooled. But, her sister has only remembered the items of dress she's had altered against Sarah's arrival in town. "Fresh growth on a yellowed ground," says Elizabeth, "the exactest description of the patterning—I knew you would like it. You have the complexion to wear yellow, and I do not."

She means well enough, Sarah tells herself, *really, she tries.*

A girl—Sarah does not recognize this one's chestnut handsomeness—is commanded to bring forth a gown of jaundiced silk, sprigged in twists of green. She takes away Sarah's teacup so that that lady might better enjoy the clever amendments to the garment. Elizabeth has commanded the insertion of panels at the shoulders and at the waist to accommodate Sarah's spreading flesh, and the fall of the skirt itself has been narrowed to suit changing fashions. "It is *very* narrow," says Sarah, examining the fabric that falls across her lap and into Elizabeth's. Her own brown travelling habit vanishes beneath a garden of unlikely blossom.

"The fullness comes with the pleats in the back," says Elizabeth.

Obediently, Sarah puts her finger to a row of careful gathers.

"And the sleeves are both scalloped *and* pinked."

Sarah takes the sleeve and inspects its layers of fabric. The skin of her hand shows, coarse and red. "One day," she says, "we will, all of us, men and women alike, wear breeches and stockings, plain coats with serviceable pockets attached. No woman will be clapped into skirts, unless she decides upon it herself. Imagine London on that day, sister, when everyone will be allowed two legs on which to stride."

"I have two legs, sister, but I wish to keep them to myself."

"And so you may, but you will not be obliged."

Elizabeth has clasped her hands together, holding one wrist—Sarah knows the gesture of old. Such thoughts are well enough in fiction—in speculation—but they have no place in this well-appointed dressing room. Her sister dismisses the girl, who withdraws, her hair, under its cap, a curl of coffee.

"The dress pleases me very much, Pod," says Sarah, hoping praise might mend what tactlessness has broken.

"No gown has ever pleased you."

"You know I am content to appear respectable rather than a la mode. Although, I do not approve this recent fashion for imaginary flowers—I prefer silken botanicals to strictly mimic those of field and wood."

"The intention is decoration, not scholarship, Sarah."

"I am already some years past any hope of appearing decorative. Nature and fortune mistook themselves with me—I ought to have been born a man and a gardener."

The women sit, divided by the ruffling expanse of Spitalfields silk. Once they were pea and pod, but now they are only sisters. Elizabeth once knew Sarah's heart, but now even Sarah herself finds it mysterious. It is, she suspects, only a cavity beneath her ribs, filled with rich, dark humus—the rotting product of leaves, stems, fruitful hulls that flourished there before. By contrast, Elizabeth's heart has been remodelled many times. She negotiates with Mr. Adams or Mr. Stuart to fill it with Chinese birds and bamboo caning. Carpet in the style of the orient. A chrysanthemum chair cushion. But this is woolgathering. Both organs are made of scarlet blood and tubing flesh, like the beef hearts Lady Barbara tries and cannot eat.

What then might that mean? On the basis of hearts—their weight and shape and colour—nobody can distinguish between sisters—or any other persons either.

The heaviness of the silk dress causes her to flush, and under her own clothing, a layer of moisture forms, a prickly dew. Sarah pushes the gown off her knees and into a chair, where it reclines like a third sister.

"You smile," says Elizabeth, leaving unsaid: *at me?*

"I smile," Sarah says, pointing, "at the part that separates us from our brothers. Who would think a few layers of boning makes so much difference in the world?"

Elizabeth does not speak, but Sarah hears her anyway. Stays do not make the difference. The palings lie deeper under flesh, a cradle of bone swathed by a rising belly. You cannot escape that girdle, Elizabeth thinks. But she is wrong.

"Without my stays, I do not feel myself," says Elizabeth.

"And I am never myself with them."

"Do not pin so tight."

"I thank you for your good advice." Sarah allows her voice to imply the opposite.

But Elizabeth is undaunted. "I thought you would be pleased to have something suitable to wear in the evenings," says she. "I have said you are coming, you know, and people are pleased."

"Coming to what?"

"Coming to London. Coming here to Hill Street."

"And?"

"Coming to my assembly tonight. Do you not long for something new to wear?"

This news comes as a little shock to Sarah, although she knew it likely.

"Then I doubt the gown will be new to any but myself," Sarah says. "Most of the party will have seen you in it before."

In reply, Elizabeth rings for the girl, who, catching her mistress' mood, takes the yellow robe prisoner. Slumped before her, the gown marches from the room. Sarah knows she behaves with insufficient kindness, but each detail of her sister's dressing room hurts her head—she cannot easily forgive Elizabeth the glinting, hovering points of light.

"This room is over-bright," she says.

"It faces north," says Elizabeth.

"It is the noise of the street. I do not like it in Bath either."

"We are not on the street," says her sister. "Why must you make problems?"

"Why must you never see them?"

Are we to fight? Sarah wonders, pinching her forehead with her thumb and forefinger. She searches out anger, crushes it, plants sisterly affection in its place, but wrath re-grows, demonstrating the persistence she lacks. She admires its tenacity, as it twines and climbs, producing blossoms the colour of a flushing face, veined with all that is unsayable.

"How do you progress with your writing?" asks Elizabeth.

Sarah takes a moment to understand she must open her mouth to answer. "The printers composite the text of my *Hall*," she says.

"You are arrived in town for a consultation?"

"I am not. They know their business tolerably well, I think."

"So, how goes the new work—you told me the title, but I have forgot it."

"The Perils of Mrs. Pauline Page: Or, Love in a Mirror," says Sarah, pleased with the lie.

"Yes, I remember now. And how does it progress? Well, I hope."

I burnt it all in the fireplace in Bath, Sarah does not say, for she burns nothing. She does not know what reply she can make. The silence pleats, folds.

"Sarah, do not shut me out. Perhaps I enquire too closely, but I have ever been a friend of your work."

"You have, Elizabeth. You must pardon my reticence. I have set those pages aside in favour of something new—the history of an orphan boy."

"Mr. Newbery will take it? When do you see him?"

"I am not here to see Mr. Newbery." Sarah decides to tell the truth, or some of it anyway. She says, "Sister, my head aches so much these days, I can no longer write as easily or as swiftly as I did. Long hours of composition are painful, and I do not expect to be much engaged with the book trade for the time being."

"Forgive me," says Elizabeth, "then I do not understand your purpose in coming to town. I showed your letter to Edward, and he could not guess either. But when you wrote, I felt some urgency behind your words. Is it Lady Barbara? Is she worse? Is it another financial embarrassment? Do you wish for me to speak with our father again? Your letter did not say, and I wish you would confide in me. You need but say the word, and I will do anything in my power to help."

What remains of Sarah's anger extinguishes. It collapses inwards and like all rotten husks, proves to have no inside. "I have come," she says, "to see you." And, as she speaks, the claim proves as truthful as anything else she might say.

Sarah Scott has taken to her bed in one of the upper rooms. Her sister's taste has made few inroads this high in the house, and so these plaster walls remain covered in the same powdered distemper they received when new. Only a mantle, decorated with insets of Sienna marble in the style of William Kent, betrays the chamber's ambitions. Well, Sarah does not have to look at it. Her room faces south, and the sun and the street filter in past the billowing red curtain, but Sarah lodges above the cares of the common man. Off her feet, fed and watered, she at last feels equal to a little warmth and life. Nobody on Hill Street cries *buy my mackerel* or *fresh country milk*—the neighbourhood is too genteel—but the nasal honking of footmen and near the constant sound of hooves still signal London.

D. M. Bryan

Two gowns, her own and Elizabeth's hopeless primrose affair, hang over chair backs, where the girl has left them against that evening's entertainment. This is not the lovely girl from the dressing room, but another—Sarah thinks her name may be Grace. Grace has asked Sarah to choose between the gowns, so that she may help Sarah dress, but Sarah—being Sarah—waved the girl away. Still, the gowns remain, awaiting Sarah's choice. How much easier, Sarah Scott thinks, if my dresses behaved more like dresses and less like unloved children.

A letter noting her safe arrival must be penned to Lady Barbara. Eyes closed, flat on her back, Sarah composes it, moving her finger a little to aid composition. *Dear Lady Barbara*, she begins. *Dearest. I have reached London after nothing more disastrous than an overturned carriage—the cause, a drunken coachman.*

What should become of the inebriated fool? Sarah has failed to take the man up with Elizabeth, just as she has not succeeded in raising the matter of Edward Montagu's shabby treatment of Mr. Gotobed. Each matter returns to the tip of her tongue, but the thought of telling Elizabeth how to manage her affairs stops her.

A drunken coachman I have decided to forgive. Absolution in his case is not especially merited as the intoxicated fellow delayed my arrival by an entire day. Nevertheless, my forbearance will be rewarded by the preservation of amity between my sister and myself.

I am writing a fiction, Sarah realizes. Epistolary nonsense. I should take my lies more seriously.

What if she wrote, *Darling Barbara, between Bath and London I saw a rhinoceros, grazing in a farmer's field just west of the Thames Bridge. This creature is known as the real unicorn to those traveling shows who advertise the living production of Camels and Zebras.*

Sarah has noticed the bills for such spectacles, posted on Bath fences and walls. The rhinoceros, with his pitted skin, seems especially worth seeing. The Zebra resembles Elizabeth more particularly, with its elegant nose and fashionable pelt. Again, Sarah writes with her finger in the air. *Elizebreth. Rhinosarah.* The camel has a mild and gentle manner, according to the printed puff. The camel is Lady Barbara, to the life. Who could capture the likeness? Why Mr. Hogarth could.

The letter to Hogarth must also be written. An obstacle to be sure, for the matter of an introduction is a tricky one. Elizabeth, if Sarah but asked her, would produce, from her many shining friends, one who might easily make the connection, but Sarah will not ask Elizabeth. "Sarah Scott," said Sarah, softly into the over-warm spring air of the little room, "wishes to do this alone." She understands why. She, active agent of so many charitable projects, cannot stand to be the recipient of one. The very sting against which she counsels her girls also torments her. And what is the name of that needling wound? *Why, it is pride that pricks me*, she writes in the air.

The wood frame of the bed squeaks as she rises, and moves to her portmanteau for her traveling quills and the carefully capped glass bottle of ink she carries. The room has no desk, so she sits beneath the window and places the leather case in her lap, writing against its surface as best she can. Filled with something resembling resolve, she quickly composes her letter to Barbara—filled with easeful half-truths and empty of beasts. She makes no mention of her project and, after some consideration, none of her accident. Barbara, she hopes, continues to feel better, sitting by a Bath window as full of city sounds as this one.

The room has no bell or cord. Unsure of how to call the girl, Sarah goes to the top of the stairs and looks around. Out on the landing, she finds only closed doors and polished floorboards. She remembers a floor cloth on this level—has Elizabeth taken it up, intending to replace it with something grander? The plainness of the stairs pleases Sarah, and she realizes her headache has eased. The twisting of her stomach no longer causes her discomfort, perhaps because while resting she allowed herself to suffer several percussive instances of those effusions unknown to ladies in public. In short, she has been farting. Sarah laughs at her own thoughts and stretches in the doorway, realizing she is still a little hungry.

After a moment, she takes her letter firmly in hand and starts down the stairs. On the first floor she calls for Elizabeth and hears no answer. She enters her sister's dressing room, which sits empty, the silver tea still upon its tray, its contents cold. The door to the bedchamber behind is closed, so Sarah moves into the long drawing room along the front of the house. In this room, the sun slips in sideways, evading the heavy curtains. Shadows stretch along the dado and cornice, reminding her for some reason of numbers entered into an account book. She goes back out into the stairwell and stumps down another flight.

"Elizabeth," she calls, remembering too late the bell pull amongst the chinoiserie of the dressing room. No matter, she has reached the ground floor, where she will certainly find Elizabeth in the hall or the dining room. But her sister exists in neither place, and Sarah will not open the door to the rear parlour, for that is Edward Montagu's private territory. Even though the man is not in London, the smell of port and leather issue past the oaken door. She backs into the dining room and rings for a servant, but nobody comes. Surprised, she rings again, and again she hears no answering tread. Then, letter in hand, stomach grumbling, she takes herself back through the hall and down the final set of stairs, to the servant's level.

How everything alters as she descends. The bright stairwell, lit by a skylight above, metamorphoses into rough-boarded steps. Now the earthy odour, underlying all other smells in the house, grows dominant. She reaches a confusing set of doorways, opening on all sides, and she chooses one she hopes leads to the kitchen. "Hello," she calls, an elderly, irritable Persephone, eager for a piece of pomegranate. Light filters from above, from windows impossibly distant. Water drips, and a draft cools her overheated flesh. A room full of bottles proves a dead end, and Sarah retraces her steps.

At last, she finds the long corridor running towards the back of the house. It carries with it the smell of cooking. Mould alters to mushrooms. She sniffs, imagining a potage of greens, of ramps and other spring plants. Voices on her right take her to a closed door, on which, after a moment of trepidation, she knocks. Every sound ceases absolutely, and Sarah hears the generalized silence which only confusion brings. Slowly, the door swings open.

The servant's hall receives all its light from a sunken well far above their heads. All this she works out later, from upstairs, where she belongs. But in the instant, she perceives, in the subterranean gloom, a wooden table and mud-coloured plates. The Montagu family servants sit at the table, pale faces aqueous. In the corner lurks a smoking hearth, its chimney and ceiling sooty. It does not draw right, and Elizabeth should see to that—thinks Sarah.

A boy comes to the door, and the girl from upstairs—the plain one with the suit-yourself face—rises to follow, yanking the knob from his hands.

"You needn't have come down." The words suggest apology, but the tone is pure correction. "Those bells," says the girl, "ain't worked right since the refitting. They broke the cords and stitched them up worse than before."

Sarah ignores the girl, hands the boy her letter for Barbara. "After dinner," she tells him, "you might post this. It needs franking," and she looks for Elizabeth's butler, who sits at the head of the table, glowing greenly by the window well. He nods, but Sarah knows she has broken the rules. Her own household is not like this. She has not been on the servant's level in a real house since she was a child.

"Upstairs," said the girl. She can command down here; Sarah must obey.

Somewhere on the stairs, under the full light of the clerestory window, Sarah turns to the girl and asks for a cup of portable soup, or failing that, a bit of bread and butter. She gets neither. The meal the girl brings up consists of dishes of conceits, one made of almond and another of caraway, and a plate of ratafia cakes. More tea. Sarah wants to complain that she is starved of real nourishment, but instead she sits under her bedroom window and chews. She takes her second tea alone. Elizabeth, it seems, is out calling.

When the girl comes to take away the empty dishes, she looks pointedly at the dresses. Sarah, ashamed of her transgressions, agrees to be put into the yellow gown. It fits snugly and the girl dresses her hair and brings her the glass. The dress looks well enough, Sarah supposes, and she accepts a portion of orange water in the folds of her arms and neck.

"You will look very fine in the candles," says the girl, and Sarah supposes this to be her attempt at a compliment. Sarah thinks to learn her name, to ask after her mother and father, brothers and sisters, but lies down in her gown and naps instead.

D. M. Bryan

Sarah wakes to the banging of footmen. The walls of her room are grey, the bed and window curtains the colour of dried blood. At the window, a gorget of dark sky shows, while carriage horses stamp and blow. In important journals and newspapers, Sarah reads of her sister's salons—the clever company and the cleverer conversation, of the ban on card play and gambling, of the over-consumption of tea. She knows some of the company, and is even reckoned of it, but Elizabeth has refurbished her guest list of late, urging greatness forward and consigning meeker souls to the lumber-room. Sarah does not yet know her own fate. Perhaps it is well she chose the primrose dress.

She goes out into the stairwell and stands looking down. Elizabeth comes to the bottom of the stairs and looks up. "Come join us, Pea. The company arrives."

"I am inconveniencing you—I should have come at another time."

"Nonsense. Follow my lead, emulate me, and you will soon feel at home," Elizabeth instructs now. She has not dressed grandly, Sarah notes, and yet looks sleeker, richer than she did before. Elizabeth's informality sets the tone for her evenings—Sarah has read so in her periodicals—and guests arrive attired so that blood may flow, setting vital thought in motion. Some of the men even wear their blue stockings. In this house, intelligence is valued. Reason praised. Wit esteemed.

Elizabeth rustles away, but then rustles back—she has not said her all. Sarah remains at the top of the stairs, forcing her sister to tilt her head. Elizabeth subjects her to a quick appraisal. "You look very well, Pea, but your hair is askew. Has a pin come loose? I will send up the girl."

Everything comes loose, thinks Sarah, *in time. All this fine company will unspool. They will unwind in the drawing room, in the dressing chamber, in the great bedroom where you receive them in sparkling groups. Bits of thread, shards of bone. Humus and mould. Fortune and nature mistake us, every one—we are all gardeners in the end.*

Elizabeth sends the girl. She comes heavily up the stairs and urges Sarah back into her room. "What have you done?" the girl says, holding Sarah at arm's length. "How crooked you are," and she sets about tugging and pinning. Taking hunks of Sarah's hair, she pulls it so tight, Sarah's face hurts.

"I suffer headaches," says Sarah. "I cannot—"

"Better," says the girl. "Your cheeks are pink."

"I do not think I know your name."

A worried line between the girl's eyes. Her behaviour borders on the impertinent, and she knows it. A true Londoner, her face creases and stays creased. "Sadie," she says.

"Sadie? Your name is Sarah?"

Sadie nods.

"Not Grace?" says Sarah.

Sadie blows out her lips in an exasperated way. "We have a Grace in this household," says she, "You saw her with the tea things." Sadie narrows her eyes. Sarah looks at the girl's hair under the cream of her laced cap. Dregs, to Grace's coffee.

"You don't like Grace," says Sarah. Not a question.

"She's my sister."

Back on the landing, the noise of the company comes in waves. Sarah stands on the top step and progresses no further. Below, a door opens and closes. Voices drift up, talking and laughing. The scent of London in spring, moist and fervent, climbs the stairs to meet Sarah. Her mouth grows cottony and fills with the taste of metal. A mild nausea sprouts and grows. Sarah, out of habit, blames her head, but perhaps too many ratafia cakes and Sadie's tight lacing are equally to blame. Still, she feels bilious.

Glancing down, she sees the wooden treads swimming before her eyes. Then they go clapping away, like crows on the wing. Like wavelets from a stone.

"You must come down, Pea," says Elizabeth, looking up. Light streams from the drawing room. "Dr. Johnson has promised to give an account of the counterfeiting of the Cock Lane ghost."

"In a moment," says Sarah.

"Are you feeling unwell, Sarah. Shall I call a physician? We have several here, all of them eminent," says Elizabeth, with an attempt at a laugh.

Sarah shakes her head. "I have a little lavender oil," says she. "I need rest."

"Oh, Pea," says Elizabeth, returning to the drawing room.

Sadie, the girl, brushes past Sarah, heading down. Sarah stops her with her roughened fingers. "Girl," she says. She won't use the name—her own name.

"Yes, madam," says the girl, bobbing neatly this time, her feet perching on the edge of the landing.

"Unpin me."

Eyebrows crinkle the tissue of the girl's brow. She says, without thinking, "But I dressed your hair. I laced your gown."

"Undress. Unlace."

"My mistress," says the girl, "instructed me to make sure you come down."

"Then we must both disappoint her." Sarah examines the girl. "Are you afraid of your mistress?" she asks.

The girl shakes her head. Sarah cannot tell if she lies.

She leads the way back into her room, and stands obediently by the bed. Then, she lifts her arms so that Sadie can better find the pins that hold the stomacher in place. "Unpin me, or find me Grace," says she. "She is the sweet-tempered sister, is she not—and you the virago."

Sadie's eyes grow wet as she undresses Sarah. Anger, Sarah thinks, not sorrow. She herself blinks and a penumbra of light appears around the candle on the ugly mantle. She thinks of Tidy in Batheaston, of Meg.

Before Sadie can finish, Sarah dismisses her, unlaces her own gown, and shrugging it off, leaves it, a pool on the floor.

The following day, Sarah calls at the sign of the Golden Head in Leicester Fields, a letter to Mr. Hogarth pinched between her fingers. It is the course of action she decides upon in the middle of the night, when she cannot sleep. She introduces herself, in her own name, writing, *Dear Mr. Hogarth, some of the world has met me as the author of The History of Cornelia and A Journey Through Every Stage of Life, although no reader knows me by name.*

She entreats Hogarth for advice on a project of her own. *I have,* she writes, *made ventures into printed pictures before, but with no success. I hope you will condescend to draw upon your expertise to help one such as myself. My aims are charitable, not pecuniary, although the scheme itself must make its own way in the world.*

The leather portmanteau remains in Hill Street. On Sarah's back is Elizabeth's primrose dress and the cloak her sister loans her when she hears Sarah is determined to go out.

Over the breakfast table, she'd apologized to Elizabeth for failing to appear at her salon, making much of her sick headache. But Elizabeth, acquainted of old with Sarah's disinclination for company, only brushed away the topic, like so many crumbs of toast. Now, in the reckoning light of morning, Sarah cannot but entertain a little regret for the brilliant company she missed. Amongst such men and women of influence, she might have advanced her own interests, with or without Mr. Hogarth. But that is not her purpose, here in London.

Dear Mr. Hogarth, I should be delighted to tell you more of my projection, should you find time to see me. I am in town for only a short while, and for this reason, I push myself forward. I am told people of business may do as much these days, although I confess I am a little shocked at my own daring. I am, sir, a lady who is chiefest amongst your admirers, and, whatever the propriety of my act, I hope you will reward my enterprise as the world has rewarded yours.

At the sign of the Golden Head, a maid opens the door and Sarah tenders her letter. She has already determined she will not wait, but says she will return for an answer in the afternoon. Then, she retreats to the square and wonders what to do with her morning.

Sarah has told Elizabeth nothing of her plans, only that she is engaged with a philanthropic matter all day. She knows her reserve injures her sister, for Elizabeth imagines herself necessary to every act of goodness Sarah contemplates. The ease with which Mrs. Edward Montagu obtains grants of money, and the size of those gifts, buys her a part in every action Sarah takes. And in every case but this one, Sarah, who understands that her pride deprives those who need help, concedes. Old women knitting gloves, poor maids sewing pockets, wronged girls righting themselves—women in scores owe much to good Elizabeth Montagu. She herself owes Elizabeth for intervening with their father over the matter of her allowance—and this itself strikes her as especially unfair. How wrong it is that Elizabeth, backed by the invisible frowning head of Edward Montagu, so commands her father's conscience, while Sarah's own pleas, undermined by George Scott's lingering, husband-shaped shadow, caused him to shrink the annuity he allows her. Without Barbara to remind Sarah of the un-evenness of life, and that she and good fortune are already acquainted, Sarah bristles, forgets to count her blessings. Instead, she remembers how she opened her mouth last night to apologize to the girl, to Sadie, but could not continue. London—or something like it—stopped her. She knows this is not the whole truth.

When Sarah realizes she has been walking with no attention to direction, she has already put Leicester Fields far behind. Now, the elegant box of St. Martin's church appears before her. She turns onto St. Martin's Lane and climbs the broad steps, to stand a while under the columned portico. The weather, so warm only yesterday, has turned, and she is glad of Elizabeth's thick cloak. Her own, thorough-ly muddied in the toppling of the coach, has been carried downstairs by Sadie or Grace—Sarah neglects to discover which—where it will be beaten, brushed, wetted, and brushed again to raise the knap. When Sarah returns to Bath, her cloak will put on a better show than it has in years. Everything Elizabeth touches is like this.

Inside the church, Sarah kneels in the black pews and bows her head. Eyes closed, she prays for as many people as she can recall—Elizabeth, Barbara, Meg, Tidy and the rest, the knitting old women, the drunken coach driver, Mr. Gotobed and his sweetheart, the sis-ters in Elizabeth's household, the guests at her salon. Mr. Hogarth, of course. She commends them all to God and blames the weather for the feebleness of her prayers. St. Martin's vaulted heavens hold clouds of damp. A chill rises from the flags.

Back in the street, the rain falls steadily, and Sarah pulls her hood up over her head. She continues down to the Strand, where she walks along graceful stone and brick buildings, all built in the new style. Shop windows vie for her attention, and she passes a wine merchant's, a cheese-monger's, and, across the narrow lane, a bookseller's. Here, the window is all leather covers and gilt pages. Sarah steps inside, but when she observes the number of books, propped upright or lying open to display title pages, she grows anxious for *Millenium Hall*. Moving from volume to volume, taking care not to drop rain on the pages, she feels a rush of gratitude for Mr. Newbery and his fine frontispiece. Barbara is right as usual—the man knows his business.

She exits the bookshop and makes her way to the front of a hatter's establishment, stopping before the window that had previously caught her eye. Between a drooping bonnet and a pert chapeau, she sees her own face reflected. She turns and reads the name painted on the swinging sign before the shop: Mr. J. Askew, Straw Hat Maker and, amused, she decides to purchase a hat for Lady Barbara.

When Sarah enters, a bell dings sweetly. A young woman, sitting in a chair at the back of the room, her elbows upon her knees and her head in her hands, rises as Sarah enters.

"Forgive me," says Sarah, casting her eye over the chapeaux perched on carved wig stands, "but might I try that one?" She points to the window, indicating the hat she means. It has a wide brim, and around the crown, a blue ribbon, finished with a bow.

The girl retrieves the pert hat and gingerly pulls back Sarah's wet hood. She settles the chapeau on Sarah's hair and pats it into place. The scent and texture of straw are not unpleasant, and Sarah is pleased with her generosity in thinking of Barbara. Her friend will protest, but then she will wear it when they next venture out to church. The blue ribbon will suit her.

A little glass, browned at the edges, sits on a curved sideboard, allowing Sarah a sight of her own face beneath its new cover. Sarah gazes but a moment before removing the chapeau. With less enthusiasm, she points to the second hat, the drooping bonnet, but the effect is the same. Straw and ribbon cannot disguise the lines in her cheeks, around her lips, the coarseness of her skin. Only the pockmarks, companions since girlhood, seem familiar.

"We can trim to suit," says the girl, pointing to a flight of feathers so airy they might yet fly up to hover at the ceiling of the little shop.

Sarah shakes her head, and the other nods. "I do agree, madam, that a simple pleated ribbon is more refined."

Sarah says, "may I try the one with the blue band again?"

It is a very pert hat, but gazing in the mirror, Sarah understands it is not the chapeau she wants to see. Rather, she longs for her own remembered face, round and solemn, dark eyed and red cheeked. She had imagined those features misplaced instead of lost. Now she knows that youthful countenance is gone forever.

"That is a very rakish headpiece," says the girl.

"What did you call it?"

"Jaunty. What the French call debonair."

Sarah removes the hat. Is that truly what people would say: oh how rakish she is in that number? How could she hold up her head after such a description?

"I should not wish to be compared to a rake."

"Truly?" said the little milliner. "It is very a la mode to be a bit of a rogue."

"Not where I come from," says Sarah. "Where I come from, we think better of amusing ourselves by pretending to be worse than we are—we are quite bad enough already."

She meets her own eyes in the mirror and feels a swell of self-pity, but it is the little milliner who begins to sniffle and wipe her eyes with the handkerchief she pulls from her pocket. It is the second girl Sarah has made cry in the space of a day.

How do I do it? thinks Sarah.

This time, Sarah does her best to condole the girl. She says, "Pay me no mind if I spoke out of turn. I did not intend to include others in my condemnation—only myself."

"No," says the hat-seller, "my mother would say the same. I should not speak so freely."

"Perhaps not," says Sarah, trying to sound mild.

"But it is London," says the girl. "It's the way people talk."

"Still, you need not adopt their manner."

"I do," says the hat-seller. "For the business, you see. It is very bad, just now. In wet weather, who buys a straw chapeau? No one." And she wipes her nose again.

I will have to buy the hat now, Sarah thinks, but when she inquires after the price, she knows she will not. Instead of a hat, Sarah buys several yards of trim in two colours—a more reasonable gift to transport to Bath. And then she goes back into the drizzle with her paper package tucked deep in a pocket of the primrose dress.

Down the Strand she continues, past a pastry cook's glazed window and the glinting interior of a sieve-wright. Tired, she pauses, wondering if she might yet return to Leicester Fields for her answer from the Hogarth household, but she knows she is still too early. While she is deliberating, the day darkens, and London gives a convulsive shake, like a wet dog. Rain flies in all directions, sprinkling her face and the shoulders of Elizabeth's cloak. The shower decides her: she will walk back as far as St. Mary le Strand, and if it is still raining when she gets there, she will go into the church. It cannot hurt to spend the remainder of the morning with her head bent, even wordlessly. Then she thinks, *especially* wordlessly.

She begins walking, but almost at once she stops. A handbill has caught her eye. It flaps wetly from the post of a railing, the ink running in the rain. Even so, the printed drawing is still recognizable, and what it shows, makes her read the type below. When she has finished, she is all astonishment—the handbill is like a signpost from God, although Sarah knows she should not entertain such superstitious thoughts. Still, has she not just yesterday imagined herself in the heavy hide of a rhino? Elizabeth as a showily striped zebra? Barbara as a camel?

She glances about, looking for the inn whose name is given in bold type. She locates instead a small boy, sheltering in an inset doorway.

"Here," says she, crossing to the child. She has not taken the sodden handbill from the post, as she should have. "Is the menagerie still about?"

"What—the one at Talbots?" says the boy, approving. Sarah nods, and for a farthing he takes her there.

D. M. Bryan

Talbots Inn, like other buildings designed for the same purpose, begins in a narrow passage and ends in a wide yard, which is tucked behind public rooms fronting the street. Sarah expects the beasts to be stamping in the court, stabled like horses in wooden-walled stalls, but the boy takes her through a back entrance and up a narrow flight of stairs.

On the landing, Sarah stops, certain of having been misunderstood. "I want to see the animals," she says to the boy's back. "I won't go up there."

In the gloom of the stairwell, the boy turns. He takes off his crumpled hat and rubs it dry against his breeches. All the buttons are gone from the knees, Sarah notices, and the cuffs flap loose. One sock sinks earthwards. "You're wrong, missus," he says. "Them creatures got their own apartments like any other guest."

"Who does?"

"What you said."

Sarah wonders if the child is simple, but instead she says, as clearly as she can, "Where is the zebra? I want to see the *zebra*." The word brings to mind the handbill's beautiful picture, flapping in the rain.

More polishing of the hat. "To be truthful, he's gone to Bristol, that zebra," says the boy, "But he was a sight when he was here. And the monkeys are gone also, which will be a sharp disappointment for a lady like yourself. Everybody knows, the ladies love a monkey." And the child gives her a leer she hopes is only mimicry of his elders.

"You should have told me the animal show is over," Sarah says, her own voice sounding childish in her ears. "They are gone to Bristol."

"Never," said the boy. "You think I'd take your coin for nothing? I'm honest, I am. And if you'll come upstairs with me, madam, you'll see how they left some of them creatures behind, for there was no room in the travelling cases for two of each. Upstairs is the Ram, from the coldest reaches of Iceland, with horns that curl and twist—they had so many of those Mr. Brooke sent some to the countryside to earn their keep. And they got a crocodile that isn't exactly alive, but is stuffed to show all his teeth. He's worth a look for his gnashers alone. Also, there's an Indian hog and some peacocks, fit for a lord's table."

"The handbill promised stupendous sights. Peacocks are hardly stupendous."

"They are to some folk."

Sarah supposed him right, although perhaps not to anyone who could afford the shilling entrance. "And the rhinoceros?" asked Sarah, expecting to be disappointed.

She was. "He's gone Bristol way. Though they was doubtful he'd survive the trip. Always sick, that creature. *And* he'd started to smell." The child shows her, holding his nose.

"In that case—" Sarah begins, turning about.

"But we got *Camelus Paco*," said the boy, all but reciting: "A native of the Mountains of Peru and much admired for his wool."

"You have a camel?"

"An alpaca they call him. Native of the mountains of the moon. Much admired for his wool. But he looks just like the camel they keep at the Tower."

The alpaca has his lodgings on the second floor, in a reeking room that looks out on to the yard. When Sarah and the boy arrive, the creature faces the window, seeming to gaze out through the glass. As they enter, it spins awkwardly, hooves clattering on floorboards. Bewigged and narrow-waisted, the creature presents such a familiar silhouette that Sarah smiles at the boy, amused by its resemblance to a frockcoated gentleman. The alpaca stands as tall as Sarah, and its coat is soft brown, like a milky cup of tea. Its face, when it looks her way, is split lipped, snaggle toothed, and wary.

Sarah decides she is glad she has come to Talbot's inn, but no sooner does she experience this small satisfaction than the boy takes up a stick leaning by the door. As Sarah watches, he commences poking the Alpaca, deep beneath the heavy woollen coat. The animal shifts away, moving toward the empty hearth and clattering behind a broken chair, which is the only furniture in the room.

"Stop," says Sarah, who hears the anxious tapping of its hooves.

"Why?" says the boy. "You can see it better this way," and he slashes with the stick across the thickly pelted chest so that the animal rears up, striking out with its forefeet.

"Stop," Sarah says again, moving to challenge the boy for the stick. To her shame, he proves the stronger, for all his small stature. Sarah loses the tussle, and the child stands in the doorway, stick still in hand.

"You must stop," she says a third, useless time.

The alpaca stalks stiff-legged back to the window, turns its face away, and starts pissing.

"Dirty," says the boy, striking it again, this time a hard blow to the hindquarters. The creature reacts, lashing out with its back feet, but the boy is faster and dodges the hooves, laughing.

Sarah can see how practiced he is. Again, she wishes she had the stick, but now she would do more than spare the alpaca.

Now, the boy approaches the animal, still with the stick in his hand. The alpaca backs away from the advancing child, the tipping of its hooves sounding on the boards.

"Watch now. I'll bring him closer," says the boy. "You can touch his miraculous wool."

"I do not wish to," says Sarah.

"He is wonderfully soft," says the boy. "More like a cloud than a sheep."

Animal and boy circle the room, the alpaca backing and the child coming on. Closer and closer to Sarah he drives the creature. She shifts, floorboards creaking underfoot, and the alpaca turns its head to regard her. She hears its breath, smells its faint woollen odour. Its eyes flicker, dark and lashed. She cannot help herself but puts out her own hand—a gesture that offers compassion and, she hopes, friendship.

The alpaca flares its nostrils and turns the sad tuck of its mouth toward Sarah. A moment later, the boy bends double with laughter as Sarah wipes disgustedly at the wet goblets that splatter Elizabeth's cloak. Genteelly, elegant as a gentleman taking snuff, the alpaca walks away. Sarah's handkerchief comes away green with spittle.

"Get on out of there," says a voice behind her. Sarah turns, standing with her handkerchief still pressed to her breast. A fine fellow stands in the doorway, scowling at Sarah and the boy. He wears riding boots and a high cut coat, but his lapels are too angled and the boots too well-oiled for Sarah to think him a real country gentleman. Also, he has taken the stick from the boy's hand.

"I'm just showing the lady around," says the boy, edging closer to Sarah. The leather soles of his shoes step in time with the alpaca's percussive tread. The beast goes one way, while the boy goes the other, setting Sarah between himself and the stick.

"I warned you to stay out," says the man.

"I only just came in. The lady wants to see the Indian hog. And the crocodile hanging from the ceiling."

"I haven't yet paid my shilling fee," said Sarah. "I shall settle my debt and go." She approaches the man, eager to leave behind the alpaca's threshing hooves and cloak-flecking bile. Behind her, the creature has begun to click in its throat, and the sound makes her step faster. As she reaches the door, her hand to her purse, the boy makes his bid for freedom. He rushes the man, who has time only for a glancing blow with the stick. Then, the child is past and clattering down the stairs.

Sarah holds out her shilling.

"We're closed," says the man. He makes no move to take the coin.

"I have seen the alpaca."

"Closed."

"Then you should bolt your doors," she tells him, tucking away her coin. "Bolt your doors and set down your stick."

She waits for the man's reply, for the insults to come, but he steps back, making way for her to pass. Sarah turns once more to see the alpaca's eyes, glinting, round as cannon shot. Then she goes, picking her way down the stairs.

D. M. Bryan

When Sarah returns to Mr. Hogarth's front door, the maidservant has her answer ready. Mrs. Jane Hogarth, it seems, is an admirer of *A Journey Through Every Stage of Life*, and on the strength of that recommendation, Mr. Hogarth will be happy to see Mrs. Scott at ten o'clock the next morning. He is happy to offer whatever advice he can provide. However, he must forewarn Mrs. Scott that he will never invest in a scheme of the sort she describes in her letter—here, his nib presses hard into the soft paper—and she must not attempt to persuade him to do so.

Sarah reads over her letter in the wet heart of Leicester Fields, then summons a chair to take her home to Hill Street. Inside the chair, a faint chemical smell tickles her nose. Through the rippled glass of the window, she views the mottled heavens. Out of the sky comes Talbots' crocodile, swimming toward her. The beast swoops up and over her head, its pale belly distending into sky. Where patches of rain fall, clouds grow dangling limbs. A bright tail coils along the horizon.

Sarah sits upright in the chair, watching the back of one of the men who carry her. She does not know if she should commend Mr. Hogarth for his generosity in agreeing to see her or find fault with his characterization of her project. She seeks no financial backing—she thought that clear from her letter. But, now she cannot remember her exact words—did she leave her motives open to interpretation? If only she had not used the word *enterprise*. Without Barbara, she is not at her best—a ship without its captain.

In her pocket, she finds the little bundle of ribbon, which she takes out now. Parting the paper with her fingers, she finds the bright stuff inside. Barbara's gift she accounts a credit, but her adventure with the alpaca must sit in the deficit column. Minute moral reckoning—that is the sort of business Sarah understands.

Her drawings, her home for harlots, ranks with the ribbons. She will explain herself to Mr. Hogarth, and he will understand. Leaning back in the chair, Sarah closes her eyes.

CHAPTER 17

"As no one is obliged to stay a minute longer in company than she chuses, she naturally retires as soon as it grows displeasing to her, and she does not return till she is prompted by inclination … "

Sarah Scott's *A Description of Millenium Hall.*

London, 1762.

Sarah dines with Elizabeth alone that evening. She has no appetite and would have been happy with a small plate of broiled fish, perhaps served in her room. Instead, they sit in state in the golden dining room, a thick-stemmed candelabra between them. Sarah has seen trees with fewer branches. A footman comes with a tray of silvered dishes, and the sisters eat in silence. The second remove follows the first without any respite. Sarah eats all, wants none. Her meat coils haunchlike on its platter. Cress soup quivers in her bowl, the exact green of *Camelus Paco* expectorant.

So that Elizabeth might not see the stain on the primrose gown, Sarah has changed back into her brown travelling dress. She has trusted the girl, Sadie, with the silk, and, with much head-shaking, the girl has borne it away. Sadie knows a laundress, she says, who can remove all manner of blotches, splashes, besmirchings, but alpaca snot—well, she will have to consult the washerwoman. Sarah is pleased by Sadie's words. She herself has known laundresses to make a difference before.

On the far side of the table, Elizabeth looks askance at her sister but says nothing. Freed of the need to be informally brilliant before her friends, she has dressed correctly for dinner, in shining blue satin and lace sleeves. Nothing at all like a zebra, obliged to lodge over an inn. Sarah sees Elizabeth's tiny hooves, clad in soft slippers, well suited to the wide oaken boards of her native land. But, no sooner does she entertain the thought than Sarah is sorry. She dislikes it when women are depicted as animals, a hesitant step on the road to creation, halfway between a slug and a gentleman drinking port. My point? she asks herself. My point, my point? Angrily, she heaps more pink mutton on her plate, sees the curving edge of each slice, fashionably scalloped.

How tired Sarah is of the company of Sarah Scott. Every word from between her lips tastes of brackish water, and even this thought sours in her mouth. She sips and sips again from her glass of elderberry wine, the fruit of the Sandleford gardens. Elizabeth turns her own glass between her fingers, examining the colour by candlelight.

Her point, Sarah thinks, is that she is about to publish *Millenium Hall*, a novel about a community of ladies, living in peace and good will, and she can't get along with her own sister. And how many other people has she offended since arriving? Sadie over the primrose dress. The straw-hat girl over straw hats. Perhaps even the laundress with the outlandish nature of her stain.

Barbara.

Sarah decides she should not have made this trip to London. She will not see Hogarth. His letter, crinkling in her pocket, will go into the fire as soon as she gets close to a blaze. Her plan, like all her schemes, is foolish. Destined to fail. A house for harlots? A reformatory for rakes? She is not practically minded, and she knows this. Her ideas ever sprout, but never flower, never fruit.

That night, when she goes to bed, she remembers Hogarth's letter still in the pocket of her gown. She wishes she had dropped it into the hot-burning fire of the dining room, or into the orange flames that licked the marble mantle of Elizabeth's dressing room. And she's not too late. Even now, a jittery blaze flickers in her bedroom grate. She can see it from where she lies, the counterpane heavy over her chest.

Invisible hands have laid that fire, ignited it, coaxed it to life. Now, she watches it throw brown shadows across the ceiling. She could easily slip from between the covers and dispose of the letter, holding it to the flame until the white page blackens. In the morning, the ash will include its fragile, pale skeleton.

This picture, provided gratis by her imagination, pleases her. Under bedclothes, she sighs, feeling comfortable at last, and Sarah, exhausted by the heavy weather of London, sleeps.

At ten o'clock the next morning, Sarah stands on Mr. Hogarth's doorstep, dressed in her travelling clothes and holding her leather portmanteau in her hands. She has his unburnt letter in her pocket. Like the day, she is brisk, renewed. Of course she will do as Hogarth instructs: seek his advice, expect nothing further—wasn't that always her intention? Even so, Sarah shifts uneasily. She rocks on her feet, shifts the portmanteau from hand to hand.

At Sarah's knock, the maid she remembers from yesterday opens the door. A moment later she is standing in Mr. Hogarth's black and white tiled hall, giving the girl her name, her cloak. She follows the slapping of the maid's leather soles, through a front parlour, full of sun and dust, and as far as an oak door, standing closed. This the girl opens, saying, "If you will go in, madam. He is in the garden with the dog. I will inform him you are arrived."

Sarah does as she is instructed and enters a dark room. A sofa appears before her, and Sarah sits, her portmanteau in her lap. While she waits, she looks around with interest. Panelled and old-fashioned, the smoke-stained chamber also boasts a battered secretary, well covered in papers—the great man's desk. Ink pens, crayons of all colours, rulers, and wooden curves cover every inch of the surface. Sarah at first ignores, then notices the drawn curtains, screening the windows. A pair of candles winks at her from over the red hearth. She sets her portmanteau aside and rises.

At the edge of the artist's desk, a leather-bound book lies open to a drawing in Hogarth's own style. The sketch gives Sarah a view

of a tilted room filled with loosely penciled figures, all men taking their ease. They eat; they sketch; they shave—drawings conveying the intimacy of friendship. Sarah looks up. From one of the secretary's shelves, a ceramic Mr. Nobody looks gravely from atop his huge trousers.

With one ear listening for footsteps, Sarah bends her head closer to the fascinating litter. Scraps of drawing paper. Little crayon sketches, some no bigger than the palm of her hand, feather the desk's hinged surface. She sees drawn hourglasses of different designs, but every one cracked, nearing empty. She sees a tiny gallows and a ruined tower. She sees the world on fire. She sees a nude male figure, reclining.

Sarah steps back.

The door opens without the preamble of footsteps. A fat-bellied pug enters, his nails clicking, tracking mud across the polished floor. At once, the small creature scents Sarah and sits, turning his goggled eyes upon her. The dog barks—intelligently, she thinks—and seems to wait for her reply.

Sarah calls the dog to her, but the pug holds its ground. She knows the artist makes the dog his emblem and prides himself on his pugnacious nature. Only, when the real Hogarth enters, he is so different she does not at first understand who stands before her. The little dog runs forward and licks his hand, so she knows this is the animal's master, but the features she knows from the engraved self-portraits are lost to old age. Rheumy eyes stare. Stained teeth protrude slightly from his drooping smile. The hairless dome of his head hides beneath a slipping headdress. His figure, still wide-shouldered and capaciously gutted, moves stiffly, an automatic Hogarth, ungreased and creaking.

There is no one to introduce them. Sarah's self-announcing letter has brought about an impossible moment—they both do and do not know one another. She bows and so does he, and then they are acquainted in a manner new to both. Sarah shivers at the success of her, yes, enterprise—she will use the word.

Hogarth seats himself in the wooden-armed chair before his desk, while the dog settles contentedly to sleep at his feet. The man gestures at the sofa for Sarah. Seated, she sinks below the artist's eyelevel, finding herself awkwardly positioned, with her portmanteau in her lap.

Still, the room is so very small, they can see each other well enough. Now, what are the words? What ought she say next? *Hello. Thank you. Good morning, Master Hogarth.*

But she has not moved quickly enough, and Hogarth both takes the trump and leads the next hand. "It is not often," says he, "I meet a person who proposes to venture into pictures." His voice comes in short, rough bursts. "What a proposition. Forgive me, madam, you do not know me. Those who do, understand how strongly I am opposed to such efforts."

What can Sarah say to such a preface? The gentleman is opposed to pictures? Has he forgotten who he is? In her head she plans words, the beginning of a long speech of respectful beggary, entreaty, correction, but instead she finds herself listing her interlocutor's works. His rushed, partial style of speaking is catching.

"Your *Harlot*, sir," says she, "your *Rake*, your *Apprentices*, idle and active, your *Beggar's Opera*, your saintly *Captain Thomas Coram*." Sarah stops for a breath. "Your *Marriage-a-la-mode*, your *Four Times of Day*, your *Stages of Cruelty*. Your *Gin Lane and Beer Street*."

Hogarth nods and smiles. "You have seen them all?" he says.

"I possess a great book at home, and I have bound up new works as I am able to find them."

"Very good," says Hogarth. "You are a collector."

"But, forgive me, Mr. Hogarth, I could not collect if you did not first venture into pictures—the very activity you say you oppose."

"Nay," says the old man, "I am not opposed to *my* venturing. I am opposed to the futile enterprise of others."

"But," says Sarah, "But."

"Nay madam. I have too long scraped, and toiled, and suffered the indifferent lot of the artist to wish it upon any other. How often I have entertained young men, here in this very room, whose parents ask—nay, beg—me to accept their sons as apprentices. I turn them away, Mrs. Scott—that's what I do." Hogarth stops and scratches his chin. "Have I offered you coffee?" says he.

"No, sir," says Sarah, "you have not."

Hogarth leans over and stiffly manipulates the bell pull. "Do you like my room?" he says, while they wait for the girl to bring refreshment. "Jane, my wife, decorated it for me when we first came to this house. She put Thornhills on the walls." Hogarth pulls a face and looks at Sarah for her reaction. He scowls when she provides none.

"Forgive me, Mrs. Scott, but I do not know your books. I have read Mr. Fielding's work, Mr. Richardson's, and Mr. Sterne's, but I do not know yours. My wife reads rather more than I do."

"I am not so much read as those authors you have mentioned, but my readers sometimes write my publisher to say my tales are not without their modest pleasures," says Sarah.

"Oh yes, that's exactly what Jenny said—your books are very proper. My pictures, you know, are not always what they ought to be. I am not the first person to say so."

The girl enters the silent room, bringing coffee in a tall silver pot. The cups are very fine, but old and a little cracked. Mr. Hogarth pours. Sarah remembers, too late, that she does not like coffee. And when she leans forward to take the cup, the portmanteau slips from her lap.

"What's that?" says Hogarth. He does not seem to remember that this is not a social call.

"I had hoped," says Sarah, "to show it to you." She realizes she must take charge of this interview or go home.

"Ah," says Hogarth, sipping his coffee. The liquid is hot, and he makes another face. At least Sarah hopes it is on account of the heat that he grimaces and glowers.

"You have been kind enough to see me, sir," she says. "I have come all the way from Bath to consult with you, and you have been good enough to drink coffee with me. My scheme, sir—I do not wish to become an artist."

"Ah," says Hogarth, holding up a finger. "I am very glad to hear you say so. Unsuitable employment for a gentleman, and for a lady—well."

"I wish to raise funds for a charitable community—women caring for other women. In order to do so, I intend to produce a series of prints, elegantly engraved, suitable for framing. Purchased by subscription."

"Subscription? Nay," says Hogarth. "You'll do nothing that way. The vogue for printed pictures is done."

Sarah sips her coffee. "I do have friends. And I had hoped to advertise in the newspapers—like yourself."

"Newspapers? Do you not see what they say of me in the broadsheets? Vulgar verse, caricatures. Jane will not let me see 'em, but I manage ... I manage."

"I would be advised by you Mr. Hogarth, and I have come to London entirely for that purpose. A recommendation for a suitable engraver. Or, guidance on placing advertisements."

"Advice," says Hogarth, putting his hands together. "I know engravers."

"I require one with a charitable heart—at least until my scheme finds its feet."

"I will not recommend a man unless you can pay him."

"And I shall pay him, as soon as the prints begin to sell."

Sarah wishes to say more, but Hogarth cuts her off. He says, "Have you any interest in signboards, Mrs. Scott?"

Sarah has never asked herself this question and has no answer, but Hogarth does not need one. "They are the original English art," he tells her. "So much communicated with a single line. A tone or a shade. A glance from a painted face. Oh, I love a good signpost, and so should you, Mrs. Scott. If you enjoy a little foolishness, why then, you must go to the Sign-painter's Exhibition. There you will see a great deal of English art that will cheer your heart, madam—I am as certain as there are three of us in this room."

Three? Does he include the dog, Sarah wonders?

"This exhibit exposes my way of working to the world, for sign-painters paint signs, and I paint sign-painters' signs—that is all I have ever done, ha! Will you promise to go, Mrs. Scott?"

"Alas, I am to leave London almost immediately, Mr. Hogarth."

"What a shame. You will miss a present-day wonder, madam, for signposts teach us about ourselves. We live in an age of combination and amalgamation, madam. We moderns are alive to variation because we know the pattern so well. We need a little difference to sustain us. And it does! Each new version is a world entire. Do you agree, Mrs. Scott?"

Sarah does. But Hogarth's volubility has emptied her of words.

The dog awakes and climbs to his feet. He stretches and yawns, and then he jumps up beside Sarah. Sarah puts out her hand so that her fingers might be sniffed before she employs them in rubbing the snub-nosed creature behind his ears. A moment later, a soft grunting signals the pug's approval.

"So you think," says the old man, watching the animal a little jealously, Sarah thinks, "the world rewards my daring?"

"I said so in my letter." She seems to remember writing that. She is, she realizes, very tired. No aching head, but a layered sadness. But for the feel of the pug's fur under her fingers, she might succumb to melancholy.

"The world cares little for my daring," says Hogarth, "My reward has been to be mocked and parodied. I am the subject of satire and faint praise. Even my defenders cavil. It is a very hard fate to live on in the heads of others."

Sarah tries to think of what she might say in reply. The differences between them appear vast.

"You are a good woman, Mrs. Scott," says Hogarth, mistaking her silence for something else. "I find I will view the contents of that leather case, after all. You may produce your designs for us, and I will help you, if I can."

Hogarth's pug rolls like a boat on a wave as Sarah rises from the sofa. Taking her portmanteau to Hogarth's desk, she removes her precious drawings and sets them before the artist. He asks her to open the heavy curtains. Grey light fills the little room.

Hogarth looks over her pictures, pulling one after another toward him. He stares. He squints. He scowls. At last, he pushes away the pages, and passes a hand over his eyes.

"I do not understand what these are," he says.

Sarah explains. "My drawings give the outlines of rooms and show what will go inside. I have seen such pictures by William Kent in books."

"Yes yes," says Hogarth, "but Kent's renderings do not look like this. What is this here?"

"It is a cheese. The product of that shed."

"And here?"

"The odor of gammon."

"And in the margins?"

Sarah cannot believe the great Hogarth does not understand what lies at the edges of her page, but she seeks to explain. "There I draw such things as do not enter into my buildings but are necessarily part of their construction."

"Such as?"

"Here, I have drawn a rake and a slipper, and over here I sketch a bumper poured in celebration of this lady's ruin."

"You have made the figures very curiously. They appear stemmed and lobed about the head."

Sarah says nothing. She remembers her glimpse of the sketches on that desk—the nude. She says, "I have heard it said that you yourself mistake the human figure."

Hogarth looks first surprised and then frowns mightily. He says, "When I was younger I did err sometimes in my proportions. I had only the artistic training a man receives in learning to silversmith."

"And I was taught to render flowers very exactly, as a lady should."

Hogarth bends his head closer to the page, frowning still. "Yes," he says, "I see what you mean. Your technique is best suited to petal and leaf. Put them away."

While Sarah restores her work to the portmanteau, she returns to the topic of a subscription. She intends, she tells him, to run an announcement in the papers, according to his model. "My drawings are highly moral," she says, "and the scheme likewise. I will sell prints by the series, just as you do."

"No," says Hogarth. "These drawings are ill-formed and ugly. Your prints will not sell. My Jane says you have a talent for novel-writing, Mrs. Scott, but you have little aptitude for art."

"I disagree."

Hogarth's face twists angrily. Sarah can see he is not used to contradiction, but he passes a hand over his forehead, smoothing signs of irritation. He tries again: "If your aims are truly philanthropic, I would imagine your sister better positioned to assist you than the print-buying public. I understand Mrs. Edward Montagu is patroness to Mr. Adams, or is it Mr. Stuart now? Such talented men might be persuaded to undertake an architectural design on your behalf."

Sarah ignores him. She will not discuss Elizabeth. She will not discuss charity to herself. He has not understood her. With care, she takes up each drawing and replaces it in her portmanteau. She fastens the lid, and sets down the leather case. Planting her feet, she says, "Mr. Hogarth, your work—nay, your Harlot has a life of her own. How often have I seen her in the street? I glimpse her bonnet in a crowd, her cape in a doorway, her fingers upon a burnished pew. She led me to believe you and I would recognize one another, but we do not, sir. And I am sorry to have taken up your time. Please do not trouble yourself to rise."

Then she exits the room.

On the stairs leading down to the street, Sarah looks out at Leicester Square. Expecting to see harlots laughing, pointing at her, she looks hard in the face of every person passing, but she sees no whores. Only respectable-looking people go by, walking arm-in-arm, exercising dogs.

Sarah tries to imagine a scene from Hogarth's pen as an end to her tale. On the illustrated page of her mind the artist examines one of her drawings, his face etched with enthusiasm. He reaches for his pen, pushing aside the unpleasant, despairing sketches that fill his desk. He draws, designing—what? The frontispiece for their published prospectus. She bids the illustrated Hogarth exult, raise the paper to the skies, but she cannot make him move. Cross-hatched and flat, he bleaches. And no wonder—what work by Hogarth has ever ended happily? No, he always concludes in funerals and murders, suicides and hangings.

Oh, she should never have come to London. On the step, Sarah puts her hands to her eyes, rubs hard. When she brings her fingers away, her lids ache. Leicester Square blurs, but there is the house she shared with her husband, George Scott. Who will forgive her? Not Barbara, who cannot see the fault. Despite the moralizing, Mr.

Hogarth's prints show great generosity to those who slip—she'd pinned so much hope on that.

She'd been better off seeking absolution from the pug, thinks Sarah Robinson Scott.

Behind her, a voice says her name. It is the maidservant, with a scrap between her fingers. A promissory note, drawn up in Hogarth's hand, for a subscription to her charitable project. The amount is not large. *I would be of some help.* Shaky, old man's handwriting.

At first, Sarah wants to crumple the note in her fist, but then she thinks better and tucks it into her pocket. Now, she is laughing. Odd.

So inconclusive. She thinks, I will write a better ending than this. Mr. Hogarth may terminate his series in bathos, but I will finish with greater cheer. I will conclude with reformation and hopeful progress. I will not resolve my story indistinctly, without resolution, in a scene both flat and inconsequential. I will not close matters thus: by leaving a room, by standing on a step, by rubbing my eyes, by ending only because someone has written

Finis.

(Nay, I must keep writing, Sarah tells herself.)

D. M. Bryan

CHAPTER 18

THE HISTORY OF GLOSSOLALIA: OR, VIRTUES VARIOUS.

THE TALE OF THE GREEN MANTUA.

London, 1746.

Glossolalia stood at the heart of Bridewell Prison and raised her eyes to the walls. Bleak stone hemmed her in on every side. Overhead, an unremitting line of slate roofs trapped even the sky within grey arms. To the lady, Bridewell appeared every bit as dismal as its reputation, and she had to sternly remind herself that she had not come to that place by accident. No, she was there because the combined influence of a laundress and Mr. Hogarth's improving prints had persuaded her to set aside those sorrows that so long held her captive in a gaol of her own devising. Having pulled down one set of prison walls, it was now that lady's fixed intention to try herself against another. And yet, Glossolalia's first sight of Bridewell was discouraging indeed.

On the far side of the prison's courtyard stood a single gateway, with a pointed and shadow-choked arch. This seemed a portal so terrible that Glossolalia suffered no little surprise when out its fanged depths a perfectly ordinary gentleman approached. He was dressed in a sober coat and a queued wig, and he was undoubtedly headed in her direction. When he came close enough, he bowed low. "Madam," said he, addressing her as if they were already acquainted, "you must not think yourself late—no, indeed, you must not." He beamed upon her.

Glossolalia put out her hand, for the gentleman seemed to expect it, and he pressed his lips to her glove. When she had been thus saluted, she said, "Sir, I do not think myself late, for I did not think I was expected at all." And this was no more than the truth, for Glossolalia had come to Bridewell without an appointment.

"Not expected?" said the gentleman. "Madame, we are more patient than that," and he bowed a second time, deeper than the first.

Glossolalia was astonished by the gentleman's forbearance—not to say his prescience. She said, "Then you have been patient indeed, for I have been a very long time in deciding to come. In truth, I have not been very heroic in my delay."

"Come, come," said the gentleman, "I will hear no excuses, for I am certain I need none. You are here now—that fact is sufficiency itself." And he smiled at her most genteelly.

The lady could not help but be pleased by this generous welcome, and so, when the gentleman offered his arm, she did not refuse. She set her fingertips lightly upon his sleeve, and at her touch, the gentleman set off, determinedly, across that fearsome yard. Gravel crunched underfoot as they walked in the direction of the central wing, a heavy fortification, pierced through with grilled glass. Her companion was, she saw, leading her towards a set of wooden doors, which stood beside a span of oriel windows.

"Where do we go, sir?" said Glossolalia, as they approached the door.

The gentleman turned to her, saying, "The child waits upstairs," and he rapped sharply on the heavy wood.

"The child?" said Glossolalia. Could this far-sighted gentleman have somehow gleaned her compassionate interest in Mr. Hogarth's picture of the harlot's abandoned boy? Certainly, it was the plight of that young person that first put Bridewell into her head—but the thought was absurd. Glossolalia said, "There can be no such child."

"Beg pardon," said the Bridewell gentleman. "There are many."

At this impasse the door flew open, and a narrow figure, dressed in a gown the shade of gloom, stood half visible in the opening. Without preamble, the gentleman spoke to this specter, whom he clearly knew and expected to see. "What do you think, Mrs. Malcolm?" said he. "The lady is come at last."

The shade named Mrs. Malcolm spoke. "I watched her arrive," said the melancholy voice. "In a coach, no less."

"I think," said Glossolalia, for the thought had begun to worry her, "there has been a mistake."

"I make no mistakes," said the woman in the doorway, and she put out a plain arm, devoid of lace ruffles, to urge Glossolalia toward her.

"In that case," said Glossolalia, "the error is certainly mine." She attempted to step away from the hand that sought her shoulder, but she found herself caught and pulled forward by fingers thin and hard as keys. "I mean," she continued, "that I am in some confusion as to my purpose here."

Upon this head, her interlocutors clearly concurred, for both nodded, but they also seemed to think her state of mind only natural. The thin woman in the murk-coloured dress pulled Glossolalia closer and examined her face with some care. A pair of large eyes regarded hers. "Leave this good lady with me, sir," said the person belonging to the eyes. "I can do for her better than she would for herself. You needn't come any further."

"Thank you kindly, Mrs. Malcolm, for 'tis a tiring climb to the top."

"Those stairs have not changed since King Henry's day," said Mrs. Malcolm, fatigue showing in her face, and a little cheerfulness went out of the gentleman as he contemplated her. "But, I don't complain," said the lady.

"No, Mrs. Malcolm, you most certainly do not," said the gentleman, and he turned to Glossolalia with such rapidity that the queue of his wig briefly took air. "The best of our housekeepers," he told that lady in a stagey whisper. "I leave you in very good hands."

"But—"

"She is most powerfully attached to the children's wards," said the gentleman, holding up his finger. "You will be well advised by her, if you but listen." Then he patted Glossolalia's hand, as if to reassure her that he could do nothing more. "I am, madam, your delighted servant," said he, and with that he bowed and vanished, the heavy wooden door falling closed behind him.

Glossolalia stood in the dark with a pair of fingers pinching her shoulders. "Well," said the firm voice that belonged to the grip. "Shall we go up?"

A long corridor led to a flight of timber stairs, rising overhead in the half-light. As they climbed step after step, Glossolalia attempted to explain that she suspected some other lady was the person expected, and that they were all mistaken with respect to her reasons for being in that place. She told Mrs. Malcolm that she had been seized by a charitable urge to come to Bridewell and arrived without an appointment, but had been greeted so kindly by the gentleman outside that she followed him in and oh—she did not understand why they must climb so many stairs. This last utterance Glossolalia delivered while bent nearly double for want of breath, and each word came as a gasp. By some miracle of persistence, she stood near to the top of the last flight, but she doubted she could go any further. Mrs. Malcolm heard her out but made no reply, except to urge her onwards, saying, "The child waits upstairs."

"I do not. Want. Child," said Glossolalia, still struggling both to speak and breathe.

Mrs. Malcolm turned and resumed her shuffling ascent, and for all she had complained of the stairs, she neither puffed nor panted. "See the girl before you make your decision," she said, speaking distinctly, and then she increased her pace so that she was climbing steadily, measured tread by measured tread. Soon, the woman quite disappeared.

The stairs ended in a mean sort of landing that opened into a long passage. At one end, a door stood ajar, daylight illuminating plaster walls and bare boards. Still breathing heavily, Glossolalia made her way down the passage and into that small chamber. Overhead, a high window emitted a shaft of daylight that glittered with motes of dust. Straw lay everywhere at her feet, loosely distributed between wooden partitions a few boards high. Woollen blankets showed that each of these was a sleeping place and had been recently used, but at this time of day, the room stood empty. The only figures were those of Mrs. Malcolm and, standing on her either hand, a pair of children, a boy and a girl.

"This is the one," said Mrs. Malcolm, her hand upon the girl child's head.

Glossolalia, approaching, glimpsed a nose, eyes, a spray of yellow hair under a tilted cap. Then she looked at the boy. Of an indeterminate age, he wore an oversized coat and breeches rolled at the waist so that they might not slide to the ground. White stockings, but not clean, stained with rust, or something of the same hue.

"Who is the boy?" she asked, for something in the child's face recalled to her mind—who exactly?

"Better ask what is the boy," said Mrs. Malcolm, placing her other hand upon his shoulder, for he was quite as tall as she. "What is he, girl?"

The girl said at once, in a lisping, little voice, "a prig, a file, a lift, Missus Malcolm."

To this answer, Mrs. Malcolm shook her head. "You've not learned your lessons," she said. "You must talk to the lady as you would the parson, or else she will not take you away with her."

The girl stared hard at Glossolalia, and then at Mrs. Malcolm, taking the measure of each.

"Mrs. Malcolm," said Glossolalia, "I have not come about this girl. And I do not care how she speaks, although I'm sure I did not catch a word of what she said.

"Why, missus," said the girl, "that's all cant. It's just the way we talk. A lift is a pickpocket—that's simple enough."

"A thief," said Glossolalia.

"The boy's the thief," said Mrs. Malcolm, pushing him a step forward. "If it's a thief you want."

"I don't want a thief—I don't want a child at all."

"You'll only find children here," said the girl. "Those older than us must go to Newgate. In Bridewell, we are only women, girls, and boys."

Mrs. Malcolm said, "The child's knowledge of such things does her no credit," but she kept her hand upon the girl's head.

"If it's a Newgate sneak you want," said the girl, "you'd better go quick, for those High Court judges hang 'em as fast as they catch 'em."

"Oh, for goodness sake," said Glossolalia. "I want neither girl nor boy. And, I don't want a thief, or a Newgate sneak, or a lift, or a file, or a—I have forgot the last."

"A prig," said the girl.

"Thank you," said Glossolalia. "I want none of those."

"No, indeed," said the girl, "nobody wants a pickpocket." And pointing to the boy, she added, "Tell the lady—you'll be a Newgate sneak yourself, the next time you're taken. Admit it."

The boy shrugged.

"He will," said the girl, "for I heard them constables arguing on the cart that brought us. One said he was too big and old, but the other said he had not a hair on his chin and so must go to Bridewell with the other babies."

"I'm sick of hearing about my chin," said the boy.

"He has hairs enough on his upper lip," said the girl. "I've seen them myself."

"Are you sure you won't take the boy, madam?" said Mrs. Malcolm. "He's a sharpish lad, for all his thieving, and will make an illustrious man an industrious apprentice. He can reckon in his head and might be indentured to a mercer, or perhaps a grocer, for there's money in foodstuffs."

"I'll be a printer," said the boy, "or I'll hang."

But Glossolalia heard little of this. Instead, she was reflecting on her reason for visiting Bridewell. The idea had seemed such a good one when first conceived. Despite the loss of her fortune, she had enough remaining to donate a sum to educating deserving children in some useful skill, like sewing or—well, sewing was as far as she'd got. Glossolalia looked at the girl and boy standing amid the straw and slanting sunlight. Were they sufficiently deserving? Who was she to decide?

"Do you like to sew," said Glossolalia to the girl.

The girl looked at Mrs. Malcolm, who nodded. "Oh, yes," said the child. "Very much."

"And what about your alphabet," said Glossolalia. "Have you learned your letters?"

"Mrs. Malcolm said, "The girl's got her letters to heart already. Though I don't fully know how she learned them."

"He taught me," said the girl, pointing at the boy. "I can read too. Show her the book."

The boy shook his head, but at the girl's insistence, he reached into his coat and took out a folded bundle. This he passed to Glossolalia, who took the pages between her fingers.

"What's this?" she said, unfolding the pamphlet and reading the words *Newgate Calendar* on its front. She turned back the first page and found a printed grid, each square holding a letter of the alphabet and a list of those sad souls doomed to execution. "John Annin, Mary Bosworth, Thomas Cappock," she read aloud. "This is your alphabet?"

"ABC," said the girl. "I got the whole book by memory." Then, the child put her hands behind her back and recited: "A is for Annin, John, from Woodstreet-Compter, Committed by Mr. Alderman Winterbottom, on the Oaths of Mary Cannier and John Jeffreyson, on Suspicion of stealing Ten Pounds and upwards in Gold, Silver, and Half-pence. That's all, but I wish I was John Annin's little girl, for that's a fine swag he took there. But he got taken, so that's that."

"Quiet, Doll," said the boy.

"It doesn't matter what I say. The lady doesn't want me, as anyone can see." Doll smiled.

"Never you mind," said Mrs. Malcolm, putting her hand beneath Doll's chin and tucking a few strands of hair beneath her cap.

Glossolalia stood in the prison room, watching the tenderness with which Mrs. Malcolm tended the child. The light through the windows shone brighter, making the straw dust glint. Glossolalia said, "It matters little whether you come with me or not, Doll. As God is good, you are worthy of love."

"No," said Doll, "I shall never deserve that happy state."

"I do not think," said Glossolalia, "you have been as naughty as that."

"Nay," said the girl, "I know what I am."

"This is not sound doctrine," said Glossolalia, looking at Mrs. Malcolm. "Such a lesson is not meet in one so young."

"It's none of my teaching," said that lady.

"Doll," Glossolalia said to the child, "people come to Bridewell in order to do some good. How can you say you do not deserve to receive what they choose to give?"

"I know what I am," said Doll again.

"What are you then, child? You have some story, I perceive."

When Doll did not answer, Glossolalia sighed. The lady spread her skirts and sat down on a battered block of wood that served as a stool, bidding the others to make themselves comfortable. Then she said, "I did not come to Bridewell for this purpose, but I fear I am less the master of my days than I imagine. Fate makes me an accidental collector of tales. I have told my own and heard several: one from my young friend Morris, and one belonging to the laundress Betty. Now I would hear yours, Doll, and if I am to be made mistress of enough stories to fill a book, how can you refuse to make me a chapter? Isn't that right, Mrs. Malcolm?" Glossolalia looked to the other woman for support.

"There's many fine books that have no chapters," said Mrs. Malcolm.

"You are very honest, dear lady," said Glossolalia. But hardly helpful, she did not say.

"I should hope so, and I am bound to observe that Mr. Swift has them, while Mr. Defoe does not."

"You are also a great reader, Mrs. Malcolm."

"I do not read but am content to be read to. Thus I know that Mr. Gulliver's tales told us where to stop, but in Robinson Crusoe's narrative, we were as lost as he."

"And have you heard this child's history yet?" said Glossolalia.

At first Mrs. Malcolm made no reply, and then she said, "I have not," in such a soft voice that Doll looked up, searching the lady's face.

Glossolalia said, "Doll, I had a daughter. You are younger than she would be now."

Doll turned from her scrutiny of Mrs. Malcolm to ask, "Where is she now, missus?"

"To preserve her life, I left her in care of another, but alas the stratagem did not succeed."

"I am very sorry for you."

"Yes," said Glossolalia. "I would not have lost her for the world."

"Was she a good girl?"

"She was like you, Doll—a good and loving child."

Doll looked from Glossolalia to Mrs. Malcolm. Then, she looked at the boy, who said nothing. All at once, the girl made up her mind. She straightened, and her air of childish innocence fell from her face, like she had removed a mask. She looked not older, thought Glossolalia, but old.

In a voice that no longer lisped but spoke clearly and a little sharply, the girl said, "You asked me for my tale, missus, and so you shall have it. And when I am done, you will certainly turn away and ask no more. I will not tell you in what parish I was born or who were my parents, for those details no longer matter. Instead, I will start my story at the moment I became the child I am now—the night I awoke to find my brother's hand over my mouth, his breath warning me of men at the door and telling me to keep quiet.

All this took place in a poor London room, where we shared the only bed—my brother Nat, myself, and my mama, when she was at home. But that night, Nat and I were the only two huddled beneath the blanket. Then, I too heard noises outside the door, although I could not guess what they might mean. I did not understand much of what happened next: the drumming footfalls, the splintering of our door, cries, and a link flaring bright in the night.

At first, I could not see the men who entered, for their light dazzled. Then one of them stuck his face very close to mine, and I could smell the herring he'd had for supper. He wanted to know where my mother was, but I could not tell him, for she was not in the bed, and more than that I did not know. Nor would Nat say a word, so they swore at us, and pressed us until we were so frightened we could not speak.

Then those men extinguished their links, and sat themselves down to be very quiet. One sat on the bed where we lay. "To keep them from warning the whore," he said. And the other perched on the chair, across from the door.

They were constables—I could see that now. They wore black coats and carried cudgels in their fists. The one on the chair had a terrible face, red and bent like the man-puppet's phiz. I could not look away from that fearsome countenance, but neither could I meet its gaze. And while I cast my eyes wildly about me, I noticed the very object I most wanted to see: my mother's gown of green wool. Her stays and hoops and petticoats were not in the room, but her sea-coloured mantua lay folded over the chair back, pressed under the buttocks of the second constable.

At last, I understood something, for I knew what the constables did not. Since coming to London, we'd fallen so low my mother had pawned her second-best gown of brown wool. I'd held her hand beneath the sign of the three balls, while she haggled the best possible price. That was the night Nat and I had fresh baked bread to eat. For herself, she bought a bottle of brownish glass. She sampled its contents while she dressed in the only gown she still owned—the green mantua she wore to go out in the street.

Now, I cried "Mama" at the sight of that gown, and Nat pushed my face hard into the straw ticking. From inside the mattress came the scurrying sound of all those creatures that live there, the mice and the beetles. I struggled under Nat's hands—I wanted so badly for my mother to hold me. Of late, she came home so soft and sleepy, fumbling to bed in her petticoats and blanketing me in sharp-scented warmth.

I pulled loose from Nat's hold and cried for her again. For my trouble, Nat pushed me down, holding me even harder against the bed. I writhed and tried to bite, and so I struggled until I tired myself. Then I lay on my side, perfectly motionless, my ear pressed to the mattress. In that position, I could not help but hear the single sound made beneath the bed. It was only the brush of flesh on flesh—her hand dislodging one of the inhabitants of the mattress above, but still I heard it. And I marked it, twisting free from Nat's loosened grip to scramble from under the blanket and down to the floor. I sought my mother in her hiding place: behind the wall of objects, beneath the bed.

Alerted by my noisy scrabbling, the constables leapt up. They pulled me out from under the bed and began to tear at the old wig box, coffer, bedpan, and broken stool that hid my mother. And when they found her, they yanked her arms and legs, pulling her along the floor so that her wails joined mine. Even Nat had begun to scream, as only a boy can.

Our room was a bedlam of cries and shouts. Free of the bed, my mother broke away from her captors, scuttling to the corner of our room, and when they tried to take her again, she stopped them with kicks from her bare legs. The constables backed away, leaving her to

D. M. Bryan

curse them at her leisure. One man put his back to the door, trapping us. The second, the one with the puppet face, had out his tinderbox and was relighting the link he'd extinguished when they thought to surprise her. Flame set the room leaping around us, and at the sight of the constables all the fight went out of my mother. She stopped cursing and kicking and a look came into her face I did not like to see. I went to comfort her, but the constable reached my mother first. He put his hand to her hair, and she came up, limp as the doll I'd seen at Bartholomew's fair.

"Here is your mama," said the constable to me. "Take your last look."

At this point, Glossolalia interrupted Doll, saying, "You were but a tiny child—you cannot imagine your artless cries sent your mother to Bridewell."

"Nay," said Doll. "No one sent her to Bridewell. When I exposed my mother, I condemned her to a different place and another end."

Glossolalia said, "Mrs. Malcolm, help me convince this child of her innocence," but the housekeeper had turned away from the company, and would not look back.

"Let Doll finish," said the boy to Glossolalia. "You have heard but the beginning."

The girl said, "You shall know the whole story. The constable lifted up my mother and took his link, holding it so close he seemed to wish to set her on fire. He leered at her teary face, and then used his light to examine her person, from her shift to her stays and hoops askew. His puppet-mouth pursed.

"Mr. Bogus," he said, as he bent to my mother's petticoats. "I've discovered a fact material to our case."

"Have you, Mr. Janus? And what might it be?"

"The person," said Janus, "has a quantity of blood on her skirts."

Bogus contemplatively spat at his feet. "Show me."

In the uneven flare of this link, Janus spun my now unresisting mother around so that some dark stain showed unevenly on the back of her outermost petticoat.

"I'll stand evidence to that," said Bogus. "Does she have an explanation."

Mr. Janus shook my mother, and she came a little alive. "Blood on your skirts," he said. "You cut the old woman's throat, didn't you? You robbed her and sliced her from ear to ear."

"I took nothing," said my mother so that I could hardly hear her.

A knock at the door interrupted this game. Bogus, the first constable, opened it a pinch and then full wide. A person entered in a coat that twinkled in the link light. I'd never seen so many buttons, and I knew he was a very fine gentleman indeed.

"We found her, sir," said Mr. Janus to the fine gentleman. "Look," and he brought the link close to the blood. Bright red it was. But the fine gentleman would not look.

"Have you recovered anything," said this splendid person, addressing himself to Bogus. "Anything at all? My sister had silver money in a leather purse and a hundred and fifty pounds in a drawer besides." A folded page emerged from his coat, which he opened to read, "Also missing: a tankard, a silver spoon, one square piece of plate, one pair of sheets, five shifts, and a ring looped with thread."

Mr. Bogus came away from the door to take up my mother's coffer box, knocked from its accustomed place under the bed. The thin brass lock gave away easily upon the first prying of the constable's knife.

From his place on the bed, Nathaniel said, "That's death when a poor man does it, but if a constable breaks a lock, it's called justice." But then, he was obliged to hold his tongue, for from the box Bogus drew a ring looped with thread.

"My sister's own," said the fine gentleman, coming forward to cradle it in his palm.

"I took nothing," said my mother, but then she set about groaning.

The coffer box held a little more: a silver spoon, a tankard, a pair of shifts.

"I am innocent," said my mother. "Given me for the keeping, all of it."

The constables looked at the gentleman, who looked very sad. They passed him the contents of the coffer, and he went away, no happier than before.

"Search her hair," said Bogus, and Janus used his free hand to root through my mother's hair, his fingers feeling obscenely beneath her tight-pinned cap. "I knew a woman once," said Janus while he worked,

D. M. Bryan

"who hid thirty-six moidore coins, eighteen guineas, twenty-three shillings, and seven crowns, all tucked in her coiffeur." He pulled out his hand, empty.

A woman peered in through our open door. I recognized her as one who sometimes went to and fro at night with my mother. "What a noise," said she. "I'm sorry to see you taken."

My mother said nothing, but Janus said, "Never mind. You may visit her at Newgate."

"Surely not," said the lady at the door in some surprise. "She only picks the pockets of those she lifts her skirts to."

"Nay," said Mr. Janus. "It's murder. Her skirts are covered in blood." And with this Janus spun my mother to once again reveal that continent of red in a sea of linen.

"Does that not strike fear into your tender heart?" said the man, his mouth jagged and wet.

"You fool," said the lady in the door. "It's only her courses. She would not come out with me tonight on account of them."

"It's murder," said Janus, dropping my mother's limp arm. "You know nothing of the law."

"Suit yourself," said the lady at the door and went away.

"Doll?" said Glossolalia, interrupting the girl again. "How do you remember so much? You are a child now and must have been an infant then."

"Nat taught me everything that happened: first came the constables with links, then they sat in the dark, and so on. And he used to tell me the story himself, when we were cold or had not enough to eat. I had a hundred questions and he was able to answer every one."

"What happened to your mother?"

"The parish prevented us from following her to Newgate, but the fame of her murderous actions put her name in all the broadsheets. An artist came to paint her portrait and make printed pictures for sale, and for a time, we saw our mother's face in whatever direction we turned. We stole a print, but we lost it later, and in truth, I have little need of a piece of paper to remember her by. Nat taught me to say every night, like a prayer, that I killed our mother, and her death is a charge upon my account."

At this, Mrs. Malcolm turned back to face the company. "Never," she said, her tired eyes red. "She is blameless. I would have her believe me." And the good woman clasped her hands together and could not say more.

"Nat and I haunted Newgate's walls, standing at its doors daily, and when the time came, we followed the cart from the open gate to the countryside. The crowd pressed us all about, but still we followed. And she saw us from the cart and wept and cursed her misfortune, and Nat said I might receive her absolution now. But then, the procession reached the Bowl Inn, and after that she would not lift her head."

"They make them dead drunk," said Mrs. Malcolm, "so they suffer less," and she crossed her arms hard against her chest.

"Nat and I were footsore and hungry, but we would not leave off, and we reached Tyburn in time to see the cart trundle to a stop near the gallows. They made us stand in the crowd with the others, and all were prevented from approaching the wagon, lest any criminal was helped to escape. Nat spoke to a man holding back the crowds, and my brother said he was our mother's son. But the man only scolded him for a liar and told him he'd have his turn on the tree soon enough. Nat cut his purse to reward him for his lack of kindness, but then we needed to move further away, for we did not want to be near when the man discovered his loss.

We heard the Ordinary's speeches only as the wind allowed, but we heard enough. We heard how our mother, like the other prisoners, repented most heartily of her crimes against God, and how she hoped to find forgiveness in the world to come. We hoped so too. Then the men geed the horses and caused the wagon to roll away from the gallows, and we saw our mother twitching upon the line like a fish. She still wore the green mantua, you see."

"Stop, child," said Glossolalia, "You have told me enough. I was wrong to let this tale continue."

But Doll would not be stopped. She said, "Everywhere at Tyburn people sold good things to eat, and we saw a man with a dogcart selling rides to other children. Nat said I might, for he had the unkind man's purse, but when I came closer, I grew fearful of such large dogs, and said

I would not get in, lest they run away with me. The dog man laughed at what he called my folly, and Nat paid instead for oranges."

Now the child stopped, and she gazed up at Glossolalia, who could not rightly say what she saw in the girl's expression.

Then it was that Mrs. Malcolm rose to her feet and stood before Doll. "Did you like the oranges?" asked that lady.

"I never tasted anything so sweet before."

"And was the sweetness punishment?"

Doll was silent.

"Nat bought you oranges. The money was stolen. The oranges were sweet. I can see no judgment in any of this, Doll."

Doll wrapped her hands in her apron and sat with her head bowed.

"Think on this, child," said Mrs. Malcolm. "It is no sin to cry out for your mother, no matter the sequel."

No noise from Doll. Mrs. Malcolm stood with her hands on her hips. She looked, Glossolalia thought, now more angry than distressed, but not with the young person at her feet. As for Glossolalia herself, she felt something go adrift in her heart.

The boy had bent his head close to Doll's, and with the privilege of childhood, lifted her chin so that he might see her face. "She cries," he announced.

Discovered, Doll showed them her face, which indeed was streaked and snotty. A little unsteady, she got to her feet, and went to Mrs. Malcolm, where she buried her face in the dark skirts. It was easy enough for Glossolalia to see how little that good woman cared that her apron would be dirtied. Her hands fluttered like pages on a breeze, then settled softly on Doll's head.

It was only a short time later that the sunlight passed from the windows, and the little room began to sink into gloom. Glossolalia, recognizing that the time had come for her departure, took Mrs. Malcolm aside. At first, she did not know how to begin, for Doll's story had put a fresh idea into her head, but at last she went direct to the heart of the matter.

"Mrs. Malcolm" said Glossolalia, "I have seen with my own eyes how you are the best kind of warder these children could hope for. But Bridewell is a vast place, with many stairs and a great deal of trouble for one as conscientious as yourself. I imagine you could use an apprentice housekeeper to run up and down the stairs for you?"

"Those stairs are wearisome, it's true, but ask yourself, madam, whether a body goes to work in such a place as Bridewell unless she finds herself pressed to it by hard necessity. An apprentice must be paid in meat and drink and apparel and lodging and washing. She must be kept from being a charge to the parish, and when she is grown, she must have a second suit of clothes, so that she has one for the working days and one for the holy ones. A poor woman could never afford all that."

"You know the obstacles to a nicety—I think you've thought before on this matter.

Mrs. Malcolm said nothing.

"The child Doll would make a suitable apprentice? Say yes or no, madam, and nothing else."

"Yes," said Mrs. Malcolm. "Truthfully, I would give much to have her stay with me and be my legs and eyes and ears."

"That's rather more than yes."

Mrs. Malcolm's look confirmed all Glossolalia suspected.

"But," said the housekeeper, "I love the child too well to wish to keep her in a place such as Bridewell. She deserves better."

"That's as may be," said Glossolalia, "but Doll does not agree—her story tells us as much. However, if we put into her head that an indenture to a Bridewell housekeeper is both salvation and punishment all in one, do you think we might convince her?"

Mrs. Malcolm thought on the proposition rather longer than Glossolalia thought necessary, but at last she nodded her head. "I do," said that good woman. "But, the meat, and drink, and apparel, and lodging, and the second suit of clothes?"

"Let me take care of that," said Glossolalia, who at last understood that the gentleman in the yard had been right all along. She need make no excuse—she had come to help at last, and that fact was sufficiency itself.

D. M. Bryan

Afternoon turned to evening. Glossolalia asked the boy to lead her to the warden. In a splendid chamber, a stark contrast to the wardrooms above, she requested that man's permission to put into practice the much-desired scheme. The warder was a brisk gentleman in a grey coat and square wig, whose chief pleasure lay in removing names from the parish books. With the gentleman's quick agreement, and Glossolalia's promise to supply everything needful for the term of Doll's apprenticeship, plus a little more besides, the indenture was drawn up. All that remained was to put the question to Doll.

Accordingly, Mrs. Malcolm and Doll were now asked to join the others in the gleaming room. Together with Glossolalia, the housekeeper described the apprenticeship in just such terms as they had previously discussed. To this discourse, Doll listened very gravely, her hands behind her back, but when all was said, the child looked from face to face, uttering nary a word.

"What do you think, Doll?" said Glossolalia. "It is hard service to stay with Mrs. Malcolm and learn her trade—no picnic, I'll warrant."

Glossolalia did not like to guess what answer the child might make—she had a mind of her own, to be sure. But Doll's only reply was more silence.

"Mrs. Malcolm will expect a great deal of you."

Still, the child said nothing.

"You must tell me the truth, child," said Mrs. Malcolm. "Would you not rather be gone from this place forever?"

This made Doll speak. "Then, I can choose to go?" said she.

"You might, Doll," said Mrs. Malcolm, "for this lady will find you a better place than Bridewell. Of this, I am certain."

Doll took a single step closer to the housekeeper. She did not look up, but said, "If I might choose, I choose to stay and by choosing make Bridewell no more a prison to me."

"Oh, well put," cried the warden, "very well put." And for all he was a man of business, he seemed to put a finger to his eye and wipe something away.

For her part, Mrs. Malcolm suffered no such wetting of the cheeks. Instead, she put her hand on Doll's cap, as she had before, but this time she fixed it there as a token of her permanent attachment.

Seeing her new friends happy, Glossolalia judged the time had come for her to leave. She picked up her skirts and made her intentions known, but Mrs. Malcolm earnestly stopped her. The housekeeper said, "Before you depart, might I know your name, madam, for I would like to know to whom Doll and I owe our good fortune."

At this request, Glossolalia hesitated, but she did not take long before she complied, giving the name she had not used in many years. Why that name seemed her own again, she could not have said, but whatever the reason, she gave her right title and felt better for it. Then, with a smile for each of the company, she again prepared to leave Bridewell.

This time, as she bade them goodbye, she found herself prevented from leaving a second time—this time by the boy. "Madam," said he, "if you'll wait just a little longer, you might hear a second story that would do you some good."

"Another story?" said Glossolalia, not at all pleased by the lad's interruption, for she was tired, and she longed for her own hearth and a pot of tea. In this frame of mind, she thought the boy looked a more hardened criminal than Doll, and she suspected him of some stratagem. She said, "I have given the warden the contents of my purse against Doll's upkeep and have only a little coin left to spare. I will give it you freely, but you need not pay me with a song."

"Ballad singing was Doll's cheat, not mine."

Glossolalia frowned at the youth's interpretation of her words. "I only meant," she said, "you may have whatever I have left, but in return, I beg you hold your tongue. I am not so innocent that I must purchase every fiction laid at my feet, and you cannot hope to better Doll's true history. Its imitation will only test my patience—not my goodness."

"As to that," said the boy, "you must be the judge."

"You are determined to speak?"

"I am."

And so, he began.

D. M. Bryan

CHAPTER 19

THE HISTORY OF GLOSSOLALIA: OR, VIRTUES VARIOUS.

THE BOY'S TALE.

London, 1746.

The boy said, "My story will not take long to tell, for much of it occurred before my birth and so is outside my knowing. I know only my mother was born into a good family but that she made a bad marriage and so lost her fortune while I was yet an innocent infant—"

"Boy," said Glossolalia, who had exhausted her charity. "I detect no especial wit in your opening, and I will not be made an audience to a romance fobbed off as ordinary life. Such a substitution is a cheat, and besides, I have read many of these amusing tales, and I am certain I recognize this one. Is it not by Mrs. Aubin or perhaps Mrs. Davys? Does not the *Reform'd Coquet* begin in a similar manner? What say you, Mrs. Malcolm?"

Mrs. Malcolm replied, "I do not know, madam, for in truth, I have not read any of those books. At home, we are reading Mr. Richardson's *Pamela*, but in five years we have only reached the scene where her master conceals himself in the closet."

"That is a very little way to read in five years," said Glossolalia.

"Indeed, I fear we might not finish before I die."

The boy, Glossolalia noticed, listened closely to this exchange, neither scowling at her outburst nor demonstrating any other kind of impatience. He stood close to her elbow, waiting to resume his speech. She turned back to him, saying "We might pass over the details of your birth to know only this: have you a locket or a cup to prove your inheritance. This is invariably the case in every romance."

"No locket or cup," said the boy.

"No birthmark? Then, I'll tell you what—if you can go to the gatekeeper and secure me a hackney coach, you might earn a coin honestly."

To her satisfaction, the boy got up at once and vanished into the yard.

Then Glossolalia took a friendly leave of Mrs. Malcolm and Doll, with many promises to visit made on both sides, and when the boy reappeared to tell her a coach waited in the yard, she was glad enough to follow him. He led her outside, where she found Bridewell's confining walls vanished in the dark of night. Only windows, yellow with taper light, marked the existence of that high barrier. For the first time in her visit to that place, Glossolalia sighted the mass of Bridewell's inmates, now released to the yard and walking to and fro in little groups. Beneath the arched doors of the chapel, women huddled close together, talking, while children played half-heartedly with stones in the mud. As her eyes adjusted, she saw, congealing from the shadows, more women, leaning up against the walls, arms crossed, and watchful. From her arrival, she'd been conscious of bells and, once or twice, the sounds of feet and voices, but the sight of so many unfortunates in one place alarmed her.

"This yard is full of inmates. Should they not be confined?" she said to the boy, who stood close by her elbow to help her climb into the carriage.

The child shrugged. "The walls stand still, missus," he replied, "and the guardroom under the arch bristles with keepers."

"Yes, but there are so many."

Our employment ends early at this time of year. The cold numbs us where we stand, and Bridewell's governors will not heat the workrooms. We are given an hour between the ending of our labours and supper to warm ourselves with walking. And some of us come out just to see the sky."

A bell rang distantly, and the yard altered like a face changing its expression. Watchfulness straightened the slack lines of bodies. The gathered women fell silent, and the silent women stretched. The squatting children gathered up their stones and filled their pockets, a squabble or two erupting over ownership. Then, slowly, heavily, a river of figures formed and began to flow into an arched passage leading to a little, steepled chapel.

"What happens now?" said Glossolalia to the boy.

"We say our prayers, and then we have our supper. Bread and cheese by the ounce, four of the first and one and a half of the other, and half a pint of beer for those of us over six."

"Will you not be late?" said Glossolalia, who preferred the coachman's solid hand to the narrow palm of the boy, and besides, the youth no longer seemed willing to help her climb into the coach. Instead, she could see that he held something pale between his fingers, a scrap of paper and no more. "You should not delay and miss your meal. I would not have you punished on my account."

The boy held out the paper to her.

"What's this?" said she, and she felt such fear of that page that she could not understand herself. She blamed her trepidation on her surroundings and on her long exertions that day. When had she herself eaten last?

"If this is some message you wish me to carry," she said to the boy, "I cannot take it. I will not do anything that might offend the law."

The boy said nothing in reply, only urged the paper into her hand. Despite the beating of her heart, she took it, feeling the rough scrape of the page against her glove. It is his face that frightens me so, she thought. His face.

"Open it," said the boy.

Glossolalia turned the paper over in her hand, finding it unsealed. But she made no move to unfold it. "I can carry this if you promise you do no harm," said she. "Now that I see you closer, I would like to believe you an honest boy."

"Open it," repeated the youth.

"I cannot read by distant lantern light. I shall look it over later, when I am nearer to a candle."

But the boy stood waiting—he would not be denied. Glossolalia could find no more excuses, and at last she opened the paper.

Bridewell's yard had quite emptied. Not a prisoner remained but the boy, pressed up against the side of the carriage. The driver, eager to be gone, looked down from his seat, begging to know if the lady needed a hand up after all. Glossolalia, with an energy she knew she possessed but found few opportunities to use, shook her head and scrambled up the step of the coach all by herself. And no sooner was she seated than she reached out and pulled the boy up behind her. He came unstuck from Bridewell's wet yard, shooting into the inside of the coach like a cork from a bottle. Almost before she knew what she'd done, he was seated at her feet, the capacious folds of her petticoats tumbling over him like a blanket. The youth's paper, she tucked into the bosom of her gown, and as she pulled her shawl straight, she felt its edge, sharp over her heart.

A knock on the wall of the coach set the contraption in motion, first rolling in a wide circle, as if to bid the prison farewell, and then trundling slowly toward the grilled arch that led out of that place.

No sooner had they reached the portcullis than a voice called loudly for them to halt. Glossolalia felt the boy stir. She put a hand out, stilling him even as the coach door swung open and a face looked inside. A guardsman, grinning so that his face seemed to split open, regarded her with a gawping stare that seemed one with Doll's puppet-faced constable.

"I know what you done," he cried, even as Glossolalia sank back against the cushions.

"What have I done?" she cried, knowing the boy wriggled at her feet, as fearful as she and for the same reason. She had never heard herself sound so guilty, so she repeated her words, hoping to force some innocence into them: "What have I done?"

The guardsman chuckled—she knew not at what. "Bless you, you don't know, madam," said the grinning figure in the guardsman's flared cap. "Mrs. Malcolm is a great favourite with all of us here, and anyone who does her a good turn is a friend of Bridewell forever." And at that he swept off his cap and bowed so low that Glossolalia could see the narrow estuary of his scalp. Behind him stood a whole clutch of guards, each with his cap in hand and each bowing and scraping as if to a lord or lady of the realm.

Glossolalia felt the heat rise in her cheeks; she felt a confession trembling on her lips. She wanted to cry: but here I am, stealing a child from under your very noses. Take me back amongst those women, for I am no better. Nay, I am as bad. Hold, I am worse.

But the pirate captain in her bade her say nothing. Her buccaneer-self gestured her thanks for the guardsmen's homage and called for the coach to proceed. The coachman geed his horses, and the carriage trundled away, into the London night.

This Glossolalia did, she and the boy.

By the time, Glossolalia at last dared sweep aside her skirts and reveal the youth, the hackney coach was a long way from Bridewell. She had the unfolded scrap of paper in her hand, and now she once again examined the crayoned sketch, made so very long ago. She saw how Mr. Hogarth had drawn her, back in the days of her youth, reclining in her chair, stretching and laughing.

The boy took his place on the opposite bench with a sort of reluctance Glossolalia could well understand. The interview that must now take place could only be painful for them both, and she must begin as harshly as she knew how.

"This drawing—by what means did it come into your possession?" she said, keeping her voice stern as if she were a judge in the Bailey. "From whom did you steal it?"

"It is mine," said the boy. "It has always been mine."

"Don't lie to me," said she. "It cannot be yours, for it was mine, and I gave it to another. Did you steal it from her? Or did you find it? Was it somehow lost?"

"It was never lost," said the boy.

"You make this into a silly guessing game," said Glossolalia, scowling. "Well, I do not wish to play along. Tell me the truth now—how did you come by this drawing?"

The boy grinned, but with no show of amusement. The lady looked across at his face and then out the window, into a lantern-smeared night. She remembered sailing northwards until streaks of emerald and lime undulated above the Ice Queen. Had that really happened? How like fiction your own past could seem—little different from something once read. Books take shape from memory. And memory gives each book its heartbeat.

The boy seemed almost to divine the flow of her thoughts as he resumed the tale she had interrupted in Bridewell. "My mother," he said, "was born into a good family, but she made a bad marriage, and so she lost her fortune while I was yet a babe in arms."

"Stop," cried Glossolalia. "I want no more stories. I am sick of them."

"It's the drawing you want," said the boy. "You asked me how I came by it." Then he stuck out his jaw at her and dared her to interrupt him again. At last, she listened.

He said, "My mother went on board a ship bound for Virginia to escape my father, who proved a wasteful rake, and I was left in the care of a very good woman, a particular friend of hers. This lady expected to hear directly from my mother as soon as she was settled, but we heard nothing for a very long time. We feared that the Primrose, for that was the name of the ship on which my mother went to sea, had vanished before ever reaching that colony. Then the name of the cursed boat appeared in the shipping news as one taken by pyrates, and we knew the worst: my mother was dead and forever lost."

Here the boy paused and bent his head. Glossolalia judged his action an easy show of emotion, designed to tug her heartstrings, although she found herself not unmoved by this account of her own death.

The boy continued. "My mother's friend proved a friend to me also, providing for me, now an orphan without a parent, as though I were her own child. My foster mother feared my father would hear of my whereabouts and steal me back, and so she contrived to keep me from him. Through cleverness and foresight, she was able to raise me alongside her own boy as safely as if I were his brother."

"So you say," said Glossolalia, "and so I discover you for a cheat. My own dear child was a girl, and your knowledge is stolen—taken from her I know not how."

"My knowledge is not second-hand," said the boy. "You have not caught me out in any lie. I seemed but a girl when I went home in the carriage with my new mother, but when next I appeared in public, I was truly a boy. The servants could not disclose my secret, for I had no

D. M. Bryan

secret to keep. I wore my foster brother's garments, for it was that lady's stratagem to introduce me to her family as a distant cousin, removed from the country and brought to London to serve as companion to her own son. He had been breeched very young, and so, without ceremony, was I. I took to the alterations in costume and form of address without complaint, and as soon as I was old enough to see the life lived by girls, I knew my new mother acted wisely on my behalf.

I was myself. I ran freely, wearing breeches and leather shoes in place of skirts and satin slippers. I kept a sparrow bone in my coat pocket and was praised for my empirical curiosity. Dirt on a girl's tucker was cause for a scolding, and inquisitiveness was pressed out of them, like whey from cheese, but that was not my lot and I rejoiced. I shared a tutor with my brother and no avenue of learning was closed to me, except for stitching on the tambour frame and dancing in petticoats. I wished to try neither, and so I was content. The only time I felt dissatisfied was when my brother, in the heat of some temporary frenzy, would hiss at me that I might again be reversed, returned to what I was not. This maddened me beyond measure, and I bruised him so often, he learned to hold his tongue.

No doubt, you will find all this impossible to believe—that a girl might be really a boy. All very fine on the stage, you will sneer, but real life defies such magic tricks. To this I say, I am not in hiding. I am not an actor in a boy's disguise. This is no magic. I am what I am—and you know who I am."

Glossolalia thought of Morris. She looked at the boy on the bench. She did not know what she thought.

"You may put your mind at ease," said the boy. "You gave me the drawing—you put it in my hand—and now I return it to you. I make no claims on your person or your precious purse. Only consider how I felt when I heard you give Mrs. Malcolm your name—my own mother, risen barnacled and dripping from her grave. I could hardly believe my ears. Like you, I suspected some imposture, but then why did you stare at me so, stealing glance after glance? Did I see a message hidden in the play of emotion on your face, like some truth written on water? It was then I decided to set you the trial of the drawing."

"You set *me* a trial?" said Glossolalia. Then, after a moment's reflection she asked, "And did I pass."

"You stole me from Bridewell, madam. Are such acts a habit with you?"

This reply forced a smile from the lady. "Truly," said she, "I have not taken anyone hostage in many years."

"I am glad to hear it," said the boy.

"But you must finish your tale," said Glossolalia. "I admit to more interest in its continuation than I at first expected."

The boy said, "Then you must steel yourself, for what comes next is not easy to tell. The illness that destroyed my foster mother did not come all of a sudden. We watched her failing long before she gave way to the urgings of those who loved her and called in the surgeons. On a wet day they came, seven of them all dressed in black, and no sooner had they entered our house than we two children were hastened out by the same door.

Our tutor put us in a carriage and took us to St. Paul's. We had a book between us, which was written for young people such as ourselves and told us everything we wanted to know—and a great deal we didn't—about that grey pile. My brother and I climbed the five hundred and thirty-four steps to the upper gallery, where London spread out at our feet like a painted cloth. Down we peered at curving lines of brick and stone, and running through all, the fat, brown slug of the Thames. But no matter the charm of this view, our thoughts flew ever westward, to where the seven surgeons bent low over our mother—for pardon me, madam, the lady had served that function for most of my life, and while I never forgot my real parent, I love my foster mother as she deserves. Descending to the whispering-gallery, we boys murmured to one another, asking was our mother cured yet? And thanks to the wonders of those curving walls we heard our tutor's sad sighs as clearly as if he sat between us.

Our mother saw us directly we returned, and this sight of her cheered us very much. She held up her head and spoke to us clearly, her eyes bright and full of interest in our visit to St. Paul's. The malignancy of those past few weeks seemed vanished, cut away by the surgeons. Indeed, the following weeks saw her rally, but it was not long before she

D. M. Bryan

sank again. Then, the servants remembered her surgery and the cries that lanced the house. Whenever our mother groaned or cried aloud, the family froze at whatever they were doing: kneading the bread, tending the fire, blacking a boot. Such pain can kill, said our servants, and we believed them.

Every morning and after our lessons, we went to see her, but then came the day they would not let us go in. Instead, we hung about uselessly, panting at her chamber door, curled like dogs on the floorboards outside her room. At last, she called for me alone, without my brother. "I have settled," said she, as I sat on a chair beside her bed, "a sum upon you that will be yours when I am gone."

I said nothing, for despite the familiar curtains—taffeta, with tiny finches—the sick chamber seemed another world. Her body beneath the covers was a stick, her face all eyes. I did not completely understand what her words meant.

She asked me if she had done well by me. "For, I would not have your mother reproach me when we reunite," she said.

"She's dead," said I, even more confused. "You can no more see her than I can."

"I shall see her soon, and I would have your blessing."

Here, the boy paused in his narrative. In the dark of the carriage, he sat swaying on the bench. His eyes were shut. Glossolalia thought: I have the same trick myself—we close out the world.

"Did she speak of the sketch?" she asked him, this time with gentleness.

"She had taken it for safekeeping, for I was a wild boy and not trusted with treasures, but she gave it to me then. She spoke Mr. Hogarth's name, and said you had been happy when he drew you that day. I took the paper, the one you have there now in your hand, and thanked her. Whatever my fortunes have been since that day, I have always kept that paper close. The lady in that drawing has been all my comfort and the whole of my consolation. I did not expect to see her appear like a ghost in Bridewell prison."

Glossolalia sat quiet. The streets outside had begun to show familiar lines in the dark.

"Long ago," said the boy, "did we have a window where I liked to stand and draw with my finger in the fog upon the glass?"

Glossolalia nodded.

"And did I sleep in a bed not my own and dream that the Primrose would sink?"

The lady said, "No one but my child and I know that. But the dream was only a fearful fantasy and not a true foretelling—the Primrose was taken, but never was she sunk. I lived to return to England and found my dear friend dead. Her household had scattered to the four winds, but I hunted them down, one by one. I found footmen and parlour maids, begging them to tell me the fate of the little girl in her care, but no one could remember any such—ah."

Glossolalia sat in the trundling coach and regarded the boy again. At last she said, "but Bridewell? How came you there?"

"It is easy enough to get to Bridewell," said the boy. "Almost no effort at all. In my case, my journey began the day of the finch-painted curtains. It was the last time I saw my foster mother in this life, for she died the next morning. My brother and I, each fitted with a new suit of black clothes, were the chief mourners. As soon as she was laid to rest, we came before the executors of her estate to decide our separate fortunes.

My brother was sent to school, and he might have gone sooner but that his mother's fondness kept him close. As for me, I was made to enter a drawing room where several gentlemen stood before the fire, having come from the city to see me—or so I was told. But when I walked in, they sent me away, asking for the girl, the foster daughter named by Mrs. E— in her documents. I went out and stood in the hallway, uncertain of what to do. I understood the frightful moment had at last arrived. I was to be reversed, to be converted to what I had never been. But I was no helpless baby—I was a lad who knew my own mind and who was content to remain in that happy condition."

A passing housemaid saw me and said, "Why do you stand there? The gentlemen wished to see you right quick."

"They want a girl," said I.

"A girl?" said the housemaid, who, like the rest of that family, knew me for what I was. "The fools—they have made a mistake," said she. "If it's a girl they want, I will go in your place, for you are to get a sum of money." And with that she opened the door and pushed me in again.

"Where is the girl?" said the men around the fire. "Did you call her?"

"Please, sirs," said I. "Consider. I am no girl. I am a boy."

"Of course you are a boy," said they. "We have eyes in our heads," and they rang for the housekeeper.

The housekeeper explained that I was the charge whose care Mrs. E— had taken up when I was orphaned—a claim the gentlemen denied, demanding to know what kind of trick she played on them. The papers, they said, were very clear: a girl, daughter to—and here they named you and my father, both deceased." The boy paused. "*Is* he deceased?"

"He is," said Glossolalia. "I attended both service and interment. I saw him waxy in the coffin and buried in the grave. He will not jump up as I have done—he cannot be hero of this tale and is done playing villain. But continue your narration, for I still cannot trace your path from Westminster to Bridewell."

"Again, it is not so far as all that. But to remove any mystery, I can tell you that the housekeeper's arrival signalled the outbreak of a quarrel that was not settled by that lady's insistence that I was indeed the orphaned child sought by the gentleman. The disputation lasted some minutes, assisted by the character of the housekeeper, who dearly loved to battle. At last, the gentlemen—growing distracted by the impossible nature of my claims—decided to take down my breeches and discover for themselves what they termed "my true nature." To this proposition, I protested most stridently. I understood what the gentlemen could not— that my true nature could not be covered or uncovered by clothing. Accordingly, I kicked and shouted and fought so violently they released hold of me, and, like trolls, they began to argue between themselves.

"It is her natural modesty that makes the child behave so," concluded one, "She is most definitely a girl."

"His violence is prodigious," said another. "A boy I say."

I'd kicked this gentleman.

"She is a lying wench and dissembles like the rest," said a third.

This one I'd bitten.

"Nonsense—the chap shows spirit, determination, grit," said the fourth, with a false smile.

"Goats. Fools. Leave the motherless babe alone." That was the housekeeper.

Under the cover of so much noise, I crept backwards to the hall, gained the street through the front door, and took off running. In dressing for church, I'd placed my sketch under my suit of mourning, next to my heart, and on account of this chance precaution, I did not lose it in my sudden departure. But I took nothing else, not even a farewell from my own brother, whom I loved dearly. So quick was I in escaping that house that I turned at the end of the street and never saw a soul in pursuit.

Madam, it would take too long to relate the misadventures that came next. Suffice it to say, I changed nothing in being a boy, but in moving from well-bred to ill-bred, from high to low, from distinguished to extinguished, I became a new creature. Slowly, painfully, I made myself over—I suffered and learned, I altered and grew, and in time I flourished. But there is no time for more, for I imagine, by the stillness of the coach, that we have arrived at your destination."

"Indeed, my destination," said Glossolalia, who felt—she could not say what she felt. Instead, she said, "What should I call you? Perhaps you might tell me the name Mrs. E— gave you. You may not remember the other."

"Useless to ask for either name, for I am neither of those persons. You must call me Cass, for that is my name now."

"Cass," said Glossolalia.

The coachman appeared, holding open the door for the lady. If he was surprised to find he had two passengers in place of one, his face did not show it.

"I wanted you to see my drawing," said Cass. "I wanted you to know I lived. But I no longer need a mother."

"Oh certainly, you need not stay," said Glossolalia, "for what business could we have, you and I, after so many years?" And she made as if to open the coach door.

Then, she said, "Where will you go?"

"I have a friend," said Cass. "I have not seen him in some time, but he will help me—I'm sure of that."

"Then you must find him," said Glossolalia. "Will you alight or go on?"

"I will get out."

They stepped down from the coach, but as soon as they stood in the street, Glossolalia found her hand on Cass' shoulder, as if restraining him, although the boy was making no effort to flee.

"Certainly, you must go," repeated Glossolalia, "but I think you might be hungry after such a day. I wonder ... bread, cheese? We might toast some. Before you go."

Cass shut his eyes—only for a moment.

"Before I go," he said, and together they went inside.

Finis.

CHAPTER 20

PUGG'S NOTE, THE LAST.

And so, we make a *finis*, but still, a little more remains to be told. I am bound by the beginning I made. Do you remember what I told you then? How I compared myself to a leather case, leashing my life to its pages? Dying dog, dying art, I said. Death launched my appeal to you and so what else but death can conclude this journey—death must stop up my mouth and close my eyes.

But I am not ready yet.

I cannot leave Sarah, standing on Hogarth's front steps, his promissory note held loosely between her fingers. I must watch as the lady's face empties itself of some blended sentiment. Pride bubbles and bursts, while ambition, always an effort, sinks like a tide. She thinks only of home and her new garden. By the time she remembers her portmanteau she is already sitting on the bed in Hill Street. She decides to petition Elizabeth to send someone to fetch it, but the request cannot be made without an explanation, which will only beget more questions. The bell goes unrung; the favour goes unasked. Later, in the coach back to Bath, she decides she will write Mr. Hogarth and herself solicit the missing object's return, but when she is finally seated at her own table the pen will not form the required words. She cringes to remember her visit to the artist's lair; she would rather forget. Shame, like a stick in her ribs, moves her sideways through the weeks, months, years, until the case is not exactly forgotten but certainly abandoned.

Then comes the day in 1794 when she receives a polite letter from a person signing himself Mr. A. Pugg. He has, he writes, a leather case he suspects may be hers. He cannot say exactly how it came into his possession, but he would like to meet her. The portmanteau contains some prints made by Master Hogarth and an assortment of other papers—an homage to the sister arts of word and picture. He is eager to speak with her further and hopes he may call.

Sarah notes the "Master" decorating Hogarth's name and assumes a former servant, a butler or footman with the portmanteau on his conscience. She does not guess the truth, not even when I appear on her front step, waiting in the chill Norfolk air.

No well-trained servant will admit a dirty stray, not even one capable of knocking with the back of his paw on the black-painted door. But as a charm against brooms or a parlour maid's boot, I am ready to beg. I have rehearsed my act, tilting my head, sitting on my haunches, holding out my paw. Tugging at heartstrings, I hope to engender sufficient compassion that I might gain entrance in the arms of a housemaid. Once over the doorsill, I trust to providence to suggest a scheme by which Sarah Scott and I might communicate.

The scene does not play out exactly as intended—how could it.

The door is opened, not by a footman or serving woman, but by the lady herself, standing on the threshold in cap and shawl. I recognize her. She is old, and the tendrils of hair about her neck have bleached as pale as the cotton from which they escape. She looks only once at where I sit on the step. Then she glances from side to side, as though looking for trick-playing children. Satisfied, she bows, a little stiffly, and invites me in.

I trot through the door, as though I know the way, and Sarah follows me down the narrow passage. Together, we emerge into the smoky warmth of the small parlour where a well-raked fire burns in the hearth. I look about me, observing the few furnishings, the chairs, the sideboard, the small bookcase. I cross to this last and look up.

On a middle shelf, with gold letters on its spine, is a bound volume of Mr. Hogarth's prints. I paw at the case and begin to bark with excitement.

"Shush," says Sarah, holding a finger to her lips. "I am only a guest in this house and unwilling to disturb my friends, who have been kind enough to make an old woman feel at home."

I stop barking at once.

"Good boy." Then she puts her head on one side and regards me shrewdly. "How come you are here?" she says. "Whose dog are you? There is an air of intelligence in your eyes I have never before observed in any of your breed—or any other breed, to tell the truth."

I paw the volume of my Master's prints.

"Hogarth had a dog like you," says Sarah, remembering. She joins me at the bookshelf and passes her fingers over the spines—tender as a lover. Slowly, she takes the gilt-lettered volume from the shelf. "It is an age since I looked at this," says she.

In her hands, the pages fall open to show a truncated stub, the edge cleanly cut by a finely made pair of scissors.

I bark again, just once, but her whole attention is absorbed by the amputation of her book of prints and she says nothing.

"I had not remembered," murmurs Sarah Scott. She takes the book back to the hearth and sinks into a French armchair. A second chair is pulled up before the fire, and I jump onto its rush-bottomed seat to wait. She settles the book in her lap and places her hand over the absence where *The Harlot's Progress* ought to begin. In another moment, she begins to turn pages, stopping to exclaim each time she finds a scene missing. In this way she discovers prints pruned from *Marriage a-la mode*, from the story of the rake, and from the tale of those apprentices, idle and industrious. Over this last she sits so long, I am forced to bark again.

"I should put you out," she says to me. "Get out of that chair." Then she says, "You have not muddy feet, I hope?"

The cleanliness of my paws interests me not at all. Only Sarah Scott commands my full attention.

The lady settles back in her chair and closes her eyes. The firelight shows me a face seamed with expression, facetted and pieced as armour. When her eyes flicker open, she starts forward, leaving age behind. For a moment, she is all cheek and chin, her flesh smooth amber, and then she sinks back into the wings of her chair. "I had drawings of my own in that portmanteau," she says. "Where are they now?"

She gazes at me, in the opposite chair, and she forgets what I am. In her eyes, I consist of dream, of loneliness.

"Where are my clippings, the letters?" she wants to know. "Where are my stories?"

I growl, deep in my throat.

"So you found them," she says. "Did you like what you read—no, don't tell me. Critics are dogs, and so are you."

She laughs at her own joke, a wheezing burst of pleasure.

"It's yours, pug—finders-keepers," she says, when she is quieter. "It was never mine to begin with. Some of it I pirated, some I had to scrub. A little is true history."

I tilt my head. I sit up on my haunches. I hold out my paw.

"Why dog," she says, "are you after more? Is that what you've come for?"

Did I bark then? I cannot remember.

"I saw them one last time, you know, the mother and son—one morning, when I was passing through Smithfield. It was a market day, blue-white and clipped with frost. Cattle lowed and men haggled. Black coated farmers stamped their feet to keep warm."

Old as she is, Sarah Scott is big with a tale. I settle myself more comfortably in my chair.

"By a barrow of apples, the first of the season, I saw them," says she. "The boy was a handsome lad, as tall as his mother and almost grown. He sat on a barrel, eating his pippin and sweet juice wetted his chin. He was gnawing its flesh to the core, as though apples had been a rare thing with him. His mother wore skirts of serviceable linen and wool, short enough to clear the Smithfield mud. When I came close, I nodded at the mother, but she did not recognize me. Then, I pretended to be busy at the costermonger's stall, while I listened to all they said.

"Have you noticed," said the mother to the son, "that young man? He follows us wherever we go."

I turned in the direction she indicated. A gangly fellow stood a little behind, grinning stupidly.

At the sight of him, the boy left off chewing, and then began again. "Gotobed, there you are," he said, as the tall lad inched forward. The

D. M. Bryan

boy spoke with his mouth full of mashed fruit, which seemed an intentional bit of cheek.

The provocation did not land. "As I live and breathe—Cass Quire," said the gangly chap, sketching out a bow. Full of good manners, he turned and bowed low to Glossolalia, for she was the lady.

Cass sighed and threw away his apple, but his exasperation was all in show. He grinned as he said, "Gotobed, this is my mother."

"Mr. Gotobed?" said that lady. "Is this the fellow you feared lost?"

To which Gotobed replied, "Feared me lost? I hope so, madam—yes, I do."

"Cass sought you in any number of stews and has scanned the newspapers daily in case of some accident. Your absence has been a matter of no little concern."

"Don't believe her," said Cass Quire.

"Indeed, madam," said Gotobed. "I *do* believe. The information is gratifying."

The lady raised an eyebrow. "And your reunification equally so, I suppose?"

"Vastly pleasant. Our unexpected separation distressed me more than I can say," said Gotobed. "I have been searching—oh, how I have searched." And he bowed again. To Glossolalia. To his friend.

"You know she is a boy," said the lady.

"Madam," said Gotobed, "none of us is perfect."

To my ears they sounded a perfect pair of Bedlamites.

When Glossolalia asked Gotobed if he would go home with them and take some tea, he agreed with so many bows, his hat fell off and landed in a steaming pile of Smithfield shit. And that was the last I saw of them."

Sarah stops talking, and I yip:

She nods. "We too should have some tea," the lady says.

She rises and sets a pot on the hearth, pouring a little water in a dish for me. Wandering about the room, she complains that the caddy has gone missing again, discovering it, at last, in the brown shadow of the window ledge. She waves the box under my nose, and I scent Souchong through the clock-shaped hole of the lock. I grunt with pleasure.

She says, "You are a good boy—a very good boy."

I bark.

She cocks her head, eyes bright with pleasure. We are obliging and respectable company for each other.

"You should bury that portmanteau, Mr. Pugg," says Sarah. "Dig a hole in the good black loam and plant it deep."

The kettle answers, steaming and hissing. She lifts it from the flame and pours. Liquid and steam part ways. While the tea steeps, she gives me my saucer of water, which I lap up greedily, for it was thirsty work to find her. She watches me, and when I am done, she smiles. Her own tea, she decants into its waiting bowl. The china is so fine, so paper thin, that her knobbed fingers, backlit by firelight, appear as shadows through the clay. I hear the old lady, smacking her lips.

When we have swallowed all, she collects our vessels, returning them to the dresser that stands in the gloom. Then, a silence germinates in that room, green and growing. I smell beeswax and mould, urine and spicy Norfolk lavender. The lady is looking at me. I watch her face as I might watch a rat, alive to its every movement. Her mouth quivers, still full of words. Between ivory teeth, her tongue glistens, moist and pale as an oyster. She has more to say.

The lady speaks. "I know a place in the garden where a shadow on an outbuilding looks just like chinoiserie wallpaper. I used to walk that way whenever I could, but now I have only to close my eyes to see. These days, I wear memory closer than peach-coloured silk. Once, I had poppies, sunflowers, and thistles. A garden with More. In Batheaston, I heard a squirrel run over the roof. Its clever, jointed toes bouncing from eave to eave. I said, "Good for you." I spoke to the squirrel, but Barbara answered. "Thank you," she said. In Bath, we washed our own linens when money ran short. We laughed at our red knuckles, our clean nails. In London, my head filled with a lopsided novel, like an amateur sketch. I folded the pages into a paper boat, bid the crew sail on. When the sun came out, I strolled Berkeley Square. Invisible sea boots set me swaggering. "Stop rolling about like that," said Elizabeth. "What on earth is the matter with you?"

D. M. Bryan

For a moment, the lady stops speaking and gazes into space. She seems to have forgotten my presence—or at least that she speaks to a dog.

She says, "Our letters, Elizabeth and I, hold empty pits, mined out sections with the words removed—the death of her son, the loss of her husband. When Barbara died, what did I say? I hardly remember. But whatever I said, Elizabeth knew. She'd always known. Those prints torn from Mr. Hogarth's book—his harlot, the rake, the unmarried wife, and the idle apprentice—put me in mind of a satirical autobiography, like something of Mr. Sterne's. I cannot help myself—I have that kind of mind. Why, Mr. Pugg, I might even write a part for you."

But then she meets my eye, and in her gaze is a transient glister that alarms me. An inky blot mars the perfect amiability of her expression.

Sarah Scott attempts to rise. She has been sitting a long time. The lady plants her slippers on the floorboards and pushes with her hands. As she struggles, she exhales angrily.

"Hogarth had a dog like you," says the old woman, "but that pug was fat and lazy."

She is telling me nothing I want to hear. My Master's fame is equal to her obscurity. I show her my teeth in what is not a smile.

"Shall I put you out?" says Sarah Scott. "It is not raining, and that is something to be thankful for."

Beyond the window, branches move.

I am growling to myself, thinking of the portmanteau. Like all novels, that leather case stinks of people, of authors stitching, starching, and copying whatever came before. The novel is an invention, like the lightening rod, the steam engine, and the self-winding clock. Its history is in its pages, and I am a faithful dog.

On her feet at last, Sarah Scott pushes open the door to the dark passage. She calls me pug, or perhaps Pugg—who can guess which—and I follow her toward the eternal glow of the entrance hall. Against the black door, with its shining paint, Sarah Scott stands in the transom's light. She lifts the latch and pushes.

Through the opening, the gravelled yard shows grey and particular. In November, at that season when wet branches bleed upwards into cloud, she will die. Then she will be forgotten.

At the door, Sarah shows me her sleeves. No ink stains the lawn fabric. "This is my last word, dog," says she, "so mark me well. The novel is *not* an invention. It is all seed, rooted, and sprouting dark tendrils like an inkblot. Its pages, like laundresses, teach the love, not of principle, but of variety, in every shape and size and colour and kind."

Then she says, "Please notice the roses as you pass. They are fragrant beyond belief."

I have reached the hedgerow and the road. A trick with a branch and a shadow reminds me of watching my Master at work. Master Hogarth is employed on the engraving he does not know will be his last, but he is tired and out of sorts. He endeavours to keep his imagination in the sunshine. I watch him using his burin, sending up arcing trails of copper. With the instrument's tip he shapes emblems of extinction: a cracked bell, a ruined tower, a waning moon, a shattered scythe. A gallows. Then, moving to the center of the composition, Master Hogarth shows even Father Time expiring. Over the figure's head he writes *Finis*. Time's last word.

The man sets down his pencil and turns to me. He says, "The deed is done, Pugg—it is all over." He gestures towards the engraving, but he seems to mean more. Ahead of us lie the vomiting, the crying out at the light, the pain, the drooping eye done in wet paint.

Every portmanteau must be opened so that we might crack its spine, slit its pages, devour its contents. Close its covers. Dying art— blank pages, unnumbered.

Dying dog. I close my eyes and the ceiling comes down to meet me—not the smooth plaster of a London condominium but a painted vault with angels and putti, spiralling like dropped feathers from the sky's blue dome. This is my death at last. Golden light picks out the odd, quadruped bodies of these divine messengers, and as they draw closer I see they have the faces of dogs. Greyhounds, mastiffs, collies, terriers.

D. M. Bryan

Now, the heavenly effulgence illuminates them to a supernatural degree. Eyes glint, diamond hard. Minute adjustments of their jewelled wings emit rays of ruby, emerald, and sapphire light. Every hair in every coat stands alone for counting. And as they descend, the dogs begin to sing in unison. An anthem of praise or welcome? I cannot tell. I prick up my ears. Closer and closer come the seraphic dogs, hovering on their wings. They hang motionless above me, like slung cattle with useless legs dangling, and their hymn piddles away into silence. Their wet noses and moist eyes stare down beseechingly.

As one dog, they begin a new canticle, a new song of praise, a new alleluia. This time, I understand the words. They are urging me forward into the light.

I cannot help myself. I am Pugg. I snort, as only a pug can. What manner of ending is that? With a kind of derision, I howl at the skies.

Hideous barking bounces off the waisted curves, the supple vines, and cascading shells of the vaulted heavens. Between wings, hackles rise and ears compress twisted skulls. Yellow fangs stretch cruelly, snatching for my imperiled flesh. Spittle flecks silver in the golden glow. And when I fear I can no longer evade the fatal attack, I open my eyes.

With a faint dripping of smoke, like the snuffing of a candle, the vision vanishes, and I am here again.

No one can compose their own death. I must go on in silence; I must go on alone. Unclip my lead. Give me my head. Watch the tip of my tail waddle off into the wide world one last time. The portmanteau is yours to keep or pass on, as you see fit. More capacious than wash water, it holds not only these pages but many more besides. Past pages, future pages. Remember how accidentally it began, invented with stitching, starching, copying. Remember how tenuously it continues, sprouting dark tendrils. Elegant inkblots. It is so generous an object that even a dog might tip pages into its accommodating cover. And now it is yours.

Keep my portmanteau various in your own way. I cannot say fairer than that.

The End

Illustrations

ACKNOWLEDGEMENTS

The eighteenth century really knew how to pen a page of acknowledgements. The language was high-flown and the purposes rhetorical. My version is plainer but heartfelt.

This novel was begun as part of the PhD requirements in the Department of English at the University of Calgary, and I would like to thank the faculty and staff for their assistance in many matters related to the completion of this book. I owe a particular debt of gratitude to Aritha van Herk for her tireless red pen, Suzette Mayr for continued support, and David Oakleaf, whose help on all things eighteenth century was invaluable. Barb Howe got me out of more jams than I can number. And, the encouragement and support of my classmates is a big deal, so thanks to all of you, with a particular tip of the hat to those who read and provided moral support: Heather Osborne, Steven Peters, Emily Chin, Emma Spooner, and Jane Chamberlin.

The Social Sciences and Humanities Research Council of Canada (SSHRC), the University of Calgary Faculty of Graduate Studies, and the Department of English all provided generous financial support, without which I could not have undertaken this work.

My family has put up with me in every kind of internal weather. The best of all parents, Lawrence and Eleanor Bryan, know when to take me to lunch and tell me it will be okay. Greg Bryan and Anne Laurent, Christine Sutherland, John and Jane Sutherland, Jim and Julia Sutherland, and the late, great Tim Sutherland have never flagged in their love and encouragement. Elizabeth, Hayden, and Jacinta Ashby provided inspiration, while George Fenwick and Mindy Andrews are simply the best. My amazing children, Aphra and Joel Sutherland, motivate me with their own scholarship and hard work—I am so proud of them. Richard Sutherland is my best friend and companion in everything, and I can never thank him enough.

Photo of Fawkes and the author by Joel Sutherland

D. M. BRYAN is a novelist, living and writing in the city of Calgary. She is the author of *Gerbil Mother* (NeWest). She holds degrees in art, film, communications, and English. Currently, she teaches writing and English studies at the University of Calgary and Mount Royal University.

BRAVE & BRILLIANT SERIES

SERIES EDITOR:
Aritha van Herk, Professor, English, University of Calgary
ISSN 2371-7238 (Print) ISSN 2371-7246 (Online)

Brave & Brilliant encompasses fiction, poetry, and everything in between and beyond. Bold and lively, each with its own strong and unique voice, Brave & Brilliant books entertain and engage readers with fresh and energetic approaches to storytelling and verse, in print or through innovative digital publication.